THE GLINTCHASERS SERIES

THEY SPLIT THE PARTY

Elijah Menchaca

CamCat
Books

CamCat Publishing, LLC
Fort Collins, Colorado 80524
camcatpublishing.com

Hardcover ISBN 9780744309201
Paperback ISBN 9780744309225
Large-Print Paperback ISBN 9780744309249
eBook ISBN 9780744309256
Audiobook ISBN 9780744309263

Library of Congress Control Number: 2022949459

Cover and book design by Maryann Appel
Map illustration by Maia Lai

5   3   1   2   4

To my Wings, who makes me feel like I can fly.

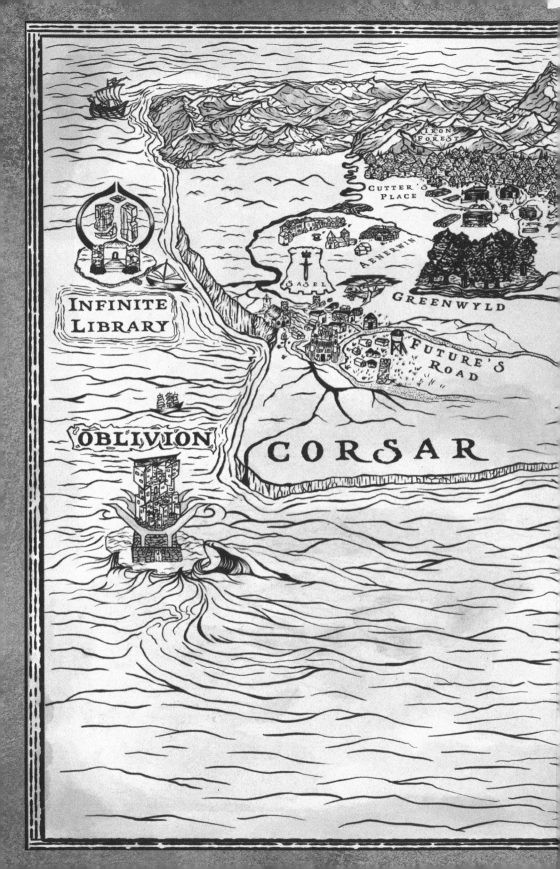

INFINITE
LIBRARY

IRON
FOREST

CUTTER'S
PLACE

AENERWIN

SAGEL

GREENWYLD

FUTURE'S
ROAD

OBLIVION

CORSAR

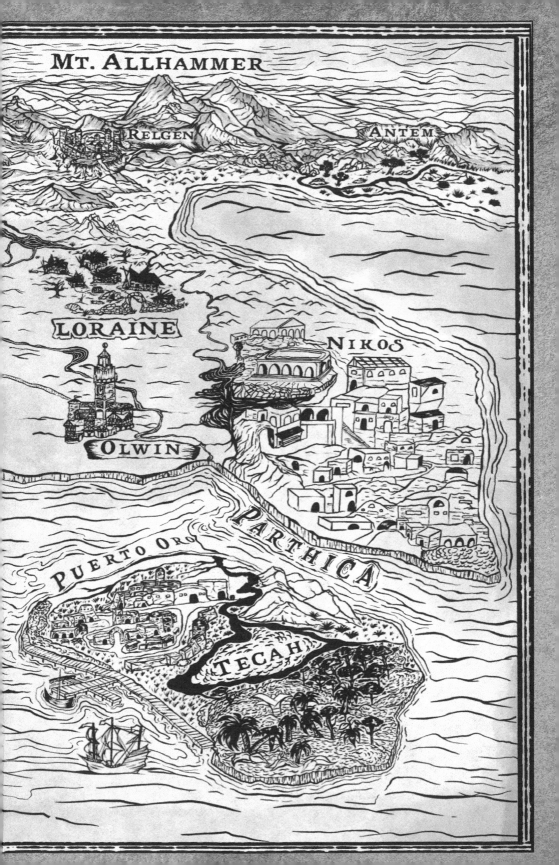

OBLIVION

It was said that Oblivion's architect had declared the prison inescapable. The prison was built on a tiny island in supernaturally rough waters; every cell constructed from floor to ceiling of solid iron. Its doors were sealed to open only at the touch of a guard. To test the architect's claim, the emperor who'd commissioned it had the architect himself imprisoned inside.

He never got out.

Ink chuckled to herself, thinking about the story. Somewhere in there, she supposed, was a moral about being consumed by your life's work. Most likely spun by someone who'd never worked a day in their lives but still felt the need to lecture others about it.

If it was true, she felt no pity for the architect. If he couldn't rise above his own creation, that was his own fault, to say nothing of his poor choice of employer.

"High Inquisitive?"

Ink was dragged back to the present by the guard in front of her, who was nervously eyeing the cell she'd requested access to. This one had to be new. Guards who'd spent any real time in Oblivion were well past the point of being afraid of the place.

"Yes, thank you," she said, waving him off dismissively. "You can go. I'll call when I'm finished."

The guard shifted nervously, like he was working up the nerve to say something, and Ink felt a wave of dread descend upon her. Hands folded, lips pressed together, she waited, silently daring him to say something.

"It's against the rules for visitors to be left alone with prisoners."

Now she knew he was new. Ink gave a sharp inhale, and the guard flinched.

Ink was beige-skinned with sharp, unnaturally blue eyes and hair that stood out against otherwise rounded features but perfectly matched the softly glowing glyphs on the sleeves of her thin-layered summer robes. She carried herself like a person of power—both the kind that made people listen to her and the kind that could turn people to ash with a flick of her fingers.

"Who dictated these rules to you?" Ink asked.

"The warden, High Inquisitive."

"And who does the warden work for?"

"The . . ." The guard trailed off. To his minimal credit, he figured out where Ink was going with this. Oblivion was operated by the Academy. Its wardens and all personnel under them answered to it. And to all but a very select handful of people, Ink *was* the Academy. "Good day, High Inquisitive."

Ink kept her face calm as the guard made a hasty retreat. It was important, she reminded herself, not to get too angry at people for what they didn't know. Otherwise, she would never not be angry.

A dark chuckle echoed from inside the cell. "You love being in charge, don't you?"

The prisoner was dressed in simple burlap, singed in several places. He was shackled by hand and foot, anchored to the floor with Old World chains. The soft orange glow from his eyes and the stray embers that trailed off his skin and hair filled the dark interior. Even from the outside of the cell, the heat inside was palpable.

"Beats living in chains," Ink mocked. "Enjoying your stay?"

"What do you want?" Pitch spat.

"Lots of things," Ink said. "There was an old shellfish place by the marina I wish would reopen. Some new perfumes, since mine are all starting to go bad. Somebody else to crack spellforging or to at least get it out of Phoenix. But really, I've just had a long week, and I figured seeing you in a cell would make me feel better. And I was right."

Pitch growled and lunged forward, immediately making his chains go taut as his eyes burned, and his shackles took on a dull red glow. Ink barked a single word in Arcania, and the chains crackled to life with electricity. He fell back to the ground, spasming.

"Down boy."

Ink didn't even attempt to hide the satisfaction in her voice. Even through the contortions and twinges from the shock, Pitch's boiling fury was plain to see. And after all the trouble he'd caused and all the years of hell he'd given her—and Renalt knew how many others—that pointless, impotent rage was delicious to drink in.

"I am going to skin you alive when I get out of here," Pitch spat. "I'm going to burn you to a crisp and piss on the ashes."

"No. You won't," Ink said. "You're going to sit in this cell until I figure out a way to get the Heart of Flames out of you, and then I will leave you to rot in here for the rest of your miserable, pathetic, angry little life. Officially, for all the murders and the assault on Olwin Keep, but mostly so you can finally stop being a pain in the world's collective ass."

"You think you're so hot, don't you?" he growled. "Little runaway girl, all grown up. I bet this brings back memories. Except now, you get to be the one on the outside of the jail cell."

Ink's hand twitched in the beginning motions of a spell before she caught herself. She was the one who got under people's skin. Not the reverse.

"Except I've moved up in the world, while you've only gotten more worthless."

"Don't pretend you're better than me," he retorted. "You act like you rose above. Like you stuck it to the world and now you're the head bitch in charge. But you haven't risen above shit."

"When I left the Cord of Aenwyn, they begged me to stay," Ink said. "They threw you out on the street like a rabid dog. And now you're in prison and I own the keys."

"And you love your job so much, you had to come visit me to feel better about yourself," Pitch prodded. "What happened? Is the Principal of Magic School being mean to you? Or is it hitting you that after fifteen years of running, you're still just somebody else's little servant?"

Ink almost took the bait, almost dove into a defense of her life and how she was not and would never be anyone's servant. But she had nothing to prove here. Their situations spoke for themselves.

"You know, you're absolutely right. I'm incredibly dissatisfied with my life, and you've cut me to my very core," she said, every syllable stitched with sarcasm. "When I go home, I will sob into my warm dinner and silk sheets, unable to think about anything other than how much better off you are than me, eating rats and shitting in a bucket. Which doesn't look that full. I'll be sure to tell the guards they don't need to clean it out."

"Don't you fucking dare."

"Goodbye, Pitch."

"Fuck you!"

He may have sucked some of the fun out this visit, but that was the only victory he was going to get from her. With a flick of her fingers, she shut the door slot behind her.

"Hey! Don't walk away from me! Ink!"

His voice echoed through the halls of the prison, hounding her, and she smiled as his frustration grew. She was done here.

She called the guard back and graciously accepted the escort out of the cell block. He was still nervous, but now he was as scared of Ink as he was of the prison.

The thought put a smile on her face.

The warden was waiting for her on the way out. A tall, broad-shouldered man with no hair and a name she didn't bother learning.

"I trust your inspection went well, High Inquisitive?" the warden asked.

Ink seamlessly slipped into the lie of her official excuse. "Oh yes. You run a tight ship here, Warden. I'll be happy to return to the Academy knowing our most important project is in safe hands."

Her sentence was punctuated by a broad smile from the warden and a sudden flickering of the lightstone in the room. There was a thud that reverberated through the walls and then a slow, building din of noise coming from the cellblocks.

Ink's own polite, practiced smile vanished. "Provided you can explain that."

The warden went pale and frantically slapped the shoulder of the closest guard. "I'm sure it's just a storm. We see quite a few of them in this region. I'll send someone to confirm it; you don't have to—"

Ink was already moving, grabbing her escort by the wrist and using his hand to open the seals on the doors as she made her way toward the commotion that was only growing louder by the second. The warden followed behind her, spinning desperate lies and reassurances she could see through without even looking the man in the eye. When she got back to the Academy, she was going to have him fired.

Alarm horns began to sound, confirming what she'd already been dreading. Escape attempt.

"High Inquisitive, I must insist that you—"

This time, the warden was interrupted by a haggard guard sprinting into the room, gasping for breath. The guard nearly ran face-first into them before Ink grabbed her by the shoulders, halting her in her tracks.

Recognition replaced panic on the guard's face. "High Inquisitive! Warden!"

"What happened?" Ink demanded.

"There was an explosion in the cellblock. She got free, started killing the guards and breaking open cell doors."

"Who?" Ink asked.

The guard answered, fear in her eyes. "Kurien."

Kurien. Of all the people locked away in Oblivion, it had to be to her. Even Ink's blood went cold.

"That's impossible!" the warden shouted, even as he was ignored. "Her cell is warded against every conceivable means of escape!"

"How many are loose?" Ink asked, trying to get a grasp on the situation.

"That's just it, ma'am," the guard said. "All of them."

Everyone in the room fell silent. Ink felt her legs shake for a second underneath her until she forced them to steady. Every prisoner in Oblivion was loose. They didn't need panic. They needed action.

She started giving orders. Establish a perimeter on the cellblock. Get archers positioned to watch the coast. Call the mainland for immediate reinforcement. The warden tried protesting early on before Ink made it very clear that this was her prison now. When everyone had their orders, she personally marched back into the cellblock to bring the situation under control.

The halls were chaos, full of everything from undead mutants to shape-shifting putty monsters. They had to cut through plant roots as thick as trees and as hard as iron. Subdue mind-controlled guards rioting even more fiercely than some of the inmates. Extinguish fires that moved like living things.

In the end, it took a full day and a hundred lives to restore order to Oblivion. Academy mages, royal soldiers, and even the knights of the Seven Gates themselves all had to be called in. Dozens of prisoners—the most dangerous men, women, and monsters to curse Corsar with their lives—were unaccounted for. And Ink, at the end of it all, was left staring at a massive hole where Pitch's cell used to be.

This was going to cause problems.

FAMILY MATTER

S parks flew from the partially dismantled fire sphere in Arman's hands as he carefully traced a handheld grindstone across its surface. If his math was right, the new grooves he was carving would make for a significantly more controlled detonation, but he wouldn't know for sure until he tested it.

All that was left to do was reinsert the core—a ball of spellforged rock and condensed fire magic the size of a grape. Everything else about the sphere—the casing, the engravings, the glyphs—was about control. The core was where the actual explosion came from, which meant it had to be handled with caution.

Half the sphere in one hand and a pair of tongs in the other, he reached over and found the core was missing. His head frantically swiveled as he worked through the possibilities in his mind. He could have misplaced it or maybe bumped into it without noticing and sent it rolling off somewhere. Considering the porch wasn't on fire, it was still stable.

But where did it *go*?

He got his answer in the form of a toddler's excited giggle. At the other end of the porch, with the core clenched in her tiny fist, was his daughter.

Robyn squealed in delight as she beheld the strange red orb. It was warm to the touch and gave off a faint glow that transfixed her attention. She had absolutely no idea what it was, but that was true about most things, and she'd yet to meet a mystery that couldn't be unraveled by sticking it into her mouth.

"Robyn, no! Put that down!" Arman yelled as he scrambled to get up.

A powerful gust of wind burst from the house, sending the front door flying open and Arman's tools scattering across the yard as Elizabeth sprinted out. Her green eyes crackled like lightning as she took in the scene, spotted Robyn, and flicked at the air with her fingers. Wind whipped around her fingertips, shooting out like a bullet and striking the core with perfect precision.

The stone shot out from between Robyn's fingers, landing several feet from the house before bursting into flames. Completely oblivious to the mortal peril she'd narrowly avoided but dazzled by the flash of light, Robyn threw her hands into the air and squealed in delight.

Concerning as it was to see a fondness for pyrotechnics manifesting in her daughter, Elizabeth had more pressing matters to deal with. Namely, glaring daggers at her husband.

"I told you to watch her!"

"I was!"

"Then why was she about to eat a fire bomb?"

"In my defense, it only blew up because you shot it. Before that, it was almost completely stable."

Elizabeth's nostrils flared as her head cocked to one side, and Arman felt himself sink into the grave she was already mentally digging for him.

"That wasn't a good defense, was it?"

"No."

Arman opened his mouth to respond but thought better of it. At this point, there was nothing he could say that wouldn't just make him look even worse. Better to accept his fate.

"How much trouble am I in?"

Elizabeth sighed as she protectively scooped Robyn into her arms. Much as she might have wanted to stay angry, Arman getting distracted and overabsorbed in his work was nothing new, and he'd already been tinkering on the porch when she left Robyn with him. In hindsight, that hadn't been the best call on her part. And damn him if he wasn't hard to stay mad at when he got that guilty look in his big, sad, brown eyes.

"Well, for starters, you can clean this up," she said, gesturing to the tools and parts she'd scattered across the yard with her entrance. All traces of venom were rapidly fading from her voice. "Afterward, *you* can start making lunch."

"That's fair."

"Oh, that's for starters," Elizabeth reminded him. "We're going to revisit this after . . ."

Elizabeth's eyes flicked out across the small village of Akers that they called home. With their house on a slight hill, it was easy to see the rest of the town and all the way out to the city of Olwin in the distance. But thanks to the Heart of the Sky, Elizabeth saw with more than her eyes. It had taken her a long time to master—to expand and contract the sensitivity of it as she needed—but her senses were supernaturally attuned to the air itself. Every sound, every smell, every movement of the air all came back to her. She could sense a storm coming from beyond the horizon. Feel a cross-breeze on a target a hundred yards out. She'd even learned to pinpoint her daughter's exact position from smell alone.

Most of the time, she kept her sphere of awareness confined to their home, but she still kept her senses peeled for a select few sounds in and around the rest of Akers. Like a carriage coming into town.

"What is it?" Arman asked before following his wife's eyes.

The carriage was drawn by a pair of jet-black horses and decorated with the royal blue crowned sword insignia of the ruler of Corsar. Only direct agents of the crown traveled in carriages like this one.

"What's that doing out here?" Elizabeth wondered aloud.

"One guess."

Arman's eyes locked on the carriage as his heart began to pound. Akers was a tiny nothing of a homestead. A dozen houses, a few farms, and a single inn that doubled as a community hub. The road it sat on wasn't even the main road to the city. It was the definition of obscure, which was exactly why he'd chosen here to live.

There was almost nothing in this town that would hold any interest to the crown or anyone else.

Nothing, except for maybe him and Elizabeth.

Sure enough, the carriage passed by every other house in Akers, continuing on until the driver brought it to a stop at the base of their hill. Neither of them moved, but Elizabeth's irises swirled and sparked as a light breeze began to sweep through, ready to pick up at a moment's notice.

The carriage door opened, and out stepped a man dressed in a tightly-tailored, black uniform with blue embroidery at the seams and shoulder, where he bore the same crowned sword insignia as the carriage. He had a light, almost pasty complexion contrasted by swept, jet-black hair. Long scars crisscrossed his sharp features, which were set in a permanent frown. An unusually short, boxlike, silver scabbard hung from his hip, standing out against the black of his clothes and highlighting the two hilts of the weapon, where his hand rested at all times.

When his gaze settled on Arman, the man's eyes narrowed.

"Phoenix," he greeted.

"Lupolt," Arman returned.

Lupolt's face contorted with rage as he threw a right cross too fast to see. Arman's head whipped to the side as the blow cracked across his cheek, and he nearly dropped to the floor before catching himself on the porch railing. Immediately, the breeze surrounding the house whipped into a full gust that shoved Lupolt back, and Elizbeth took up a defensive posture, positioning herself between him and her family. In her arms, Robyn began to cry.

"Back off!" she shouted.

"No, it's fine." Arman raised his hand. "He needed that."

Arman winced as he gingerly touched where Lupolt's fist had connected and came away with blood on his fingertips. "Good to see you too."

Lupolt grunted in disapproval. For his part, he had already regained his composure, straightening his stance and resetting his expression to a stoic neutral.

"That was for my home," Lupolt stated, deadpan.

"I figured."

"Lupolt. Did you come here for *a reason?*" Elizábeth asked.

"I did," Lupolt said. He took a moment to collect himself, drew in a long, deep breath, and met their eyes. "Lady Elizabeth, Arman Meshar. On behalf of the kingdom of Corsar, I have come to ask for your help."

AENERWIN

Arno's boots squelched against the mud as he walked, still blinking the sleep from his eyes. It was too early in the morning to be visiting the jailhouse. He tried not to think about the tea he hadn't gotten a chance to drink before being called out. That would only make him feel more tired.

"Jailhouse" was a bit presumptuous a name for a repurposed shed built next to the watchman's house, but it was all the town of Aenerwin had. The watchman was sitting out on his porch when Arno arrived, idly sketching in his notebook. He snapped the book closed when he saw Arno, tucking away his pencil into his cap like a feather, and stood up to greet the man.

"Morning, Vicar," the watchman greeted.

"Good morning, Clyde. I heard you've got someone for me."

"Mm-hmm." Clyde gestured for Arno to follow him to the jail. "Got brought in last night during the ruckus with the Henleys' wedding."

"What ruckus?"

"Right. Forgot you turn in early for a man your age. Couple hours after the ceremony, the whole party got a little out of hand. People getting too drunk and loud, breaking shit. Had to chuck the ones who didn't get dragged home in here."

In the holding cell was Arno's former companion Brass, sporting an ill-fitting and utterly ruined white wedding gown, its skirt torn and caked in mud. The gown was especially loose around the torso, awkwardly dangling off the man's body and exposing a toned chest decorated with multiple scars and an elaborate tattoo of a hawk. His curly hair was flopped to one side, giving him an off-kilter, disheveled look. When Arno and Clyde came in, he was telling a story to his only cellmate, a much more soberly dressed if no less unkempt-looking young man hanging on to every word.

"—and at that point I had two options: I could keep using my old sword, which, you know, was *fine*. Or I could fuck a merman," Brass recounted.

"And?"

"And it wasn't nearly as clammy as I expected."

Brass's cellmate howled with laughter, and Arno shook his head.

"I don't even know where to start," the vicar said.

Brass's eyes lit up as he finally noticed Arno, and he threw his arms in the air. The bodice of the gown slipped even farther down his chest.

"Church! Are you here to bail me out?"

Arno's lips pressed into a thin line, and he said a silent prayer begging Renalt for strength. "Brass, why are you wearing a wedding dress?"

"Oh, funny story, that," Brass said, pulling the dress back up. "See, I was at this wedding, and I told the bride I loved her dress. She said she loved my outfit, so I said we should switch, and we did! It was great. I danced with the groom, the bride's dad . . . Of course, then her mother took a swing at me for ripping the skirt, which was an accident. She missed me, hit some other old lady. That person yelled at her, some spouses got involved—it's a bit of a blur, but I think I accidentally unearthed some deeply buried unpleasantness there.

"Anyway, the whole thing ended with these two guys chucking the heaviest shit they could find across the square to prove a point. One of them tried to throw *me*, which I was down for, but he lost his grip on the backswing, and I ended up going through somebody's window."

"The bakery," Clyde specified.

"Miraculously, not a scratch on me anywhere important," Brass said. "So, I got up, and I yelled, 'free cakes for everyone!' I was joking, but other people took me seriously."

"Stole every baked good on the shelves," Clyde said.

"And that's when Pencil Hat over here found me," Brass said, pointing to Clyde. "Weird look by the way. Don't think I could pull it off, but you make it work."

A part of Arno considered leaving Brass, but he couldn't in good conscience make Brass someone else's problem. "Thank you for . . . containing him. I'll take him from here."

Clyde grunted in acknowledgement, unlocking the cell and turning Brass over to the vicar. Not wanting to get into an argument in front of Clyde, Arno kept his lips sealed and motioned for a smiling Brass to follow him out.

"Hey, speaking of looks, you wouldn't happen to know where the newlyweds live, would you?" Brass asked. "I gotta return this dress at some point. Then again, I don't want to interrupt the honeymoon. Maybe wait a few days."

"Are you completely incapable of not upending every place you set foot in?" Arno asked.

"Oh, come on," Brass said. "I went to *one* party."

"And somehow managed to ruin a family heirloom of a dress, start a brawl between two elderly women, and incite culinary larceny."

"It was a good party." When Arno wasn't amused, Brass held up his hands in surrender. "Look, I'm sorry if I caused trouble."

"No you're not."

"Not particularly, no. Except the bakery thing. That seemed expensive," Brass said. "I'm just bored, all right? I've been here for months now, and I'm starting to go stir crazy. The bar barely imports anything, nobody sells drugs of *any* kind, and there's only one hooker in town that everyone has to share. I'm not made for places like this."

"You were the one who wanted to come here," Arno said.

"I mean, I mostly just needed a ride out of Olwin before Vera got impatient and had me castrated, but helping Ruby get her life back felt like a nice thing to do," Brass said. "I didn't think it would take you this long to exorcize one girl."

"Well then, you're in luck," Arno said.

Brass's eyebrows shot up as the vicar piqued his interest. "You did it?"

"No. But the ritual scrolls I asked the Church of Avelina for finally came in," Arno said. "It should be exactly what we need to break whatever curse has dug itself into Ruby. It's a bit involved, so I was *hoping* you could be there to keep her calm. And then when it's all over, we can all get back to our old lives."

Brass's eyes lit up, and he immediately pulled the priest into a hug. "Church, I could kiss you!"

"I'd rather you didn't."

"Okay." Brass nodded as he broke off the hug. "Absolutely, I'm there. But can we wait a few hours before we do it?"

"Why?"

"I smoked a pick-me-up last night to keep myself going, and I think I added too much leria root to the blend, because I *still* haven't come down, and when this crash hits, it's going to hit hard."

Arno sighed. The sooner he helped Ruby, the sooner Brass would leave, and the sooner he would get his quiet, peaceful town back. But he'd endured three months of Brass's unbridled chaos. He could handle a few more hours.

RUBY

The ceremony room of the Church of the Guiding Saint was a much smaller, more intimate space than the knave. With the sun long since set, the room was illuminated by a spread of candles, whose soft light lent the space a cozy, calming air, only enhanced by the scent of a spring breeze that gently wafted off sticks of burning incense.

And Ruby was still a nervous wreck. The girl kept a brave face about it as best she could, but her stomach was twisting in knots, and her fingers unconsciously reached for her hair to twirl some of her red locks around her fingers.

Brass picked up on her discomfort without her saying a word.

"Having second thoughts?" he asked.

"No." She didn't even know why she was nervous. Having a curse latched onto her soul was something to be afraid of, but she'd taken that in stride without batting an eye. Lived with it in the back of her mind for months. But somehow this moment, getting the curse removed, was the part that had her sweating. It would have been funny if she wasn't so anxious.

"Will it hurt?" It was the first thing that came to mind, but even as she said it, she knew that wasn't what was bothering her.

"It shouldn't," Arno offered before his lips pursed and his eyes drifted to the side. "Well, actually, it might."

Ruby sat upright, suddenly much more concerned. "What?"

"You know how it can sting when you wash a cut?" he asked. "This is sort of like washing a cut on your soul. So it might . . . sting. I don't know for sure; it's not mentioned in the ritual notes."

"Wait. You haven't done this before?"

"I've removed dozens of curses. But not one like yours."

"What's wrong with mine?"

"Well, for starters, it isn't trying to kill you."

"That's bad?"

"Not to put too fine a point on it, but there's demonic influence latched onto your soul. It's doing *something* to you, and whereas normal curses leave people sick or dead, yours . . . I don't know what it's doing. And that's what worries me."

"Oh."

Arno was pretty good at comforting people who were afraid, but he was honest to a fault. He told people the truth, the whole truth, and nothing but the truth, even when it wasn't what they wanted or needed to hear. He did his best to deliver it as gently as he could, but he'd never learned the lesson that sometimes what people really needed was a nice lie to cling to.

"But it's fine, because we got it covered now, right?" Brass said, gesturing to the scroll Arno had brought with him.

"We should." Arno unraveled the scroll. "This ritual was made to purge curses and influences from a soul, regardless of what they are or what they're doing. It's basically built for someone in your shoes."

"See?" Brass said. "You're gonna be back to your old life in no time."

As soon as Brass said it, Ruby finally understood at least part of her worries.

Before getting a demon stuck to the bottom of her soul, or whatever she'd done, Ruby had been an escort working out of a high-end hotel in the city of Olwin. It wasn't the most respectable profession in Corsar, but it was good money, she was good at it, and her boss had always made sure she and all the other men and women working for them were well taken care of.

Until the fire. Until a madman had reduced her world to ashes and left her to pick up the pieces. She'd come to Aenerwin with Arno and Brass to get whatever was wrong with her fixed, but the truth was, there wasn't really anywhere else to go. Her job and home were gone. Her friends were all dead, missing, or had moved on. She didn't have any family. A church run by a former glintchaser had been as good a place to hole up as any, even if it was in a town so small, you could stand in the middle and throw a rock all the way to its edge. Getting the mystery demon curse sorted was barely more than an excuse.

When this was all over, she didn't have a life to go back to. She'd be starting completely from scratch. And that was terrifying.

"You're in the best hands in the business," Brass assured her. "I'd be dead a million times over without this man."

Ruby tried to look convinced as she watched Church make his preparations: lighting sticks of incense, setting up a small symbol of Renalt on a pedestal, and somehow changing the color of the candle flames in the room from orange to silver. Prior to coming to live in one, Ruby hadn't attended church much, and even now, she still hadn't seen much in the way of divine magic. A healed wound here, some sickness cured there, but nothing like this.

The uncertainty was what was getting to her, that was all. Uncertainty in the ritual. Uncertainty in her future. That was nothing she couldn't manage. She just had to suck it up and take the plunge.

Except, there was one more uncertainty she was having a harder time explaining away. A recoiling in the pit of her stomach strangely *other* in origin, like a kind of secondhand anxiety. Some part of her that didn't even feel like her did not want to be around Church and his divine powers. And the further along he got in his preparations, the stronger that feeling became.

With a flick of his fingers, Brass produced a tightly rolled nail seemingly from nowhere.

"Take the edge off?"

Ruby checked Church's face to see if this would somehow interfere with the ritual, but though he frowned in disapproval, he said nothing, so she snatched the packed herb from Brass and lit it on the nearest candle.

Brass's drugs worked fast. After only a couple drags, she could feel her hammering heartbeat calm, and her stomach settled. Not completely, but enough that she didn't feel a pressing need to run out of the room.

"Okay," she said. "Let's do this."

Finished with his own preparations, Arno nodded. "Go ahead and step back, Brass."

Ruby felt another brief pang of worry, wondering why this ritual had a minimum safe distance, but stayed still as the vicar began to recite a prayer in the language of the gods. She'd heard him say a prayer before, but those were never more than a few words long. This one was involved, giving her time to take in every melodic, sighing syllable and the inhuman power that resonated from them.

It was a beautiful language the gods spoke. The feeling in her stomach grew stronger and yet simultaneously had lost the urgency underpinning it. Actually, *everything* had lost some of its urgency.

Saints, Brass's stuff was good.

A warmth slowly spread across her body, pooling in her chest before spreading out. It took her a few seconds to figure out whether it was the drugs or the prayer. It was the latter. It was comforting for a moment until it started to tingle. When a ring of light drew itself around the sofa and bathed the room in a golden glow, it started to sting. It was like her whole body had been scraped all at once and the air was biting at every inch of her, inside and out.

"Hang in there. You're almost done," Brass reassured her, no idea whether or not he was lying to her. "Church?"

The vicar kept praying, presenting his amulet forward as he did. A shimmering sword of pure light appeared in the air above Ruby, point leveled at her chest, and her eyes went wide. Dimly, a voice in the back of her mind told her to run, but she couldn't move. The pleasant fog in her mind evaporated as pain gripped her entire body. A tug came from deep inside her chest as if her heart were about to wrench itself free of her body, and a scream tore itself from her lips.

Arno faltered. With sudden fear and confusion, he whispered, "What?"

Ruby screamed again as more pain exploded along her back. Something lashed out, Brass and Church were flung backward, and every light in the room snuffed out at once.

Ruby panted as the pain in her body faded to a stinging tingle, and she sat up, feeling the sofa rustle and scratch beneath her. She was sweating, surprised by the sharpness and clarity of the world around her. It took her a few moments to realize that it wasn't just that the effects of the nail were gone, but that even in the darkness, she could see everything around her.

After a few seconds of fumbling in the dark, Arno managed to find and strike a match to relight a candle. As light returned to the room, he froze, and Brass swore.

Ruby cocked her head, confused, until she realized what they were staring at. She was still sitting on the sofa, but now a tangle of thorny vines slick with blood spread out underneath her. Scorch marks ran along the sofa wherever the vines touched it as wisps of smoke curled off of them. When she caught a whiff of the smoke, she almost gagged on the smell of sulfur.

"It didn't work, did it?" Brass asked.

"No," Arno said. "It didn't."

Ruby sat on the front steps of the Church of the Guiding Saint hugging her knees and staring at the dirt. Her head was spinning, and since Arno and Brass had looked like they had a lot to talk about, she'd decided to get some air.

She was marked by something from the hells, and it turned out two of the most competent and experienced people she'd ever met had no idea what to do about it. Their big plan to help her had literally blown up in their faces, with nothing to show for it but a burnt sofa cushion, some dead thorns, and a sourceless feeling somewhere deep inside Ruby that they had made something angry. The front doors of the church opened behind her. She expected Brass but was greeted by someone else.

He was a slim, sandy blond-haired young man, maybe a few years younger than her, dressed in the plain tunic of an acolyte of the church. There were a dozen or so people living and working in the church under Arno, most of them older, quiet folks who Ruby hadn't really gotten to know, and she could honestly barely tell apart. But she remembered passing this boy in the halls a few times or seeing him talking with the vicar after dinner.

"Oh." She didn't mean to sound as disappointed as she did.

"The vicar and Brass are still talking," the boy said, somehow reading her mind. "But . . . I overheard how things went today."

As soon as he said it, his eyes widened, and he hastened to add, "I wasn't trying to eavesdrop or anything! I was cleaning the hallway and—"

"It's fine," Ruby reassured him. Three months in a small town as a mysterious newcomer—she was used to being an object of curiosity by now.

"Are you okay?"

Ruby's head perked up, caught off guard. She'd been expecting him to pry her for details or try to confirm some rumor about her being from another world or secretly sleeping with the vicar. Concern was new, at least from someone other than Brass or Arno.

"I don't know."

Gossip aside, the last three months had been unexpectedly nice. For the fuss Arno made about how dangerous it was to have a demonic curse latched onto her, it hadn't really been doing much. Until recently, the only evidence of it being there at all was the fact that she was fireproof. Meanwhile, she lived in the church for free with no obligations but occasionally talking with Arno and answering a few questions.

It was like a vacation.

But today, for the first time, she'd gotten a taste of another possibility. That there was no other side to this mess. She'd felt the ritual prying at her soul, trying to wrench out whatever was inside of her, and it had felt like she was being torn apart. It hadn't felt like it was pulling at something in her; it felt like it was pulling *her*. Whatever this curse was, it was a part of her now. And it was going to keep changing her.

One day, fireproof skin. Today, spontaneous vines and thorns. Tomorrow . . . Arno may not have known what was happening to her or what was coming next, but after today, in the pit of her stomach, Ruby knew that someday soon the changes would become unpleasant.

The boy stood, awkwardly avoiding eye contact as the silence between them grew.

Bart. She remembered his name now. They had spoken at the dinner table a few times and when Arno was handing out chores to the acolytes.

"You know," Ruby said, "all my life, everyone always told me to stay away from glintchasers. That they're nothing but walking trouble."

"I might believe that if Brass was the only one I'd met," Bart said. He paused, asking with his eyes for permission to sit down next to her. Ruby scooted to the side, offering him space on the steps. "But the vicar was one. And there was another one I met before. He saved me and the vicar and this whole town. For what it's worth, I don't think you're making a mistake trusting them. I know today things didn't work out, but if anybody can help you, it's them."

"You really believe in them, don't you?"

"Yeah. I do." He sounded like he was only now realizing it himself. "I know everyone always says glintchasers are trouble, but I think they're just the ones who stand up to trouble. And that gets them caught in it sometimes. I mean, you got caught up in trouble, and you're not a bad person."

"How do you know?" Ruby asked. "You just met me."

"I don't know," Bart said. "You just . . . seem good."

"Why do I feel like I'm being damned with faint praise?"

"No, really," Bart said. "It's like . . ."

"Like what? Come on, don't leave a girl hanging."

Instead of answering, Bart pointed up to the sky. High above the town of Aenerwin was a dark-bearded man in a leather coat, riding in on a flying board with a shimmering golden sail. Flying next to him, even more spectacular to behold, was a woman in hunter green leather, wind whipping through her hair as a pair of feathered, ethereal green wings gently flapped behind her. The pair touched down in the evening streets, looking like something out of another world entirely.

"Bart, right?" the man asked.

Bart was too stunned to speak, so he nodded.

"Could you get Arno for us?" Phoenix asked. "Tell him Arman and Elizabeth need to talk."

MONICA

Monica was fairly certain this man was trying to rip her off. The too-wide smile was the first clue. The fact that she could see him weighing her coin purse with his eyes was another. Then there was the way he kept trying to bury her in proper nouns.

"This stuff comes all the way up the coast from Puerto Oro," he said, affectionately slapping one of the barrels of rum he was selling. "I can't just give it away."

"Not asking you to," Monica said. "But fifty crowns a barrel for rum?"

"Rum?" The man looked offended. "This is genuine Techan product, aged in petalwood barrels that they import from the Blossom Forests all the way in Hidora. Five thousand miles were traveled to put these barrels together and bring them here. Fifty crowns is a bargain."

Monica was a tall, dark-skinned woman who wore her hair in thick ringlets that came down to her shoulders. Her clothes were plain and loose-fitting, save for the bright red sash wrapped around the waist of her tunic. She looked like any ordinary day laborer who had probably never even heard of Hidoran petalwood and would be suitably impressed by a man rattling off exotic sounding places and materials.

But looks were deceiving.

"I can get booze for half that somewhere else," Monica said, unimpressed.

"But as fine as this?" the man countered.

"Probably," Monica said. She glanced at the barrels. "Hidoran petalwood?"

"Yes! It's cut from the mystic forests in a land across the Oberin Sea," the man said, punctuating his words with a flourish of his hands.

"Mm-hmm," Monica said. "Interesting choice for a rum barrel. Since the sap's toxic."

The man's smile dropped as his eyes darted around to see if anyone had overheard her. Nobody was looking their way, but he still tried to salvage the lie anyway.

"Ah, they dry it out before they make the barrel," the man quickly stammered. "Makes it perfectly safe, but it gives the rum a special kick."

Monica folded her arms, letting her unmoved expression speak for itself. The merchant's Adam's apple bobbed as he swallowed, hard.

"How about a discount?" he asked, changing the subject. "Forty crowns a barrel?"

"Twenty."

The man grimaced and looked like he wanted to protest, but he held his tongue. With a grumble and a shrug, he agreed, and Monica tossed the money onto the counter of his stand.

"You can bring over your wagon, and I'll help you load it," the man said.

"I'm good," Monica dismissed.

With a casual stride, she strolled to the pile of rum barrels next to the man's stand and, without effort, hoisted one onto her shoulder, exposing her well-muscled arms. The man's eyes went wide, flitting between Monica and the barrel before he quickly and quietly tucked away his payment and bid her a good day.

There were dozens of settlements running along the coast of Corsar, varying from tiny fishing villages to actual beacons of trade. Rockshore was in the middle of that scale. Built along the shoreline of a sheltered bay, it was big enough for some traders to justify making stops and close enough to the capital to be comparatively safe, but not so big or close to put on most people's maps. The skies were overcast, the air smelled like salt, and everything was made of cobblestone, save for the boardwalk docks. Monica crossed the street, partly to get to her meet-up spot with Thalia faster and partly to avoid what looked like trouble up ahead. A ragged man, dirty and drenched in seawater, was staggering down the road, growling and grunting incoherently at anyone who came near him. Her guess was a shipwreck survivor washed ashore in shock or maybe, worst-case scenario, a kraken cultist driven mad by what he'd seen beneath the waves. Either way, he wasn't her problem.

"What did you get?" a wry voice asked her.

Thalia was a light-skinned woman with dark curls tied back and held at bay with a handkerchief headband. She was a full head shorter than Monica and a lot spindlier in terms of muscle, but that didn't stop her from carrying two massive armloads of food in oversized canvas bags.

"Rum," Monica said, hefting the barrel. She looked at the bags the smaller woman was carrying. They were slipping. "Need help with that?"

"No, no." Thalia shook her head and adjusted her grip. "I've got this."

"It's a long way back to the Star."

"Carry your fucking barrel."

Monica chuckled, and the two women fell into step together, following a street that hugged the water's edge, a rope barrier all that separated them from the short drop into the tides below. The splash of waves crashing against the rocks left Monica with a pang of nostalgia. It had been a long time since she'd lived this close to the ocean.

"We got another letter from your friends this morning," Thalia mentioned as they walked. "When are they coming to visit?"

"I don't have friends."

"Fine. Your companions."

Monica shrugged her shoulder that wasn't supporting the barrel. "I don't know. Depends on if anything comes up, I guess."

"You did tell them we're not in Glassburrow anymore, right?"

"I'm not that much of an asshole."

"If you say so," Thalia said, and Monica flipped her off with her free hand. Thalia laughed.

"And what do you mean you don't have friends?" Thalia asked. "What about me?"

"You don't count. I pay you."

"Who says you can't be friends with your boss?"

"Your boss."

"Whatever," Thalia dismissed. "You love me."

Despite herself, Monica smiled. Out of all the bartenders she'd employed over the years, she had to admit, Thalia was her favorite. Even after everything she'd learned about Monica, she was never intimidated by her, and she never needed much excuse to speak her mind. She liked that kind of backbone in a person. At the same time, she never pushed too hard, always respecting Monica's boundaries, often without even needing to be told what they were.

Thalia caught Monica's smile, and a victorious smirk spread across her face. Monica was about to tell her not to let it go to her head when she heard panicked shouting coming from a street away. Monica felt a flicker of warmth in her chest and willed it to extinguish. If there was trouble, she was determined to react like a normal person.

"We should get home," she said.

"What's going on over there?" Thalia said at the same time, already walking in the direction of the noise.

Of fucking course.

"Thalia." Monica had to resist the urge to physically drag her away from the scene. "Fuck are you doing?"

"If something's causing trouble in a place I want to live, I want to know what it is."

"It's probably just some idiots getting in a fight," Monica lied. She was a shit liar. When a brawl broke out in a port town, people jeered or encouraged it, and those weren't the kind of shouts they were hearing. No, whatever was happening, people weren't annoyed or entertained. They were afraid.

Thalia kept walking toward the commotion, and Monica hurried after her.

"Thalia." Monica was still trying to reason with her as they rounded the corner. "This isn't—"

She forgot what she was going to say next, and Thalia read her mind. "Holy shit."

Except for a few brave souls brandishing fishing spears and old swords, everyone on the street was running. A man—a thing—with a disproportionately bulbous arm growled and thrashed at everything around it. Where it wasn't covered by tattered, wet rags, the creature's form was red and sinewy, like swollen, exposed muscle. Every time its oversized fist crashed into the ground, nearly flattening someone, it came away with cobblestones stuck to its skin.

Thalia stood frozen in fear. Monica froze too, but for a different reason. The giant arm and rippling flesh were new, but she recognized what was left of the same man she'd avoided in the street. And that wasn't the only reason she recognized the monster. In another breath, Thalia's fight-or-flight instinct would have sent her sprinting in the opposite direction, but the monster was faster. Its retreat from the town's defenders put it on a collision course with her, and it reared back its rapidly growing arm to swat her out of the way. The bartender swore, backpedaled, and tripped.

Instinct took over, and the warmth in Monica's chest spread like wildfire through her body. The rum barrel crashed to the ground as she caught Thalia, yanking her back with one arm. With her other arm, she shoved the creature into a wall.

Instead of smashing into it, the monster's entire body briefly pancaked and flattened against it, rippling like a water balloon that had been struck. His skin ripped open as his whole body expanded, and what was left of his human form transformed into a massive, hulking creature of stringy, crimson flesh. It was still humanoid in shape but easily over ten feet tall with just as wide of an arm span. Its skin glistened like jelly and reeked of citrus with a pointed head and webbed, pudgy hands. Two bulbous green orbs Monica could only assume were eyes swiveled in their sockets, and rows of teeth began to grow into place along the sides of a mouth wide enough to swallow half a person.

As the creature picked itself up off the ground, its skin stuck to the street, stretching like putty as it hefted its considerable bulk. It let out a deep, bellowing sound somewhere between a wheeze and a roar.

Monica had never fought the monster personally, but she'd shared drinks with the people who had. Lexos, the human mimic. Part man, part shape-shifting monstrosity dug up from a forgotten lab buried in a mountain. It had made quite the payday for the glintchasers who'd caught and sold it fifteen years ago. The thing was, the monster had been sold to the Academy, which meant it should have been locked up in Oblivion with every other monster they'd collected.

Before she could decide whether to kill the monster or give it a wide berth, it made the decision for her by lunging toward Thalia.

Monica's eyes flashed with golden light as a burning halo materialized above her head, and she attacked. Searing heat spread through her whole body like a fire in her veins, and she let out a feral shout as she delivered a punch, driving Lexos's face straight into the cobblestones. Letting her momentum carry her, she pivoted into a kick, sending it rolling.

"Monica—" Thalia started, only to be cut off by Monica grabbing her by the sleeve and hauling her to her feet.

"Run!" Monica ordered. Her voice seemed to echo itself, as if there were two of her speaking at once. Thalia listened.

Monica spun around just in time to catch the creature running at her on all fours. Her body wreathed itself in light, and the heat inside her turned to burning pain. As the creature lunged again, Monica delivered an uppercut, stopping it in its tracks. Throwing her full weight into her next punch, she landed a blow square in its chest, sending it crashing into another building.

It was a stupid, amateur mistake not recognizing the man wasn't human the first time she saw him on the street. His movements should have given it away—jerking and floundering like he was uncomfortable in a bipedal body. If she'd realized what it was then . . .

She took her frustrations out on the creature itself, which was getting back up. It grew thick, bony plates across its forearms, trying to armor itself. The plates shattered against her next fist.

She was better than this. Smarter than this. She'd heard the sound of a crowd suddenly confronted with a monster more times than she could count.

She should have known what they were walking into before they'd even gotten around the corner.

All she would have had to do was keep Thalia back, tell everyone to stay back, and wait for someone else to handle things. She didn't have to be fighting this thing. She'd counted at least five people trying to fight the monster before her. More than enough to handle something like this.

Maybe. If they were smart. And careful. And lucky.

Or maybe they'd have gotten themselves killed.

What was her problem? Why couldn't she just, *for once*, stay out of something like this?

Lexos switched tactics, growing tendrils from its back and using them to drag her toward its gaping maw. Monica thrashed against the creature, but the more she did, the more tendrils it grew to try and hold her. Running out of options, she wedged her arms between its jaws, doing her best to hold them open to stop the thing from biting her in half. Its teeth dug into her, but she ignored them.

Every fiber of Monica's body screamed from the white-hot heat coursing through her. Light cascaded off of her, bright enough to turn the creature translucent. With a roar, Monica's vision went white, and twin streaks of light flashed from her eyes, burrowing straight down the monster's throat and flash-searing everything it touched. Monica swiveled her head, slicing the creature in half lengthwise with the beams until all tension in its body vanished and she tore herself free.

Monica's halo dissolved into the air, taking the light wreathing her body and the heat searing her from the inside out with it. She was left standing over the remains of the monster, panting from exertion, blood running down her arms from rows of teeth marks. The two halves of the creature spasmed once before beginning to melt into a thick sludge, with foul smelling smoke like spoiled citrus and burnt meat curling off of it.

As Monica caught her breath, she finally took notice of the people around her, all staring in slack-jawed awe and horror. The monster may have been beyond their comprehension, but Monica saw recognition in some of their eyes. A burning halo. Heavenly golden light. Impossible strength. There was only one thing she could be.

A sentinel. A warrior of heaven, incarnate in the flesh, standing right before them. Even the ones who wouldn't know the exact legend would already be making assumptions from what they'd seen. And then, even worse, came the *real* recognition.

A dark-skinned woman who wore a golden halo and blazed like the sun. Only one woman in all of Corsar fit that bill, and there were few who hadn't heard the stories. She was Angel, one of the most infamous glintchasers in Corsar's history.

So much for sticking around this town.

COLD-BLOODED

S creams echoed in the darkness of a freezing cold basement as Julian ran for his life. He could feel his heartbeat in his ears, and his whole body was numb. Maybe from adrenaline, maybe the cold. He didn't know and barely noticed.

All of the lanterns were out, leaving him to stumble near blind, guided only by a faint crack of light along the gap in the trapdoor that led upstairs. He banged his shin on the leg of a table and nearly fell. Suddenly losing all traction on his next step, he went sprawling. He nearly bit his own tongue off when his jaw cracked against an icy floor.

This was wrong. All of it. Why were the lights out? Why were his bodyguards begging for their lives? Why did his basement feel like the tundra when it was supposed to be the middle of summer?

His ears rang and his body ached, but more screams from behind him spurred him to scramble to his feet. Out of the basement. If he could just make it out of the basement, he could get out of this cold, out of this darkness, and out of danger.

Someone behind him begged for their life before their pleas turned to a muffled wail of pain. There was a thud. A crash. The sickening squelch of a blade burying itself in flesh and slicing through tissue.

A sound like a thousand glasses shattering in rapid succession.

He doubled his pace up the ladder to the trapdoor, cracking his knuckles against the rungs more than once until he was close enough to claw for the handle and push with all his might.

It didn't budge.

Julian shoved on the handle with increasing desperation, nearly throwing himself from the ladder as he tried to shake the door open or even loose, but it remained frozen in place. The handle itself was cold to the touch, to the point where if he hadn't been so afraid, he might have recoiled at the sting. He tried to reposition his foot on a rung for better leverage, only to find it too slick with ice, and his feet slipped from under him. With a panicked yelp, he tumbled back to the ground. He hit his head twice on the way down and landed in a crumpled heap.

One final yell came from behind him before being cut off with a wet gurgle. A deathly silence fell over the basement.

Julian slowly pulled himself off the ground, feeling warm, wet blood trickling down his forehead. His eyes were adjusting to the darkness, but he could still make out terrifyingly little. He was trapped in the basement with something, and he couldn't even see what it was.

He crawled and fumbled in the dark, trying to remember where the lantern closest to the ladder was. He tried and failed to control his stammering whimpers.

Light. He needed light.

He made it to the wall where the lantern should have been, and after a few misses, his hands clasped around it. He grabbed a match from the tray mounted beside it and shakily relit the lantern, banishing the darkness with a soft orange glow.

Finally able to see, Julian dared to turn around. His breath caught in his throat.

The entire basement glittered in the lamplight, coated with a thin layer of frost like grass on a winter morning. Swaths of ice spread out from the doorway to the next room, and at the edges of the light, he could just make out one of his bodyguards, lying face up, eyes wide, in a frozen pool of their own blood. Standing in the doorway itself was a lithe, deathly pale woman clad in a dark blue hood and leather jerkin. Frost covered her extremities and the blades of the daggers she held in either hand, and, along with her dark hair, it framed her white, pupilless eyes.

Terrified recognition dawned on Julian's face as he slowly backed away until his back hit a wall. A lump formed in his throat that he tried and failed to swallow. His knees turned to jelly, and he had to brace himself against the wall to stay upright. He wished it had been a demon. A ghost. Anyone or anything but her.

"Snow."

His voice came out in a hoarse whisper. His mouth was dry. His pants were wet.

"Hello, Julian." Her voice was hollow and glasslike, as if her vocal cords themselves were made of ice.

Julian cleared his throat, trying to regain his voice. "Y-you're not dead."

"No. I'm not."

"G-good," he stammered. "I was worried. S-sorry about the guys. They, uh, they must've not known it was you. Did you need something?"

"A rat told me you were one of the brokers who circulated the contract on me," Snow said. There was no emotion in her voice. No malice. Just a statement of fact.

"It was a Handler contract! I have to circulate those, you know that! Nobody crosses him."

"Nobody crosses *me*, Julian."

"So, you're both scary! What, you want me to pick?"

"You did pick. And you picked wrong."

Julian made a break for it. He didn't know where he was running to, just that he had to run away.

Before he made it three steps, ice spread out from Snow's foot, reaching Julian and rooting him to the floor. He tripped, but with his foot frozen in place, his ankle couldn't follow the rest of his body, and there was a loud pop as he hit the ground.

A scream raced up his lungs but got stuck in his throat, coming out as little more than a hoarse, keening whimper. Snow stalked toward him, the temperature seeming to drop with every step until Julian could see his breath. She loomed over him, crouching low and close to his face.

"Whatever you want, name it," Julian begged. "You want to kill the Handler? I'll help you kill him! Glint. Name your price, I'll triple it!"

"I don't want money or the Handler," Snow said. "I want the one who put the contract out in the first place."

"What? *I* don't even know who that was! I swear!"

"You run every stop on Future's Road. You know everyone who comes through and where they're headed."

A glimmer of hope raced through Julian's veins. "I do! I do! Whoever you wanna find, if they used a road, I've got them! Tell you where they are, where they're going, the name of their favorite hooker! Anything! Just gimme a name! I'll find them!"

The color of Snow's eyes shifted ever so slightly, going from white to a pale, icy blue. The barest hint of anger crept into her previously emotionless voice as she said the name of the man she had been hunting for three months.

"Silas Lamark."

When Snow emerged from Julian's roadside stop, she saw a blue-haired woman in a set of cerulean mage's robes waiting for her outside.

"You've been busy," Ink said, casting a glance to the frozen windows.

"Lots to do."

"I imagine. You know, I'm genuinely surprised you kept the beacon like I told you to. I was expecting to have much more trouble tracking you down."

As a condition for not being thrown into Oblivion for her numerous crimes, Ink had given Snow a small arcane beacon to carry on her person at all times. According to the High Inquisitive, all it did was give off a unique magic signature Ink could use to home in on for teleportation and scrying. As long as Snow carried it, Ink could find her with ease, which would come in handy if the wizard ever needed a favor from Corsar's most notorious assassin.

It would seem that day had come.

"What do you want, Ink?"

"Why does everyone always jump to that question with me?" Ink asked. "It's like you all think I can't make a purely social visit. We're friends. In a roundabout sort of way. Acquaintances at least. Maybe I just wanted to chat."

"Do you?"

"Of course not. But it's rude to assume."

Snow resisted the urge to groan in exasperation. The timing wasn't perfect—she wanted to stay on Silas's trail—but if Ink *was* calling in her favor, this was her best chance to get out of the High Inquisitive's debt and be rid of the damn beacon. Ink had assured her she was the only one who would be able to track it, but Snow had been using shadow magic to cloak her movements from magical sight since she was seventeen. *Anything* being able to track her felt wrong. Not to mention that if Ink was asking for Snow's help, it meant that whatever was going on was big and probably interesting.

"What's the job?"

SASEL

Arman and Elizabeth sat in the back seat of a hired carriage as it bounced along the stone-and-gravel road, rattling their bones with every bump. Future's Road, the artery that linked Corsar's capital city to the rest of the interior, was about as nice as roads got within the kingdom, but that still left plenty of room for dips, catches, and potholes that had made the last few hours uncomfortable at best and painful at worst.

"I hate carriages," Arman grumbled.

"Could have flown in," Elizabeth reminded him.

"It'd be too much of a scene," he said. "I'm trying *not* to broadcast that I'm coming here."

Elizabeth rolled her eyes, resisting the urge to thump her husband on the arm. "Then stop complaining."

Arman gave an annoyed grunt and went back to watching the ocean from the window. The chop of the water's surface broke up the light of the afternoon sun that glinted across it, creating a shimmering tapestry that stretched out to the horizon. The view and the scent of saltwater sent him straight back to his childhood, a time when anything seemed possible.

How far away that all felt now.

"Are you okay?"

"It's just a city," Arman said. "I'll be fine."

There was a furrow in her brow, and he took a guess that she didn't believe him. But before he could reassure her, her eyes lit up, and she pointed back to the window.

"We're here."

As the carriage crested a hill, the city of Sasel finally came into view.

Three grand stone bridges linked the mainland to the island on which the city rested. Sloped walls encircled the island, topped at regular intervals by towers mounted with Old World cannons. Beyond the walls, the city itself rose up, a veritable mountain of stone and glass towers with rivers of flying skiffs soaring between them.

This was the capital of the kingdom, the City of Yesterday and Tomorrow, unmatched in all the world. It was here that the collected resources and knowledge scavenged from the Old World had been collected, their wonders implemented or even imitated. A city of merchants and collectors. Innovators and historians. The home of the Academy, the crown family, and the First Church of Avelina. In all his years, Arman had never been able to see it as anything other than the city of his dreams, a place he felt with his whole soul that he belonged, even before he had ever set foot in it. He was not fine. Not when he knew that he would never call this place home again.

Elizabeth squeezed his hand, dulling the ache in his chest with her touch. She'd known he was lying about being okay.

Their driver pulled their carriage into the line of travelers waiting to get into the city, barking out that it would be just a few more minutes. Arman took the time to try and compose himself.

In seven years of exile, it had never really struck him how much the city meant to him. In the earliest days, he'd been too consumed by guilt and grief to even think about it. Then he married Elizabeth. His family had moved to Olwin to be closer to him. Robyn arrived. And so the Jewel of the Coast had faded from his mind.

But now that he was back, staring at brilliant blue banners and the proudly displayed sword and crown crest of the city and the small fleet of multicolored vessels from across the globe in the harbor, he felt what he had lost.

"It's ridiculous," he muttered.

"It's not," Elizabeth said.

"It's just a city."

"Not to you."

He frowned, swallowed a lump in his throat. How did she do that? How did she bring him to the verge of tears with as simple a gesture as giving him permission to feel sadness? It made him feel so vulnerable. And selfish. And *seen*.

"Thank you."

She said nothing, instead cupping his cheek in her other hand. He leaned into it for a moment, letting her steady him until he could finally draw a breath without shaking again.

"I'm okay."

"Okay."

"ROLAND!"

Elizabeth pulled away, surprised by the sudden shout from a new, unfamiliar voice outside. There was a warbled, bellowing quality to the voice that made it sound inhuman. And Arman recognized it.

"ROLAND!" the voice shouted again, nearer to their carriage this time.

"What do they want with the king?" Elizabeth murmured. She called out to the front of their carriage, "Driver? What's going on?"

"Some vagrant's trying to cause a ruckus on the bridge," their driver called back. "Looks like the gatekeepers are coming out."

Arman was barely paying attention, digging through his bottomless bag for his coin purse. Sifting through everything else he had stored away, he dug out a fistful of glint, dumped it across the back seat, and climbed out of the carriage door.

"Arman?"

"Come on!"

Elizabeth followed her husband out onto the bridge, joining the crowd of people, carts, and animals all crossing in both directions. Before she could ask what they were doing, the stones beneath her feet began to shake.

"WHERE IS THE COWARD WHO FLED HIS DUTY?"

The voice was coming from farther back down the bridge, toward the mainland. Already, guards of the city's gates were pushing their way through the crowds toward it, but they were still a ways out, having to fight for every foot of progress they made through the massive stream of people in their way.

"WHERE IS THE TRAITOR WHO CALLS HIMSELF KING?"

Arman pushed aside his coat and drew his wand from the holster on his hip. The cylindrical chamber in its base spun before clicking a power cell into place, and the wand's tip began to spark bright white.

Seeing where this was going, Elizabeth drew her twin scimitars and pressed their pommels together. In a flash of light, the blades transformed into an elegantly sculpted hunting bow.

The crowds in front of them forcibly parted as a tall, twisted figure shoved its way forward. Standing head and shoulders above anyone else, the figure was draped in a faded, moth-ridden purple cloak, which sat awkwardly on a pair of broad, hunched shoulders and did little to hide the disfigured, bark-like skin beneath. Faceted eyes like a fly's peered out from beneath hair of moss and vines, and they blazed with rage.

"BRING ME ROLAND!" the figure roared.

Somewhere along the bridge, one of the guards yelled for the figure to stop.

In response, it raised two gnarled, twisted arms toward the sky, and the stones of the bridge began to shake. An instant later, plant roots as thick as a man burst out from the water below the bridge, crashing into the stone. The shock reverberated through the entire bridge, and cracks raced along its length. Confused gasps were replaced by screams.

"Who in the hells is that?" Elizabeth asked.

"Edelfric, Scourge of the Iron Forest," Arman said.

"Who?"

"One of mine," Arman said. "He's got a grudge against Roland's father going back decades."

Edelfric had been a servant of King Roland I once but fell defending his king during a trip to the Iron Forest. He should have died. Instead, the magic of the forest had bonded to him, twisting him into a crazed plant monster who believed himself abandoned and betrayed by the crown. He'd spent years terrorizing both the royal family and the settlements along the forest until the Starbreakers had managed to tear him to splinters and toss what was left into Oblivion.

"You could have just said 'bad guy.'"

"Fine! He's a bad guy!"

Elizabeth rolled her eyes and crouched down. From out of her back, a pair of ethereal, bright green feathered wings burst out, expanding out to their full wingspan and pushing back people all around her.

With a single flap, she catapulted into the air, kicking up dust in her wake. Immediately, people began to point her out in the sky.

"By the gods, look!"

"The Winged Lady!"

"It's her! We're saved!"

As the people cheered at her arrival, Elizabeth faded away, and the Winged Lady emerged. She was the knight of the crown, defender of Corsar. And down below, her husband slipped back into his old instincts like a familiar coat.

The Meshars were gone. In their place, Phoenix and Wings went to work.

Edelfric's head whipped toward the sky, spotting the flying archer as her first salvo of arrows sailed toward him, splintering harmlessly against his skin. Thorns grew out from his body and the surface of the giant roots, slowly digging into the bridge. When they were the size of daggers, they started launching themselves at Wings.

As Wings nimbly weaved through the air to avoid Edelfric's assault, Phoenix took in the rest of the situation. The guards from the gate were nearly here, for all the good they could do. With this many bystanders around, neither he nor the city itself could bring down any heavy weapons on Edelfric, which was what they needed. And if the Scourge wasn't removed from the bridge, the roots he was summoning could tear the whole thing apart. The structure was already unstable, bits crumbling off and splashing into the water.

In only a few seconds, he pieced a plan together and rushed to meet the oncoming guard.

"Tell the cannoneers to get ready to fire!" Phoenix shouted. "We'll give them a clear shot!"

The guards stared back at him, confused. At least one of them worked out that by "we," he meant him and Wings, but even that guard didn't take any heed in his instructions.

Phoenix groaned, worried for a minute that he'd have to do everything himself, when another root burst through the bridge between him and the guards. As they shouted in panic, he reacted. He aimed his wand straight into the base of the root and fired a blast at full power that punched a hole into the outer bark. With his free hand, he dug out a fire sphere and threw it straight into the hole he created, blasting the root apart in a ball of flame.

As the flaming remains of the tree root rained down around them, the guards adjusted their assessment of Phoenix. Someone ran off to carry his message.

In the air, Wings flew in a tight loop, narrowly avoiding a wooden tendril reaching out to grasp her. Below her, Edelfric literally dug his heels in, a tangle of thick roots and vines securing himself to the part of the bridge where he chose to make his stand. She loosed another arrow in response, this time propelling it forward with a burst of wind.

It barely sunk into Edelfric past the arrowhead.

Edelfric answered her attack with another hail of thorns that launched themselves from his chest, but they never even came close as Wings used a gust of wind to blow them harmlessly off course.

They were at an impasse.

"Wings!" Phoenix shouted to be heard over the sound of screams and stone cracking. "We need to clear the bridge!"

Wings looked down, taking in the sheer number of people still on the bridge. If the task daunted her, she didn't let it show on her face.

"Keep him busy!"

Wings shot higher into the sky, disengaging from her fight with Edelfric and leaving Phoenix to face him alone. His faceted eyes bore into Phoenix, his head listed to one side in recognition. Good. Phoenix could use that.

"YOU. BOY GLINTCHASER. HAS ROLAND CALLED YOU TO FIGHT HIS BATTLES YET AGAIN?"

"A lot older than a boy now," Phoenix said. "And Roland abdicated. His son wears the crown."

"SO HE IS EVEN MORE A COWARD THAN HE WAS BEFORE!" Edelfric lumbered forward. "AND STILL YOU SERVE HIM."

"Actually, we're kind of on the rocks these days," Phoenix said. "I guess you don't get much news in Oblivion. How did you get out anyway?"

"I WARNED YOU BEFORE. NO PRISON WOULD HOLD ME."

"I guess you were right," Phoenix admitted. He could feel the wind beginning to pick up. He didn't need to stall for much longer.

He armed another fire sphere and threw it at the same time that Edelfric launched another barrage of thorns. The attack was swallowed up in the explosion, and Phoenix threw up a force shield from his bracer to protect against what little got through.

Edelfric roared in fury, his whole body beginning to grow as the plant life he had summoned over the course of the battle began to wrap itself around him. As another massive root broke through the bridge and raced out to meet him, Phoenix braced himself to take the blow on his shield.

It never landed.

Twin beams of light flared to life, searing into the oncoming root and splitting it in two before it could ever reach Phoenix. When the beams vanished, Phoenix turned in time to see Angel step out of the crowd, a radiant glow rapidly fading from her skin.

Phoenix didn't even have time to be surprised.

"Nice timing," Phoenix greeted before pointing his wand at the ground and firing a string of spider silk from it to anchor himself to the bridge. "Now, hold on to something!"

Angel cocked an eyebrow but only until she glanced up, after which she immediately dug her fingers into the stonework of the bridge.

Wings dove through the air, straight toward the bridge as all around her, the winds whipped into an impossibly strong gale. When she landed feet first on the bridge, the winds rushed out from her, sweeping across the bridge and scooping up each and every person still on it. Hundreds of miniature cyclones formed, keeping everyone aloft high above the field of battle.

Sweat beaded on her forehead. Her whole body shook, and her heart fluttered like a hummingbird's, but she held them. All of them.

On the walls, the guards saw their opening. Two of the cannons along the wall pivoted, making final adjustments to their trajectory before both firing. Twin balls of pure white arcane fire tore through the air, landing direct hits on Edelfric's form. Bits of wood and stone sprayed out as the Scourge's body was wiped off the surface of the bridge in an instant, leaving behind nothing but a smoking crater.

The blowback from the blast snapped Phoenix's anchor line like a piece of twine, and he went cartwheeling over the edge of the bridge. For a moment, he tumbled end over end, too fast to even make sense of which way was up.

Then, all at once, he came to a sudden stop as a pair of strong arms scooped him out of the air. When the world finally stopped spinning, he was in Wings's arms as she very gently guided them through the air back down to the bridge.

"You couldn't have just backed up before the blast?" she asked.

"I knew you'd catch me."

"I should drop you just for that."

As soon as they landed and Phoenix was set down on his feet, Wings practically collapsed into him, exhausted. All around them, people were gently drifting down, guided to safe, solid ground at either end of the bridge.

Angel dusted off her hands on her shirt, sauntering over to join them. Elizabeth flashed her the biggest smile she could manage.

"Hey, stranger," she greeted.

"Hey, yourself," Angel replied with a nod of respect. "Hell of a move."

"I have my moments."

"So, you actually got my letter?" Phoenix asked.

"Contrary to whatever Brass might tell you, I do read my mail. Actually came at a pretty good time. Was looking for an excuse to get out of town," Angel said. As she looked around, her face's normal resting frown deepened. "We might wanna talk about this later though."

Phoenix looked around. From the guards to the civilians, every single pair of eyes were on the three of them as an awestruck silence fell over the bridge. In another second, it gave way to cheers.

"Well," Phoenix muttered, "so much for keeping a low profile."

THE CALL

*A*fter everything they'd accomplished, the Starbreakers had earned the right to think of themselves as important. But they weren't "ignore summons from the King and Queen of Corsar" important. So when a squad of royal guardsmen showed up at their collective home in Sasel and said their presence was required in the Pearl Palace and that they should come at once, they dropped what they were doing, grabbed their gear, and they went.

And that was how, for the third time in their lives, the five glintchasers found themselves face-to-face with the Crown of Corsar—King Roland and Queen Katherine. Even now, in their later years, the pair was as beautiful and fierce as they appeared on coins and in artwork. Their hair, though graying, remained the kind a painter could get lost in. The skin around them had more lines now, but their eyes were as sharp as ever. Both of their outfits, finely tailored and exquisitely decorated, also bore minor accents of armor, lending them the air of soldiers who hadn't quite made the transition from fighting to ruling.

Then there was the third face.

With his wavy, burnt umber hair, piercing blue eyes, small nose, and strong jaw, Roland II managed to be the spitting image of both his parents, though he'd traded their quiet intensity for an infectious spark of life and energy. His legs, or rather, the devices attached to them, whirred as he walked. A few years ago, an assassin had targeted the crown prince. The Starbreakers had prevented the assassination and saved Roland's life, but it had been close. Roland's spine had been injured, and by the time healing prayers could be administered, too much time had passed to restore full functionality.

The prince could not, would never, walk unassisted. But rather than crutches or a chair, he made do with a set of arcane braces for his legs and back, designed and built by Phoenix himself.

Roland II shook Phoenix's hand, nodding to the others. "Thank you all for coming."

"Well, twelve people with magic spears didn't seem like the sort of invitation you politely decline," Brass pointed out before being elbowed by Angel.

Roland II apologized anyway. "I'm sorry if that gave the wrong impression. The situation is urgent."

"What is it?" Phoenix asked.

The prince stepped aside to let his parents speak.

"We received word this morning that a machine of the Old World is attacking the kingdom," Roland's father said.

"What, like all of it at once? Think we'd have noticed that," Brass said, earning another elbow.

The king continued. "It was found in Red Gorge, a mining town in the far east. The machine awoke and began attacking indiscriminately. In a matter of minutes, the entire town was destroyed."

"The people?" Church asked.

"We hope and pray, but for now, we can only confirm one survivor," Katherine said. "They were a member of the freelancer company the town had hired to protect against anything the miners might encounter. Their account is the original source of the information, though, scrying has since confirmed the town's fate."

Katherine tapped at the table in the meeting room's center, and arcane glyphs and grooves carved into its surface lit up. In a brief shower of light particles, images took shape in the air.

The Starbreakers were treated to a gallery of the utterly destroyed remains of a mining settlement. Buildings toppled, flattened, and burned. Rock faces shattered, or in some places, sheared glassy smooth and still glowing at the edges. It looked like

Red Gorge had been hit by a thunderstorm, earthquake, and lance of divine light all at the same time.

"Red Gorge was only the first. We've already received distress messages from several neighboring settlements. Scrying shows the same results in every one of them," Katherine said. "We're still determining what exactly the machine is. But from everything the survivor and his company saw before the attack, we believe it might be something called a Servitor."

"Renalt preserve us," Church whispered.

The others were silent, but eyes immediately fell onto Snow, who just last year had become infused with the power of a Servitor Heart. She ignored them, staring straight ahead.

"We've already discussed the threat with our own forces and the Academy. But our son put forward your names as another option worth exploring."

"Our best option," Roland II corrected.

"Why us?" Phoenix asked.

It wasn't that he thought they weren't up to the job. After Snow had absorbed the Heart of Ice, Phoenix had learned everything he could about the Hearts and the machines they were made to power. If anybody could be called an expert on Servitors, it was him and his company. But Roland didn't know that.

"Because freelancers have more firsthand experience and knowledge about the Old World than anyone else, and because the five of you are the best freelancers there are," the prince said. "At least that I know of."

"Well, you're not wrong about that first part."

"Or the second," Brass added.

"But even we can't take a Servitor," Snow said, breaking the cold silence she'd been maintaining at the back of the group.

Katherine's ears homed in on the knowing tone in Snow's voice. "You know what this machine is?"

Phoenix briefly explained his research into Servitors and their Hearts. He even talked about how he'd looked into ways to drain the power of the Hearts, though he left out the part about how that last line of inquiry had become one of the many wedges that had driven him and Snow apart.

"*The point is, one Heart could count among the most powerful artifacts ever discovered, and Servitors had multiple Hearts,*" *Phoenix said.* "*If we want even a snowball's chance in the hells against this thing, we'd need . . .*"

"*What?*"

"*A lot.*"

"*Every resource we have is being devoted to fight this monster,*" *Katherine said.* "*If you're as knowledgeable about this machine as you say you are, you'll have whatever you need.*"

Phoenix tried and failed to keep his expression neutral as one of the sovereigns of their homeland pledged them her full support. The Starbreakers were no strangers to gratitude from important people, but this wasn't gratitude. This was deference.

He tried not to let that thought overwhelm him.

He looked back to the others. "*Guys?*"

"*I think Roland's right,*" *Church said.* "*With everything we know about the Hearts, we might be the kingdom's best hope.*"

Snow shrugged. Phoenix wasn't great at reading her shrugs, but it wasn't a no.

"*Oh, come on,*" *Brass said, grinning like an idiot.* "*Do you even have to ask?*"

"*Fuck it,*" *Angel said.* "*Let's kill this thing.*"

Roland II beamed. "*I knew we could count on you.*"

ASSEMBLED

It was a short but tense flying skiff ride from the city gate to the Pearl Palace. Lupolt, who had come to bail them out of jail, kept his eyes fixed straight ahead, silently simmering the entire time. Not trusting himself to say something that wouldn't just make things worse, Phoenix opted to keep quiet.

The skiff brought them to a small landing platform tucked away in the back of the palace, far from any major crowds and out of sight from most of the city. Only two guards were waiting for them, and they were all ushered inside without a word. Two empty hallways and a secret staircase kept them out of sight of anyone else inside. A lot of planning and effort had gone into making sure their arrival at the palace was as secret as possible.

And after the business at the gate, it was probably all for nothing.

The next door they walked through took them into a sitting room with no windows but several lightstone fixtures, including a crystal chandelier that kept the interior bright.

Three people were already waiting for them, and one in particular leapt out of his seat to welcome them.

"There they are!" Brass announced. He held his arms out for a hug, but a glare from Angel convinced him to instead fold his hands behind his back. "I heard all of you got arrested without me! I don't know whether to be impressed or hurt."

Behind him, Arno stood up as well while Ink remained seated. The young-faced priest gave the group a soft, relieved smile as they arrived, as if he'd been worried about them.

"Hi," he greeted, uncertainty tinging his otherwise cordial voice.

"Church." Angel nodded to the priest, pointedly ignoring Brass.

Arno took note that Angel was still using his old freelancer name rather than his real one. "It's good to see you again."

"Yeah, well, it's not like we're all here just for a reunion," Angel said, eyeing Lupolt meaningfully.

"Lupolt," Phoenix said. "We've played along this far. Can you tell us what's actually going on now? Because if you called for *us*, I'm guessing it's important."

"Has he still not told you?" Ink asked. "How rude."

Lupolt's jaw set, and he glanced at a grandfather clock in one corner of the room, mentally calculating something. He grunted, clearly not liking whatever answer he came up with, and then folded his hands as he spoke in a quick, detached voice.

"One week ago, there was a security failure in Oblivion. The integrity of some cells was compromised, and a riot ensued. As of right now, there are dozens of inmates unaccounted for. Most are likely still somewhere on the island, but we believe a significant number have escaped into the world. I've called you all here to ask for your help recapturing them."

Angel's eyes went wide for a moment, genuinely caught off guard. After the incident at Rockshore and Edelfric's appearance at the bridge, she'd already assumed there'd been a slip up at Oblivion. But she hadn't expected it to be on a scale like this. The others wore similar expressions. The only exception was Brass, who looked less stunned and more quietly excited.

"How many?" Phoenix asked. His voice shook.

"Until we've tracked down every inmate loose on the island, we don't know," Lupolt said. "All we have are assumptions and scattered reports from places where escapees have been spotted."

"What kind of prison island can't get a headcount?" Angel asked.

"It's not so simple," Lupolt defended. "Several inmates are experts at avoiding detection. One was already found in the walls. The island itself is so shielded against scrying and divination that the guards' only option is to physically search every inch."

"Tried using dogs?" Elizabeth asked.

"At my suggestion," Lupolt said, bitterly. "They went two days without thinking to."

"Wizards," Phoenix scoffed. If there was one thing mages were absolutely terrible at, it was thinking up solutions to problems that didn't involve magic. He suspected there were students at the Academy who couldn't open a jar without casting a spell.

"I'll pretend I didn't hear that," Ink retorted.

"Some of the escapees could cause crises all on their own. And there may be dozens of them at large," Lupolt said. "The Order of Saint Ricard is refusing to leave their post in the mountains. Seven Gates are the only knights left in the kingdom qualified to face this. And they are not enough. If we're going to resolve this before any lasting harm is done, we need help from people who have already proven they can handle the kind of monsters locked in Oblivion. We need all of you."

Silence gripped the room. Phoenix surprised himself by being the one to break it.

"Why didn't you lead with that instead of a right cross?"

"I was waiting to discuss it in a secure location," Lupolt said. "Which would have been this room before the mess at the gates."

"What do you mean?"

"Because of your fight, hundreds of people saw you and Angel outside the city gates. Because you were arrested for defying your exile, I had to issue orders for your release. And all of that means it's only a matter of time before Roland finds out that all of you are in the city and that I'm the one who brought you here."

"Wait. You didn't tell Roland you were bringing us here?" Church asked.

"No. He didn't." The clack of crutches may as well have been a strike to the back of Lupolt's head for how much he flinched. The doors of their impromptu meeting room were pushed apart by a pair of royal guardsmen, who made way for the man they escorted.

Roland II looked tired. Permanent dark circles hung under his eyes, accompanied by lines in his face that had no business on the skin of a man only just entering his thirties. His clothes were new, still brightly colored, stiff, and spotlessly clean, but for how he wore them, they looked like a fresh coat of paint on a derelict house. His head slumped, as if the crown on his head were made of lead.

He bore nearly all that weight on a pair of crutches strapped to his arms. He didn't wear the braces Phoenix had made for him.

He hadn't for seven years.

Roland didn't so much as glance at anyone else in the room, focused purely on Lupolt.

"Who told you?" Lupolt asked.

"Who refused your order to lie to me?" Roland retorted. "McCarter."

"She's fired."

"She's promoted. Good soldier. Organized. Loyal to her king." Roland stressed the last point. Lupolt winced.

"Roland—"

"No." The single syllable matched the punch Lupolt had given Phoenix for its measured brutality. Roland's voice held almost no emotion, save for flat, simmering anger. "I don't want excuses. I don't want an explanation. I want them," he pointed to the four former Starbreakers, "gone."

"Well how's that for royal hospitality?" Brass said, immediately making Phoenix and Church both cringe and making Angel want to punch him through a wall.

Roland finally looked at them and glowered. "My hospitality is not having you thrown back in prison for violating your exile. My hospitality is letting you leave this palace, now, and go back to whatever holes the lot of you were hiding in."

"Hey, he's the one who asked us to come!" Brass pointed a finger at Lupolt.

"In defiance of the law . . . and me," Roland said, eyes back on Lupolt. "If you were anyone else, you would be going to jail with them."

"I'm not," Lupolt said.

"Excuse me?"

"I'm not anyone else," Lupolt repeated. "I am your most loyal and faithful servant. Everything I do, I do for you and for this kingdom. You know that. And you know that I am not a puppet either. Whether you like it or not, I brought them here because we need help."

"Not *their* help! Not again."

"Okay, fuck you," Angel interrupted.

The entire room sucked in a breath.

Roland blinked. "What?"

Angel held her head even higher.

"Fuck you, you ungrateful sack of shit," Angel said. "I didn't even know if I wanted to help with your bullshit, but I was at least going to let your lapdog finish talking before I flipped the bird and went home. But I'll be damned if I stand around listening to one more second of you trying to get up in arms about 'our help' like it's the fucking shit you scraped off your shoe."

"Angel . . ." Church tried to talk her down, but she was on a roll now.

"'Our help' is why you still have a castellan in Olwin instead of a Clock-tower patsy. 'Our help' is why the Servitor didn't carve an end-to-end canyon into this country. 'Our help' is why you're still fucking breathing. The crown wasn't too good for our help for years. You were fine with it, risks and bent rules all included. You gave us medals for it. But we make one mistake—we lose one time—and you throw us to the fucking wolves."

"My father's home died!" Roland nearly fell as he stamped one of his crutches. His voice reverberated off the walls. "Every soul in it, gone! I owed my kingdom due diligence for what happened. The council wanted your heads, but I gave you all a fair trial that still found you innocent even though half of you never bothered to show up!"

"Innocent of mass murder," Angel corrected. "Guilty of endangering the kingdom. Stripped of all holdings, banished from the city, and blamed for everything that happened and the shit laws you threw up to act like you were doing something. That was our thanks for seven years of saving your collective asses. Forgive me for not falling over myself in gratitude, Your Magnanimousness."

"Get out," Roland repeated. His voice was lower but shaking now. Angel was already walking away. The other Starbreakers swiftly followed. "All of you, get out."

Ink raised a finger. "Does that include—"

"OUT!"

Lupolt was the last to leave, hovering in the doorway for a moment. He looked about to apologize, then thought better of it.

When the last person had gone and the doors had shut behind them, Roland collapsed into the closest seat, completely drained of his strength and will to stand.

THE CASK

"Well, that went well."

Brass broke the silence before it could settle onto their table, and for once, everybody was grateful for it. Angel had gotten everything she'd needed off her chest, but the rest of them remained tense for the entire exchange with Roland. They needed time to talk, to relax.

They needed to drink.

The Broken Cask was one of the few taverns in Sasel that didn't use lightstone, instead making do with lanterns and the light of its twin fireplaces. It gave the place a warm glow, accentuated by the deep, rustic hues of its wood paneled construction. Fiddle music and raucous laughter filled its dining hall as the working people of the city gathered to drink and sing away the worries of the day.

"Sorry," Angel muttered insincerely into her beer. "Someone had to say something, and you were all just sitting there taking it like Sicaran whores."

"Hey now," Brass protested. "I've known plenty of Sicarans that were very active participants."

"He's just hurting," Church said, choosing to ignore Brass. "This whole situation has to be stressful for him, and his best friend went behind his back."

"He's king, of course he's stressed. That's the job," Angel said. "No excuse to act like a dick."

"You're one to talk," Phoenix said without thinking. He practically spit out his drink when he registered his own words. "I didn't mean—you know, sometimes you just . . . shit."

He scanned Angel's face, trying to work out if he just needed to shut up or if ducking and covering was in order. One of her eyebrows twitched, and he flinched.

And then she laughed.

"Probably right," Angel admitted, taking another drink. "Still. Fuck him if he thinks I'm just gonna let him talk about me like that after all the shit we've done for him. For the whole country. Whole world."

"We could've used you at the trial," Phoenix said. "When we were in there, we just . . ."

"Took it like Sicaran whores?"

". . . yeah."

The Cask's beer always did have a way of making things better. It had been a natural choice to come here. After leaving the Pearl Palace, the four former companions and accompanying knight of the crown had been in the mood for a good drink and whinge, and none of them had felt much like walking all the way out of the city back to the Rusted Star to get it.

It was the first tavern the Starbreakers had ever stayed in when they'd come to Sasel as a company, when they were still five idiot teenagers. Since that first night, the tavern had played host to some of their best bar fights, one-night stands, and drunken song renditions.

There were a lot of memories in this place.

Given their reputation these days, it was also probably the only place they wouldn't be kicked out of if they got recognized.

Which they were, almost immediately after Brass and Phoenix called for another round.

A short boy dressed in grubby wools and carrying a serving tray, who could have passed for twelve, spotted them, did a double take when recognition dawned on his face, and immediately abandoned his attempts at flirting with two women at another table to come over.

"Avelina's ass, if it isn't the Starbreakers!" the boy swore. Phoenix reflexively winced at their name being shouted in a crowded place since it was still a crime for them to be in the city. He needn't have worried. The sounds of gambling, arguments, and off-key singing drowned out any chance of recognition from the surrounding tables. "Wow, you guys got old. I thought you all were dead or something."

"Or something," Angel said.

"Also, technically, we're not here, and you definitely never saw us," Brass added.

The child gave a conspiratorial nod as Brass slid him a few extra glint. "Not hide nor hair of ya. Shame too. You were always my favorites."

His gaze settled on Elizabeth. "Hang on. You look different. What happened to the ice and the knives?"

"Snow's not here," Phoenix said.

"Oh. Well then. Are you gonna introduce me to your new friend?" the boy asked, winking at Elizabeth.

"Simon, this is Elizabeth. My wife." Phoenix took extra care to stress that part. "Elizabeth, this is Simon."

Simon's face fell immediately. "Fucking save some for the rest of us, jackass. Most of us are lucky to pull one beautiful woman in our life. How the hells you . . ."

Simon trailed off as he reexamined Elizabeth and recognition slowly dawned. The green armor with a knight's emblem on the shoulder. The quiver of arrows. Eyes you could see a hurricane in if you dared to look. "Sweet blistering saints' asses, the Winged Lady's in my bar."

He paused, a new wave of realization following the first. "You married the dragon-pegging Winged Lady?"

"Got quite a vocabulary for a kid your age," Elizabeth said.

"Oh, hang on now. Don't go getting cute with me Little Miss Feathers," Simon said, jabbing a finger at her. "Just because you're a town hero doesn't mean I won't deck ya."

Elizabeth suppressed a laugh. "Sorry?"

"Simon was cursed by a witch to age in reverse," Church supplied. "It was eleven years ago? It actually got worse when we went after her too."

"That's a funny way of saying they pissed her off, and I started shrinking by the hour. If they'd been any slower about killing that old bag and breaking the curse, I'd have had to go back to sucking on my mom's tits," Simon said.

"Oh. Wow," Elizabeth said, immediately banishing every mental image that story created. "So how old are you, actually?"

"Old enough to be some of these young people's father," Simon spat. "Most men my age are buying things they don't need or sleeping with somebody half their age to make themselves feel young. Me, I'd kill to have hair anywhere besides my head."

"Look on the bright side," Brass offered. "Once you get through second puberty, you're gonna be back to that handsome devil you always said you were when you were younger."

"There is that." Simon chuckled, rubbing his bare chin. "Still can't believe you're actually here. Knew all that bullshit the crown said about you wasn't true."

An uncomfortable silence fell on the group as Brass and Elizabeth both flashed awkward smiles.

A restrained, professional voice saved them from having to disappoint Simon.

"Excuse me. Could we get two more chairs for this table?"

Simon cast a confused eye at two new arrivals who approached the table, which changed to suspicion when he saw the surprised looks on everyone's faces.

Lupolt pulled back his hood to reveal his face, which was full of barely disguised contempt for the bar's unruly atmosphere. Behind him, smiling from beneath her own hood, Ink looked right at home.

"You know these two?" Simon asked, offering to have them kicked out with a raised eyebrow.

"We do," Elizabeth said. "They're . . ."

Brass cut in as she searched for an appropriate word.

"Also not here," he said.

Simon looked from the table to the new arrivals and cocked his head. "You know you fuckers can meet somewhere other than taverns, right? Especially if you want to be discreet."

Brass tossed another stack of glint on the table.

Simon shook his head but took the money and sauntered off, muttering under his breath, "Glintchasers."

"I'm glad you're all still here," Lupolt said once the boy was out of earshot.

"Does your father know where you are, young man?" Brass mocked.

"His Majesty's time is more than occupied for the day, and I have no shortage of duties to explain my absence if and when it's noticed," Lupolt said, pulling up a seat. "Try not to make a scene here as well. We have a lot to discuss, and moving this conversation *again* is going to waste time we don't have."

Five pairs of eyes exchanged glances. Elizabeth spoke first.

"Lupolt, this is—"

"Defiance. Insubordination. Possibly treason, if you wanted to be liberal with your interpretation of the word," Lupolt finished for her.

Next to him, Ink's smirk only grew. "I tried to tell him. But he's like a dog with a bone."

"I know exactly how serious a crime I'm committing even coming here to talk to all of you, let alone conspiring to bring you into this," Lupolt said. "I also know my king is waging a war against the worst thieves, murderers, monsters, and warlords the kingdom has ever faced, and he cannot win it with the forces he has, especially not when he is due in Parthica in only a few weeks."

"The fuck is he doing leaving the country in the middle of a crisis?" Angel asked.

"The first ever international summit of Asher is occurring in two weeks in the Parthican capital of Nikos," Lupolt stated flatly. "It's the first move toward multinational, global cooperation in modern history, years in the making. Leaders and representatives of Iandra, Gypten, and Parthica are all confirmed for attendance. Cooperation on that scale could completely revitalize this kingdom and help us truly begin rebuilding what we've lost in these last years. Patrols for the roads. Protection for the fringe settlements. Advancement in arcane studies. The escapees could kill thousands. But the summit could save hundreds of thousands. Roland has to go."

"That's a pretty good reason," Church said.

"And it is all the more reason for the escapees to be dealt with swiftly," Lupolt said. "If the rest of the world learned of our crisis and that we couldn't respond to it—"

"You'd be really embarrassed at the next dinner party," Angel surmised.

"Essentially, yes. Which is not to discount the damage the escapees themselves will do if left unchecked," Lupolt said. He splayed his hands out across the table. "I will say it as much as I have to: We need you. For the sake of the world, the kingdom, the people. For Roland's sake and mine." He took a deep breath. "Please."

Contemplative silence fell on the table as the five original occupants exchanged looks. Worried, wordless conversation passed between husband and wife. Eager anticipation on Brass's face met admonishment and trepidation from Church's. Angel's typical frown deepened, threatening to become a full scowl.

Brass answered first.

"A job offer from the crown to chase down the worst of the worst? That is top-tier money and exposure. Couldn't ask for a better comeback."

"The goal of this operation is discretion," Lupolt said with a glare. "The less word spreads about the breakout, the better. And your affiliation with the crown on this matter must remain strictly secret."

"But we're still getting paid, right?"

Lupolt's lips pressed into a thin line, and his eyebrow twitched, but otherwise, he kept himself in check. "You can name your price."

"Then I'm in. Guys?"

"Retired or not, I don't think I could go back to Aenerwin knowing people were in danger and that we might be the only ones who could do something about it," Church said.

With a nod from Elizabeth, Phoenix gave a hurried answer, "We're in too."

Ever since Lupolt had first explained what the threat was, Phoenix had looked uncertain about the whole enterprise. But as soon as Church had mentioned returning home, knowing he'd walked away, his eyes had snapped into focus. "Roland might be king, but Corsar's my home. And I've got people I need to be able to face too. We'll need to make a stop back in Olwin to tell Wings's family they'll be taking care of Robyn a little longer than we thought. But we're in."

That only left Angel, who was staring at all of them with a half-incredulous look.

"Just so we're clear," she said. "You're asking us to stick our necks out for a king and country that actively hates us and does not want our help?"

She'd have laughed in Lupolt's face if the look on it wouldn't have made it feel like kicking an already injured puppy. She wasn't *that* mean.

It was almost impressive, though. The sheer gall of Lupolt, to ask her to help ease Roland's burden when Roland didn't give half of an ungrateful shit what happened to any of them.

She wasn't heartless but she wasn't so much of a saint that turning her back on this fight would cost her sleep. And unlike Phoenix and Church, she didn't have a bunch of townsfolk or a wide-eyed toddler she might have to worry about letting down.

The only person she'd have to face was Thalia.

The decision was obvious. Let the king solve his own problems with his handful of knights and overstretched army, while people all over the kingdom who were just trying to live got their shit ruined by a bunch of bad guys she'd helped put away in the first place.

And what was with that anyway? It was the Academy's job to make sure Oblivion was secure. Ink should have been begging them to help cover her people's mistake just as much as Lupolt was. But she didn't have a care in the world, if her smile was anything to go by.

Clearly, everything was *fine*.

This *wasn't* her problem.

"Fuck Roland all the way up his ungrateful ass." A good start. If she'd left it there, she'd have been free. But for gods knew what reason, she kept talking. "He doesn't get to tell me who I can and can't punch, and he doesn't have a monopoly on protecting the country."

"I mean, I think he technically can. And does," Brass said. "You know, being king and all."

"You know what I fucking mean."

"You're joining a fight against the most dangerous individuals on Asher . . . out of spite?" Ink asked.

"Got a problem with that?"

"Oh no. It's very on brand."

And like that, Angel was in. Out of spite for Roland, and no other reason.

"If we're all in agreement then, we should get started," Lupolt said. At a nod from the king's right-hand man, Ink dug into the bottomless bag at her hip and began producing folders of stacked parchment.

"The palace and the Academy both have extensive records on escapee sightings and probable land routes, but it's still largely conjecture, and most of that information is in the palace. Arakawa and I could only smuggle copies of so much of it here. We are working from limited data to track moving targets across the largest landmass on Asher. This will not be easy."

"That's an understatement," Phoenix said.

"I've been thinking about that," Church said. "Since you mentioned having trouble finding the escapees back at the palace. If we really need to find out where they all are, there is one person we can ask."

Phoenix cocked his head, mentally sorting through a list of every person they knew to try and figure out who Church could be referring to. When he finally hit a name that fit the bill, his eyes went wide.

"You think he'll actually help? He *hates* us."

Church shrugged. "I don't know. But he *would* know where every prisoner is. And he's helped us before."

"Under very different circumstances. Like, we had Snow, for starters."

"Would you two mind sharing your idea with the rest of the class?" Ink asked.

Phoenix sighed, rubbing the back of his neck. Lupolt already looked intrigued.

"The Oracle."

The High Inquisitive of the Academy balked. Around the rest of the table, eyebrows shot up. Even though the Starbreakers had been the ones to defeat him, everyone at the table knew who the Oracle was and, more to the point, how dangerous he could be, especially when they didn't have a thief who could hide even from magical sight.

"Really wish Snow were here right about now," Brass said.

KINDRED SPIRITS

The Dice House looked like a stiff breeze could knock it over and smelled like sweat and booze. But it was one of the last rest stops on the roads east of Olwin until the border with Parthica, and it was where Snow had come to find passage to complete her new mission.

Ink hadn't recruited Snow to help with the Oblivion breakout—at least, not with recapturing the escapees. Instead, the High Inquisitive had Snow chasing a lead on the potential plot *behind* the breakout, and it hadn't even altered Snow's plans all that much. It turned out she and Ink were both after the same thing. Or rather, the same person: Silas Lamark.

Silas was a wanted man for the string of contract assaults, kidnappings, and murders he and his late master, Sir Haegan, had orchestrated and which Snow herself had been a target of. Apparently, Ink and the Academy's difficulties scrying on the Oblivion escapees bore an eerie resemblance to the difficulties they had scrying on Silas and his remaining allies.

Add in the fact that Silas and Haegan's ultimate goal in their previous plot had been to collect Servitor Hearts and that one of the missing escapees was Pitch, a man infused with the Servitor Heart of Flame, and there were too many coincidences for Ink to rule out. Especially when everything she knew about Oblivion said that the breakout couldn't have happened without outside help.

The only actual change in Snow's plans had been that now, she was trying to take Silas alive rather than kill him on sight. Ink wanted answers, thought Silas could give them to her, and wasn't willing to risk losing those answers to a botched resurrection attempt or the vagaries of a grave speaker.

Snow agreed, but she was still planning on murdering Silas once Ink was done with him. The bastard and his friends had put a contract on her head. And not just her head. All of the Starbreakers. He'd made her and her old company targets for all the underworld. She refused to let that go unanswered, Ink's investigation be damned.

According to Julian's contacts, Silas was headed for the southeastern border to cross into Parthica. He had some kind of deal waiting for him there in the capital city of Nikos, but what it was exactly, nobody seemed to know. It didn't matter to Snow. She had her heading, and somewhere in this dive, there was bound to be someone she could hitch a ride with. One of the servers was already asking around for her.

All she had to do now was wait.

She took another sip from her glass of gin, the liquor rapidly cooling as it passed her lips. It had a sweeter taste than she'd expected.

"They started cutting it with syrup here a few years back," came the explanation as she stared at the glass. "Gin's only gotten more expensive since Relgen."

Snow looked up from her drink to see a slim, meticulously fabulous individual being shadowed by a towering brick house of a half-orc.

"Good to see you, Vera," Snow said.

"Right back at you," Vera said as they took the seat next to Snow. Their half-orc friend stayed standing. "Buy you another round?"

"What for?"

"Just a gesture for an old friend. And maybe to say thank you," Vera said, already waving a bartender over. "I heard you killed Pitch."

Snow nodded her understanding. "Oh. No, he lived. They threw what was left in Oblivion."

She opted not to add that he'd also since escaped.

"Oh," Vera said, clearly disappointed. After a moment though, they shrugged. "Close enough, I suppose. Drink's still yours."

Vera handed off a short stack of glint, and a second glass was deposited in front of Snow.

"I heard about the fire," Snow said. Sympathy had never really been her strong suit, especially after the Heart of Ice had taken hold, but since Vera was buying her liquor, she did her best. "If it makes you feel any better, he got his ass handed to him."

"It does, actually."

Vera ordered another glass of gin, this time for themself, and took a deep swallow from it. They shook their head in frustration.

"It cost me damn near every favor I had just to get back on my feet after the Lilac went up," they said. "And I'm *still* not back in the black."

Snow cast a glance toward the gambling tables that gave the Dice House its name. "Not sure this is the best place to help with that. Unless you're trying to drum up business."

"No. I'm just here to unwind before my next business trip," Vera said. After a pause, they flashed Snow a knowing look. "Although, if you're interested, I *do* have some company that's your type. Lanky young gentleman, likes to talk. Farm girl with good, strong hands . . ."

"I'm fine right now, thanks," Snow said. "Maybe next time."

"Excuse me, um . . . madam?" The server Snow had sent to ask about traveling parties returned, looking anxious. Even more than people usually did when talking to her. "I asked around about any traveling parties going to Nikos, but it seems like there's no one going quite so far that way. If you'd like, I could see about renting a room for you, and you could stay here until something comes through?"

"No thanks," Snow said. "I'll just get a horse and go myself."

"You're going to Nikos?" Vera asked.

"There's someone there I need to kill," Snow explained.

At the word *kill*, the server quickly turned and walked in the other direction.

He hadn't been working here long, but he'd still learned it was for the best to keep his nose as far out of this kind of business as possible.

"For business or pleasure?"

Only Vera would have phrased it like that.

"It's personal," Snow said.

"Sounds fun." The one-time hotel owner batted their red-lined eyes. "Would you like a lift?"

Snow cocked an eyebrow, and Vera elaborated. "As it happens, that business trip I'm going on is in Parthica, and Kratz is many wonderful things, but a conversationalist is not one of them."

The half-orc, who had not stopped hovering a vigilant three feet behind Vera, grunted.

"You're literally in the business of providing people with company, and you didn't think to bring someone to talk to on the road?" Snow asked.

"All right, you caught me," Vera said. "The truth is, it's a long, unpatrolled road to Nikos, and a single half-orc isn't always enough to dissuade the desperate. I can always try and hire some glintchasers, but you're probably worth a whole company of amateurs by yourself. And it's always better traveling with people you already know."

"Oh, I see. You're just using me for my daggers."

"Don't make it sound so crass; we're using each other," Vera retorted. "You need a ride, I need some travel insurance. Everybody wins. And I *would* honestly love to catch up. So, what do you say?"

Snow's usual reasons for traveling with others were practical: whenever she could, she preferred to conceal her movements inside those of others. She didn't do it for the company. But there were certainly worse people to travel with than Vera. Hells, she'd spent seven years traveling with four of them. All things considered, it was a decent deal.

When Snow still hadn't answered, Vera added, "I've got wine for the trip . . ."

Snow sighed. "What vintage?"

"Atta girl!"

ENTRAPMENT

A throbbing pain in Pitch's temples greeted him as he came to on a hard stone floor. The last thing he remembered was that Ink had paid him a visit. A few minutes after she left, everything had gone nuts. Cells were busted open. Inmates rioted. Magic started running wild. Something tore the door off his cell. And then, nothing.

No. There was something else. A voice.

You're coming with me.

Pitch groaned as he tried to stretch out the kinks in every one of his muscles. With every pop of his joints, a little pulse of warmth radiated through his body as the Heart of Flames slowly woke up within him. He was in a small room with three solid walls and one with a row of iron bars, eliciting an annoyed scoff from him. From one cage to another.

Except this time, none of the other safeguards from Oblivion were in place. No guards in sight. No enchanted chains. Whoever put him here was about to feel very stupid.

The fiery orange of Pitch's eyes began to dance as his excitement grew and flames licked at his fingertips. Both of his hands completely began to glow; first a dull red orange, then brighter orange. Finally, just as they were reaching near white-hot heat, he swung the flat of his hand like a blade, cleaving through the bars of his new cell as if they weren't even there.

With a second slash, the bars fell away, smoking at their ends, and he was free.

With a chuckle, Pitch sauntered out of the cell and into the wider hall beyond. He couldn't see any windows, but the space was generously lit by multiple lightstone fixtures in the walls and ceiling.

The hall was a short one, ending in a single door. But as soon as he set his sights on it, panels within the ceiling slid open, and loaded crossbows descended from them before training on him.

With a high-pitched whistle, both weapons loosed bolts that transformed into balls of pure force, striking Pitch dead in the chest and knocking him onto his back. The flames on his hands snuffed out, and a hoarse wheeze came from his throat as the wind was knocked from his lungs. He spasmed on the ground, trying and failing to suck down air.

The crossbows reloaded themselves, their arms pulling back of their own accord as energy coalesced along them into newly loaded bolts.

"Don't get up, or they'll shoot again."

The door opened, and a short, somewhat haggard-looking man entered. He was light-skinned, with sand-colored hair shaved on the sides and cropped short on top. He wore a chain vest over a loose-fitted shirt while a pair of shortswords joined by a cord hung from his hip.

Pitch's wheezing turned to coughing as he gagged on his own spit, but finally as his throat cleared, he was able to draw a normal breath. His eyes flitted between the stranger and the crossbows in the ceiling still aiming for him. Catching his breath, he decided not to immediately kill the man.

"Who the fuck are you?" he coughed.

"Someone who needs to ask you some questions."

Pitch was absolutely dumbstruck. He was no stranger to rude introductions. In fact, he was usually the one making them. But between the cage, the crossbows, and whatever the hell had been done to him to make him feel like his head was full of bricks, this had to be the crowning achievement of bad first impressions.

"Fuck off."

The man frowned. "Loose."

The crossbows shot a second round of bolts, knocking Pitch flat on his back again. As Pitch rolled on the ground, his new captor crouched down next to him.

"I'd prefer your cooperation. But I don't need it. Give me what I need, and I can let you go."

Pitch glared at the man, feeling the heat in his chest sputtering and struggling to grow without a proper breath. The crossbows reloaded once again.

"Anyone ever tell you that you're an asshole?" Pitch asked.

"Several times."

"Yeah, well, they were right."

The man shook his head and stood back up, putting a bit of distance between him and Pitch.

"I hope you understand this isn't personal or vindictive. Given your imprisonment, speaking with you was difficult to arrange. Considering the circumstances and your . . . volatile nature, it was safer to contain you until we knew you could be trusted."

Pitch recalled the chaos in the prison in the moments before he'd blacked out. Had this man arranged that? In spite of the pain from the last volley of shots, his curiosity was piqued. Not to mention, given the choice between more crossbow bolts or hearing out the jackass, he was willing to choose the latter. For now.

"Trust, huh?" Pitch glanced at the crossbows again. "You know that goes both ways."

The man narrowed his eyes. A long silence passed between them as the two sized each other up, not breaking eye contact.

"Disarm."

The tension in the crossbow arms relaxed, and they retreated back into the ceiling, panels sliding back over them. The man folded his hands behind his back.

Pitch staggered onto his feet and dusted himself off. "You got a name?"

"Silas."

"Great," Pitch said. "What do you want?"

Instead of answering, Silas turned back to the door behind him, the only visible way out of this place.

"Bring it in," he ordered.

The door opened again, and a pair of identical women wearing matching bracelets entered. One of them carried a segmented bronze cylinder about two feet long and two inches thick. She handed it to Silas without a word, and, after casting a wary look toward Pitch and a gesture from Silas, they both left the room as quickly as they'd entered. As much as Pitch wanted to ask about them, he had a more pressing question.

"What the fuck is that?"

"It's called an extractor," Silas said. "It's modeled after the original vessels of Servitor Hearts and designed to siphon the energy of a Heart from its current vessel into itself."

Pitch took a step back. "Not happening."

"You should let me finish."

"I don't need to," Pitch said. "This power's the best shit I've gotten in years. No way in hells am I letting you take it."

"I will do it by force if I have to," Silas said.

"Try it," Pitch warned, his eyes flashing a blazing orange. He was still feeling a little off, but with every second, more heat radiated through his body, loosening his stiff muscles and filling his veins with fire. If Silas wanted a fight, Pitch would give him one.

"I don't believe I have to," Silas said. "Not if I can make you understand."

Flames burst back to life, licking up the sides of Pitch's arm. "I think I understand just fine. Now get out of my way before I turn you into a roast dinner."

"If you leave here with the Heart still inside you, the only place you will end up is back inside Oblivion. And it will be because of your own actions," Silas warned.

"The fuck's that supposed to mean?" Pitch asked.

"This device came from the Academy," Silas said, holding up the extractor. "The very same people who were keeping you imprisoned. They could have taken the Heart from you at any time and left you powerless in their prison, but they didn't. What does that tell you?"

The flames running along Pitch's arm dwindled as his brow furrowed. The pieces were moving in his head, but Silas could tell already he wasn't going to complete the picture on his own.

"The power of the Servitor Hearts was not designed to be kept inside a human body, but it has happened. It happened to one of the Starbreakers, a woman they could never hope to catch. But then it happened to you, a prisoner hand delivered to them. You are a chance for the Academy to study the phenomenon of Servitor Hearts inside humans. To weaponize it. And that makes you impossibly valuable to them. This place is shielded against scrying. But the moment you leave it, they will hound you. They will do everything in their power to reclaim their prize. Unless you're no longer worth pursuing."

"If they wanted it that bad, they'd have gone after Snow by now, and she's still walking free," Pitch said, though he sounded like he was trying to convince himself.

"You are not Snow," Silas said. "You never received a parade in your honor for saving the crown prince. You weren't even with the Cord of Aenwyn at Loraine. *She* has powerful friends. You have done nothing but make enemies your entire life. They won't touch her. But they *will* come for you."

Pitch's face twitched as Silas laid out everything Snow had that he didn't. But, crucially, he didn't disagree.

"You're a man who values power," Silas said. "But you value freedom even more. It's why you left the Cord. Why you never returned to Antem."

"How the fuck would you know why I did anything?"

"I've learned that if you're going to be dealing with someone, it pays to understand them," Silas said. "I've studied every note the Academy has ever written about you so that I could make you see that getting rid of the Heart is your best chance to have what you really want. You'll never be free as long as the Academy thinks it can use you. But with the Heart gone . . ."

Pitch's mouth opened, but no words came out as he simply gave Silas another once over. The atypical, almost leaf-shaped blades of his swords screamed of being not just from another place but another time. Old World weapons, almost certainly enchanted. His posture, rigid and yet still almost spring-loaded in its tension, made him out as a trained and disciplined soldier. If Pitch had seen him on the street, he would have guessed he was a knight. But he was also a fountain of Academy secrets, willing to negotiate with the assassin he kept in his personal dungeon.

A knight. An Academy expert. A captor trying to do his prisoner a favor. Silas was a mass of contradictions.

He didn't have Pitch's trust.

But he had his curiosity.

"Okay. So that's why I'd give it up," Pitch said, "but why do you want it so bad?"

Silas's jaw tightened for a moment. "The Hearts are extremely powerful artifacts. With them in our possession, we could rewrite this kingdom's future. Bring order to chaos that has been eroding it from every side."

"How?" Pitch pressed.

Silas was silent.

"Oh, come on, now you stop talking? You were just getting interesting."

"By using them to combat threats to the kingdom," Silas said, choosing his words carefully.

"Like what?"

"What are you trying to learn?"

"What you're trying to hide."

"Monsters. Warlords. Entities beyond the stars," Silas said. "While the crown sits behind its city walls, we will take the fight to these threats. We will do what a proper ruler would already have done and defend these lands and their people."

Pitch nodded, a smile slowly spreading across his face. "Son of a bitch. A fucking coup."

"What?"

"Oh, don't play dumb with me. It's obvious," Pitch said. "You're scooping up power. You're making friends in weird places. Using plural pronouns like you're already a part of something. Talking about saving the world and slagging off the people in charge. Not exactly a lot of places for those roads to lead."

"My only concern is Corsar. My home."

"Uh-huh." Pitch nodded with obvious disbelief. His smile only grew as he began to slowly pace around the room, thinking out loud. "So, I give you the Heart, I get the Academy off my back, and you get one step closer to kicking the Cripple King down a flight of stairs and taking his hat. Am I reading this deal right?"

Silas was quiet for a moment, and he stared at the ground. There was shame in his eyes but also a sense of grim determination. He didn't like any of this. But he was still going to do it.

"And if you are?" Silas asked.

"Then I think you're even crazier than me," Pitch said. "But the less reason I have to ever see Ink's face again, the better, and it's been a while since I helped overthrow a king."

"Is that a yes?" Silas asked.

"I give you the Heart, I walk?"

"You have my word."

Pitch narrowed his eyes, searching Silas's. There were two kinds of people in this world: those whose word meant something and those whose didn't. Pitch was usually in that second category. And he liked to think that gave him a leg up on detecting people like him.

"Fuck it. I miss cold drinks anyway," Pitch said. "You got a deal."

"Good."

Silas twisted the extractor, causing its segments to begin separating from each other to reveal an empty glass container in the center. The bottom end of the extractor expanded out, forming a tripod while the top end began to slowly rotate.

Pitch took a half step back. Silas placed the extractor down, making sure its legs were firmly planted and stable.

"This could be uncomfortable."

"How uncomf—"

The rest of Pitch's words were cut off as the extractor let out a deep, pulsing thrum from its spinning portion, and a sensation like the marrow trying to escape from his bones exploded out through the assassin's entire body. He dropped to his knees screaming, and his eyes became orbs of solid, blazing orange. Flames spread across his entire body, completely engulfing him and forcing Silas back. All the while, the extractor's head spun faster and faster.

Slowly, the flames on Pitch began to curl toward the extractor, as if being sucked into a cyclone, and the glass container in the center of the extractor began to glow a dull red. Pitch's body spasmed, his screams only growing as he made a desperate attempt to try and swat at the device. Silas moved in a flash, grabbing Pitch's arm to stop him from interfering. The flames seared Silas's hands and quickly began igniting his clothes, but he did not falter, holding Pitch still as the extractor continued its work. Pitch wailed and howled, practically deafening Silas, but his agony left him too weak to meaningfully struggle.

With every passing moment, the flames on his body diminished, and the glow from the device's center grew brighter until finally, the last traces of light left Pitch's eyes and their color changed from their previous amber hue to a dull, dark brown.

The assassin went limp in Silas's arms, and a hush fell over the room, broken up only by the faint whine of the extractor and Silas's own ragged gasps. Silas released Pitch's body as he collapsed onto the floor. Smoke coiled off of Silas; his flesh was sizzling and black in several places. He grit his teeth, trying to stay conscious as his whole body shivered with pain. He very nearly couldn't.

The doors burst open again, and the twins standing guard outside rushed in.

"Sir!" René shouted, immediately crouching down next to Silas. Her hands hovered over him, but she hesitated, uncertain if he should be touched.

"Stay with him," Rosa said, already turning to leave. "I'll get a priest."

René nodded before returning her attention to Silas. "You're going to be all right, sir. Just hold on."

Silas grimaced as he placed a hand on his own burnt chest and held it as tightly as he could. With every ounce of will he could muster, he reached out for the power of the Renalt as he had been taught, letting the divine energy flow into and through him. After a moment, the burns on his chest began to mend themselves. The effect lasted only a short moment, and even when it was done, they were still only partially healed, but it was enough for him to sit up.

"I'm fine, René," he insisted. "The Heart?"

The device's top portion had finally come to a stop, its work seemingly complete. The center was now an incandescent, bright orange, roiling like a tube of flaming gas. It was done. The Heart of Flames had been taken from Pitch.

"It worked, sir. We have it."

Silas nodded, finally lying down for a moment. His skin was still screaming with pain, but it was a manageable pain now. He could stay conscious until a priest arrived. For now, he would rest.

In all this time, Pitch had not moved, though his eyes remained open and his jaw was slack, as if he was still frozen in a scream. Silas's brow furrowed, and when René followed his eyes, she, too, frowned. Hesitantly, she reached out, checking Pitch's neck for a pulse.

"He's . . . dead."

Silas closed his eyes. "Maybe that's for the best."

"Sir." René's voice was wary. "When you told him you would let him go, were you lying?"

"If he had survived, I would have let him go," Silas said, carefully.

"Did you know he wouldn't?"

Silas was quiet.

René nodded, though she did not meet Silas's eyes. Silas frowned, recognizing the early seeds of a shaken will. Doubts, he had learned, were always best dealt with openly and quickly. Festering inside, they could only grow until they consumed everything else.

"Is everything all right?" he asked.

"We do what we must," she replied, trying to steel herself.

Silas grimaced, saying nothing. It was true. There was still so much work to do before they could save Corsar, and much of it would be unpleasant. The breakout at Oblivion was only the latest in a long line of sins their order had committed. But it had brought them a Servitor Heart. The chaos the other escapees caused would be the perfect smokescreen to mask their activities and draw resources away from the hunt for them. And before too long, it would bring them an arsenal fit to take back a kingdom. The destruction and loss of life that occurred from it would be worth it, in the end.

It had to be.

THE SANCTUM

B rass was freezing his ass off. Even through a fur-lined coat, a thick doublet, and long underwear, the frigid air was biting into his skin. Flecks of ice had already formed in his mustache and eyebrows, and he was starting to lose feeling in his toes.

And yet, he couldn't help but smile.

He had missed this. A foreign land's air in his lungs, his company at his side, and a ticking clock over their heads. Replace Wings with Snow and pretend Ink wasn't tagging along, and it was just like the good old days.

In some ways, it was even better, since with Wings around, the howling winds that whipped through the mountains never hit them as anything more than a gentle breeze.

"We couldn't have gotten any closer before we had to start walking?" Church muttered into his scarf.

"Talk to Phoenix," Angel said. "It's his map."

"It's also twelve years old," Phoenix said. "Not the easiest thing to use to track a moving target."

"Are you even sure we're close?" Angel asked.

"We're in the neighborhood. My math's not perfect, but it's still good," Phoenix said.

"Truly, a fountain of confidence," Ink taunted from the back of their group.

The six of them picked up the pace, making their way up the snow-covered slope of the small mountain ridge until they finally reached the crest and were met with a sweeping view of the horizon beyond.

A wide expanse of flat tundra stretched out below them like a patchy white sheet going all the way to the horizon that was almost oppressively bright to behold. All save for one dark, near-perfect circle of a shadow situated directly beneath their destination.

It was a village-sized hunk of rock, shaped as if sheared off the top of a mountain, suspended hundreds of feet in the air, draped in stalactites of ice and dusted in its own blanket of snow that trailed off of it in gentle, waterfall-like drifts.

Capping its very top was an alabaster keep, made of three massive struts that all converged in a single, crowned structure in the center. The Sanctum of the Oracle—a floating fortress of ice and rock built by a world long dead, held aloft by magic lost to time.

"Oh."

The word slipped from Wings like a gasp as she stopped dead in her tracks, and for just a moment, she was seventeen again, seeing the world beyond her parents' farm for the first time, and her stomach fluttered with a thrill of drinking in the new and unknown.

"Now, this is worth the trip," Ink said, a look of unqualified delight slowly spreading across her face. "Imagine what there is to learn from something like this."

"Nothing good," Phoenix said.

"Oh, there's Sir Hates Progress," Ink said. "I was wondering when he'd come out."

"Just get us on to it so we don't have to keep walking," Angel interrupted before they could start arguing.

"Right, well, now that I actually know exactly where I'm aiming . . ." Ink said.

A trail of bright white sparks etched themselves in the air in front of them, accompanied by a sound like glass being cut. The trail traced out the shape of a doorway with the space inside it becoming a two-dimensional, milky white void.

"Ooh, you do portals now?" Brass asked.

Ink froze, her hands still mid-gesture. A confused expression took over her face. "I didn't do that."

"Oh," Brass said. He looked to Phoenix, in case he was trying to one-up Ink again, but he was just as surprised as her.

It was Church who pieced together what was happening first. "We're being invited in."

Wings glanced between the doorway and the Sanctum of the Oracle floating off in the distance. It was miles away from them.

"That's not creepy at all," she said.

"Welp," Brass said, stepping forward. "Nothing ventured, nothing gained."

"Brass, wait," Phoenix said. "We don't actually know if—"

And before he could get out another word, Brass had already stepped through the portal. Phoenix groaned, burying his head in his hand before dragging his hand down his face.

"Why do I even bother?" he muttered.

THE ORACLE

Angel stepped into a room with scuffed, white granite walls as the arcane doorway flickered shut behind her. The freezing wind shear of the mountain vanished, replaced by a hanging chill. Aside from the faint whistle of a draft moving through the room, her breathing and footsteps were the only sounds. There was no sign of the others.

Terrific.

She moved through the halls slowly, her fists clenched as she rounded each corner, ready for a fight that she never found. Instead, she was greeted by snowdrifts piled against pillars, cracks and holes in the ceiling that let sunlight and chilling wind slip through, and broken piles of stone that were once sculptures. This was always the part about ruins she hated. The utter haunting emptiness of them.

It was almost a relief when the hallways she was following finally led her outside to a wide, high-ceilinged veranda offering a soaring view of a surrounding mountainside and the sheer cliff that gave way to the open sky with the tundra slowly drifting by far below.

"Angel?"

Her body reacted to the sound, and she took a fighting stance before she even finished registering the voice. At the other end of the veranda, Phoenix immediately threw his hands in the air. Angel relaxed.

"Just you?" she asked.

Phoenix nodded, lowering his hands once it was clear Angel wasn't about to pulverize him. "So far, yeah."

A cold crosswind blew through, drawing their attention back to the view.

"At least we know where we are," Phoenix said.

"Where else would we be?"

"We went through a nondescript magic portal and came out surrounded by Old World architecture with a draft. We could have been in any above-ground ruin in the world."

She shrugged. "My money was still on here."

"How do you figure?"

"Context."

Phoenix opened his mouth to argue that while the circumstances might have strongly suggested their location, there was a difference between knowing and suspecting, and it was entirely possible that the portal had been completely unrelated to the Oracle. But Angel wouldn't care. At the end of the day, she'd figured they were in the Oracle's sanctum, she'd been right, and that would be good enough for her.

"Well, if it was the Oracle, then he brought us into the sanctum but not directly to him. And he separated us," Phoenix said. "He's up to something."

"He's a thousand-year-old, half-insane, omniscient wizard. Probably just bored," Angel said. "What does he even do up here all day?"

"I watch infinity unfold."

This time, both Phoenix and Angel whipped around ready to fight.

The Oracle was exactly six feet tall, most of his narrow form swallowed by frayed white robes trimmed in long-faded black. His dark-toned face was slender and smooth with large pointed ears accented by tarnished silver jewelry along the tops of their helixes. Dark, thick ringlets of frizzy hair cascaded down one side of his head, while the other was decorated in rows of loose, unkempt braids.

In many ways, he was like the sanctum itself. Imposing, majestic, but weathered away by a particularly unkind passage of time. A fitting, even natural appearance for one of the very last living elves in the world. What wasn't natural were the hundreds of luminescent threads following his every move that all converged in his eye sockets, giving him the appearance of a puppet held aloft by a massive web of strings. The threads stretched off into the ceiling, disappearing somewhere above, whirring softly as they extended and retracted to keep up with his teetering movements.

The Oracle shuddered in naked disgust, making the threads connected to his eyes dance.

"Always violence with you. You bring it with you, so you assume others bring it too."

"We're usually right," Phoenix said.

The Oracle's lips curled back as he stalked around them in a slow circle. "Yes. So much blood. I see it over and over. You fight and kill and fight and kill and kill and die. But my tomb has no violence but what you bring. No harm but what you do."

The Oracle's head listed to one side. He was facing them, but he wasn't looking at them, not really. His voice quivered with both malice and uncertainty. "What *will* you do?"

"Don't you already know?" Phoenix asked.

"I see you so many times. Too many times. Too many lives and lies and life and death. What is one day, and what is the next? The past and the present?" the Oracle muttered. He was drifting, but as another shimmer traveled down the threads into his eyes, he seemed to refocus. "How long is it for your eyes? Which one is this day? Fight or talk? Live or die?"

Phoenix and Angel exchanged a glance, before very slowly lowering their guards just enough to convey they weren't immediately going to start a fight. Angel kept her weight on her back foot, and Phoenix's wand stayed out of its holster.

"We need your help to find some people," Phoenix said. "There was—"

"Oblivion." The Oracle interrupted Phoenix with an excited gasp. His angular face bent into a wicked smile. "*These* days. Yes. Good. Yes yes yes. GOOD!"

For a ragged wisp of a creature, the Oracle moved quickly, swiveling around to stand between the two of them and throwing his arms around their shoulders. Immediately, Angel twisted out of his arms, but before she could shove him away, he was gone. He was standing at the far end of the veranda, leaning over the edge of the railing and kept from tumbling over only by the threads burrowed into his eyes.

"You're all alive, then," the Oracle said. "None of you stay dead before Oblivion. Not *before*."

Angel pointedly ignored the bait in that. If there was one thing they all knew painfully well by now, it was to never ask the Oracle about the future. "Disappointed?"

"I have watched you die, Exile. I have watched the deaths of the very last living things to ever know your names. My joy in your passing has come and gone. You cannot change that by standing here." The Oracle pulled away from the edge, or maybe the threads pulled him. It was hard to tell. "But there are other joys."

"What do you want?" Phoenix asked.

"You ask. Such kindness." Sarcastic venom hung on the words. "You have no thief to hide from me. No priest to twist my tongue. You ask because you cannot take!"

"You want to test that theory?" Angel's eyes briefly flashed golden.

"You threaten me?" The Oracle snarled. Then he laughed. "You threaten me! With death? Violence? I see you from cradle to grave. You bring death, death, death, all the way down. But not for me. My life is not *yours* to take. What do I want? For you to see."

Another doorway swept over the Oracle, taking him away in an instant as their surroundings melted to an empty, black nothing. Angel called to Phoenix, only to watch him fade away along with everything else while Phoenix watched the same thing happen to Angel.

In another second, both of them were alone in an empty, silent void.

Phoenix set his goggles to detect magic and was nearly blinded as his eyes were filled with nothing but pure white. Everything around him was magic. An illusion then. Angel was still here somewhere, they were still in the sanctum's heart.

Unless they weren't and the illusion of the void was just to hide that. His mind raced with possibilities, doing his best to recall the layout of the sanctum and think where they might be. He worked through his options for dealing with the illusion, locating Angel, neutralizing the Oracle.

And then a voice ground his thoughts to a halt.

"I will never be good enough for you, will I?"

Snow's voice cut through the void around Phoenix. Something in his chest froze. He remembered those exact words, that exact tone. Even now, he could still remember her eyes, bright and full of pain, from that day.

The day he broke her heart.

Angel searched around herself. Her best guess said the void was an illusion, though, she kept "pocket dimension" in the back of her mind as another possibility. There was no immediate need to worry. She knew a threat when she heard one, but if the Oracle wanted to fight, she was more than ready for that. The annoying part would be making sure not to hurt the bastard too much so he could still answer their questions.

"Monica, you unpack that bag, and you sit down now!" Her mother's voice shrieked out of the darkness. *"You are not going to just quit and leave. Monica!"*

"Shut up." The words came out of Angel like a reflex.

"Just shut up already, okay?" a younger version of herself echoed. *"I never asked for any of this! I'm done! I hate this, and I hate you!"*

"Monica! Get— MONICA!"

Angel felt the crash as much as she heard it of a woman being flung into a bookshelf and it toppling over. She heard herself running, heard the wails of her mother calling her name. Her fists clenched.

"See it," the Oracle instructed. "See the hurt you bring. The oaths you break."

Trapped in the void, unable to see the Oracle or each other, Angel and Phoenix both were met with a barrage of voices and faces drawn from their pasts. Angel got to relive the day she fled the Order of Saint Ricard. Phoenix, the day he was expelled from the Infinite Library. He showed them the fallen at the Battle of Loraine. He showed them themselves after the fall of Relgen.

"See your failures."

Phoenix's heart hammered in his chest, his eyes shut to try and block out the noise, the pain. Without thinking, he found himself backing away in a panic until he bumped into what felt like a wall of solid muscle.

"Phoenix!"

In a blink, Angel was there in the void with him again, looking just as surprised to see him as he felt to see her.

"Broken lovers. Abandoned homes," the Oracle crooned, finally materializing in front of them. "You like it that way. That's why you do it. You hurt and lie and fail. And now you see."

"He's messing with us," Phoenix warned. "He wants a reaction. We only win by not playing his game."

Angel nodded in agreement, even as her fists shook. "You had your fun. Help us or not, I don't even care. But quit fucking around and wasting our time."

The Oracle laughed, staring past them as the strings attached to his eyes shimmered once again. "Or what? You'll hurt me? Like you did before when you plunged me into infinity? I remember. I screamed so long I tasted blood. Do you know what it sounded like? The hurt you gave me? It sounded like *this*."

A scream echoed through the void. But it wasn't the Oracle's. It wasn't Angel's mother either. It was a shattered, grief-wracked shriek of a young woman, desperate, terrified, and pleading for her father's life.

"Go back! Put me down! Please! Monica! Go back, go back! I hate you! Go back!"

Phoenix reached for Angel, hoping to calm her down or hold her back. But she was already swinging.

Her fist sailed straight through the Oracle's face, which collapsed in on itself like smoke along with the rest of the black void around them. In a sudden rush, as if swept away with a wind, the void was gone—along with Angel.

Phoenix was back on the veranda, exactly where he'd been before the Oracle had arrived. Where Angel had been, there was only a milky white, two-dimensional doorway. The Oracle walked out from behind it, smiling.

"No violence here but what you bring. And it leaves with you." The Oracle paused and frowned. "But there are so many days, all so different and yet so hard to tell which is which. Tell me. Can she fly yet?"

Phoenix looked from the Oracle to the portal to the view of the open sky the veranda had and quickly connected the dots. Then he pulled down his goggles and dove headfirst through the portal.

It vanished behind him, leaving the Oracle standing alone on the veranda, giggling to himself.

"Two come, two fall."

KIRA

Under different circumstances, Ink would have been elated. She hadn't been in an Old World ruin in years. One as pristine as the Oracle's sanctum? Over a decade. The part of her that still remembered the thrill and discovery of being a glintchaser was over the moon.

Unfortunately, that excitement was tempered by business and the fact that an extremely powerful *elven* mage was fucking with them. The good news was the Oracle didn't want them dead. Not when he just as easily could have teleported them to the bottom of the ocean and been done with it. But sometimes an enemy wanting you dead was easier. It was straightforward, predictable, and usually solved rather neatly with a well-placed lightning bolt. An enemy after something else was far more troublesome to deal with. And there were some things worse than dying.

Ink and Elizabeth had found each other quickly, but it was the others that were proving difficult. The sanctum was warded against scrying, shutting down any hope Ink had of just solving the issue herself. That only left exploring and hoping they got close enough for Elizabeth to sense something.

"Still nothing?"

"Ink, if I get anything, I promise I will tell you."

"Fine, fine," Ink said. "You just found me so quickly, I figured you would have gotten *something* by now."

"You were closer. And wearing perfume," Elizabeth said as she checked around the next corner. "Which kinda smells like it's losing its kick by the way."

"I keep meaning to get new ones, but work always has me busy," Ink lamented. "And I do not trust aides to pick good perfumes without getting scammed."

Elizabeth smirked.

"What?" Ink asked.

"Nothing," Elizabeth said as her smirk grew into a wistful smile. "You just remind me of a friend of mine."

"From the Broken Spear? Or someone you met after you got the Heart of the Sky?" Elizabeth's eyebrows shot up, and Ink rolled her eyes. "Oh, come now, you didn't actually think I didn't recognize you, did you?"

"No one else did."

"I'm not anyone else."

The Servitor that had attacked the ruintown of Loraine ten years ago had been powered by four Hearts. In the aftermath of its defeat, the Heart of Life had been donated to the Church of Avelina. The Academy had claimed the Heart of Force for itself for the purposes of study and containment, both of which they failed at after it ended up in the hands of Sir Haegan of Whiteborough. The Heart of Shadows had been taken by the Cord of Aenwyn as compensation for their services, even over the vocal protests of the Academy and the Starbreakers. Officially, the Heart of the Sky had been destroyed in the battle. In reality, Phoenix had reported it destroyed to cover up that he'd used it to save Elizabeth's life, and, in doing so, give her the power to become the famous Winged Lady of Sasel.

The source of the Winged Lady's power was a mystery to the public. Some people thought she was a sorceress or druid. Others thought she might be a full-blown nature spirit or at least the scion of one. Surprisingly few people guessed that she was an angel, which would've been Elizabeth's first choice. No one but the Starbreakers and the surviving members of the Broken Spear knew the truth. Or at least, that was what Elizabeth had thought.

"How long have you known?"

"I admit you had me at least a little fooled back when you were first knighted," Ink said. "I *recognized* you, but the glowing wings threw me off. I kept wondering where a warden from a second-rate company would come into power like that. Of course, once I learned you and Phoenix were an item, it all made too much sense. He was the one who told everyone the Heart was destroyed. And he has a pattern of sleeping with women infused with Servitor Hearts."

"*Two* is not a pattern."

Ink shrugged. "Maybe not. But if you ever meet another one, I'd keep him on a short leash."

"Anyone ever told you you're incredibly rude?"

"Numerous times. Usually when I'm right about something," Ink said. "You can relax by the way. I haven't told anyone else, and I do in fact seem to be the only person in Sasel who has ever heard of the Broken Spear. Your little secret is safe."

Elizabeth was still annoyed over the insinuation that her husband would cheat on her, but decided to set that aside. "Why?"

"Because knowledge is power," Ink said. "I don't like sharing power. And someday, I may need something from you. When I do, I will have one more chip to bargain with."

"I don't respond well to blackmail."

"I'll keep that in mind."

Dormant lightstone flickered to life in stages, banishing the darkness and revealing a space filled with rows upon rows of giant spools of luminescent thread, each one tethered to the next and all humming with energy. Even with only a vague understanding of the Oracle and the sanctum, Ink was certain. This room was a part of what gave the sanctum its power. Free and total knowledge of past, present, and future. An impossible miracle, and yet just another in a long list of miracles the elves had accomplished.

"The whole world used to be like this," Ink whispered in awe.

With some trepidation, Elizabeth said, "And it paid the price for it."

"Look at this place. Think about what it can do. *Imagine* what we could be capable of if we had their secrets," Ink said. "We could change the world. Remake what the elves did. Go beyond them!"

"Or burn down the little we have left."

Ink let out a disappointed sigh. "Now *you* remind me of someone."

"Arman isn't the only person who knows the Old World wasn't perfect."

"All the more reason to try to build a better one."

"Grand dreams," a new voice interrupted, "for a human."

The Oracle glided across the floor, held aloft by the strings coming out of his eyes. They followed the strings to try to find the source but they led nowhere; they faded away to nothingness near the ceiling. The elf cocked his head as he looked Ink and Elizabeth up and down while pacing in a slow circle around them. He walked behind one giant spool and disappeared.

"The Oracle, I presume?" Ink asked.

He was behind them now and closer too. "I think I have seen you. Wizard and warden. But it's so hard to tell. Is this now or later?"

Ink took a moment to parse the elf's words. "This is the first time we've met, yes."

"Ah," the Oracle agreed readily. "Later then, are the things to come."

"That's generally how the future works, yes." Ink was starting to wonder if it had actually been a good idea to come here. Not because the Oracle frightened her but because he was clearly a few cards short of a fortune teller deck, and she wasn't sure what, if anything, they could actually gain by talking with him. It didn't matter if he knew where the escapees were if all they could get him to say was gibberish.

"You don't know the meaning of the word!" the Oracle snapped. "You are small and blind! You do not see what I see!"

Ink's lips pressed into a thin line. Condescension irritated her, but rationality told her to be careful. Mad or not, the Oracle was on his home turf and had centuries worth of greater magic than hers.

"Where are our friends?" Elizabeth interrupted.

"Close," the Oracle answered, intentionally vague.

"*Where?*"

"You will see them again," the Oracle said. "I do not want them. I have seen them over and over. But this—you—are new. I have seen so little of you. And I want to see more."

He leaned in close to them, tilting his head as his string-filled eyes searched them. The corners of his open mouth turned up. "What do you want?"

"We need you to tell us the location of every escaped prisoner from Oblivion," Ink said immediately.

The Oracle grunted, and his lips curled in a sneer. A multicolored flourish of lights traveled along the threads connected to his eyes. "I see. You are like *them*. Like all the maggots that come here. Asking for little things for their little minds."

Elizabeth saw the tiniest of shifts in Ink's posture and knew the Oracle had struck a nerve. She immediately tried to intervene. "Ink—"

Ink held up a hand to silence her, which only made Elizabeth more sure things were going to take a turn for the worse.

"He's trying to—"

"I know what he's trying to do."

"Then don't fall for it!"

Ink rolled her eyes and waved two fingers in a quick glyph pattern. The world around Elizabeth went completely silent. She looked around, tapped her swords together, opened her mouth to speak—nothing. Ink had literally silenced her.

Elizabeth glared and mouthed, "You bitch."

"Now, let's get something straight," Ink said to the Oracle. "You don't know me. Because if you did, you wouldn't be playing with fire like you are right now."

Another shimmer ran down the strings and into the Oracle's eyes, and he chuckled. "I see you. The little girl who runs from master to master."

"I don't have masters." Ink bristled. "I have patrons."

"You come on the whims of others. You hunt their quarry, you ask their questions."

"I want the same thing they do. That doesn't make me their servant," Ink said.

"Then I give you one more chance, little dabbler," the Oracle said. "For you, for me." The Oracle ran his fingers through the web of threads coming from his eyes, singling out one and pulling it away from the others to hold out toward Ink. "Past. Present. Future. I see it all. You can see your master's quarry. Or you can see whatever piece of eternity you desire. But only *one* of these. Which will it be?"

The single thread glittered between his fingers, and though Ink thought she knew better, she stared at it. Any secret. Anything to ever happen. Anything that ever would. Right in front of her. The location of long lost, legendary artifacts. The secrets of spellforging that would let them create their *own* artifacts. The real, full truth about what caused the Collapse of the Old World. The sheer scope of possibility was dizzying.

Ink caught the eyes of Elizabeth, who was furiously shaking her head.

Painfully, Ink forced her professionalism and logic to take back the reins of her mind from her bruised ego. She and Elizabeth both knew the Oracle was intentionally trying to bait her.

It wouldn't do to play into that.

"Sorry, but I came to do a job," Ink said. "And I pride myself on getting the job done. Maybe next time."

"No," the Oracle snapped. "I see every face that comes to this sanctum. Every face, every time. You are never among them again, wizard. This is your time. Your only time."

Ink looked from the Oracle to the thread and back again. A part of her found it hard to believe that she'd never come back here, treasure trove that it was, but the Starbreakers had warned her the Oracle was never wrong, and they knew him better than anyone else. Her resolve wavered. And then she struck upon an idea.

He thought he had her. But she didn't have to take this arrangement on his terms. Not when whatever answer she might want was already somewhere in his mind.

One of the few spells she'd learned to cast without any physical components let her reach into the minds of others with her own. If she stayed close enough to the surface, he wouldn't even be able to feel her probing. All it would take would be a few hypothetical questions to bring the right topics to the forefront of his mind, and she could glean whatever she wanted all on her own. It was the perfect way around his little game.

At least, she thought so. Then her mind touched his, and fire erupted in her skull.

In horror, Elizabeth watched as not one but dozens of threads lashed out from the Oracle's eyes, burying themselves in Ink's. The High Inquisitive recoiled, and the threads from the Oracle retreated from her, only for new ones from the surrounding spools to take their place. Ink fell to her knees, screaming. The silence spell on Elizabeth fizzled out.

"Ink!"

Elizabeth's eyes became swirling orbs of green, and with a massive gust of wind and the return of her wings, she rushed forward with her swords ready to cut the threads.

"You cut the strings at her peril," the Oracle warned. "Only her own will may release her mind."

He smiled as Ink thrashed and clutched her head, still screaming. "What is left of it."

Elizabeth slashed through the air, sending out a gale of wind toward the elf. An arcane doorway swept over him, taking him away before the wind could touch him. When he didn't reappear, she turned her attention to Ink. She knelt down, grabbing the wizard's head in her hands.

"Ink, listen to me!" she shouted. "You have to let it go! Whatever you're seeing, let it go!"

Ink thrashed against Elizabeth's grip, not seeming to register the words. Ink wasn't there. Whatever she was seeing, it had left her completely cut off from her surroundings and trapped inside her own head. The only solution now would be to go in after her. But if Ink's current state was anything to go by, it was going to be unpleasant.

Taking a deep breath and gritting her teeth, Elizabeth touched her fore-head to Ink's and manipulated her presence to let her own being mingle with the wizard's.

It was like sailing a raft in a hurricane—waves tossing her one way and the other, each one sending her to another place, another time. Like being pelted with sheets of rain coming down hard enough to blind her, every raindrop its own voice and face and life story. This was everything. Absolutely everything that ever was and is and would be.

And it was drowning her.

It was impossible to track who or where or what was happening. It was all happening, all at once. Mixed in with it was her past, her present, her future. It was too much, and yet the more it confused her, the more she instinctively reached out to it, trying to make sense of it all. It was an endless loop—a confusing barrage of scenes, a desperate need to understand, and then another barrage, even more disorienting than the last.

She just needed to understand. To sort through it all. Separate the pieces and put them together. And more pieces. More pieces. More pieces—

Let it go.

For the briefest, fleeting moment, the words cut through the noise of infinity. They were desperate, they were pained, but they were there. They were real. And they came from her. But they didn't. They were and weren't her. Who was she again?

You don't need this. You don't need any of this.

Let it go.

She wanted to listen. Tried to listen. But there was too much at once. She couldn't see. She couldn't think.

One piece. Think of one piece. Bury yourself in it until it drowns out everything else. One piece. One vision. One memory.

She was trapped.

Trapped.

She remembered what it was like to be trapped.

She was curled into a ball, her knees jammed against her chest and her head buried between them. Splinter-riddled wood pressed against her from all sides, offering no room to move. Her body ached, stiff and sore, and her stomach churned with the constant, undulating rhythm of the world around her. She could see only darkness. Hear only the groan of wood and waves of the ocean. A seagull cried somewhere in the distance as men and women argued.

"We already got paid. Let's dump her and be done with it before the Imperials catch up to us."

"We don't even know they're chasing us!"

"Of course they fucking are. Do you know what that girl is? *What it means to them if she makes it to foreign soil?"*

She wanted to vomit, to cry, to scream. She forced herself to do none of them. Either they would hold up their end of the deal and take her to Corsar or they would kill her. And either way, there was nothing she could do about it, so there was no sense crying over it. She knew the risks when she ran.

Focus. Don't let anything else in.

The voice sounded so much like her. Was it her? It was so hard to tell. The memories weren't hers, but they were. Who was she?

No. One thing at a time. Focus. We're trapped. So get us out.

Out.

She remembered getting out.

The barrel and the ship were gone, replaced by the interior of a luxury suite. A dark-skinned man with short, curly hair and a fine beard stood before her. She avoided looking him in the eyes. She knew what she'd see if she looked. Betrayal. Disappointment. Heartache.

"The Headmaster made me an offer." Her throat was drier than she'd expected.

"What kind of offer?"

"High Inquisitive. Head of the Academy's intelligence."

She waited for him to say something and was rewarded with silence. He was a smart man. He had to know everything else she was going to say now. But he was going to make her say it.

"I'm taking it," she said. "The offer. I'm leaving the Cord."

"All right."

"That's it? That's all I get?"

He stood up a little straighter, held his head up. Standing like a soldier to hide the pain. "What do you want me to say?"

"Whatever you're really thinking."

He frowned. "Why?"

He wasn't asking why she wanted to know. He was asking why she was leaving.

"Because I have to. Because I was made to be more than a glintchaser. Because I need more than the Cord can give me."

"More than I can give you."

The words went through her like a knife. But she didn't falter.

"Yes."

"Is there anything I can say to change your mind?"

She risked a look at his eyes and regretted it. They were already red and glossy. Exactly like she'd pictured them and yet somehow even worse to actually stare at. She nearly lost her nerve seeing them.

Nearly.

"No."

"Then I won't try. Goodbye, Kira."

"Goodbye, Quint."

The threads broke away from Ink's eyes, retreating into the spools as Ink and Elizabeth collapsed onto the floor. Tears were running down both of their faces. Ink coughed. Her throat was raw from screaming.

"What did you do?" Ink asked. She had been completely overwhelmed by the sanctum's visions.

And then, there had been a presence that cut through the storm and guided her back to herself. At once, alien and familiar, like a stranger she'd known her whole life.

"Total empathy," Elizabeth said, still lying down. "It's a . . . druid technique. Mixing my presence with yours so we could share the burden and I could get you out."

"Is that why I suddenly miss a child I don't have?"

"Sorry. Two-way street," Elizabeth explained. "And full disclosure, it's not really supposed to be used on *people*, but I figured out how to twist it a while back. It'll pass in a few minutes, just . . . ignore any thoughts that feel out of character until then."

"Lovely."

Ink rubbed her temples, which were still throbbing. That . . . had not gone how she'd expected. But even with only the briefest of glimpses into the Oracle's mind, she knew it was *exactly* how he'd planned it.

"I'm sorry. Even just brushing the surface of his mind—"

"I know."

Ink looked around. "Where did he go?"

Elizabeth sat up and shrugged. "Don't know. Bounced as soon as I tried to take him."

"Well, this has been a productive day."

Elizabeth grunted as she pushed herself up onto her feet and extended a hand down to help Ink. "Come on. We need to keep looking for the others."

". . . Elizabeth."

"Hm?"

"About whatever you think you saw while you were inside my head . . ."

Elizabeth gave her a look that nearly shattered her. Never in Ink's life had she ever felt so understood, so seen, as she did in that moment. Elizabeth knew. She knew *everything*. The irony wasn't lost on the High Inquisitive, who had only minutes ago held Elizabeth's secrets over her head. Which only made Elizabeth's next words feel even kinder.

"What do you mean? Didn't see a thing."

THE PRIEST

Keep moving downward, don't panic, and don't touch any of the threads. With those three rules running a loop in his mind, Church managed to make his way down to the lower levels of the sanctum. At the very bottom of it all would be the heart, the source of its power and the place where they'd beaten the Oracle the last time they'd all met.

The separation had to be a play at leaving them all vulnerable. Short of finding each other, the best counter to the Oracle's play would be to go where he would be the most vulnerable, too.

Church's palm rested on the hilt of Zealot as he rode another elevator. He sincerely hoped he wouldn't have to use the sword.

The elevator let him out in the core at the end of one of three walkways that all converged at the nexus of the threads. All around, spools, rods, and pulleys kept the threads taut and organized, like components of a giant loom. Faint, unintelligible whispers came from the strings, like voices straining to be heard.

Besides that, silence.

Experimentally, Church called the Oracle's name. "Apollius?"

The name reverberated in the room, off the walls and tightly wound strings of the sanctum's mechanisms. The air thrummed at the sound, and Church's hairs stood on end.

A cold whisper slid across the back of his neck. "Give breath to a demon, and it shall appear."

Church turned on his heels as the Oracle materialized behind him. A cruel, malicious sneer tugged at the elf's features as light rippled along the strings embedded in his eyes, producing a subtle strobe effect across his face.

Church held his ground in spite of the stone in his gut. "But a prisoner of the devils, I shall not fear."

The Oracle's eyes narrowed. "Prisoner. Yes. My devils are children playing knights."

"Is that how you see us? The devils to your demon?"

"The sanctum is my tomb. The stock for my gluttony. My death, should I end my feast," the Oracle said, throwing his arms in a sweeping gesture. "Feast of the eyes. Of time. Here, you trapped me. Here, you torment me. My mind entwined round and round the spools, it turns. I see it all, and it is all I can see. Devils, yes. My devils, you five were and are and will always be."

"We had to stop you."

The Oracle's voice boomed as he snapped. "You *chose* to stop me!"

He surged forward, and it took every fiber of Church's nerve to resist drawing Zealot.

The elf loomed over him, his whole frame bent with pain and rage. The strings anchored in his eyes quivered, as if barely restraining him. Power and malice radiated from the elf so strong Church could feel it as their faces came within inches of each other. But Church held his ground, and his sword stayed in its scabbard.

"Ungrateful maggots! You roll in filth and call it civilization! I would have brought back the sun!" His voice shook and with it, every string on every spool and pulley all the way back to the central orb. And yet, even before they had gone still, his face fell. "No. Not the sun. Never the sun. Never for me." The shimmer in the threads dulled, and the Oracle's mouth hung open. A whimper, barely audible, escaped his throat. "Why? Why did you do this to me? WHY DID YOU MAKE ME SEE!"

The Oracle pressed forward, forcing Church back. "Little minds call it fate, so they can blame something else. They come here, thinking there is some warning to be found, some plan to be subverted. But fate did not bring you here on that day, did not tie me to this place and leave me screaming. No great other moved your hands or mine! It happened, all things happen, because we are who we are!"

"We?" Church asked.

"You!" the Oracle howled, but the shimmer in his strings flickered. He repeated himself, some of the fire dying in his voice. "You . . . me. The sanctum. I wanted to see." The words came again, a hollow croak from a confused, old, tired creature. "I wanted to see."

Church still didn't know if his plan would work, but he didn't think he was going to get a better opportunity than this. As the strings in the Oracle's eyes dulled and his face took on a lost, sad expression, the priest clasped his saint's talisman and spoke a prayer.

Renalt's power, supplied by Saint Beneger and guided by Church's will, flowed over the Oracle's mind in a gentle, slow-moving tide. For a moment, as the prayer made contact, Church could feel the Oracle's being, the frantic mad energy of it. A constant state of overwhelmed confusion and pain, directionless and omnipresent. The whole world blurred as a dozen different moments of the same space filled his senses. The room was empty and full. Pristine and ruined. Brilliant and dark.

The prayer pressed on, wrapping like a blanket around the Oracle's shivering mind, bringing it slowly to stillness and calming the storm of his thoughts. The world came back into focus. Everything was smaller. Quieter. Gentler.

The Oracle's mouth hung open, lower lip quivering. Church held his breath, waiting.

And then the strings detached from the Oracle's eyes, receding into the air and vanishing. The elf's dark chocolate irises became visible again for the first time in nearly a decade. His whole body shook, and he let out a hoarse, keening sound as he wobbled unsteadily on his feet. His open-mouthed cries grew steadily louder until his legs gave out from under him completely, and he fell into Church's arms, shuddering and sobbing. The priest caught him, arms strong and gentle as he guided them both to the floor.

"Blind," the elf whispered. "I cannot see. I am blind."

Despite his words, the elf's eyes locked on to Church's, and the priest understood what he meant. The young man nodded. "You're free."

Still supporting the elf with one arm, Church took up his talisman again. "I'm sorry. I would let you rest, but we need to talk."

When Church finished his next prayer, he was glad they were already on the ground. He wasn't sure he'd have trusted himself to stay standing after using so strong of a healing prayer immediately after stemming the sanctum's onslaught. Hot flashes plagued him as he finished his work, a sign he was beginning to overtax his body's tolerance for divine power, but the elf in his arms stirred, clutching his temples as the restorative power helped to mend a decade of mental strain.

The older the damage, the less clean the results of healing prayers. The Oracle, Apollius, would carry the scars of his time tethered to the sanctum for the rest of his existence. But at the very least, he'd be able to think straight again.

Apollius shrugged out of Church's arms with a grunt, drawing himself up into a seated position a few feet away. For a time, neither of them spoke.

"You would come to the one who knows everything and give him ignorance?" Apollius's voice echoed in the chamber, which seemed emptier now than it had before.

Church shrugged. "It was the only thing I could think of that you might want."

"You are a fool," Apollius said. "You've released your greatest foe from his bondage. You've freed him to enact whatever he desires on your pathetic people."

"If you were going to hurt someone, you'd have done it by now, trapped in the sanctum or not."

"Are you so arrogant as to proclaim to know me, mongrel?"

"The last time we fought, you saw something," Church said. "I saw it in your face right before Snow destroyed the sanctum's safeguard. You saw something you didn't want to see. And you stopped fighting."

The elf kept his back to Church. He did not respond.

"You just froze, right in the middle of everything. No one else even noticed it happen. But I saw. You looked . . . defeated," Church said.

Apollius sat hunched, still refusing to look at Church.

"You still look like that."

He let the words hang, and the silence drove them home even harder. When Apollius finally spoke, there was no pride in his voice. No sense of superiority. Only low, rumbling bitterness.

"Of all my devils," he said, "I despise you the most."

He glowered at the young man, an ember of his old bearing in his eyes.

"The others are disgusting and insufferable in their ways. The pathetic tinkerer playing at intelligence. The perversion of the divine order. The prattling swordsman and that thrice-forsaken *thief!*" The embers flared up as he put extra venom into his final word, but they died out again just as quickly. He had run out of will to be galled. "But I could only hate them as I hate the rest of your kind. Your world. Skittering around the bones of something you did not build, pretending to be more than the petty little scavenger animals you are.

"I hate you differently. Because you are different. The other mongrels come with all their pettiness on full display. Their vapid, tiny thoughts, fretting over their meager little handful of years as if they could eke out a few more or moaning endlessly of the ones they have already lost. They are so simple to unravel. You are . . . *human*. In the old meaning of the word. Even with the sanctum, I could never find the pettiness of other mongrels in you. The fear of their own insignificance. I do not understand it, and I hate it. But most of all, I loathe that you are right."

The words came out like a puff of air from Apollius, and he deflated even further after speaking them. His head drooped below his sagging shoulders, shaking in meek self-contempt.

"I lose. Each and every time I make war on your kind—and make no mistake, I *will* make war on your kind again. When you are dead and gone, when I have forgotten this day and that the sanctum is never wrong, I will feel the fire of my ambitions and disgust, I will bring my heel down on the neck of this world—and I will lose. Always. That is what I saw, *human*." The elf's lips curled. "I despise your people for taking that word. I despise you all the more for living up to it."

"We do our best."

Apollius grunted in contempt, turning away again.

Another silence passed between them, which Church did not try to break. He wasn't Snow or Angel or Phoenix. He couldn't simply brute force the elf into giving information with violence or logic. He couldn't talk circles around him until he tricked Apollius into telling him what he wanted to know like Brass would.

All he had was understanding and patience.

Finally, Apollius spoke again. "It's so . . . quiet. I'd forgotten what that was like."

"I'm sorry I didn't come back sooner."

"This was always when you would have."

"You saw?"

"No. Or perhaps yes. It was difficult to parse—what was what, and what was when. But that's how it works. How it all works. Events transpiring as an inevitable consequence of trillions on trillions of things being what they are, because in any given moment, they can be nothing else."

"But people can change."

"Yes. But *how* they change is a product of who they are and events that transpire around them because of who other people are. Things seem mutable because of limited information. Mortal creatures do not fully know one another or even ourselves. So, we can be surprised. But the sanctum knows. It knows everything, and everyone, and the concert of it all moving together." A wistful smile touched the elf's lips. "Damn it all. We could have been gods."

"How much do you remember? Of what you saw?" Church asked.

"Save your breath, priest," the Oracle sighed. "I know why you and yours are here. I know I give you what you want. And I know how it all ends." A dark smile crept across the elf's features. "Which is exactly *why* I give it to you."

DEPARTURE

Phoenix's first sign that he'd slowed their fall in time was that he was still conscious. The filter of his goggles shifted erratically, turning his vision into a strobe of blue, orange, green, and black. Dirt and snow had crept down his collar, into every crevice in his armor, and coated his beard. He lay flat on his back, staring up at the silver streaked clouds. Far, far above, he could just make out the tiny square of the arcane doorway they'd fallen out of as it winked out of existence.

Angel was on her feet a few yards away, a slight dent in the earth around her. The divine glow faded from her skin, and the gravity disc he'd slapped onto her shoulder clattered to the ground in a smoking heap.

The Oracle's sanctum sailed lazily overhead—a peaceful, quiet monolith of rock and ice topped with sloped spires of glass and stone. Framed against the clouds with snow gently trailing off of it, it looked beautiful.

He never wanted to go back there ever again.

Angel hooked her arm under his and hauled him to his feet. Though parts of him screamed in protest, he accepted the help and forced himself to stay standing over the aching in his everything.

"You're crazy," she said.

"Probably."

"The hell were you thinking?"

"That he'd just dropped you off a cliff and you weren't gonna survive the fall, mostly," Phoenix said. "And he left the portal open, so . . ."

Angel looked at him, both bewildered and impressed. She became quiet, not saying anything until she looked away. "Well, thanks I guess."

Phoenix had to remind himself not to make a big deal out of Angel saying thank you.

"You're welcome."

She joined him in looking up at the sanctum. "We're kind of fucked for getting back up there, aren't we?"

"I left my sky surfer in the Star."

"Figures," she muttered. "Well, what now?"

"We hope the others have a better time than us," Phoenix said. "And that Church checks in soon."

"Tan-fucking-fastic," Angel said as she sat down.

They sat in silence, catching their breath and trying to stay warm. Angel emitted a soft, golden glow, using just enough power to warm herself. Phoenix went to work, taking apart one of his fire spheres to expose the core at its center. A few minor tweaks to the sphere and some scrap parts from his belt and he'd converted it into a tiny space heater. Warmer than a campfire, no chance of being snuffed out by wind, and only a slight chance of destabilizing and exploding.

A wistful smile briefly crossed his face, remembering Robyn's own near miss with a different fire core. Maybe someday he would teach her how to work with enchanted objects.

Assuming he lived that long.

"Hey." Angel drew him back to the present. "When you jumped into the portal after me, how did you know you weren't just jumping into a volcano or something?"

Phoenix smirked. "Context."

"Very funny."

A new doorway sparked to life in front of them, and the two of them exchanged looks before standing up.

"He doesn't have a high opinion of us if he thinks that trick will work twice," Phoenix said.

"So, we're ignoring this one?"

"I didn't say that." Phoenix began tapping glyphs on the back of his gauntlet, preparing a spell to identify the portal and figure out as much as he could *before* going through it.

Before he could even finish, however, Ink and Elizabeth stepped through the portal, followed by Church, and then, finally, a snow-covered Brass, who face-planted on arrival as the portal shut behind him.

Brass shook the snow off himself like a dog as he sat up. "Was I the only one who was portaled to *outside* the sanctum?"

"Probably just didn't want to deal with your bullshit," Angel mused. "Honestly relatable."

"Did you guys get anything out of him?" Phoenix asked.

"A splitting headache and some bad metaphors," Ink said.

"I got what we came for," Church said.

Phoenix's eyes widened. He hadn't expected anyone to actually say yes. "How?"

Church didn't answer immediately, and he wore an expression Phoenix didn't know what to make of.

"I gave him what he wanted," the priest said and offered no further elaboration. "Come on. We've got a lot of work to do. And there were two escapees the Oracle couldn't find."

"Who?" Ink asked.

"One of them was Pitch. And the other . . ." Church's face took on a grave expression. "The other was Kurien."

Kurien, also known as the Prince Killer. One of the people the Starbreakers had personally sent to Oblivion. The woman who crippled Roland II.

THE PRINCE KILLER

Lord Roso didn't know which was making him sweat more—the sweltering humidity or the fact that Kurien wasn't saying anything. Everything about the assassin unsettled Roso—the overly long steps she took that gave her movements an unnatural bob, the owlish mask obscuring her face that she never removed, or the fact that she was wearing a full bodysuit and shawl on a tropical island in summer—it all just came across as artificial and wrong.

To top it all off, she was immune to Roso's powers of fiendish persuasion. He knew of blessings and other magics that could shield a person from his words. But Kurien's immunity was a complete mystery, like everything else about the woman.

If she even *was* a woman and not an inhuman monster.

Roso cleared his throat. "Is there something else you wanted? Money? Manpower?"

"Do stop groveling before you damage your appeal."

The Prince Killer picked an expensive glass sculpture of a crane off Roso's desk, holding its head gingerly between two long fingers. She cocked her head to the side, shrugged, and flung the crane into the corner of the room. Roso flinched as the glass shattered.

"An Iandran Lord should be suave. Sophisticated. Sociable." The Prince Killer's voice resonated through her mask. Every word punctuated by a flourish of her hands. "Not a sniveling coward hiding behind the devil blood in his veins. But then, I suppose you're not a lord, are you?"

There were eyes painted on the Prince Killer's mask. Two wide, white circles framed in a black outline mimicking the look of a barn owl. They stared at Roso, unblinking. The hellborn shifted uncomfortably in his chair.

"To your question, no," Kurien said. "I don't use money, and all the others are already providing suitable distractions for the king's protectors. What I need is something unique. Something . . . unforgettable."

"I would think killing a king would be unforgettable enough by itself, but I did my best," Roso said. He opened the latches on a large carrying case and turned it around to show off the contents—a dozen different Old World weapons nested in a bed of straw and wrapped in leather. "Old World artifacts routinely pass through this port while moving from one land to another, but it took some doing to find someone who had suitable goods and . . . to persuade them to part with them. I've had an attendant select what he thought were the most interesting pieces."

"Well done," Kurien congratulated. "Now, what are our choices?" The Prince Killer removed and unwrapped the first weapon, revealing a two-foot blade attached to a spear shaft with a deep groove running the length of the weapon. "A Late Dynasty sword spear. Elegant but a bit simple, don't you think?"

Roso dutifully nodded. He didn't know what the Late Dynasty was or what the spear did, just that it wasn't good enough. "Of course."

"Oh, now there's something interesting." Kurien withdrew a bronze chakram from the case. "I killed the son of Duke Rojdero with a weapon like this. He was quite the talker. So, I took his throat. A perfect orbit around his neck, a single unbroken slice. I almost missed, you know. A little higher on the neck and he would have died too quickly to register what happened. The spray of blood was something to behold."

"So, do we have a winner?" Roso asked.

"No," Kurien said. "I never reuse a scene. A proper story must rhyme, not repeat itself. Difficult as it may be in as long and storied a tale as mine. But we must— Oh my."

Kurien flicked the bladed ring aside, embedding it in the wall. And then, very gingerly, she lifted out a large, oddly shaped weapon. It resembled a crossbow but with a basket guard around the handle and a long, narrow gem embedded along the top instead of space for a bolt. As she tested the grip, the weapon whirred to life with a condensed ball of white energy crackling at its tip.

Experimentally, Kurien pointed the weapon at a wall and pulled the trigger. With a sound like glass shattering underwater, a blast of barely visible force shot from the weapon, punching a small hole in the wall. The Prince Killer gave a dark chuckle from behind her mask.

"Do you know what this is?" she asked.

"N-no." Roso tried and failed to swallow the lump of fear in his throat.

"This . . . is no Old World weapon," Kurien said. "It was built by a glintchaser—a crow, as they say in your country. It's modified from something scavenged, of course, but so much his own design as to be indisputably his. It was one of his earliest works."

"How did a crow build something like that?" Roso asked.

"He was like me. A visionary ahead of his time. He used this to slay countless monsters. Save countless lives . . . including Roland II. It was the only target I ever had who survived," Kurien said. The more she stared at the weapon, the heavier her breathing became. "Roland's savior made his end. My enemy, the enabler of my art. It's *perfect*."

Roso nodded again, even more enthusiastically. "Wonderful. I'm so happy I could find something to your tastes, as repayment for . . . your help, securing my freedom."

"Yes. Your freedom," Kurien mused, inspecting the sights of the weapon. "Well, this for that. Our debts are balanced, Lord Roso, which means our partnership is concluded. Do try to enjoy yourself."

"I intend to," Roso said. He paused for a moment, and silence fell over them. Kurien wasn't leaving. "So. What will you do now?"

Roso could not see the Prince Killer's face, but he heard the smile in the assassin's voice.

"Are you familiar with the Cord of Aenwyn?"

Roso shook his head. "I can't say I am."

"They're another band of crows. Unlike most companies, they travel the whole world. If I've not been misled, they're currently here in Tecah. And they have something that I require."

"What is it?"

"Shadows." Roso shrank back under the sadistic glee in the Prince Killer's voice. "My dearest Lord Roso, how would you like for *me* to be in *your* debt?"

ON THE ROAD

I f Vera considered themself tight on money, Snow wondered how well off they had been before the fire. Their carriage was, without exaggeration, one of the nicest Snow had ever traveled in, and she'd once been given parade honors by the royal family.

The carriage interior was upholstered for comfort and style with ample leg room, stained wood paneling, and plush leather seating. State-of-the-art suspension and axles made for a ride smooth enough to sip wine without spilling, and the whole ensemble was pulled by a pair of handsome white driving horses.

It was no magic carpet or flying skiff, but as far as landlocked transport went, it was top of the line.

"Of course, I meant it at the time. But I mostly just needed someone to blame. And truth be told, I was angry at myself for getting involved with him in the first place," Vera said, wrapping up their story. "After all, Brass is trouble, but I can't fairly give him all the blame for a fire someone else set. So, if you see him, tell him he's more than welcome back in the Pale, and I won't kill him if he gives me three hundred crowns."

"I'll pass it along," Snow said.

Vera reached for a new bottle of wine and held it out toward Snow. "Would you mind?"

Snow obliged, tapping the bottle with her finger and chilling its contents in the span of a few seconds. A smile spread across Vera's face.

"Avelina bless your heart. You're going to become my favorite at this rate."

"Who's your favorite now?"

"The priest."

"Seriously?"

"It's his face," Vera lamented. "Perfect kind of boyish handsome. Used to get me every time I saw it. How is he, by the way?"

"Fine," Snow said. After a moment, she added, "Still ace."

Vera sighed in disappointment. "That figures."

Snow shrugged.

"You're a wellspring of conversation."

"I told you talking isn't really my thing."

"Well, what is your thing these days?"

Contract killing, if she wanted to go by what she spent most of her time on. But that was a job. It paid well and she was good at it, but it wasn't exactly what she did for fun. But then, neither were the gambling, wine, and one-night stands when she wasn't working. That was more for passing the time. Turning herself off for a few hours.

She couldn't remember the last time she'd actually just enjoyed herself.

That bothered her more than she expected.

"Doesn't matter," she deflected.

Vera narrowed their eyes for a moment before giving a dismissive shrug. They'd never really had the patience for breaking down people's walls. And they had more pressing matters than grilling an antisocial assassin over her hobbies.

"Why are we slowing down?"

"Sorry, boss," the driver barked. "Some kind of toll stop up ahead."

"Toll stop? Since when did the crown start giving a damn about the roads again?"

Snow sat up in her seat as her fingers wrapped around the hilt of her dagger. "They haven't."

Picking up on the edge in Snow's voice, Vera pulled aside the curtain on the carriage's window.

A couple hundred yards down the road, a ramshackle outpost and barricade had been erected out of what looked like bits and pieces of broken vehicles. There were half a dozen people or so manning it, some of them wearing scraps of mismatched armor, a pair of them on horses, all of them armed.

A road gang. Probably assembled out of a bunch of thieves and brutes run out of nearby towns that couldn't be bothered to keep them locked up or ship them to prison with a few army deserters thrown in for good measure. Just one of a dozen things that made territory beyond city lands such a hassle to get through.

And just when Vera was beginning to think it would be a quiet trip.

"Avelina spare us," Vera muttered. "Looks like you and Kratz are about to earn your—"

They stopped when they realized Snow was no longer inside the carriage. Vera shot Kratz a questioning look, but the half-orc looked just as confused.

Vera pulled the curtain shut and sank back into their seat, arms folded. Decisive action was nice, but that was just rude.

Glintchasers. Always so fucking dramatic.

Two of the gang approached the carriage as it pulled to a stop just short of the assembled wooden barricade, hands resting casually on the hilts of their weapons so as to draw attention to them. On the small platform erected just off the road, a woman sat on a stool, cradling a loaded crossbow.

The driver tried not to look nervous. He failed.

"Afternoon," one of the leads greeted upon sidling up to the window. He was the shorter of the two with a patchy beard and a silver tooth. "Sorry to trouble you folks on your trip. Just a bit of routine customs and fare collection."

Vera rolled their eyes as they drew back the curtain again. "Spare me. This is a holdup."

"Let's not go using flamery language," Silver-Tooth said, either mispronouncing "inflammatory" or just not knowing the actual word. It was always hard to tell with the backwater types. "We're just honest working men and women collecting funds for essential services."

"Like what?" Vera asked.

"Maintaining the roads," he declared. "Keeping them marked. And making sure folks traveling them are protected from any unfriendly types."

The man next to Silver-Tooth gave a half chuckle, exposing his own golden incisor.

"Last I checked," an icy, hollow voice cut in, "that was the crown's job."

Snow stepped out from behind the carriage, causing both men to flinch in surprise. She hadn't been there a second ago. And, seeing her pale face, they weren't convinced she wasn't a ghost.

"The fuck are you?"

"Security. You're not with the crown. Step away from the carriage and get your sticks out of the road."

Silver-Tooth collected himself best he could, but his eyes remained a little wider than they'd been before. He wanted to keep control of the situation, but he was nervous now. Indignant victims he could handle. But he didn't know what to make of Snow yet—or the magic looking symbols on her naked dagger.

He held up his hands and took a few cursory steps away from the carriage to try to pacify her. But he made no move to clear the barricade.

"There's no crown out here, Miss Security. But I don't think any of us want any trouble to come of this. So, let's call it." Silver-Tooth paused, looking over the exquisite craftsmanship of the carriage and the understated but still clearly imported clothes of Vera. "Two hundred crowns a head, and we inspect your luggage for any . . . contraband . . . and you can be on your way."

"Two hundred—" Vera nearly flew off the handle before restraining themself. Much more composed, they said, deadpan, "Fuck off."

Snow took that to mean they wouldn't be paying.

"Counter offer," Snow said. "You let us pass. You all live."

"All right, now." Silver-Tooth took a half step back to adjust his footing. Next to him, Gold-Tooth tightened his grip on his spear while others drew their own haphazard collection of weapons and repurposed farm equipment. "Maybe you should take a good look around before you try to start something."

The other members of the gang had slowly begun to fan out, encircling the carriage and cutting off any easy escape. They could try to just bull-rush past them, but two of them were on horseback. Hard to outrun an enemy when you're pulling a vehicle and they're not.

Snow cocked her head slightly, as if disappointed. The color drained from her eyes, the bright blue irises becoming paler by the second. At her feet, frost slowly spread out across the ground.

"Maybe *you* should."

Silver and Gold both recoiled, caught off guard. Panicked, Gold-Tooth brandished his spear in defense, trying to ward Snow off. She grabbed the spear just below the head, spreading ice along the haft until it reached Gold-Tooth's hands and made him howl from the sudden sting of cold.

Seeing her comrade attacked by some kind of magic, the archer on the platform panicked and loosed a crossbolt straight at Snow's head. Snow was moving before it had even started flying, and the bolt whizzed past her, burying itself into the dirt. Her expression remained unchanged, but she slowly corrected her stance and drew a second dagger.

Vera backed away from the window, knowing what came next.

"Kratz!"

The half-orc shifted forward, enveloping Vera in arms like worked stone and shielding them with his body. Outside, curses and screams began to fly, accompanied by the rasp of metal on metal. The crack of ice, the thump of a crossbow. And over and over again, the sound of skin and muscle being separated by a blade.

And then, it was over. Horse hooves thundered off, fleeing the scene. But otherwise, it was quiet.

Hesitantly, Kratz loosened his hold on Vera and began to sit up.

Snow's face appeared in the window, flecks of frozen blood dotting her face like freckles.

"Hey. Give me a hand with the barricades."

Kratz looked to Vera, who nodded.

Outside, a dozen or so gang members lay dead, scattered around the scene along with their weapons and several patches of frost. Most of them had only a single, neat wound—a slashed artery or a stab through the eye. But Silver-Tooth himself was suspended a few feet in the air, impaled on a spike of solid ice that jutted out from the ramshackle shooting platform.

"Avelina . . ." Vera swore. "Is this all of them?"

"A couple took off on the horses. Didn't feel like stopping them."

"Lucky them."

Snow shrugged and, with Kratz's help, began clearing away the barricades the gang had assembled on the road. Vera couldn't take their eyes off the bodies.

"Feels a little wrong just leaving them out here."

"Their friends will come back for the bodies if they give a damn," Snow said, barely glancing over. "Or something else will eat them. Either way, it's not our problem."

Finding it hard to argue with Snow in that moment, Vera had their driver get them underway shortly thereafter.

Roughly an hour passed before Snow was proven half right, as something else did come across the bodies, but it was neither to eat them nor bury them. Instead, the single-hooded figure that found the carnage stopped only briefly to assess the aftermath of the slaughter. It made notes of everything it saw, internalized those facts, and moved on. It was aware of both the cultural stigma of leaving corpses unburied as well as the practical risks. But it had priorities which superseded the issue. Namely, following the signature of a magical beacon currently carried by a master assassin.

A BAD IDEA

At her earliest convenience, Ruby found an excuse to slip away from the chaperone Church had left her with in his and Brass's absence. Not that she didn't love getting secondhand anxiety from a priestess who was clearly afraid of her but Ruby had other plans for the afternoon. After making sure no one saw her leave, she made her way into the woods behind the church.

The clearing wasn't that far of a walk. In fact, if she looked hard enough, she could just make out the church through the trees in the distance. But it was far enough away that she could be sure she wouldn't be disturbed.

Bart was already waiting for her.

"Hi."

"Hey."

The two of them stood about an arm's length apart, neither saying anything for a moment. Out of everyone in Aenerwin, Bart was the one who reminded Ruby the most of Church. He was the only person who hadn't treated her any differently since Church had left, who still saw the person behind the mysterious demon magic. Partly because of that, and partly because she wasn't exactly spoiled for choice, he was the one she'd trusted to bring into her plan.

She was still a little surprised he'd said yes though.

"Are you sure about this?" Bart asked.

"No," Ruby admitted. "But we're here. Let's do this."

Ever since Church's failed ritual, she hadn't been able to get it out of her head. Even more than the pain or uncertainty the night had left her with, though, there was this sense, growing stronger by the day, that there was something there. Inside her or connected to her maybe, she wasn't sure. But it was there. And it was calling her.

She'd wanted to talk to Church or Brass about it, but they'd both left for the capital, leaving her with only two options: she could ignore this feeling, let it remain this mysterious thing that only scared her more the longer she left it alone, or she could confront it herself, head on, and stop letting it keep her up at night.

It was an easy choice.

If she could figure out whatever sort of magic had its hooks in her, maybe it wouldn't scare her anymore. And her gut told her the best way to figure it out was to explore it. The memory of when the thorns had come out of her—the pain, the power—played over and over in her mind. She wanted to try to do that again. On purpose this time.

"All right. Well, I got you some targets." Bart stepped out of the way and gestured to the setup he'd prepared for her—a fallen log and a row of partially broken clay pots set on top of it.

"Thanks."

"So, what now?"

"I don't know," Ruby admitted. "Just . . . stand there and look pretty. And if something goes horribly wrong, go get help."

"Right." He took another half step back. Ruby could see the same thought she was having written on his face.

Maybe this is a bad idea.

She ignored it, extending her hand out toward a target and closing her eyes. Then, after considering it might be hard to aim with her eyes closed, she opened them again. The sun was almost perfectly positioned overhead to cut through the gap in the trees above, bearing down on them. They hadn't been outside long, and already her shoulders and hair felt hot. Sweat was collecting on her forehead and the back of her neck. A stray fly zipped past her face and briefly landed on her collarbone. Even after she shook it off, she kept feeling like it was still somewhere on her.

Focus, damnit.

She closed her eyes again, aim be damned. She breathed, letting out the tension in her shoulders on the exhale. She tried to take herself back to the night of the ritual, to remember the tipping point that had drawn the vines out. She tried to recall that presence, that sense of something else inside her.

"Anything?"

Ruby groaned as she opened her eyes again. "I'm trying to concentrate."

"Sorry!"

"Just give me a second, all right? I think I've almost—"

She was cut off as the ground beneath her feet exploded upward, and she was sent cartwheeling through the air as out from the earth burst a fully constructed, two-story tavern complete with intricate stonework and a rusted iron sign over the door.

Ruby landed flat on her back with a grunt, the world spinning and the wind knocked out of her.

"Ruby!" Bart was at her side in an instant, helping her sit up. When she signaled she was all right with a nod, he turned his eyes to the newly sprung-up building in front of them.

"Did you . . . mean to do that?"

"I don't think I made that. Or, if I did, I'm both better and worse at this than I thought."

With Bart's help, she staggered onto her feet, taking in the sight of the building. Her eyes fixated on the sign over the door.

The front door of the Rusted Star flung open as Angel marched outside, checking to see who she'd just hit with her tavern and quickly spotting the two dumbstruck young people covered in dirt.

"Oh, shit. It's Ruby, right? You and your friend okay?"

Before Ruby or Bart could pick their jaws up off the ground to answer, the doors of the Star opened again, and more familiar faces came walking out. Brass and Church, the former looking very excited while the latter looked worried on multiple levels, and Ink, looking slightly impatient and as self-satisfied as ever.

"We're ba-ack," Brass announced, before noticing the dirt all over Ruby and Bart. "Oh wow, what happened to you two?"

"The . . . thing," Ruby said, gesturing to the Rusted Star as she forgot every synonym for the establishment.

"You can run people over in this thing?" Brass asked, looking over the Rusted Star with renewed interest.

"Hey, I specifically parked us where Church said there wouldn't be anyone," Angel said. "This is not my fault."

"We're fine," Ruby said. "Just standing a little too close when it came up. More startled than anything."

Church nodded, looking relieved. A moment later, though, his expression switched to curiosity. "What were you two doing out here anyway?"

It was a moment of truth for Ruby. As much as Church had been trying to help her, and as kind as he had been, she wondered if it was the best idea to admit to a priest's face that she was intentionally experimenting with demon magic. Of course, part of the reason she'd even considered experimenting was that he was gone, and if he was back, then maybe she didn't have to try anything. Maybe now, there was no point in even mentioning what she'd been up to.

And what if she told him and he started treating her the way everyone else in Aenerwin had?

She cast a quick glance to Bart to gauge the boy's reaction. He idolized Church, and she half expected him to immediately tell the vicar everything. But to her pleasant surprise, he met her gaze, asking her with his eyes how she wanted to play this.

Ruby cleared her throat. "Just going for a walk."

"Oh. Is that all?"

Church's brow furrowed, and Ruby silently cursed. Not once in the months she'd been here had she ever seen someone successfully lie to the vicar, and she wasn't breaking that streak today. He knew she was hiding something.

Her heart began pounding in her chest, feeling seconds away from being exposed. Her mind raced to come up with another lie, another layer of obfuscation or else just some kind of way to get Church to drop the subject. And then, Brass came to her rescue with the exact wrong read on the situation she needed.

"Uh, Church, maybe we let the people alone in the woods together have their privacy?"

"What?" Church asked, not getting the hint.

"*What?*" Bart echoed, going beet red. "No, that's not—we weren't . . ."

He looked to Ruby for help, but she kept her eyes straight ahead and took a half step closer to the cleric in training.

It wasn't the cover story she would have picked, but it was one she could sell.

And if it got Church to stop asking questions, she was going with it.

With an elbow to the ribs and a series of meaningful eyebrow waggles, Brass finally managed to get the message through to Church, and realization dawned on the vicar's face.

"*Oh.*"

Ruby couldn't tell who looked more embarrassed, Church or Bart. Meanwhile, everyone else in the clearing beside her was wearing a grin and barely containing their urge to laugh. The vicar was suddenly in a hurry to change the subject.

"Well, we're going to go," he said. "We're not actually back yet, we're just picking up some things."

"Wait, what?"

"Glintchaser stuff," Brass explained. "I am really sorry to just leave you hanging like this, but it's a whole thing. Bad guys on the loose, people in danger, money to be made. You know the drill."

"For how long?" Ruby asked.

"A few days?" Brass guessed. "Weeks? Don't know. But the point is, we're gonna have to pause the whole demon-magic-removal thing for a bit. Are you gonna be okay?"

There was a moment of emotional whiplash as Ruby went from disappointed that Brass and Church were leaving, to remembering she'd already been making plans to sort this out without their help.

"Yeah," she said. "I'll be fine. Go save the day or whatever."

"We'll be back as soon as we can," Church reassured her. "In the meantime, don't worry. You're in good hands with Sister Laurel. If anything happens, she can handle it."

Ruby fought to keep a neutral expression at the mention of her chaperone at the church. At the too-fresh memories of being treated like she could explode at any moment. Of all the times the priestess had been just checking in. Just wondering what she was up to.

Just suffocating her.

Weeks more of that. Of an entire town full of people terrified of her. Of having to sneak out into woods just for some space and sanity. She couldn't do it. She *wouldn't* do it.

"Come now, we're burning daylight," Ink insisted, leading the way toward the town. "Let's get what you need and get on with things."

"Duty calls," Brass said. With a wink, he added, "Enjoy your walk."

With that, the four of them all made their way back to Aenerwin proper, leaving Ruby and Bart alone in the woods with the Rusted Star.

"Well, that happened," Bart said when they were all finally gone. "Should we move somewhere else or just go back to—Ruby?"

The young man looked around, just in time to spot Ruby ducking into the Rusted Star. He reached out as if to stop her, already far too late. His outstretched hand clenched into a fist, and he bit back a curse. He knew how she felt about Sister Laurel. About how the whole town had been treating her ever since the ritual had failed and the vicar had left. And knowing that, he had an idea of what Ruby was planning.

He looked to the Star, then back in the direction of town. And with a sigh, he followed her into the tavern.

He was going to be in so much trouble when the vicar found out about this.

ESCAPE

After they collected the rest of their things from the church in Aenerwin, and Angel warned Church not to let Brass get him killed, Ink teleported herself and the two men away, leaving the sentinel behind. With a sigh, Angel began to make her way out of the church. There were a few clerics here, but most were scattered around town right now, shopping, eating, or just visiting people, and the halls themselves were quiet. The lack of people present in the church made it a little more comfortable for Angel as she walked it. But only a little.

The nave was empty but clean and already lit by candlelight. Whatever altar kid Church had on duty was on top of their chores. Without meaning to, she cast her eyes toward the altar at the front and instantly regretted it. As soon as she laid eyes on the altar, she felt it. A slight tingle on her skin. A fluttering warmth in her chest, like the first wisps of flame in a fireplace. This was a holy place, belonging to Renalt and his saint. And her own nature was reacting to it. A nature she preferred to keep buried.

She turned her back on the altar and tried not to think about it or what it stood for as she walked away. But partway down the aisle, Angel stopped. Despite her own internal protest, she turned back around, coming face-to-façade with the altar. Staring at it, the silence in the nave somehow deepened. There was a feeling, one that had followed her all her life, of eyes looking down on her, expectant.

"What the fuck do you want?" Angel asked.

The altar remained silent. But there was no denying its presence. It was a symbol of the patron god of Corsar, of truth, justice, and benevolent strength. Symbols had power. And power always carried a hint of its source.

"Come on, say it. What am I doing wrong this time?"

Most churches didn't depict Renalt directly. The traditional altar, instead, went for his symbol—the downward sword inside a ring. The sword stood for power but wielded in protection rather than aggression. The ring, a watching eye, casting light on the darkness.

The symbol looked more like him than any statue or painting that gave him a face. Angel didn't even know how she knew that. Even the one time she'd visited the heavens in the flesh with the other Starbreakers, she'd never seen the god. But she knew all the same. One more part of herself that felt like it came from someone else.

She weighed the pros and cons of smashing it.

As a Sentinel, she was neither human nor divine. A disappointment here and a joke up above. Maybe she was the one who'd chosen to be born—she still wasn't sure she bought that, whatever the legends about Sentinels said— but Renalt was the one who created her as someone who wanted to be like this. Her life was his fault.

But smashing an altar like that was probably a pretty fast track to invoking the wrath of the god. Which would probably get her killed, which would mean she would end up back in the heavens. And she had no intentions of going back so much as a second sooner than she had to.

The stone sculpture lived to see another day, and she unclenched a fist she hadn't even realized she'd made. She swore it seemed unimpressed by her, which should have just made her angry all over again.

Instead, it just hurt.

She could have just walked away. The altar couldn't follow her. But fuck that. If it was going to stand there and judge her, she had some shit to say to it, and it was going to listen.

Renalt was going to listen.

"You know what the worst thing is?" Angel asked. "All the shit I've gotten because of you, all the pain, everything I've been through . . . and I still want you to be proud of me."

She felt pathetic saying it out loud. Pathetic and betrayed. "But I don't know what you want me to be. It wasn't a knight. It wasn't a glintchaser. And it's not this either, is it? I can't just live a normal life and keep my head down. Well, I'm out of ideas, okay? I don't know what'll make you happy. But I'm done trying to find out. At least this way, nobody else gets hurt."

She stood in the center of the nave, waiting. Daring some saint or even Renalt himself to come down and say something. To argue with her, to tell her what they wanted, or even to just admit she was never going to make them happy so she could at least be free.

No one came. No answers. No judgment. Just a big empty room.

She shook her head and turned for the doors. "This is why I don't go to church."

———

Angel had left Thalia in the Rusted Star to finish the job of clearing space in the backroom, just in case they ended up needing to transport a prisoner themselves. As usual, she worked fast. By the time Angel made it back to the Star, she was already back behind the bar.

"Hey," she greeted. Her casual smile immediately vanished once she saw Angel's expression. "What happened?"

Skipping over asking if something was wrong; she already knew.

"Nothing," Angel said. "Sentinel stuff."

Thalia's face said she wasn't satisfied with that answer, but she shrugged. "You're the boss."

Angel placed both hands on top of the counter. "We good to go?"

"She's ready to burrow. Where to?"

"A village down south of here. To catch a mole man."

"Is that like a man-sized mole or a mole-sized man?"

"Both? Look, he's short and ugly, and he likes to dig holes and eat kids. Come to your own conclusions."

"You have the weirdest life."

"Had," Angel corrected. "This is a one-time gig. We're done, we go back to normal. For good this time."

Angel concentrated her will into the Rusted Star, focusing her thoughts on the location Church had given them. It was a little harder to steer somewhere she'd only ever heard of, but she had more than enough practice moving the tavern.

As she breathed in, the whole of the inn breathed with her, and as she breathed out, she could feel it. Her hands connected to the counter. The counter to the floor. Floor to foundation, foundation to dirt, dirt to rock. Finally, her senses converged on her destination, and with a single mental push, the ground beneath the Rusted Star opened up and swallowed it whole.

The windows went dark as they were buried, and then, a moment later, they burst to life again with sunlight. With a final lurch in their stomachs, the journey ended. Thalia was a little more unsteady than Angel, not nearly as used to the sensation, but she was still smiling.

"You have got to teach me how to steer this thing."

"It's pretty intuitive," Angel said. "Just sort of think about where you want to go and—"

She was cut off by a sudden crash coming from upstairs.

"Did you remember to secure the rooms upstairs?"

"They've been secured since Rockshore," Thalia defended. "Not like we've had any guests since then."

Before Angel could make a retort of "clearly not," there were more sounds upstairs. Scuffling and bumps, starting and stopping. That wasn't loose furniture.

"Did something get in before we left?"

"All the windows should still be locked," Thalia said. "So, unless one of your friends left the door open on the way out . . ."

"You were in here the whole time."

"I was in the back for most of it, and you can't hear shit in there."

Angel rolled her eyes as she climbed the stairs, picking up a broom on the way up to deal with whatever animal had made its way into the inn. But when she reached the top of the steps, she caught the sound of whispering.

Not an animal.

A switch flipped in her mind as Angel realized someone had broken into the Rusted Star. Maybe it was just an innocent, curious person from Aenerwin. But maybe not. And years as a glintchaser had taught her to always be ready for the worst. Her body tensed as she stalked down the hall toward the voices, ready to spring at the first sign of an enemy. She reached the door of the guest room that was the source of the sounds, threw it open, and came face-to-face with an overturned nightstand and Bart and Ruby in the middle of a furious whispered debate.

"Oh, you have got to be kidding me."

The two of them froze like startled deer for a moment before Bart sputtered out, "Okay, this isn't what it looks like! We—"

"Stowed away inside my inn."

"Oh. I guess it is what it looks like."

Ruby stepped forward. "I can explain."

"You ran away from the church because they were driving you insane."

Ruby's mouth hung open for a moment, looking somewhere between annoyed that she'd been interrupted and surprised that Angel had figured it out so quickly.

"That's the gist of it, yeah."

"You do remember you've got a demon thing going on, right?" Angel asked. "If you just ignore that, it's gonna end badly."

"I'm not ignoring it."

"You ran away from the place that's supposed to help you fix it."

"*Church* is supposed to help me fix it," Ruby corrected. "Not Aenerwin."

"Yeah, he's busy and also not here. What was the plan here, exactly?"

"I just need to get away!" Ruby snapped. "Church and Brass . . . they've been fine. But everyone in town is afraid of me. And now, when he's not there, everyone just looks at me like a monster. The ones that don't run or say prayers to try and ward me off are following me, everywhere, just watching me, waiting for something to happen. I can't *breathe* in that place. I'm sorry for breaking in, even though the door was unlocked. But I couldn't stay there. At least not until Church and Brass get back."

Angel rubbed her temples with her hand to try and preempt the headache she was sure this was going to cause her. "Look, kid, I get it. Small-town people can get really dumb about stuff. Double when it's religious small-town people. But you can't stay here, all right? I'm on the same job Church and Brass are on. And I know for a fact Church doesn't want you just running around wherever with some kind of demon mark on you, because if it doesn't get you hurt, it'll probably hurt someone else. Someone's gotta keep an eye on you, so as much as it sucks, Aenerwin's where you need to be right now."

"So, you're taking us back?" Ruby asked. "You're just going to leave me there to deal with all of them?"

Angel clenched her jaw, curled her fist, and took a deep breath. She knew where this was going, could see it coming from a mile away, and she hated it. She hated how easy a mark she was for this. She wanted to put her foot down, just to show she could.

To say Ruby was going back to Aenerwin and she didn't care if the girl didn't like it because sometimes what you want and what you need are two different things.

But then she would actually look at Ruby, and the only thing she could see was a scared girl, in over her head with a bunch of magic bullshit that had just been dumped on her, suffering because all people saw was that magic bullshit instead of her. And fuck her if it wasn't like looking in a time-warped mirror.

She refused to look at Ruby, instead bearing down on Bart, who held up surprisingly well under the Sentinel's irritated glare. The boy had more backbone than he let on.

"And I'm guessing you want to stay, too?"

"I promised Ruby I'd help her figure out what was happening to her while Vicar Arno was busy," he said, his voice only slightly quivering. "So yes."

Angel stared up at the ceiling, counted to ten just like Sir Richard had taught her, and gave up on trying to not give a shit. With a deep sigh, she raised a hand to the messaging coil on her ear, muttering to herself.

Ruby's eyes brightened as she dared to hope. "What are you doing?"

"Talking to Church. I better tell him I'm taking you before someone in Aenerwin has a panic attack."

PUERTO ORO

The sun above Puerto Oro was brighter than it ever looked over Corsar, and its light cast a shimmer across the crystal-clear waves just off the coast. Brick streets, flanked on either side by multicolored adobe buildings, were choked by buskers, merchants, and messengers, amplifying the already humid atmosphere into something swelteringly alive with activity. It was the kind of vibrant, vital place that demanded movement and music and provided both in spades. Church was doing his best to contain his discomfort.

The streets were loud and overwhelming in a way even Sasel couldn't match. And even after time to adjust and buying new clothes better suited to the climate, he still felt constantly covered in partially dried sweat. The only thing that made him feel even a little bit better was that now, a few weeks since their arrival in the city, he and Brass were almost done.

The only escapee left was the one who'd brought them here: Lord Kaiden Roso, an Iandran hellborn. Lord Roso was adept in the use of the Hell Tongue, a fiendish power that let him control others through verbal commands. In Iandra, he'd used the power to gain a noble title, as well as a substantial power base. The Starbreakers hadn't personally brought him down, but they'd been in Her Lady's City when he was captured and got to hear the story first-hand of how he'd been stopped by an intrepid freelancer group armed with a ball gag.

Brass and Church didn't have a ball gag—at least, in Brass's case, not anymore—but Brass did know a blend of smoking herbs that rendered the mind immune to charms and control like the Hell Tongue, and Church had both prayers to shield his mind and the backing of divine will. If anyone could resist Roso's power, it was them, which was why they'd chosen to handle the Oblivion escapees on Puerto Oro.

Per others they'd already recaptured, Lord Roso had taken the initiative during the breakout to bend many of his fellow inmates to his will to protect himself, aid in his escape, and serve as his personal muscle in the outside world. He'd come to the trade port of Puerto Oro to build up a fortune and powerbase near Iandra until he was secure enough to make a move to reclaim his old glory in Her Lady's City.

Church and Brass had steadily been grinding away at those plans, capturing one escapee after another. Roso had even saved them quite a bit of time and effort by sending several to try and kill them, which so far was the closest they'd come to actual danger. By now, the only thing actually slowing them down was the difficulty Church had at keeping Brass on task.

Brass hadn't even bought new clothes. He'd simply stripped a few layers of his ensemble and called it a day. He walked with a spring in his step. Almost every block, he found someone attractive to throw a sly wink to. Twice, Church lost him in the crowds, only to find him dancing with other passersby to the tunes of street performers.

"You do remember we're here for a reason, not just a vacation?" Church asked.

"You should know me better than that. If I were treating this like a vacation, I wouldn't still be dressed," Brass retorted. "I'm scouting. Getting a lay of the land before we barge in on our bad guy."

"Have you learned anything useful?"

"So far? Nothing specific. Unless you count Ylonda's affair with a guitar player as useful," Brass admitted with a shrug. "But you've got to trust the process with these things."

"Your process looks like indiscriminate partying."

"Well yeah, that's the point. If I *looked* like I was scouting, I'd stick out like a sore thumb, and whatever spies Roso's got in the streets would see us coming from a mile away."

"What spies? We've already taken all the others. He's the only one left."

"Only Oblivion breakout left, maybe, but come on. He's literally all talk and no fight. Guys like that *always* have spies."

Church conceded the issue. Brass was right. In their experience, people like Roso *always* had more help. They'd do well to be prepared for that.

Down a flight of steps and through a narrow alleyway, they reached the cramped doorstep of their destination, a gambling house with a massive painted sign of a woman in a wide hat and low-cut dress hanging over the door. According to everything they'd learned from his captured lackeys, Lord Roso would be waiting for them inside. Well, not literally waiting for them. Hopefully.

A line of people sat in front of the door, fenced in with velvet rope and kept at bay by a pair of imposing men. People at the front of the line would step forward, usually hand over a stack of coins, and get ushered in. The few who didn't were decisively turned away.

Church grabbed at his coin purse, only to find it feeling much lighter than it should have. Brass gave him an apologetic look.

"Sorry. I was a little light on funds, so I borrowed some of yours to make a few purchases."

"What kind of purchases?"

"Some street corn, a few glasses of a citrusy drink, a song request from a busker . . ." Brass trailed off briefly as he slowly withdrew a pre-rolled nail from his vest pocket, gave it a light, and took a long drag. ". . . some hard drugs."

"What?"

"I needed local ingredients for the blend!" Brass said. "If you want to get the kind of high that lets you shrug off mind control, you need ingredients that breathe the same air as whatever's doing the controlling."

"I told you I could shield us with a prayer."

"Eh, you fight brainwashing your way, I'll fight it mine."

If Church were a pettier man, he would have used a prayer to cleanse Brass's mind of the drug's influence right then and there. Instead, he let out a frustrated sigh and said a prayer to shield only himself. If nothing else, it was a little less strain.

"Well, we're going to need another way in now because I don't have enough left to pay for entry," Church said.

Brass waved his free hand dismissively as he continued to smoke. "Relax, I got this. Just be yourself and let me do all the talking."

In short order, they reached the front of the line. One of the bouncers gave them a grunt.

"Ten sails a head."

"You've got it, my man. Coming right up!" Brass said. There was a lazy drag to his words, and he wobbled on his feet, playing the part of a man who'd already had a few drinks. That or maybe whatever he was smoking was kicking in.

He fished through Church's coin purse, which the priest did not remember handing him, his exaggerated smile fading as he counted coins.

"Uh, right up," he repeated. "Right . . ."

Brass faltered. Church wanted to believe it was part of the act and whatever plan he had in mind. But it was hard to tell the difference between Brass pretending he was in trouble and Brass actually being in trouble. "Brass?"

"It's cool, we're cool," Brass assured him, waving Church off before turning back to the bouncer. "Hey, listen, we're a little strapped right now. How does eight glint for the both of us sound?"

"Ten sails. Or twelve glint. Per head."

"Oh, have a heart. My buddy here's getting married tomorrow! You're gonna deny a man his bachelor night over four glint?"

The bouncer was unmoved. "Get out of the line."

The brick wall of a man on duty took a step toward them, and Church's fingers curled around his amulet. But Brass was faster.

"Haven't you ever had a friend you knew you were going to lose?" Brass asked, suddenly switching to a desperate tone.

The bouncer raised an eyebrow, looking at least a little intrigued to hear where this was going. The other held his position, waiting for a signal one way or the other from his partner. Brass saw his opening and threw everything he had into his performance.

"You used to be real close, you did everything together, and you had more stories than you could ever tell. But then their life went one way and yours went another? And you saw it coming, but you just wanted to hold on? Just a little longer? You don't know my friend here's fiancée. Once they tie the knot, I'm never going to see him again. This might be the last night we ever get together. My last chance to get into some trouble with him. And then he goes and lives his happy married life, and I'm all on my own again. Come on! Show a man some compassion."

Brass managed to put a real quiver in his voice as he pleaded his case. He almost had Church convinced.

The bouncer cocked his head slightly. If he felt any pity for Brass, his face didn't show it, but his gaze did slowly track over to Church.

The priest was a terrible liar. When he was born, the gods had neglected to include a single dishonest fiber in his whole being. Still, he did his best to at least wear an expression that said Brass was telling the truth. His face settled on a cross between earnest and embarrassed.

The bouncer was unimpressed.

"Where's the ring?"

Brass blinked. "I beg your pardon?"

"You said he's getting married tomorrow. Where's the ring?"

Brass whirled around to look at Church, eyes darting up and down on the priest. Church could see the wheels spinning behind Brass's eyes, trying to work out an explanation. A new lie to find his way out of the hole in his last one. But his eyes were off, a little more distant than they should have been, and the wheels were turning slower than they should have. Now the drugs had really kicked in.

"He . . ." Brass paused, fishing for words, finding none, and decided to just go with whatever came out of his mouth next. ". . . ate it."

Both of the bouncer's eyebrows went up this time, but he looked no less amused. "Fuck off."

"Hey, wait—"

Before Brass could get another word in, the other bouncer closed the distance between them, grabbed him by his vest, and hurled him across the alleyway. Sober, Brass would have landed on his feet, sword drawn. As it was, he managed a halfway decent tumble that ended with him upside down against a wall. The bouncers turned their attention to the priest.

Church sighed, his hand once again finding his amulet.

So much for talking their way in.

LORD ROSO

The inside of the Red Lady hummed with the activity of dozens of different tables, where clinking coins changed hands over the clatter of dice and slap of cards. Attractive servers dressed in aggressively sensual outfits mingled between the patrons, handing out drinks and sultry looks. The smell of tobacco and alcohol hung in the air while in every corner people shouted, laughed, and swore.

But then the front door crashed open, and everyone froze as one of the bouncers was flung backward into the room, blood streaming from his nose. A hush fell over the crowd, save for the sound of one roulette wheel still lazily spinning away. Brass sauntered into the room, twirling his rapier with a flourish before leveling it at the bouncer's throat as a warning to stay down. The defeated man got the message, throwing his hands up.

Church marched in a moment later, now sporting a breastplate and chainmail. His amulet shone like the sun in the notch in his breastplate, while the angelic sword Zealot remained sheathed at his side.

"Sorry to barge in like this," Brass apologized. "But could someone point us in the direction of a Lord Roso? The boys out front weren't much help."

"May I ask who's calling?"

At the far end of the room, sitting in a booth with one arm around a woman and another holding a delicately thin cocktail glass, sat Lord Kaiden

Roso. He remained seated with his legs crossed, resplendently dressed in elaborately dyed linen robes that contrasted with his bright red skin.

"Sorry, my manners always seem to go when I'm high," Brass lamented. "My name is Brass, and this handsome gentleman here on my right is Church."

Lord Roso's eyes gleamed with anger even as he smiled. "The Starbreakers."

"The very same. I take it you've heard of us?"

"Your names have spread quickly as you took my loyal servants from me. I was wondering when you would dare to come here, to me. But even before, I had heard of you. There isn't a prisoner in Oblivion who hasn't. You who put away so many of my cell neighbors. I couldn't have avoided learning about you if I tried. Not when I was surrounded by so much bitter whining."

"Sorry about that. We kicked a lot of ass back in the day."

"And I would love to hear all about it," Roso said, lowering the pitch of his voice. He licked his lips, tilted his head back ever so slightly, and while looking at them through hooded eyes, murmured, "Come sit down."

Instantly, Church felt his stomach twist into a knot and his heart race. Roso's words flowed like honey, slowly rolling into his ears and down his spine. His face, his whole body, felt a kind of heat completely unrelated to the humidity, and his legs suddenly felt impossibly heavy. Sitting down sounded nice.

Too nice.

Even with a prayer to shield his mind, Roso's words hit Church hard. He grit his teeth and hardened his resolve. With a discipline drilled into him by the Guiding Saint himself, the priest focused on the image of the words and his feelings as separate from himself and walled them away where he could ignore them. The room felt like it was spinning, but it did the trick. His will was his own.

Next to him, Brass showed absolutely no signs of feeling Roso's words at all.

"Are you buying us a round? Because otherwise, I think we'll stand, thanks," Brass said. "You should probably get up too, seeing as, you know, you're coming with us."

Roso's face twitched with annoyance before his mask of confidence resolidified. It didn't quite reach his voice as he congratulated them. "So well prepared."

"Well, we didn't get this far completely by luck," Brass said.

"No," Roso agreed. "But neither did I. Everyone?"

In perfect sync, every single head in the gambling house pivoted toward Roso, staring at him with rapt attention. Without a word, Church and Brass took a step toward each other, turning back-to-back. Both of them took a quick count of just how many people were in the Red Lady.

"Kill them."

It was like someone threw a switch. Moving as a single tide, staff and patrons alike bore down on the two of them. Some grabbed bottles and furniture to use as weapons. Others drew blades. And the rest just charged empty handed with murder in their eyes.

Church finally drew out Zealot, and the milky white blade of the angelic sword flashed as it was freed from its sheath. Instantly, the spirit within awoke, taking in the situation through Church's senses and thoughts.

Masses afflicted by the touch of fiendish control. Let them be purified by a divine edge!

"No purifying!" Church had worked with the sword long enough to know what it meant by "purify," and it was not something to be doled out to innocents taken by mind control. With effort, he turned the hilt in his hand and swung with the flat of the blade to smack aside the closest card dealer.

"What?" Brass asked, thinking Church was talking to him.

"The people! We can't kill them!"

"Speak for yourself. Their stances are all shit!"

"Brass!"

"Yeah, I know! No killing the innocent bystanders, even if they're trying to kill us," Brass said, rolling his eyes even as he neatly dropped a man with a slice to the knees. "I swear, these people are lucky I like a challenge!"

As the two of them fought off the rest of the Red Lady's occupants, Lord Roso stayed seated, sipping his drink and watching the chaos unfold with a smile. The Starbreakers may have kept their minds, but they would at least give him a show.

"Crows." Roso made a *tsk* sound. "Always the same. Arrogant, greedy, and so predictable."

Church was too busy holding his own to pay Roso any attention, beating people back with the flat and pommel of Zealot while cycling through whatever prayer best suited his needs in a given moment.

Blind the people at a distance. Drain the strength from the big ones. Put the rest to sleep. Don't let them get—

"You in the corner there," Roso called out, and the person he was talking to froze. "Slit your own throat."

Church's stomach wrenched as he watched the person, a young male waiter in an open vest with bright caramel skin, break the bottle he was holding on a table and bring the jagged glass up to his own neck without hesitation.

"NO!" Church screamed. All thoughts of strategy and prioritization vanished. Even as the blood began to spill from the man's neck, Church used a healing prayer to seal the wound. And while Church was distracted, a cocktail waitress brought a bar stool down on the back of his head.

"You make this too easy!" Roso howled with laughter. His eyes locked on the waitress who'd just bashed Church across the skull. "Girl. Run yourself through on his sword."

With instant compliance, the cocktail waitress threw her barstool aside and dove for Zealot. Church could scarcely contain the shock and horror racing through him. His heart was hammering so hard, he could feel it in his ears. This man, this monster, was twisting everyone around him. Trying to turn them into their own murderers. Trying to put their blood on his sword.

"What are you doing?!" Church shouted. "These are *people*!"

Church yanked his sword away while he used a prayer to put her to sleep. It stopped her from hurting herself, but it left him completely open, and in seconds, the mob was on him.

He managed to pray to make his skin as hard as stone just before people's blows and clawing hands reached him, which saved him from being torn apart.

But he was pinned down, and with his head throbbing and people battering him on all sides, to say nothing of the cold fury racing through his veins, it was increasingly difficult to keep his concentration on his mental shield.

"There are always more people to serve," Roso said, unmoved by the priest's indignation. "If I kill this whole port, there's always the next tropical paradise. But my freedom? My dignity, as a Lord of Her Lady's City? That is precious to me. That, I will gladly kill for. Not that I need to. They'll all do it for me!"

Across the room, Brass was in his own predicament. He rolled to avoid a chair somebody had thrown at his head, took somebody's legs out from under them while he was down on the floor, and sprang back up to grab a bottle of liquor and piff it into someone's head just hard enough to rattle them. He shoved that person over, kicked another in the stomach, and flicked a marble from his vest pocket into the eye of the third.

None of these people were particularly dangerous on their own. Even against this many at once, he was pretty sure he could have taken them all down, as long as he didn't mind killing most of them. But he sort of did mind, and Church absolutely did, so he was having to improvise. Pull his punches. Be extra careful with his swipes and thrusts. And the fog in his mind, good as it was for keeping Roso out, was shit for his reaction time. If this kept up, either they were going to have to start murdering people or they were going to lose.

Or, alternatively, they could try to end this quickly.

"Church, keep them busy!" Brass shouted.

Somewhere beneath the pile of people trying to kill him, Church yelled something back that got lost in the noise.

Brass flashed a thumbs up. "Just like that. You're doing great!"

Brass jumped onto the closest table and, after kicking a waiter who got too close in the face, took a running leap off its edge. He sailed through the air above the crowd of people trying to make a grab for him, landed on a person's shoulders, and skipped off of them onto the next table all while barely breaking stride.

He repeated the trick, over and over, bounding from table to person to table, making a beeline straight for Lord Roso.

The smile vanished from the hellborn's face as he watched Brass approach. "Keep him away from me!"

Several people converged on Roso, forming a wall of human shields just as Brass landed on a table full of hors d'oeuvres. Brass threw his sword like an improvised javelin, skewering one of Roso's shields through the knee and dropping them to the ground; Church could probably heal that once this was over. At the same time, he stomped hard on the edge of a plate of miniature taquitos and caught one as they were flung into the air. With a split second to aim, he hurled the finger food through the gap he'd made in Roso's defensive line of thralls and straight into Roso's open mouth just as the hellborn was about to call out another order. The command collapsed into a violent choking sound, and Roso doubled over, gripping his throat.

"Church!" Brass shouted, even as the patrons began to swarm the table he was on. "Roso can't talk!"

Still trapped under a mob, and now curled into a ball to try and protect himself, Church only barely managed to hear Brass.

No danger of Roso's voice meant he could stop trying to concentrate on shielding his mind. And that freed him to concentrate on other prayers. It was a long shot. But it was their only chance of ending this quickly and cleanly. His mental shielding fell away as he started speaking in the language of the gods, even as he was being pummeled and slashed at from all around. The prayer to reinforce his skin gave out under the onslaught—he was amazed it had held out as long as it had—but he kept praying, even as the attacks began to actually hurt. Someone kicked him in the teeth, filling his mouth with blood. He kept praying. Someone got something around his neck—a towel or maybe a shirt—and was using it to try to strangle him. He continued to choke out the words.

Every syllable was agony, and he could feel his whole body heating up by the second, but finally, as the mob rolled him onto his back and a woman prepared to cave his skull in with a chair leg, he gasped out the last words.

The roof of the Red Lady exploded in a hundred different places as rays of divine light pierced through the ceiling. Raw, divine power cascaded down and slammed into each and every one of them. As one, the crowd screamed in shock and pain, and as one, they all collapsed to the floor. The rays of light vanished, and once more, silence took hold in the gambling house, a faintly sweet smell lingering in the air in the aftermath of the divine power. Partly from the air having been expunged of any trace of smoke, partly from every stain in the room being suddenly cleaned and all the water having spontaneously turned into wine.

Brass found himself suddenly more alert and aware. Just being that close to the prayer had completely sobered him up.

Church felt a wave of mind-numbing fatigue roll through his entire body, starting in his head and washing all the way out to his extremities. That prayer was meant to be used to defend a god or saint's home territory, a temple or a shrine. Consecrated ground at the very least. Using it just out in the world was beyond exhausting—from the way his head spun and cold sweat broke out across his forehead, it had nearly killed him.

But it did the job.

Everyone in the crowd was subdued and unconscious. They would hurt when they woke up. But they would all wake up. They were alive. They were safe. Roso couldn't hurt any of them anymore. He wasn't going to hurt anyone else on this island. The relief of that thought alone made the agonizing fatigue worth it.

His hand rested on the saint's talisman embedded in his breastplate as he whispered, "Thank you." Saint Beneger's presence washed over his mind, accompanied by a feeling like a strong hand on his shoulder.

"Nicely done!" Brass congratulated. As much of a wet blanket as he could occasionally be, Brass really did love being friends with a priest. "Got a little touch and go for a second there, but I think we pulled that off rather well. Let's get this guy tied up and ready to hand off."

"Just . . . give me a second," Church panted, hands on his knees as he tried to stay upright. He willed his legs to move. They refused. "Need to . . ."

"No sweat, I got this," Brass assured him as he made his way to an unconscious Lord Roso. "Gotta say, it was a good thing we saved him for last. Can you imagine how this would have gone if he had actual backup?"

The beautiful thing about reflexes, especially sober ones, is that they're actually even faster than the brain. Touch a searing-hot pan and a hand will pull away before its owner can even register the heat.

When the back door of the Red Lady flung itself open, Brass caught the briefest glint of the sun reflecting off polished metal, and his back started bending even before he could finish processing what was in front of him.

A thin stripe of blood materialized across the tip of Brass's nose as a spear, flying impossibly fast, sailed straight through the space his head had just been. It buried itself into the wall behind him, so deep, only the last two feet of the shaft were visible. His back bend turned into a full flip, and he came up, sword at the ready, and finally took stock of the new threat in front of him.

A dark-skinned man in sleek, form-fitting white and bronze armor strode through the door. In each hand, he wielded a Kaberian short spear. Short segments of more spear shafts lined his belt with the Arcane symbol for the number five serving as the buckle. On his exposed right shoulder, he bore a tattoo of a pair of crossed spears encircled by chains.

The symbol of the Cord of Aenwyn.

UNEXPECTED REUNION

It was never just good news in the life of a glintchaser. It was always good and bad, and the bad was always worse. Church had actually managed to subdue the people inside while sparing his conscience, but he looked absolutely winded. They'd taken down Roso, and now a new problem had arrived.

Brass threw a nervous smile to the newest arrival to the Red Lady. It had been a long time since he'd seen Quint.

From their very first meeting, the Starbreakers and the Cord of Aenwyn had been bitter rivals, fighting over the same artifacts, jobs, and prestige. Somebody had to be the best freelancer company in Corsar, and neither group had been willing to cede the issue—at least until the Cord left Corsar and the Starbreakers collapsed. In all the times the two groups clashed, Brass and Quint had been each other's responsibility. Brass had won their last fight, but their overall record stood at an even three to three.

Quint looked good. Strong, confident, lethal. Everything the leader of the Cord of Aenwyn should be. A shame Brass was currently on the wrong side of his spears, and even more of a shame that he'd just come off the back of fighting an angry mob.

"Hey, Quint, been a while. How's it going?"

Quint reversed his grip on one of his spears, preparing to throw it. "I am Lord Roso's protector. All who threaten him will die."

"I was afraid you were going to say that. But does god-lasering someone really count as threatening?"

Quint seemed to give that a half second of thought before he hurled his spear, which tore straight through Brass's vest as he barely managed to side-step it.

"It was worth a shot!"

Just like that, Quint was on him, his remaining spear's shaft lengthening to a full-sized version of the weapon. The first clash of their weapons sent a hard vibration up through Brass's entire arm. He nearly dropped his weapon right then and there but forced himself to maintain his grip. For a single moment, as he braced his blade against Quint's spear shaft, their eyes locked.

Quint had the eyes of a rabid, desperate animal trying to catch a meal before it starved to death. Brass wasn't sure exactly what being controlled by Roso felt like, but if the look in Quint's eyes was any indication, it wasn't fun.

They pushed off each other, and both of them became a blur. The clang of steel on steel echoed as the two dueled, constantly moving, dodging, and lunging. Off to the side, Church was trying to use Zealot as a crutch to help him stand, but Brass almost wished he'd stay down. In his state, there was no way the priest would be anything but a hindrance.

"Brass, Church, which one of you has the coil?"

Brass's ears perked up as Ink's voice came through, slightly metallic but otherwise as if she was standing right next to him. He'd forgotten he was wearing that thing.

"That'd be me," Brass answered, not breaking his rhythm in the fight. "Something we can do for you?"

"I'm checking in on everyone's progress with their targets. You and Church haven't reported anything since the jewel thief two days ago."

"Well, we ran into a bit of trouble. Actually, can I call you back? We're kind of in the middle of something."

"What's going on?"

"Nothing too major," Brass told Ink as he fought for his life. "Just Quint trying to kill us."

"What?"

"Small world, right? It looks like Roso got to him, too. Anyway, I gotta go, your ex-boyfriend is kind of kicking my—"

His words caught in his throat as Quint's spear skidded past Brass's guard and stabbed him through the shoulder. Fire exploded along his nerves, and this time, Brass couldn't hold on to his sword. He jumped back, yanking himself off the spear and saving himself from being run clean through, but his shoulder throbbed, and moving it sent spikes of pain all along his body.

No time to think of how much of a problem that was going to be. Brass drew his knife in his off hand and kept fighting. He was moving without thinking, trying to match Quint's mindless, relentless speed.

He tried to parry and get inside Quint's reach. The first half of that plan worked, but Quint reacted too fast for the second, and Brass was rewarded for his efforts with a spear shaft to the nose and a slash across his wrist. His knife clattered to the ground.

It didn't matter. He couldn't afford to let it.

With a click of his heel, Brass extended the concealed blade in the toe of his boot and kicked, actually drawing blood from Quint's thigh and managing to force him back. He jumped and kicked again, drawing a second gash on Quint's cheek.

On his third kick, though, Quint locked his leg with his spear, twisted, and sent Brass to the ground. Before he could roll away, Quint's boot came crashing down on his chest, pinning him.

A sensible man would have feared for his life or may have been too stricken with pain to think at all. Brass was mostly annoyed that his record against Quint was now three to four and liable to stay that way.

Church finally forced himself onto his feet once again, shakily raising Zealot. He might be able to buy them a few more minutes of life, and Brass would certainly take every second he could get. But if he was being completely honest, he was pretty sure the both of them were dead. Light glinted off Quint's spearpoint as he raised the weapon, and Brass grimaced.

Well, shit. There go my summer plans.

Quint drove his spear downward, and Brass made a move to catch it. His hands whiffed through empty air.

Quint's spear had stopped short.

Glowing blue threads wound tight around Quint's weapon, holding it back from reaching Brass. Standing in the doorway of the Red Lady, holding tight to the other end of the threads with both hands, was Ink. For the second time inside five minutes, Brass felt an utter elation race through his body. He loved being friends with a wizard.

"Ink?" Quint's voice was lost.

"Hello, darling," Ink greeted. "So sorry about this."

A crackle of lightning raced out from Ink's fingers, across her threads, and into Quint. His body jerked, and he flew off his feet and headfirst into a wall before slumping to the ground.

Brass sat up, shaking off any lingering peace he'd come to with his own mortality. "Has anyone ever told you your timing is immaculate?"

"My *everything* is immaculate," Ink said.

"I couldn't . . . agree more."

Even groggy and rasping, Lord Roso's voice was intoxicating, and both Brass and Ink's gazes fixated on the hellborn as he struggled to sit up. Somewhere in their minds, they both knew they needed to act. But Brass was sober now, and Ink had teleported in expecting a fight with Quint, not Roso, and hadn't thrown up any shielding against his power. His absolutely hypnotic power.

A victorious grin spread across his face as his eyes locked with Ink's. "From now on, you serve—"

He never finished the command, as Church's gauntleted fist connected with his jaw, knocking him back out. The priest swayed on his feet, and his breathing was still ragged. And yet, he couldn't have felt more satisfied. Roso, a man who preyed on everyone around him simply because he could, was going back to jail where he belonged, and they were the ones who'd made sure of that.

If only to himself, he could admit, he missed this part of being a glint-chaser, too.

THE DRUID

For most of his life, Phoenix had never really thought all that much of flying. There'd been an initial spark of interest the first time he'd read about
Old World sky ships and there was the novelty of riding in a flying skiff for
the first time through the skies of Sasel. But past that, it hadn't really felt like
anything special, especially once he'd gotten his sky surfer. The oblong board
with attached enchanted sail made flying little more than a quick, efficient way
to get around.

But when he was with Wings, flying became the most amazing thing in
the world.

Cool wind whipped into his face and through his hair as billowing
mountains of white towered all around him and an endless ocean of fields and
trees stretched out below. And in the middle of it all was her.

Wings soared through the clouds, ethereal green wings spread wide as she
banked, dipped, and darted around them. With her wings tucked tight against
her, she performed a spinning dive and disappeared straight into a cloud bank.
She came out the other side in a burst of speed with little wisps of cloud still
trailing off her wingtips and a smile of childlike wonder on her face, and he
fell in love with her all over again.

As if she sensed his eyes on her, Wings slowed down, eventually drifting
alongside him. Her eyes were impossibly bright green with irises that swirled

like tiny cloudbanks all their own, and her hair somehow managed to billow in the wind without once ending up in her face or getting blown into a frenzied mess. She smiled at him, and he nearly melted off the sky surfer.

He had to remind himself they were still working. They'd recaptured every other escapee assigned to them, leaving only Edelfric, the Scourge of the Iron Forest.

What they had faced at the gates of Sasel was not the true Edelfric but an extension of him, grown from the original and turned against the city. One of his "seedlings" as the Starbreakers called them. The Oracle had confirmed the real Scourge was already back in the Iron Forest, and Phoenix knew from experience that taking Edelfric down inside the forest would not be easy, even for them.

Fortunately, after everything Phoenix had told Wings about his last encounter with Edelfric, she had formed a theory about his power. All signs pointed to Edelfric making heavy use of druidic magics to draw strength from the Iron Forest itself. She was certain there was a way to exploit that, but Wings had only ever studied druidic magics to supplement her own survival skills. To actually take advantage of any potential weakness, they needed an expert.

Luckily, Wings just so happened to know one.

Wings's eyes trained onto the forest below them, taking on a more serious expression.

"We're here."

She made a sharp bank away from him into a rapid descent, and he followed her lead. The bright, open freedom of the skies vanished as they dipped below the tree line, leaving them enclosed and cut off from the rest of the world.

Phoenix brought the sky surfer to a stop about a foot off the ground before deactivating it, letting it drop the rest of the way down with a soft thud. The magical force anchoring his feet to the board faded, and he stepped off to fold down the surfer's mast and sail and get the whole thing back into his bottomless bag. Next to him, Wings finished her slow, graceful descent with a few beats of her wings before touching down. Her ethereal wings dissolved away, taking the faint light they gave off with them and leaving them with only the dim haze that managed to filter through the branches overhead.

Phoenix had never been comfortable in forests. It was disorienting, being surrounded on all sides by identical trees. But this forest felt particularly wrong, like it was sneaking around behind his back. Compelled by curiosity, he set his goggles to detect magic. There was nothing to see through the arcane filter, but as soon as he switched to the divine magic setting, every branch, shrub, and stone was suddenly linked by a flowing river of bright white light that passed through the whole of the forest, like blood vessels in an animal. This place was alive with magic.

Wings placed her hand on the trunk of the tree. Even without magic detecting goggles, her eyes followed the same trail as his.

"Sinnodella's close," she said. "This way."

After more than seven years together, Phoenix knew enough about his wife's past to have a basic grasp on who Sinnodella was. The elven druid who called the Greenwyld home, who'd first trained Wings in druidic magics and put her on the path to becoming the warden she was today. But he'd never actually *met* the elf before now.

He'd studied the elves and the Old World extensively during his time at the Infinite Library, but reading about a culture through scholars' words was a far cry from actually talking to someone from it. He'd only ever met one elf in the flesh: Apollius, the Oracle. That had been a comparatively brief and extremely antagonistic encounter that offered surprisingly few cultural insights. So, when he'd first learned that Wings had spent an entire year studying under an elf, the first thing he'd asked was what she was like.

After a pondering silence, her answer had been, "Lonely."

That was all he had to work with in terms of mentally preparing himself. He checked himself over a few times as they walked, picked out the stray pine needles that had gotten in his hair during their landing, and imagined possible conversations so he could mentally rehearse what he might say. He'd never been great with first impressions, but he wanted to try and make a good one. Sinnodella was someone Wings respected, and he didn't want to mess up whatever bond might be between them. Also, if this went well, maybe he could talk to Sinnodella on his own and learn about the Old World from her own firsthand accounts.

But that was getting ahead of himself.

"So, is she going to be happy to see you?" Phoenix asked.

"If she wasn't, we'd know by now."

"She knows we're here?"

"Relax. She's a *friend*," Wings said. "You've got absolutely nothing to worry—"

Phoenix didn't catch the rest of the sentence, as the wind was knocked out of him by something hard and heavy slamming into him and sending him sprawling into the brush. There was a big, dark shape, then crushing weight. Hot, sulfurous air crashed into his face and filled his nostrils. By the time the world stopped spinning, he couldn't breathe, and he was staring down the coppery length of a reptilian snout. Pale, sickly green eyes the size of his fist bore into him with predatory intent as a single, massive clawed hand held him to the ground.

A cavernous rumble echoed up the creature's throat, and Phoenix felt his blood turn to ice.

"Stixy! Down!"

Wing's tone mimicked the one she used when chastising Robyn for trying to eat something she wasn't supposed to. The creature obeyed, removing its claw from Phoenix's chest and backpedaling away, bowing its head in submission. Phoenix gasped for breath as sweet air rushed back into his lungs, though, it quickly turned to coughing.

It was only slightly shorter than a horse, but twice as long, with four legs and massive, leathery fringe along its side, which took Phoenix a second to recognize as wings, folded against its mottled copper-colored body. The beginnings of spines were forming along the edge of its jaw, which looked like a cross between a crocodile and a bird of prey. Phoenix had seen a creature like this only once in his life, only it had been much, much bigger.

It was a dragon. And Wings was currently giving it scratches under its chin, to which it responded by closing its eyes, upturning its head for easier access, and enthusiastically pawing at the ground while letting out a sound that was just close enough to a purr to be disturbing rather than endearing.

"Good boy, Stixy," she murmured to the beast. "That's a good boy. You remember me? You remember, don't you? Good boy!"

"Is that a *baby dragon*?" Phoenix asked when he finally found his voice.

"It is." A new voice cut through the forest as the shrubbery itself parted to make way for a new arrival. She was lithe and tall like the Oracle, but her skin was a lighter, ruddier color, and she had bright auburn hair that came to her waist, except for the small portion of it that had been braided like a circlet wrapping around her head. Her eyes were a golden hazel color, matching the trim on her flowing white shawl and burgundy tunic.

Sinnodella offered him a cool, reserved smile. "You're very lucky you have so much of my Sable's smell on you, or Stixaxlatl might have eviscerated you before I could say hello."

"Sinnodella!"

Wings walked into the waiting arms of the elf, and the two exchanged a fierce hug that Phoenix knew from experience would leave Sinnodella breathless.

"Oh, my girl," the elf cooed softly. "It's so good to see you again. Every time I turn around, you're a whole new woman."

"Well, we can't all be ageless druidic masters," she teased.

"Perhaps not," the elf said with a smile.

When her golden eyes landed on Phoenix, his mind went completely blank. Whatever rehearsing he'd managed had been knocked out of his head by the business end of a dragon's claw.

He tried not to panic, unsure if his efforts made it to his face as the elf offered him a lukewarm smile. "You must be the Phoenix I've heard so much about. You wouldn't happen to be immune to fire, would you?"

"Resistant," he said, thinking about the variable enchantment on his armor. "Sometimes."

She pressed her lips together in consideration. "Rebirthed then? Back from the doors of death?"

"Well, yes, once, but that's not why I took the name." He realized where this was going. "It was more metaphorical. I—"

"Oh, splendid!" Sinnodella interrupted him. "I love a human with a grasp on dramatic device. Too many of the ones I meet are painfully literal. Hammers looking for nails, every one of them. But you're a complete workshop, aren't you?"

Phoenix guessed that was a compliment and nodded, but it was a pure guess. People were hard enough to read as is. He couldn't tell if Sinnodella was genuinely happy, about to murder him, or seconds away from bursting into tears. She might have been all three for all he could tell. A bead of anxiety formed in the pit of his stomach, which he did his best to ignore. It was like he was five years old again, too terrified and confused to speak.

"Please, both of you come with me. We can talk more over dinner."

With a quick wave of Sinnodella's hand, the shrubbery parted once again, and they followed the elf deeper into the forest.

Dinner was smoked salmon, honeycomb, and blackberries served on worn wooden plates with rocks for chairs and only a campfire and fireflies to replace the last traces of dusk. There was no cutlery, and yet the elf managed to make eating with her fingers look delicate and refined. At her motion, the ceiling of interwoven branches above parted, letting out the smoke and giving a clear view of the sky as the first stars of the night became visible.

Stixaxlatl curled by the fire, a low rumble accompanying the rise and fall of its massive form. Phoenix thought he was asleep until Sinnodella casually tossed a whole salmon in the creature's direction, and his head lunged to snap it out of the air and happily gulp it down, little electric sparks dancing from his jaws. It all reminded Phoenix of his earliest days as a glintchaser, camping on the road between gigs, only somehow, even more rugged. Back then, they'd had a cart, supplies from town, bedrolls, and a tent. Sinnodella was living completely off the land.

"My dear Sable, it is good to see you again and to see the woman you have grown to be," Sinnodella said. "But neither of us has ever given company to the other as a gift. What is it you need?"

Elizabeth faltered for a moment, maybe feeling embarrassed or called out, but she told Sinnodella the short version. Edelfric was at large, and they needed help to stop him. Sinnodella had seemed dismissive at first, but as Elizabeth described Edelfric's bond with the Iron Forest, she sat up and took notice. "I was hoping you knew something we could use to find him quicker or to make fighting him easier," Elizabeth said. "Whatever else he is, Edelfric's using druidic magic. And there's nobody better at that than you."

"Oh, I'm sure there is, dear. There were certainly others before me. And by your gods' will, there will be again," Sinnodella said with a wave of her hand. "But I take your meaning. And there *is* a way to defeat this Edelfric in a much shorter fashion."

"How?"

"You are dealing in the realm of groves now, my dear Sable. A grove is a druid's wellspring, and the Iron Forest is Edelfric's. Threaten his hold over it, and he will race to you to defend it. Seal off the well to him, and he will wither to dry, dead weed that scarcely need be plucked."

Phoenix had a little trouble following that chain of metaphors, particularly because, given what Edelfric was, it was hard to know how much of it was literal. But he wasn't about to ask Sinnodella to clarify when she'd already praised him for his grasp on figurative speech. At least Elizabeth still understood.

"But how do we do it?" Elizabeth asked.

"Simple. You make it yours."

Sinnodella stretched out her hand toward the center of the clearing, and the earth began to rumble. Faintly at first, but growing steadily stronger until there was a jolt that nearly toppled Phoenix off his rock and a thick, sinuous plant stalk burst from the ground. It was capped by a bulb the size of Phoenix's head, emitting a dim light that cast the entire clearing in a soft orange glow.

The bulb slowly bloomed open, revealing at its heart a pit the size of a fist, glowing golden orange in its seams and crevices.

"A groveseed. An extension of its creator's presence and will, through which a bond can be forged between druid and grove. With it, you could match your will against Edelfric, overpower it, and overwrite his claim to the forest. He will lose all power that he draws from it and have nowhere to run."

"So, we just need this thing?" Phoenix asked, pointing to the glowing seed unfurled before them.

"You misunderstand, little bird. This is *my* groveseed, through which I have taken root in this place. And those roots have grown deep. I cannot move it any more easily than you could tear off your own arm," she said. Elizabeth's eyes were already widening, as if she knew what Sinnodella would say before she said it. "You must make your own."

"I can't." But Elizabeth's eyes were already faintly crackling, and the corners of her mouth were twitching upward. She didn't believe that. She was excited that maybe she could.

"Are you not my apprentice? Did I not teach you to harness the magic of this world as your own?"

"Yeah, but I just make things grow out of my arrows or heal a few cuts or talk to squirrels. I've never done something like that before."

"But you can," Sinnodella insisted. "It is druidic magic in its simplest form. Will and being and connection. There is no need for advanced technique or greater knowledge. It is fundamentals and power. And you, my Sable, have both in spades."

A warm summer breeze swept through the clearing as Elizabeth stared down at her hands. She looked to Phoenix for a moment, clearly hoping for something. What she wanted, or needed, he wasn't sure, but he gave what he could. He nodded, and he put all of the love and admiration he had for her into that nod.

You can do this, he tried to say. And it worked. By Avelina, it worked.

Elizabeth's eyes were fully alight now, bright and roiling green, and a smile settled onto her face. There was the face of Wings, the savior of Sasel.

There was the woman who'd slain a dragon.

"Okay," she said. "Why not?"

Sinnodella smiled and rose from her rock.

At its core, druidic magic was using your own being to manipulate the natural forces of life all around you. Creating a groveseed, Sinnodella explained to Wings, was as simple as focusing her will and essence of self so strongly as to physically manifest a piece of it. Using the seed required planting it, spiritually as much as physically, in the location she wished to bond with and exerting her will through the seed to form the connection.

A simple process in theory, but not one to be attempted for the first time in the heat of battle. At the elf's insistence, everyone but Elizabeth left the clearing to give her room to work. Stixaxlatl was annoyed to be woken up from his nap but complied. Phoenix made sure to keep Sinnodella between him and the dragon, just in case.

Elizabeth knelt in the center of the clearing, eyes closed and her hands stretched out in front of her. The breeze was constant now, gently brushing through the trees, waxing and waning in time with the rise and fall of her own shoulders. In only a short time, a small, spinning orb of light began to take form between her hands. Tiny, but growing, ever so slowly.

Phoenix watched the entire process from just beyond the trees, mesmerized. When he examined the scene through the filter of his goggles, he could see magic traveling down Elizabeth's body, out from her chest, down her arms, and into that single point out in front of her. That point, he could feel, even from here, was pure *her.*

He'd seen her do magic before, but she'd never done anything quite like this. Something so primal and raw. It hardly felt right, calling both something like this and the arcane manipulations of Academy mages "magic." Such was the world he lived in, full of so many different and varied powers, all pushing and pulling in a million different directions. He forgot, sometimes, how spectacularly varied and beautiful the world could be. But in moments like this, he remembered.

"How long will she need?" he asked, keeping his voice low.

"It's different for everyone who attempts it. Perhaps a few seconds. Perhaps a few hours," Sinnodella said, just as transfixed on Elizabeth as he was. Her small smile broadened as she finally pulled herself away. "Come. We shouldn't disturb her."

He nodded, but his heart was beginning to pound now. This was it. He was actually talking with a living elf, alone. And as far as he knew, she didn't want to kill him. He said his next words five times in his head before he had the confidence to say them out loud.

"You know, you're nothing like the elves I met before."

"You've met others?"

"Two. Well, one in person, and one . . ." Phoenix struggled to find the words to describe the first elf he'd met. ". . . a recording. A really advanced recording."

"And how were they?"

"Well, the one I met in person tried to kill me. Which was disappointing," Phoenix said. "But the recording taught me a lot. About the Old . . . about his time. His technology, his magic."

"Vulcan, or one of his disciples, I'd wager," Sinnodella guessed, correctly. "They would be the only ones whose repositories would open themselves to a human."

"He did seem upset that it was me he was teaching."

"And he made you swear to guard his knowledge like a secret, pass it only to one, that it may live on, but no further. Meanwhile, the one you battled would not stop his talk of a glorious empire to be restored, order imposed, and your people brought back to their natural place."

"How did you know?"

Sinnodella rolled her eyes.

"By the end, my people were an embittered and desperate one. Some could never accept our fall from grace. They broke themselves on the cliffs of our ruin, trying to scale back to our previous summit. The world was their child; grown and changed though it was, they could only see what it had once been. Your foe was one of many like-minded. But they all fall, in the end.

A grown child cannot be forced back into the womb. Trying only kills the mother," Sinnodella said. "It was different for others. For the school of Vulcan, spellforging was a spurned lover. Both beautiful and the cause of their woes. They believed it ruinous, the source of all the harm in the world. And yet they could not bear the thought of a world without it. Such is the contradiction of one hurt by who they love."

"How did *you* take it? The Collapse?"

She frowned, and her eyes drifted.

"I was not yet born. Those were the days of my mother," she said. "She was one of the few who saw the path my people marched for what it was—self-destruction. She saw no virtue in such a path. So, she abandoned it and came here, carrying me with her. From the people of this world, she and I learned natural magics. Ones that drew only on the power of the world and the self. In time, we buried those that taught us. And their children and their children's children. Until one day, I buried my mother and I was alone. And so I have lived ever since. Apart from the visitors that come to my forest . . . every so often."

She cast a look back in direction of where Elizabeth was working. "You inspire her, you know."

Phoenix blinked. "What?"

"I have forgotten much. But I remember the young girl who entered my forest with half a quiver of arrows—lost, terrified, and determined to make something of herself. I remember training her, and I remember all the times she has returned since. In her trials, her doubts, she thinks of you. What you would do, or what you believe of her. And she perseveres. You inspire her."

Phoenix wavered between being impossibly flattered and thinking the very idea of him inspiring anyone, let alone Elizabeth, was just wrong.

"She inspires *me*."

"Good." Sinnodella nodded. "My Sable is a great woman. She deserves nothing less than a great man by her side."

"I know."

"Tell me. The oath you would have sworn to the repository. Have you kept it?"

"Yes."

"Why? What do you owe a dead spellforger?"

"Well, he made a pretty convincing argument," Phoenix said. "He told me spellforging made it too easy to put too much magic in too many people's hands, and the more spread out magic like that gets, the higher the odds that something goes wrong."

Something like Relgen.

The great bastion of the north had been wiped off the map by the Ending, an Old World weapon built with spellforging. No mage could ever do something like what the Ending had done. Maybe a few hundred could, if they were willing to kill themselves trying. But in the Old World, you didn't even need to be a mage to kill a city. You just needed an arcane bomb that could fit in a messenger bag and a stomach for mass murder. No spellforging meant no bombs and no catastrophes.

That was the idea anyway.

"So, you've taught no one?"

"I used to imagine I'd have a child and pass it on to them," Phoenix said. "But now I have one, and I couldn't imagine putting something like this on her. Sometimes I think about maybe writing it down or making my own recording. Sometimes I think it'd be better if I just never taught anyone."

"Do what Vulcan and his disciples could not, and let the art of spellforging die," Sinnodella mused. "Perhaps that is how you'll be great. By ridding the world of power."

Phoenix frowned. There hadn't been any obvious malice or contempt in Sinnodella's face or voice when she said that, and yet he couldn't help but feel like he was being criticized. But then again, that might have just been projecting.

Was that really what he wanted to do? The mark on the world he wanted to leave?

A flash of light came from the clearing, and Elizabeth gave a cheer.

She'd done it.

Because of course she had.

She was Elizabeth, the Winged Lady of Sasel. Who even now acted as a one-woman knightly order, working and fighting every day to make Corsar a better, safer place.

And who was he, standing beside her? The man ridding the world of power by doing nothing but waiting to take a secret to his grave. He'd spent so many years defending his decision to not share spellforging with the world. He'd made several enemies over that decision. He'd cited his oath, the risks to the world, the dangers of the science itself. It had always seemed like such a monumental task, guarding the secret. Now, suddenly, that "task" felt oddly insubstantial. Like he could, *should*, be doing more.

He just wasn't sure what.

THE CULT OF STARS

The first bandit encounter had only been the start of their troubles. It also set the precedent for how those troubles were handled. Whether it was more brigands trying to hold them up, a wild land shark they set up camp too close to, or a witch that tried to lure them into her hut, it only ever resulted in a brief inconvenience and Snow doling out swift, decisive violence. Kratz was no slouch, but his job in situations tended to default to body blocking for Vera. He had earned Snow's respect, though, after breaking a troll's neck with his bare hands.

Kratz and the carriage driver got the campfire started, but the fire was more for light and scaring off wolves than for warmth. The summer air was plenty warm on its own, even with the sun going down—so long as nobody sat too close to Snow.

In a few days or so, they would enter the nation of Parthica, hopefully have fewer problems on the roads, and make it to the capital city of Nikos by the end of the week. But "hopefully" was a dangerous word, and Snow didn't trust it.

She'd taken to doing a quick patrol of their surroundings when they set up camp each night. She was no warden, but it gave her a little more peace of mind at least knowing the terrain. If nothing else, she'd know what direction trouble would be most likely to come from and what it might use as cover.

They were camped just off the embankment of the road in the remains of a weathered, sun-bleached stone foundation that might have been a ruin a hundred years ago. It gave decent cover, but it also left them at an obvious height disadvantage to anyone on the road.

Snow didn't like it and hadn't taken her eyes off the embankment since they'd settled in for the night.

"I think you can probably stop glaring at it now," Vera teased her as they poured themself a glass of wine. "Come and have a drink."

"You're the one who wanted protection on the road," Snow said. "And I don't get drunk on the job."

"Now, far be it from me to criticize a woman's professionalism or claim that the roads aren't dangerous," Vera said, "but we both know there's nothing out here you couldn't take even if you were smashed."

"Keep talking like that, and I'm going to start feeling underpaid."

"All right, let's not get ahead of ourselves," Vera said. "I just thought I'd make sure you knew you could if you wanted to. You're making *me* tense."

"Do you try this hard to get your half-orc drunk while he's working?"

"Oh, Kratz couldn't get drunk off a whole barrel of wine if he wanted to," Vera said. "Too much of his mother's blood in him. Isn't that right?"

Next to Vera, Kratz grunted an acknowledgment. Snow had yet to hear him actually *say* anything.

The truth was Vera was probably right. Lots of things preyed on the roads, but that was a threat of quantity, not quality. Really dangerous things didn't stalk the roads. They hid in the dark, in the depths of wilderness far from civilization or at the very top of its power structures, where they watched the world and waited for the chance to take what they wanted.

Or they were like her. You weren't randomly visited by the Cold-Blooded Killer on the side of the road. She came for you for a reason, in the dead of night, usually preceded by a week of suspicion and rumors that something was coming for you. Usually because somebody paid her to, but sometimes just because you'd tried to have her and her old company killed, and she was very upset about it.

But no one like that was coming for her any time soon. She'd seen to that personally, spending the last few months putting the fear of her wrath back into the underworld.

Until they got to Nikos, there wouldn't be much for her to do but keep the brigands off their backs, which was more exercise than anything.

She eyed the wine bottle and the extra glass Vera had already set out and relented, letting Vera pour her a drink. She might as well relax while she could.

A third glass got poured for their driver, and all three of them clinked their glasses together. It was tart and earthy but still light, especially at the end of the sip.

Vera knew how to pick a good bottle.

"Nothing like wine and a fire to keep you company on a foggy night," the driver said.

Snow's cup stopped halfway to her lips at the mention of fog. Sure enough, as she looked around, she could see the first wisps of a thick, silver-white mist curling across the ground. Except that it wasn't mist or fog. It was the wrong season, the wrong temperature, the wrong place for something like that. They weren't even near the river yet.

Snow stood up, drawing the attention of the others.

"Snow? What's wrong?"

She didn't answer, transfixed on the slowly thickening, smoky haze that crept ever closer to them from all sides. It was descending on them now, too, swallowing their surroundings. She'd seen something like this before, but she couldn't believe it was here now. It couldn't be. It was impossible.

"Snow?"

As the smoke began to sweep into the camp itself, she lost sight of her own feet. When she stomped on the ground, she *heard* the scuff of dirt, but she *felt* a cold, wet splash.

A tingle ran up her spine, and her stomach dropped. She knew what this was. She knew *who* this was.

"Snow?"

"Get to the carriage!"

Her voice echoed all around them as if they were in a canyon, and now everyone began to scramble to their feet. There was only one problem.

They couldn't see the carriage anymore. In fact, they couldn't see anything but each other and the all-consuming silver smoke, pockets of it crackling and flashing around them. The others stared down at the floor as they moved, experiencing the dissonance of hearing solid ground but feeling water beneath their feet.

"What am I stepping in!" Vera shouted.

"Damn it," Snow muttered. "Kratz, cover them!"

The half-orc grunted, his gaze sweeping around them. Meanwhile, the assassin drew both of her daggers.

"Chloe Guerron . . ."

A hollow voice reached out to her through the smoke. It echoed like everything else, but Snow was getting better at picking out the source of sound. She threw her enchanted dagger, Companion Piece, straight into the smoke in the direction of the voice. There was a brief squelch of steel sinking into flesh, and when the dagger returned to her hand a second later, the blade was wet with blood. Silence for a moment, then a new voice from another direction.

"Starbreaker . . ." It growled in displeasure. She threw her dagger again, hearing another hit.

"You're all supposed to be dead!" she shouted.

"And yet," a third voice taunted, "I draw breath."

Another throw, another blade burying into an unseen person.

"Your hunt for Silas Lamark cannot be allowed to continue."

"Why the hells do you care about him?"

Finally, shapes began to emerge from the smoke. Twelve people advanced in a ring around them, each adorned in long robes. Three of them were already bleeding from open wounds, but if they noticed, they didn't show it. A twelve-pointed star had been carved on each of their foreheads.

The one closest to Snow spoke. "It pleases me for his work to continue."

The last traces of doubt of who these people were left Snow's mind. The Cult of Stars was standing before her, back from the dead.

Kratz let out a low snarl as Vera and the driver took refuge in between Snow and the half-orc. Vera brandished the wine bottle like a club, ready to swing.

"Then prepare to be disappointed," Snow said, her voice like shattering glass as her irises faded to pure white.

She shot forward, daggers flashing, and behind her Kratz let out a roar as he swung his hammer for all he was worth.

The cultists moved in perfect sync, stepping backward and drawing blades as one before rushing back in. Her daggers danced between all of them, blocking, parrying, and darting in for a kill. Nothing short of a killing blow put any of them down. Any less and they wouldn't register the wound at all, continuing right on fighting with half a dozen holes in their ribs.

They were fast, and on a home field advantage in the smoke. Multiple times as she or Kratz went for a strike, their target would vanish into the smoke, reappearing behind them or off to the side. Kratz did his best to keep up, but it was Snow who matched them, blinking around the fight just as often as they did.

She threw a knife at one cultist's head, only to watch the weapon disappear into a pocket of smoke and come whistling straight back at her from behind. She sank a blade into another, only for them to dissipate like smoke around her dagger. She'd lost count of how many she'd killed, partly because some of them kept getting back up, but she knew it had to be more than they'd initially seen circling them.

It should have been frustrating or terrifying. Going off the reactions of Kratz and Vera, it was both of those things. But Snow felt neither. Her chest became a cold, bottomless pit as the Heart of Ice spread itself through her. Its cold was her shield and her edge, numbing out every feeling, every distraction, until all that was left of her was lethal intent.

With a sweep of her foot, ice spread across the ground in front of her, rooting several cultists in place. She took a step, blinked out of sight, and reappeared behind the closest one before losing herself in a rhythm of violence.

Slash, duck, blink, stab. Blink, throw, dodge, slash. Duck, slash, blink, stab.

Six more dropped to the ground, puddles of their blood freezing solid around them. And then, suddenly, a dull ache appeared in her stomach, and she couldn't move correctly. She glanced down to find the point of a sword protruding out between two of her ribs. It didn't hurt, not with her body consumed by the cold, but it was hard to turn around when you were skewered at the end of a blade.

Her attacker's voice breathed into her ear, a mix of spite and satisfaction. "Now I remove you, like the splinter you are."

Snow grabbed the blade with both hands, spreading ice down its length and back to the wielder. He grunted in surprise, but before he could take so much as a step, he was completely encased in ice. She pulled herself off the sword and spun around just in time to watch Kratz take the man's frozen head clean off with a swing of his hammer.

Snow's legs collapsed out from under her, scattering the smoke around her as she fell. Blood streamed briefly from her wound until both sides of it froze over, sealing it shut. Sensation slowly began returning to her body, and now it hurt to breathe. But the camp had gone silent, and after a few seconds, the smoke began to dissipate, revealing their camping spot once again—but not a single dead body. Aside from the splashes of frost, the frozen blood that now littered the area, and the gore on her and Kratz's weapons, there was no sign their fight had ever happened.

Kratz looked to Snow, and Vera put a voice to the question in his eyes. "What the fuck was that?"

Snow panted as she clutched her wound to try and keep it numb.

"Did any of us ever tell you how we got the name 'Starbreakers'?"

BAD MEMORIES

"They called themselves the Cult of Stars."

After the attack on their camp, there had been a brief debate about whether or not they should move to somewhere safer. Snow insisted there was no point. If the Cult of Stars wanted to attack them, they would. Relocating to a different spot on the side of the road wouldn't make any difference.

Snow was back to not drinking, which suited Vera just fine now that they were gulping down the rest of the wine. The driver claimed to have gone to bed, but it was easy to tell he wasn't going to sleep at all tonight.

"Supposedly, there were these . . . things. A long time ago. The Cult calls them the Starborn and thinks they came before the gods. They want to bring them back to power or something. I never really grasped their whole plan beyond killing a bunch of people. Phoenix was the one who'd actually studied them," Snow recounted.

Her head swam at the thought of the Starbreakers' very first encounter with the Cult, how long ago it had been, and how woefully unprepared they all were. It was a miracle any of them had survived, let alone gone on to as successful a career as they had. But then, the Starbreakers had always had luck on their side. Until the day they didn't.

"We fought a bunch of them in Aenerwin, when they were trying to sacrifice the town to the Starborn. Afterward, we took a few more jobs to root out any problems that sounded culty. More for branding than a grudge. But by the end of the year, we stopped finding more of them, and we figured we got them all."

No company could last forever just wandering around the countryside looking for work, even one with a budding scholar specializing in locating lost ruins and artifacts. Eventually, you needed to start getting hired, and that was where reputations were invaluable. It was why companies had names to begin with. And as the newly christened Starbreakers, it wouldn't have been right to let anyone else stamp out the remnants of the Cult of Stars.

"You figured wrong," Vera noted, pouring themself another glass. They were going to have a prodigious hangover come morning, but at least their hands had stopped shaking with lingering fear.

"Not the first time," Snow muttered. "We ran into more a couple years later. I'd just gotten the Heart of Ice, and it was causing . . . problems. Phoenix was trying everything he could think of to come up with a solution, even going back to the library. And when we got there, the Cult was there too. We killed them all, again. But we never found out what they were after. At least, not until a few years later. When they turned up at Relgen."

It should have been the easiest job in the world. Phoenix had tracked down an artifact called the Ending to a ruin somewhere beneath the city of Relgen. Find the ruin, deal with whatever was inside, recover the artifact. They'd done jobs like it a hundred times.

But the Starbreakers who went to Relgen were a very different group than the ones who built a reputation as the finest freelancers in Corsar. Snow had officially broken things off with Phoenix for a dozen different reasons that all boiled down to them having different ideas of what was right and wrong and what did and didn't count as looking out for each other. Phoenix himself had only just come back from his own personal endeavor—helping a fellow freelancer named Sable make the transition from survivor of the battle of Loraine to the Winged Lady of Sasel. Church was thinking of quitting the group altogether and accepting the offer of knighthood they'd all been given. Angel had been reading the writing on the wall and had started pulling away from the others in preparation for the day they'd say goodbye. Only Brass really still had his heart in the company by the time they entered the city of Relgen.

Old emotions dredged themselves to the surface as Snow's head throbbed.

So many stupid, small mistakes had happened that day. But small things piled up. The Cult of Stars returning again, stealing the Ending, and setting it off over Relgen had been the world-shattering capstone to one of the worst days any of them had ever had. And instead of going their separate ways like adults and promising to keep in touch, the Starbreakers broke apart in a flurry of guilt, grief, and pent-up frustration. A five-way brawl that left them all bitter, bleeding, and alone.

The last nail in the coffin was the trial.

Phoenix and Church had been the only ones with enough shame to return to Sasel and explain what had happened. Snow knew better than to show her face in the kingdom's capital, and Angel wasn't even in the country by that point. Brass eventually got caught by the authorities during a weeks-long bender, completely oblivious that there had even been a warrant out for his arrest, but by then the judgment had already been handed down.

Maybe it was because of all the good they'd done, but the Starbreakers weren't found guilty. They *were* found to be negligent, reckless, and dangerous. They were ordered to disband, barred from ever setting foot in Sasel, and all of their possessions and holdings in the city were seized. To limit freelancer activities in the kingdom and prevent anything like Relgen from happening again, all agents of the crown were forbidden from ever soliciting the services of not just the Starbreakers but any freelancers.

It was the end of an era.

"All this time, I think we all thought that the one silver lining was that the Cult died with the city," Snow mused. "We should have figured that was too good to be true."

"So, what now? Now that you know they're still around?"

"We fucking kill them all, for good this time," Snow spat and was surprised by the amount of venom in her voice.

There had been a point in her life where she hated the Cult of Stars with every fiber of her being. But hate was an emotion that took a lot of effort, and the Heart of Ice had been numbing her emotions for a decade now. She should have been annoyed or maybe even indifferent, not furious.

They were a pain in the ass, and they were in her way, but she knew what to do with things in her way, and it wasn't to get irrationally angry. Something was throwing her off, upsetting the normal steadiness to her emotions.

Her head really was swimming now.

"Can you even do that?" Vera's skepticism was rooted in what she'd been through. Seeing the Cult of Stars in action for the first time was unsettling. They seemed inhuman. Invincible.

Snow knew that better than most. She also knew they still died just like anyone else if you stabbed them hard enough.

"They've got a lot of tricks, and they caught me by surprise this time. That's it," Snow said. "I literally made a name for myself hunting these bastards. I know their tricks. If they think they can . . . think . . ."

Snow lost her train of thought as she tried to remember what her actual plan was. The Cult of Stars were after her because of Silas. She was after Silas. Why was she after Silas?

"Snow?" Vera sounded wrong. Farther away than they should have been. Or maybe too close.

There was something Snow was forgetting. Silas. No, not Silas. The Cult. The Cult and their tricks.

She pulled open the gash in her armor the cultist from the fight had left her to inspect the wound left behind. Her wounds froze over quickly, and one of the perks of the Heart of Ice was that her flesh could heal just fine even frozen and quicker than a normal person's at that. Sure enough, the stab wound was already closed up by a thin, icy scab. But spreading out from all around it were discolored veins.

With more effort than it usually took, Snow willed herself to go cold, and her eyes snapped from pale blue to pure white. All feeling, physical and emotional, vanished from her mind. No distractions, no weakness, just stark, crisp clarity. With that clarity came a memory, one she should have remembered the second she'd been stabbed.

One of the cultists's favorite tricks was poisoned blades.

Suddenly, everything she'd felt in the last few minutes was recontextualized. Her head swimming. The anger. The confusion. All telltale symptoms of early stages of mindfire poisoning.

"Shit."

CORDS THAT BIND

Quint woke up to a tingling sensation all across his wrists and midsection as he found himself tied to a chair by a tangle of Ink's glowing threads. His hands were bound tight behind his back, his ankles were secured to the chair legs, and his whole body was pinned against the chair's back. Ink sat in a chair across from him, legs crossed.

"He lives," she greeted. "I was starting to think I'd overdone it."

"What did you do?" Quint asked. He'd spent the last few days with a fire inside his skull, burning, driving him forward after whatever Roso had ordered. The hellborn's every word had been his obsession. Now, his head only hurt in the regular, familiar way.

"Roso's control is like a blade. It leaves a wound, but the weapon itself doesn't stick around. And no lingering magic means there's nothing for me to dispel. So," Ink gave a playful smile, "I had to knock the sense back into you."

"You knocked something, for sure."

Ink chuckled, and her eyes drifted to the floor. A silence took hold of the room for a beat. She folded her hands. Kicked at the floor. When she finally looked back at him, she wore a confident smile that didn't quite reach her eyes.

"It's been a long time since one of us tied the other to a chair, hasn't it?" she teased.

"It has." He didn't fight the small smile that crept onto his lips. "It's good to see you, Kira."

"I know," she said. After a pause, she added, "You too."

"What are you doing here?" Quint asked.

"My job," Ink said. "Well, actually, I suppose right now I'm not. But I heard Roso got to you, and . . . I figured you could use my help."

Quint slowly raised his eyebrows. "How far did you teleport to come save me?"

"Oh, shut up before I zap you again. Harder this time."

"Is that a promise?"

"Are we interrupting something?" Brass's voice cut through the tension in the room as he and Church stood in the doorway. "Because we can come back later."

"No," Ink said. She cast a quick glance back to Quint. "Come in."

The shift in her voice was subtle but powerful. A little bit faster, a little bit tighter, and it was back to business. Stray thoughts of the past vanished from Quint's mind, as if she'd thrown a switch in him. And she didn't even need a demon's voice to do it.

Quint started with something that had been in the back of his mind since waking up. "Where are we?"

"A tavern just up the road that wouldn't ask questions when we brought in a tied-up, unconscious mercenary," Brass answered. "By the way, do you still want to kill us?"

"No more than anyone else who has to deal with you, I imagine."

"How are you feeling?" Church asked.

"Like I was kicked by a camel."

Church nodded. With a quick prayer, Quint felt a warm, comforting sensation roll through his skull, like the world's greatest head massage. His head stopped hurting immediately. His relief was short lived, though, as he saw the slight strain on the priest's face and remembered how utterly winded he'd looked earlier.

And how he'd tried to kill him.

He had tried to do that in the past as well, but that had been intentional. This time it hadn't.

"Thank you," Quint said. "I'm sorry. For before."

"You weren't in control of your actions," Church said. "You have nothing to apologize for."

"I don't know about that," Brass said. "Wounds heal, but do you have any idea how hard it is to get blood out of a white shirt?"

Quint gave a half-amused grunt. A lot of things had changed over the years. But the Starbreakers, it seemed, were not one of them.

"Roso's not talking," Ink said. "What happened?"

Quint's expression hardened into a deep frown. "We've been working in Tecah, clearing allosaurus nests for a jungle expedition group based here in the city. We'd just wrapped up our last trip when a messenger came to us asking if we'd hear out their master's business proposal. We were on our guard but . . . all he had to do was say a few words. Ever since then, he's had the entire Cord doing his—" He stopped, suddenly worried. "The rest of the Cord. Are they—?"

"Sorry, it was just you," Brass said. "We figured you could tell us where they were. Me and Church have been going through his underlings like wet tissue paper. I'd have thought if he had the Cord in his back pocket, he'd have used them by now."

"He held me back as his personal bodyguard. If the rest of the Cord wasn't with me," Quint said, sounding more concerned by the second, "and they haven't come looking for Roso, then they're still on the last assignment he gave them."

Out of all of them, Ink was the one most rattled by Quint's distress. "What are they doing?"

"Roso loaned them out. To the Prince Killer."

Ink was the first one to recover from the stunned silence. "The Prince Killer. As in Kurien, attempted assassin of Roland II. That Prince Killer?"

Quint gave a nod. "From everything I gathered, she was the one who got Roso out of Oblivion. She's after arcane weapons. More than even she could ever use. And Roso gave her the Cord to help shake down the artifact collectors and importers here in Puerto Oro. They've been helping her amass an arsenal for weeks now."

"Kurien's *here?*" Ink asked. "And she's got the Cord of Aenwyn for backup?"

"Worse," Quint said. "When Roso gave Kurien the Cord, he had us give Kurien the Heart."

Every pair of eyebrows in the room shot up. There was only one Heart that Quint could have been talking about. The one that the Cord of Aenwyn had taken in the aftermath of the Battle of Loraine.

"Kurien has the Heart of Shadows," Church breathed, "That's why the Oracle couldn't see her."

Several things came into stark focus at once. The Prince Killer was the one who'd gotten Roso, and presumably all the other inmates, out of Oblivion. She'd unleashed chaos on the world stage, and now, as all of Corsar's defenders were racing around desperately trying to control the situation, she was amassing an arsenal of arcane weaponry with the Servitor Heart of Shadows to serve as its crown jewel. She'd be invisible to any attempt to track her with magic, and, even if they found her, Kurien had been one of the most dangerous people ever thrown into Oblivion *without* a Servitor Heart.

Five minutes ago, Church, Brass, and Ink had thought they'd taken care of the last of their problems in Puerto Oro. Now, they had what was possibly the biggest problem of the entire breakout to deal with.

"Well . . ." Ink began. "Fuck."

BROKEN GATES

Angel cut a relentless pace through her portion of the escapees, tunnel-porting across the kingdom from one fight to the next. She never took on less than six in a day, and her record so far was twelve.

Bart and Ruby hadn't been nearly as much of a hassle as she'd worried. Church hadn't been *happy* to hear they were with her, but he was sympathetic to Ruby's plight with the people of Aenerwin, and Angel might have accidentally said some bullshit along the lines of a promise to keep them safe. Apart from occasionally spectating her louder and more obvious fights, like the one with the Thunderer, they stayed out of her way and even helped Thalia around the kitchen. Funnily enough, the bartender was actually the closest thing to a problem Angel had on the job.

"Don't take this the wrong way," Thalia said when Angel finally decided to ask what was bugging her, "but I've never seen you work yourself like this. You're running yourself ragged, forgetting to eat, barely stopping to catch your breath . . . You're taking on more work than any of the others *and* moving faster. Why are you in such a rush?"

Angel wished she'd just left it alone.

"I'm fine," Angel dismissed. She knew immediately that wasn't going to fly, so she switched tactics. "I just want to get this over with, okay? And the closer I get to the end, the more I just want to hurry up and finish."

"You said yourself most of these people aren't causing real trouble yet," Thalia said. "You can afford to slow down. To rest a little."

"I'm fine," Angel stressed, as if repeating it would make it more convincing. "The only people left are chumps and pushovers. I won't even need to turn the lights on to take them down. And I'm almost done. A couple more names to cross off and then I can stop, and we can all move on with our lives."

If she wasn't already so close to the end, Angel might have taken a nap right then, just to make Thalia feel better. But she was so tantalizingly close to being free again.

From the fight. From Renalt. From herself.

Rest could wait just a little longer.

It was when she was in her home stretch of escapees that she got the message from Ink. A contingent of the Seven Gates, the order of knights who served the crown and the vanguard of the king's own efforts to round up Oblivion escapees, had failed to check in during their latest assignment, and everyone else—including Ink herself apparently—was too wrapped up in other issues to find out what had happened to them.

Before the Seven Gates of Sasel had ghosted Ink, they'd been on their way to apprehend Wendel Lestrade, an Oblivion escapee who'd been incarcerated for stealing the secrets from the Academy's original Disassembly Council and then murdering every single one of its members.

Before their unfortunate end, the Disassembly Council had been tasked with keeping dangerous artifacts secured from the rest of the world. With them dead, Lestrade was the only man alive who knew the location of the Black Vault, where all of the artifacts in the council's charge were stored.

Lestrade was dangerous and valuable for what he knew, but he was a scribbler first and a half-rate necromancer as a very distant second. The Oracle had given them an exact location and heading. For the premiere knights of the crown, he should have been an easy grab.

But "should" was always a dangerous word.

The Seven Gates's last known location took them to a winding limestone gorge, deep enough for the sun to have already disappeared behind the top of the ridge and cast the entirety of it in shadow. One step out the door of the Rusted Star, Angel knew something was wrong.

It was quiet in the gorge, the air still and heavy, like it couldn't escape the confines of the surrounding ridges. The only sound came from the occasional cry of a distressed animal echoing against the rocks coming from somewhere deeper within the gorge. High overhead, vultures circled.

That's not a good sign.

"Stay here," Angel ordered. No one argued.

She advanced slowly down into the valley, the silence making the scuff of her boots against the rocky ground seem deafening. With every cry from whatever panicked animal was waiting for her, she winced.

She quickly found the source of the cries—a horse, straining against the lead that tied it to a lone tree. It was laden with heavy saddlebags decorated in the heraldry of the Seven Gates, but there was no sign of its rider. There were two other leads tied to the tree, but both of them were frayed at the ends.

As soon as the horse saw Angel, it let out a panicked whinny and thrashed its head, trying to break free and failing.

"Easy, easy," Angel said, running her hands along the mount's neck to try and calm it down. "Don't suppose you know where your owner went?"

The horse let out an unhelpful whinny, and Angel sighed, giving it a pat. "Yeah, I didn't think so."

There were no more bends in the gorge, just a gentle slope down as the mountains of the gorge converged. Down at the very bottom at the end of the gorge was an intricately-carved stone facade framing a wide, open set of doors and a pitch-dark corridor beyond them. The entrance to an Old World ruin.

"Be back," she told the horse.

As she approached the entrance, a faint glow began to flicker at her fingertips as a flutter of warmth spread through her chest. Deep inside her, something instinctually curled in disgust. She could feel it in her soul. This place was stained to the bones by something foul.

The interior quickly swallowed up any light from outside, leaving every-thing inside in complete darkness. Her eyes adjusted to it after only a moment, and the world came into focus in an eerie black and white. Sharp, angular Old World stonework greeted her with shallow grooves running through it that once held lightstone. Cracks had formed in several places in the stone, and wisps of black smoke trailed out from each and every one. She nearly gagged on the smell of rot and mold.

The only sound was the echo of her footsteps and her own breathing. The back of her neck prickled at the dead stillness of this place, and the warmth in her chest was spreading to the rest of her body. Every step carried a slight sting, like her feet were rejecting the floor itself.

There was a lot of dried blood on the floor.

An open vault door of solid, ornately decorated steel greeted her in the next room, flanked on either side by modern lightstone lamps bracketed into the walls. As she approached, the wall next to the vault doors lit up with glowing text in a dozen different languages. In every one Angel could read, it said the same thing: CLASS 1 IMMUTABLE: HELM OF THE DREAD KNIGHT. SEALED FOR SAFETY. DANGER! DO NOT OPEN!

There was nothing inside the vault but an empty podium and broken glass. The stench of death was so strong, she couldn't even set foot inside it, but she could still clearly see, on the back wall, a mural of an undead horde tearing into panicked masses with a single, black-armored individual at its center. Mottled black wings fanned out from its back, and its face was obscured behind an ominous, spiked helmet.

She activated her messaging coil.

"Ink, it's Angel. We've got a fucking problem."

THE WARDEN

When Phoenix had last been here, Cutters Place had been barely more than a village. Clinging to the edge of the Iron Forest, it was one of a few dozen places along the forest's edge where loggers brave and stubborn enough to deal with it lived and worked. In the eleven years since then, however, the tiny community had grown into the largest settlement on the forest's edge. It was their last stop before plunging straight into Edelfric's home turf.

It looked like it had seen better days.

The defensive wall facing the road into the forest was battered and worn down. Several structures near it had holes in their roofs, and others had collapsed altogether. The ground outside the wall was absolutely littered with scraps of wood, twisted gnarls of dead plants, and deep scores in the dirt.

Phoenix wanted to keep a low profile if they could, but Wings was a knight of the crown, so of course, as soon as she saw signs of recent battle, she flew straight to where the damage looked the most severe.

By the time they touched down, a crowd had already gathered in a circle around them. Voices came at them like waves, too many and from too many directions to make out even half of what they were saying. Phoenix took an unconscious step toward Wings, who was trying to get everyone to calm down, when a sharp whistle silenced the crowd.

"Everyone, back off! Give them some space!"

A young man pushed his way through the crowd, nudging people away and waving them off as he went. He couldn't have been older than twenty, but he wore a breastplate over well-worn leathers and a cloak that was frayed at the edges and held in place with a scratch-covered silver pin of two crossed axes. His deep-brown face was furrowed, caught in a nebulous territory between fear and hope.

"I'm guessing you're the Winged Lady, then," the young man asked.

"Lady Elizabeth Meshar, Knight of Sasel," Wings introduced herself.

"Please tell me you're here to help."

"We are now." She looked at the surrounding damage. "What happened here?"

"What hasn't? We've been—" The young man stopped when he finally took notice of Phoenix. The boy had been carrying himself with a certain confidence up until now, standing tall and speaking with authority. But when he saw the spellforger, his eyes went wide, and he suddenly looked very young. "You're back."

Of all the things Phoenix could remember with perfect clarity, faces were not one of them. The young man was familiar, clearly from here, and he knew Phoenix.

Given the circumstances, he had to be someone Phoenix met the last time the Starbreakers had come through here. But for the life of him, he was drawing a blank.

"You probably don't remember me. My name is Dietrich. The Starbreakers saved me from goblins when I was eight."

Phoenix was confused for a moment because he did remember rescuing captives from a goblin camp back then, but those had all been *children*, and this man was . . . probably exactly the right age to have been one of them. As soon as Phoenix did the math, everything clicked—including, it felt like, his joints. It was one thing to know in his head that he'd taken up glintchasing fourteen years ago; it was another thing altogether to see a child he'd saved now standing in front of him as a grown man.

"You grew up," he said when he finally found his voice again.

Dietrich gave a soft chuckle. "Yeah." He looked around at the eyes of the crowd still on them. "Maybe we should go somewhere to talk."

After urging people to disperse, Dietrich led them off the streets and into a cabin deeper in the city. The whole walk over, people kept flagging Dietrich down with questions and concerns. It turned out he was the town warden, charged with protecting Cutters Place from everything that came out of the Iron Forest.

That was supposed to mean dealing with things like goblins, ogres, and the occasional fey creature.

But now, Cutters Place was under siege from Edelfric.

"According to him, we're encroaching on 'his' forest. We've gotten runners from surrounding villages saying they've been attacked once or twice, but he's hitting here the hardest. We're the biggest target along the forest's edge, and he's sent copies here every day this week so far." Dietrich closed his eyes for a moment, rubbing his temples. "How is this happening? How is the Scourge back?"

Phoenix sighed. "When we stopped him last time, we burned him down to his core, but killing that last part of him was harder. Nothing we tried worked, so eventually," he paused, thinking of how to explain, "we locked him up as far from the forest as we could get it. But he grew back, and then he got out, and now he's here again. Which is why we are too."

"So, are you a knight now, then?"

"Uh, no."

He'd been offered the job once, after the Battle of Loraine, but turned it down. It had made sense at the time.

"Just married to one," Wings said, squeezing his hand to bring him back to the present.

Phoenix squeezed back in thanks. "How have you been holding up so far?"

"The first one was more of a surprise than a problem. It barely scuffed the walls before I killed it. But they've been getting stronger every time. The last one, I couldn't even scratch until we doused it in mushpowder."

"Sorry?" Wings asked.

"A compound we use to weaken ironwood. It makes it easier to work and harvest," Dietrich explained.

Phoenix tried to give the boy a reassuring look. "You don't have to worry anymore. We'll take care of Edelfric."

"Let me help."

"You don't have—"

"I do," Dietrich insisted. "Up until a few months ago, I was the warden's apprentice. Then, one day . . ."

His eyes briefly drifted downward. "I was promoted to this job a lot sooner than I expected. A lot of people around here aren't convinced I can do it. And that was *before* Edelfric came back. If you two take care of everything, that saves today. But tomorrow, when the next monster comes out of that forest and you're not here . . ."

He let the hypothetical hang a moment before continuing. "Relgen's gone. People in the north need to feel like they're safe to live up here, otherwise they'll just pack up for Olwin with everyone else. So, I need to help. I need to prove to this town that I can keep it safe."

The words stuck like a barb in Phoenix's mind, a problem staring him in the face just daring him to solve it. Elizabeth was looking at him like she'd already made up her mind to say yes. But just saying yes felt like a half measure. What good would it really do this town if Dietrich helped them fight Edelfric? Maybe they'd believe in him. But unless you were a priest, belief didn't really count for too much on its own.

"Do you think you can?" Phoenix asked.

"I think I'm the best-trained fighter in this town and the only one besides our deacon with any magic. I think if I can't, then this whole town's on borrowed time. The crown's stretched too thin. The knights and the army only cover the big cities. Nobody's in a hurry to move up here. It's got to be one of us. So, it's got to be me. And besides," Dietrich added. "I still owe you for saving my life."

Phoenix frowned. Dietrich was positioning himself as the bastion between his home and any danger the wilderness of Corsar could throw at it. His resolve was there. And the warden had to have skill to have lasted even as long as he had. Those two things would do a lot of work. But not all of it. Phoenix couldn't help but wonder if maybe the people of Cutters Place were right to be afraid of staying here. If maybe they should just pack up and find somewhere closer to the crown's dependable sphere of influence. They'd be safer.

And they'd be refugees, like so many others that had been displaced by the fall of Relgen.

He tried to push the thoughts out of his head. They were here for Edelfric, not to pass judgment on the viability of local settlements. And in that regard, an extra body that knew the local terrain would be invaluable.

"We appreciate the offer," Phoenix said. "It's been a long day for us. First thing tomorrow, we can go after Edelfric."

Dietrich nodded. "Thank you. You don't know what this means to me."

"Don't thank me yet," Phoenix said. "You've been fighting Edelfric here. You haven't seen what he can do inside the forest."

Elizabeth dusted off her hands as the fireplace lit up, bathing the room in a dull orange glow. Their room for the evening was small, but the wooden walls, furs, and firelight made it cozy.

Arman sat at the little writing desk next to the fireplace, using a tuning fork-shaped device to clean his coat and armor. A faint hum came from the fork, and wherever he waved it over his things, dirt simply scattered and dissolved. Arman had never been one for neatness—the usual state of his workshop attested to that—but his hands always sought out tasks when there was something on his mind. The slight frown on his face only confirmed Elizabeth's intuition. Something was bothering him.

She half leaned, half sat on the corner of the desk. When he didn't notice her, she switched to the direct approach.

"What is it?"

He twitched in surprise, as if suddenly remembering she was there with him and looking briefly embarrassed that he'd forgotten.

"I was thinking," he said, "about what's going to happen to this place once we're gone."

Elizabeth gave him a puzzled look. "They go back to living their lives, minus a crazed tree man trying to kill them."

Arman shook his head. "They can't though. Not for long, out here, alone. This whole town . . . it's too small to defend itself but too big to go unnoticed by everything in the forest. One warden can't protect it alone. Which means it's only a matter of time before *something* swallows it up. They can't stay here. It's suicide."

"They have to try," Elizabeth said. "Somebody has to try."

Now it was Arman's turn to look confused.

"Wilderness is always advancing," Elizabeth said. "Everybody just stays where it's safe? Sooner or later, there's nowhere safe left. Living out here on the fringes like this is dangerous. But if they can survive, make it work? That's how new, safe places get made."

She paused for a moment, studying his reaction to her words.

"But that's not what's really bothering you, is it?"

He shook his head. She'd known even before he did. Like usual.

"This place is like this because of Relgen. Because of *me*. And it *was* my fault, at least a little. I thought I made peace with that. I thought I could live and . . . maybe not do better but not do anything worse. But I don't want this to be the world I leave Robyn. I made her world more dangerous. And I don't know how to fix it."

Elizabeth ran a hand along his cheek, hoping to ease his mind. "We make it better. How we can, where we can."

Arman sighed, leaning into her touch and nodding. "Make it better."

He sat upright, his gaze locking straight ahead, staring into space. His hands froze in their work.

"Arman?"

"I need to talk to Dietrich," he said, immediately getting out of his chair, donning his coat, and starting for the door.

"What?"

He paused at the door for a moment, then turned around and planted a kiss on her confused lips. His voice came out both relieved and excited. "I love you. I'll be back."

And then he strode out, leaving his stunned wife in his wake.

A bleary-eyed Dietrich answered the knock at his door with his armor on and his sword in hand, only to find himself faced not with a panicked townsperson but Phoenix. The warden hesitated, unsure what to make of his bearing. He looked like a man on a mission.

"I've got a plan," Phoenix stated. "We're going to save this town. Not just stop Edelfric but really *save* it. Give it a fighting chance to turn into something."

"Okay," Dietrich said, not precisely following. "Do you need something?"

"A few things, actually," Phoenix said. "A forge, some materials, and somebody who can explain to me how you make that powder you use to weaken ironwood." Phoenix glanced down at the weapon in the warden's hands. "And I'm going to need to borrow that."

EDELFRIC

Elizabeth had spent a lot of time in forests. She used to play in one behind her family's farm as a child. She'd lived in one while training with Sinnodella. Her old company, the Broken Spear, had taken a lot of jobs deep within them, and they often cut through them instead of sticking to the roads to save on travel time. If there was any place where she should have been comfortable, it was a forest.

But the Iron Forest was anything but comfortable. The near pitch-colored bark of the trees seemed to swallow all light, leaving the forest dark and unnaturally cool even though she knew somewhere beyond the smothering canopy, the sun was high in the sky. The ground was a gnarled mess of roots and black mud. A musty, metallic stench hung in the air, like wet, rusted iron. And no matter how many times she checked over her shoulder or reached out with her senses and found nothing, she could not shake the feeling she was being watched.

A grove was a reflection of its master, and its master in turn reflected the grove. Elizabeth thought back to the twisted, gnarled shape of Edelfric's seedling and the mad fury he'd displayed. She could see that same twisted, angry, insane nature in the forest around her.

Arman was even more on edge than her.

"You okay?" she asked.

"Nervous," he admitted. "We're taking a risk here. Even if we win today . . ."

"Hey." She reached out, gently guiding him to look her in the eye. "It's going to be fine. You're smart, and I'm stubborn."

The words put a reserved smile on both of their faces. It was their secret code. A reminder in their most uncertain times that each of them was a force to be reckoned with and that together, they could do anything.

Phoenix and Wings took their positions. Him standing next to Dietrich, both men with weapons at the ready. Her resting on her knees, bow placed down in front of her.

"Whenever you're ready," Phoenix said.

Wings closed her eyes, held her hands out in front of her, and breathed. As Sinnodella had taught her, she manifested a groveseed—a tiny, glowing emerald ball of life and power spun from her own presence. Then, pushing with her will as much as her hands, she forced it into the ground and took hold of the forest itself.

Instantly, things felt different from her practice run in the Greenwyld. Then, she'd only tentatively brushed the life force of the place and had been met with the calm, warm presence of Sinnodella and the Greenwyld. Now, burning, splitting pain raced along her skull as her essence touched that of the Iron Forest.

Every feeling it had given her before was magnified a thousand times. Cold, hard, twisted power met her, carrying with it agony, anguish, and betrayal. A taste of metal and rot filled her mouth, and she had to resist the need to vomit.

"Wings?"

"I'm okay!" she gasped.

She steeled her stomach and pressed on, sifting through everything it was giving her. The energies of Edelfric and the forest were hopelessly entangled, but the more she prodded, the more the differences began to take shape. Some of what she touched, she could feel writhing and convulsing. But in other places, it simply stood firm, monolithic, and unbending. With time, she began to feel out what was the pain and anger of a man and what was the power of the forest that bent to nothing.

She made her first effort to pry at the connection between the two, and the entire forest shuddered.

That was fast.

"Wings?"

"He knows. He's coming."

"Where?"

"Everywhere."

She doubted it was a helpful answer, but it was all she had. That and whatever was coming was either big, numerous, or both. Already she could hear the twisting and snapping of branches far off in the forest. Probably Edelfric on his way. But it was too far for her to get anything precise from sound alone, and the forest was shrouding everything else. Edelfric and the forest were still too alike for her to tell which was which.

THIS PLACE IS MINE!

Wings reeled as Edelfric's resistance filled her mind. At the same time, something wrapped around her throat, and she was lifted off her feet. A gnarled root had burst from the ground, and her legs thrashed and spasmed as it tightened around her neck.

A gust of wind swept across the forest floor, sending her bow flying toward her outstretched hand. Midflight, the bow broke apart in a flash of light, turning into a pair of scimitars that continued spinning through the air.

From off to her left, Phoenix let loose a jet of dull-pink powder from the tip of his wand, spraying the length of the root just before her swords reached it, allowing the weapons to slice cleanly through. The grip on Wings's windpipe slackened, and sweet air rushed into her lungs as she tore what was left off of her.

She fell onto her back, coughing and sputtering. Her skin itched like it was made of dried leaves, her bones ached, and the back of her mind buzzed with a constant, simmering rage. Most of all, though, she felt like a piece of herself was missing.

She couldn't feel the forest. Her forest. Without it, she felt naked and starving. Weak and wilting.

And then her husband was at her side.

"Are you all right?"

Her throat felt like one giant bruise. The lingering aftertaste of Edelfric's thoughts still clung to her and made her skin crawl. But for just a moment as she met Arman's eyes, Elizabeth felt the world go still. It was a moment of peace, like coming home just in time to get out of a storm, that immediately centered her and helped her sort out which thoughts in her head were actually hers.

"Fine," Wings said. "He's fighting me harder than I expected."

"The forest is coming alive!" Dietrich shouted a warning. "He's close!"

Phoenix's look hardened with a tactical resolve. "How long do you need?"

"As long as you can give me."

"Done."

Phoenix stood up, briefly flicking the chamber of his wand open to eject a spent cell and load a fresh one before snapping it shut. The cylindrical chamber spun, clicked into place, and a tiny flame danced at the wand's tip.

"Dietrich! Circle around wide and come at him from behind! I'll draw him in!"

The warden of Cutters Place cast the spellforger a wary look but took off in a sprint.

Phoenix glanced back at Wings. There was no doubt in his eyes. Only a promise and absolute trust. Wings gave him a clear, concise nod to signal they were on the same page, and then he was off, running through the trees, slapping devices from his belt onto the trunks as he ran past.

They were doing their jobs. Time to do hers.

She took a kneeling position again and drew in a deep breath. She reached out to her groveseed, still buried in the soil, and once again, Edelfric's will pressed against hers, trying to snuff out her presence with his own. His pain, his rage, everything that was him choked in all around her. She grit her teeth and met it with everything that was her.

This was more than a simple contest of will. Claiming a place through a groveseed was about imprinting your identity on to the land and making it into an extension of you. As the claim of her groveseed crashed against Edelfric's, what mattered was whose presence could make the strongest impression on the forest itself.

Edelfric was anger. Pain. Possession. He had fallen in this forest and believed he had been left to die. Its own natural power had rebirthed him. There was little of the man he'd once been in him now, but what remained was single-mindedly focused. He would wipe Roland and his kingdom off of the map if it took a thousand years. It was who he was.

It was all he was.

She called up the memories and experiences that made her who *she* was. She thought about days long behind her with the Broken Spear. Meeting them in the Greenwyld, fighting beside them. Living and laughing and singing and sobbing together. She thought about her family. The light that could gleam in her husband's eyes when he was deep in thought. Her daughter's laugh and smile. She thought about the enemies she'd faced. Reth, the warlord whose spear she'd shattered. The Servitor, whose advance she'd helped halt. Ixnikol, the dragon she'd struck from the sky.

She was Sable, explorer and warden of the Broken Spear. She was Elizabeth Meshar, wife and mother. She was the Winged Lady of Sasel, knight, and keeper of the Heart of the Sky. Different names, different times, different roles. But always adventurous, and always a protector. She was Wings.

And she was too much for Edelfric.

His presence failed to repel hers, and a pulse of energy rippled through the forest as it accepted a new groveseed. With every passing second, Wings's connection to the Iron Forest grew stronger, and Edelfric's weakened.

The entire forest shook around her as Phoenix came running through the trees. A giant figure followed close behind him.

Edelfric stood over twenty feet tall, his towering form reminiscent of the copy he had sent to attack Sasel but somehow even more warped and twisted. He did not walk so much as wade through the ground. When he clenched his fist, whole trees responded, stooping to swipe at them. A dozen devices spread across the trees lit up with silver glyphs a moment before exploding in unison, releasing a single pink cloud of mushpowder equivalent to what Cutters Place usually produced in a year. Once Dietrich had taught him how it was made, most of Phoenix's preparations had been rush-designing and building a device that could produce the powder as quickly as possible, refining it from local silt and plant matter. The fruits of that effort were now on full display as Edelfric's entire lumbering form was swallowed in the cloud of the blast.

"Light him up!" Phoenix shouted.

The tree line erupted in a shattering staccato as Dietrich arrived with Phoenix's next contribution—a dozen modified crossbows, now slinging bolts of pure force and being carried by the bravest that Cutters Place had. At Dietrich's command, they focused their fire on Edelfric's legs, shredding the newly softened ironwood limbs and causing them to snap out from under him.

Edelfric crashed through several trees and gouged the earth where he fell, but already, the pieces of him that had been knocked away were regrowing. As long as he remained connected to the forest, it would sustain him. But now, Wings had a connection to the forest too.

And with a flex of her will, she severed his.

Her groveseed pulsed with power, burning away Edelfric's influence like a wildfire clearing brush. The atmosphere of hostility and rot vanished in a breath, replaced with a sense of ironclad safety and refuge. The Iron Forest was hers.

"NO!"

The Scourge's bellows shook the ground, even as bark and brush sloughed off his form. Wings held out her hands, and the wind carried her swords whistling into her waiting palms.

"Yes."

With rapidly fading size and strength, Edelfric swiped at all of them. Wings leapt clear of the blow, Phoenix blocked it on a hastily erected force shield, and the citizens of Cutters Place scattered.

All but Dietrich, who ducked beneath the attack and charged.

The Scourge of the Iron Forest struggled to stand, losing so much of himself that he now stood only twelve feet tall. Thorny spikes grew all along his arm, and Dietrich drew the weapon Phoenix had spent the last two days forging for him.

It had started life as a single-edged shortsword but now sported a wrapped grip on either side of an axe-head crossguard, so it resembled a fusion of axe and sword. Magic pulsed down the grooves carved into the edge of both the sword and axe blades, and Arcania runes spelled out the weapon's name along the flat of the blade. *Cutter.*

Dietrich danced around Edelfric's clumsy swings, hacking into the man's barkflesh with ease until a lucky swing knocked him back and put a dozen bleeding holes in his arm guard. He barely slowed down, flipping the weapon around to wield it like an axe.

He swung, and the axe head flew off the weapon, pirouetting through the air before burying itself in one of Edelfric's faceted eyes. With a scream, the monster lashed out with a whip-like limb. Dietrich dodged, undeterred even as he was forced further back. He gripped the remaining piece of his weapon in both hands and fingered an activation glyph in the hilt.

The axe head, still embedded in Edelfric's eye, lit up with arcane glyphs etched into it, as did similar symbols on the rest of Cutter in Dietrich's hand. Dietrich was lifted off his feet, carried through the air by his weapon as it flew to reunite with its missing piece.

Just as he closed the distance, Dietrich deactivated the pull and instead tumbled underneath Edelfric's attempts to bat him out of the air. He came up in a roll behind the monster and stabbed him through the back.

He danced around to Edelfric's front as he activated the weapon again, and this time, the axe head yanked itself free and flew to rejoin the rest of the weapon. Then Dietrich set to work.

His first swing cleaved an arm at the elbow. The next took out both the Scourge's kneecaps. With his third, he cut a gash deep into Edelfric's chest, exposing a glowing, sickly green bulb buried within. Edelfric's heart. His own twisted version of a groveseed.

The Scourge finally managed to bash Dietrich back with his remaining arm, but he struggled to stand and regrow what he had lost. He was the same height as the warden now. And as Dietrich got to his feet, he held out Cutter.

The axe head crossguard was missing from the weapon again. Because it was embedded in Edelfric's heart. Dietrich activated the weapon, and the axe head was yanked back—taking the heart with it. Edelfric let out a last, gargled cry as he desperately groped the air. The wooden, warped frame of his body creaked, stiffened, and then went still. The iridescent sheen of his eyes faded until they were nothing more than two hunks of dried, cloudy amber.

Stunned silence gave way to the cheers of the townsfolk as they surged forward to embrace Dietrich. They congratulated him, slapped him on the back, shouted his name. One particularly bold woman grabbed him by the face and pulled him into a kiss, which only made the townspeople cheer louder as he kissed her back. Phoenix felt like he was watching the entire town celebrate.

They had needed help to do it, but the people of Cutters Place had stood against the Scourge of the Iron Forest and won. The new mushpowder production machine was going to revolutionize the pace they could harvest ironwood. They had brave, competent defenders armed with arcane weaponry that could stand up to whatever the forest threw their way.

He was looking at the future of this place. A bright future that he'd helped build. That future would persist and grow, even without any further input from him. In the grand scheme of things, he hadn't done much, just given the town a few tools. But they were going to make a world of difference.

It terrified him, in some ways. He'd never intentionally built something for someone else with the express purpose of having this kind of impact. But it also excited him. It felt good. It felt *right*.

As if sensing that things were going too well, Ink's voice crackled into his messenger coil.

"Tell me you at least have some good news."

Phoenix's smile vanished at the exasperation in Ink's words.

"Edelfric's taken care of," Phoenix reported. "What happened?"

"What didn't?

INDEBTED

This wasn't Snow's first time being poisoned without Church or Phoenix on hand to take care of the problem. She was an assassin; it came with the job. Unfortunately, out of all the poisons she did have antidotes for, mindfire wasn't one of them. In her defense, she'd thought the only people that knew how to make it were dead.

Delirium in a few hours, total catatonia in twelve, death in twenty-four. That was the prognosis for a normal person poisoned by mindfire. But, as her first stroke of luck would have it, Snow hadn't been normal for more than a decade.

Even without actively channeling power from the Heart of Ice, her body ran incredibly cold, and her heart beat impossibly slow. Since realizing she'd been poisoned, Snow had been keeping herself as cold as possible without freezing herself solid. It dramatically slowed the spread of the poison and gave her enough clarity to think straight, but even that would only buy her time.

In a city like Nikos or Olwin, she could easily find the reagents needed to create an antidote or a priest who could expunge poison. But even running cold, she'd never make the trip. She needed someplace closer but well versed in dealing with weird shit and frequented by freelancers and the itinerant workers who tended to follow and profit off their exploits.

She needed a ruintown.

And that was her second stroke of luck. Because even though they hadn't been close to Nikos when the Cult of Stars attacked, they were close to the most renowned ruintown in East Corsar—Loraine, the town where the Servitor fell. At Snow's insistence, they'd diverted course, making a beeline for the town while she was still conscious. Even now, she could feel they were cutting it close. Her head felt sluggish. Wrong. A few more hours and the mindfire would become debilitating.

Crumbled remains of buildings dotted the road leading into town, breaking up the farmland. At the outskirts, there were little more than overgrown foundations and the odd hunk of a stone support, easily mistaken for a stray rock, but as they neared the town proper, entire walls and even a handful of mostly intact buildings stood, hollow and stripped of any salvageable materials.

"So, where to now?" The driver tossed the question out, unsure whether he was directing it at Vera or Snow.

Vera pulled open the curtain, eyeing the assassin. "So, don't take this personally . . ."

"You want me to leave before the cult takes another shot at me."

"I knew you'd understand," Vera said. "I like you, I really do, but not so much that I want any part of this."

It *was* understandable, from a cold, detached perspective. The Cult of Stars tested the nerve of anybody who came across them. People had gone *mad* contemplating the things they served. She couldn't blame Vera for wanting to get as far away from anything to do with them as possible. Even if having someone to watch her back while she was wounded would have been nice.

"I can manage from here."

She hopped clear of Vera's carriage, leaving behind frost on the seat cushion. Her movements were slow and plodding now. She was a step above a frozen corpse, only able to move thanks to her bond with the Heart of Ice. And even then, only barely.

That probably should have concerned her.

"If you survive, look me up in Olwin sometime. I'll buy you a round of drinks," Vera offered.

As Snow left, Kratz cast a glance at his employer, who immediately glared at him.

"Oh, don't look at me like that," Vera said. "She's a smart woman. She'll be fine. The last thing we need to do is get mixed up in cult shit. I've got plenty of my own nightmare fuel to deal with."

Nearly every structure in town was reclaimed from the original ruins the town had been founded on. Some were beautiful restoration jobs, with expertly remodeled architecture and cracks in old structures filled with brightly colored materials and metals, giving them the appearance of veins. Others were more haphazard with hastily slapped together scaffolding and precarious braces holding things up and mismatched thatch covering up holes in roofs.

The second kind still dominated the town, but there were a lot more nice-looking buildings now than there had been the last time Snow had been here. Ruintowns often initially exploded around large sites as collectors and rippers did their work and other people came in to supply and profit off them. But the sites were usually abandoned once everything useful had been extracted. Loraine was looking to be one of the rare examples that bucked the trend. The biggest scavengers were gone, but plenty of other people had chosen to stay, put down roots, and adapt their business models to be less directly dependent on the ruins.

It didn't change the fact that Loraine was still a ruintown in its bones. This was a place glintchasers and other opportunists had frequented, digging up and attracting all sorts of trouble and strange occurrences, and that left a mark on a settlement even after those glintchasers and opportunists moved on. You could always count on a ruintown to have things a normal town might not, to say nothing of the townsfolk who'd seen some shit and learned to deal with it. Snow was confident she could find what she needed *somewhere*.

Stopping on a street corner, she didn't immediately spot a church or alchemist. But what she did see across the street, standing still while the tide of foot traffic flowed around him, was a man in a hooded cloak staring directly at her. On its own, that might not have raised any alarms—she was a human cold front in the middle of summer, and she looked like a walking corpse right now. Even in a ruintown, that would at least draw eyes. No. What set Snow off was the tip of a familiar scar on the man's forehead just barely peeking out from under his hood.

Once she saw him, it was easy to spot the others. A woman peering out from an alleyway where people were hanging laundry to dry. Another man standing amid a crowd of people waiting for a food cart to serve them. All dressed in the same robes, all sporting the same carving on their forehead, all looking right at her.

The Cult of Stars had come to finish the job.

When Snow moved, so did they, keeping on her trail without getting too close. Even moving slow, with a constant bubble of space around her from people avoiding her, she could lose one or even two of them for long stretches of time as she ducked through alleyways, clumsily clambered over fences, and slipped in and out of establishments. But she never lost all three of them, not for long.

And now *she* was lost. No matter where she looked, she was never quite sure if she'd seen a location before or just something like it. Slowing a poison's spread wasn't the same as neutralizing it, and the mindfire had been in her system for a while now. She was sloppy, unfocused, and only getting worse with every passing moment.

It almost took too long for her to realize they were corralling her away from the heart of the town, where there would be fewer people to get in the way of any potential murder. Already, the crowds had thinned, and her pursuers were growing bolder, getting closer.

In response, she moved *farther* away from the protective cover of witnesses and then down the first alley with no easy way out, effectively cornering herself. Then, all she had to do was wait.

The man came around the corner, knife already drawn, and she stepped forward to meet him.

She'd never be able to fight properly this stiff and cold, so she didn't try. Instead, she came at her pursuer as open-stanced as she could and let him stab her straight through the chest. Two benefits of turning herself into a walking icicle: no fear and no pain.

She took the knife without so much as flinching.

For his trouble, her pursuer got to watch as ice crawled up his knife, freezing his hand to the hilt.

Without malice or even much rush, she jammed her own blade up through the man's jaw and into his brain. Frost spread out from the point of entry, and by the time she withdrew her dagger, the man's head was frozen solid.

She pulled herself off the man's own knife, closing the wound up with more ice.

One down.

Her head was starting to swim again. Not much, and only fleetingly, but it was enough to remind her that kill hadn't cost her nothing. She was trapped in an alleyway with no way out but through her pursuers, she had a new hole in her chest that was only temporarily sealed, and there was even more mindfire in her veins.

She didn't have the time or emotional capacity to be worried about that.

By the time the other two cultists came into the alleyway, Snow was nowhere to be seen. The two of them stopped for a moment until the woman had the idea to glance up in time to see Snow, sticking to the side of the building by her frozen hands and feet.

Snow pushed off the wall, dropping down on the both of them with a dagger in each hand. It might have worked against people who were easier to kill. But nothing ever seemed to phase the Cult of Stars.

The man and woman both leapt clear of Snow's ambush before immediately reengaging. In any other circumstance, she'd have simply blinked out of the way. But she couldn't blink. She could barely move. So instead, Snow froze the ground around her, locking both of the cultists in place just before their weapons could reach her. Then she covered herself in a protective layer of thick frost and made a clumsy grab for the woman's throat.

Ice spread where she touched as the woman immediately began slashing. The frost armor did its job, blunting the woman's strikes enough to keep anything from going too deep. And all the while, Snow kept spreading ice across the woman's face. Completely freezing a person from the outside took a good amount of time—too much time, usually. But Snow wasn't trying to freeze the woman's whole body.

Just her throat.

The woman's mouth opened, but no sound escaped it as her windpipe froze shut. She flailed, jerked, and stabbed for all she was worth. She left Snow's face and arm a crosshatched mess of frozen blood. But none of it changed the fact that she'd already drawn her last breath.

Two down.

Snow staggered away, aware in the back of her mind there was something she was forgetting just as a cloud of silver smoke appeared in front of her, and from it emerged a man's hand, holding a stiletto knife on a collision course with her face.

She took another step back away from it, only for a pair of arms to wrap around her from behind as she backed straight into the waiting arms of the last cultist.

He had to be giving himself frostbite with every second he was touching her, but if he felt it or cared, he gave no indication as he drove his knife into her chest. She froze the knife in place, if only to keep him from stabbing her again. He switched tactics, coiling an arm around her neck.

Her body was surviving with virtually no circulation. She wasn't going to suffocate anytime soon. But, she realized too late, he could probably still break her neck before she could freeze him solid.

She stabbed once behind herself, hoping to get a killing blow and missing. A second attempt took out his eye but didn't go deep enough to kill. He adjusted his hold and lifted her off her feet as he prepared for the final jerk.

And then, in Snow's third and final stroke of luck, a large metallic arm shot out from the corner of her vision, transforming into a gleaming blade that cleaved through the cultist's arms at the elbows. Snow dropped away from the man, along with his severed limbs, and rolled away in time to spot a familiar face beneath the hood of a cloak. Autostructs were seven-foot-tall machines that walked like people, and this one in particular had crossed Snow's path more than once. Its body was different now—a cobbled-together construction of different design styles, some parts made with ornately carved ceramics, others with scraped and bare steel—but its face was the same. Like a metal approximation of a human face with a hinged jaw and two glowing, golden orbs for eyes. Gamma swiped his armblade, cutting a thin line along the cultist's neck. The man gurgled once and collapsed into a pool of his own blood.

Three down.

"I request that you do not decapitate me as you did in our previous meeting," Gamma said flatly as his arm transformed back into a normal hand. "It would be counterproductive."

In reply, Snow blacked out.

DRESS REHEARSAL

nk, Quint, Church, and Brass stood outside of a large dock warehouse in Puerto Oro that ostensibly stored sugarcane and coffee. According to Quint, this was where Kurien and the Cord had been consolidating the weapons they'd been collecting over the past weeks. Assuming they weren't out collecting more right now, this would be where to find them. As a precaution, Church and Ink had asked local town watch and clergy to clear the area of foot traffic which had left the entire section of the dockyard eerily quiet, save for the cries of a few seagulls and the creak of a ship's hull.

Ink stepped to the front of the group, arcane sigils slowly spinning up around her hands as blue sparks began to leap between her fingertips. "Seeing as surprise is definitely out with an evacuation this obvious, we might as well just knock."

With a single ear-splitting boom, a bolt of lightning arced out from Ink's outstretched fingertips, blasting the warehouse doors—and a sizable portion of the walls—to smithereens. Chunks of stone and wood rained down in the aftermath of the blast, and fire licked at the edges of the massive hole left behind.

Terse shouts rang out from inside the warehouse as unseen people called out their status movements to one another, using quick, efficient phrasing that gave away as little information to the attacking freelancers as possible. It was the coordinated communication of a trained fighting force. Of the Cord of Aenwyn.

Quint tightened his grip on his spear. "Here they come."

Church tried to remember the names of the Cord that Quint had given them as they emerged from the smoke and flames. Spike—a muscular girl sporting a pair of knuckle dusters. Drummer—a big, old man with a big, old hammer. Squid—a sea sorcerer with blue skin. There was a figure dressed in all white with a Faceless mask. Their name, he forgot. There was an archer with too many quivers, a woman with too many knives, and a man with an unusually long rapier. Sting, Point, and Fang, though which was which, he wasn't clear.

And bringing up their rear, swathed in a flowing purple and white shawl with her face obscured behind her mask, was Kurien, the Prince Killer herself.

"How spectacular!" Kurien cackled before bowing with a flourish. "My deepest welcome to my greatest adversaries! And you've brought friends! Oh, I would love to stay and reminisce, but sadly, I must be off. I have a show to prepare for."

"You're going nowhere!" Quint growled.

"Not to worry! I never leave an audience without a performance to enjoy. Everyone?"

The Cord of Aenwyn's heads snapped to her as one.

"Stick to the script. Kill them, and leave the cargo to me."

With a flourish of her shawl, the Prince Killer vanished. The Cord of Aenwyn charged.

Brass crossed blades with Fang and Point, holding his own until Fang opened his mouth and breathed fire.

Ohh. Fang as in dragon. Shit.

Zealot and the sword's ethereal duplicate were a blur around Church as he faced off against the masked Faceless, who fought with a pair of scythed blades and seemed to anticipate Church's every move before he made it. Quint found himself somersaulting to dodge both hunks of earth and arrows while Ink was wielding her threads like an impossibly long, constantly twirling whip to keep both Squid and Spike at bay. As the fight raged on, a hole burst open in the warehouse's roof as an oversized chest flew up from inside. The chest froze in midair, hovering over the warehouse, until it was joined by another chest bursting out of its own hole in the roof. Then came another and another until there were dozens of chests all hovering above the warehouse.

When the chests finally stopped emerging from the warehouse, Kurien herself rematerialized on the roof, arms spread wide in an invitation to behold her.

"Lovely rehearsal, everyone!" the Prince Killer cackled. "I look forward to seeing you all onstage!"

Then, with a snap of Kurien's fingers, the chests flew out over the dockyard, rushing for the deck of a ship moored at the edge of the docks. One of the chests dipped lower as it flew, and Kurien leapt on top of it as casually as someone taking the next step on a flight of stairs. The chest flew off to join the others on the boat, taking her with it.

"She's getting away!" Church shouted.

"Stop her!" Ink shouted. "Quint and I will handle the Cord!"

"All yours!" Brass shouted.

With Ink and Quint covering them, the Starbreakers disengaged from the fight to race after Kurien. The mind-controlled members of the Cord tried to pursue, only to meet a wall of magic and spear points.

"You realize it's now seven against two, correct?" Quint asked.

"Well, darling," Ink said as her threads crackled with lightning, "for both our sakes, let's hope you've let the Cord fall to shit while I've been away."

"You know I haven't."

Ink smiled. "Hm. Let's take the children to school anyway, shall we?"

Kurien's ship was already moving as Church and Brass neared the end of the docks, but neither of them slowed down as they approached the edge. With Church saying a prayer to grant them strength, the two men leaped after the parting boat. They soared out over the water, cleared the ship's railing, and landed on the deck with their swords drawn.

"You know, it's customary to ask the captain permission before coming aboard her ship."

At the sound of Kurien's voice, Brass and Church drew close to each other. It sounded like it came from everywhere at once. In searching for the Prince Killer, they both made a startling realization about their surroundings.

A ship as large as this one should have had a crew of around a dozen sailors, but there was no sign of anyone on deck. The only sounds were the groans and creaks of wood, the rustle of wind on the sails, and the sound of waves crashing against the hull. Meanwhile, rigging tugged and secured itself, adjusting the sails as the ship pulled out of the harbor, and at the helm, the wheel was rotating of its own accord, steering the ship clear of any obstacles.

The ship was sailing itself.

"Though, I suppose I'm willing to forgive the slight given the joyful circumstances."

Again, Kurien's voice resonated from seemingly every direction, impossible to place. They could hear the smile in it, the wicked delight she was taking from their confusion.

Church exchanged a look with Brass, who jerked his head. Together, the two of them advanced along the deck of the ship, keeping their eyes peeled.

"Really?" Brass called out, trying to keep Kurien talking. "What's the occasion?"

"Why, our reprisal!"

Kurien's laughing voice danced around them, like she was circling them, always staying just out of sight. "The greatest artist to ever take the stage of murder, reunited with the only foes who ever made for her match. I knew when I embarked on this journey I would find enemies. After all, what's a villain without heroes to challenge? But I was preparing to have to make due with whatever scraps could be pulled away from the task of pursuing my fellow inmates. Not in my wildest dreams did I imagine *we* could be together again. Please, tell me the others are with you. On their way now?"

"Sorry. Just the two of us," Brass apologized. "Everyone else was busy."

A deep, sorrowful sigh. "Shame. But the show must go on. And with any luck, we can bring them back into the fold before the final act."

"Are you sure you want that? I mean, we were a lot worse at this the last time we stopped you," Brass mused. "If all of us turned up, that's your show over."

"Ah, but I've also honed my craft. There's not much else for one to do in Oblivion but think and reflect. I've reviewed all my performances—every step, every angle, every drop of blood. I've focused my art within my mind's eye, expanded its potency. It's precision. Look around you! Controlling this entire ship is *nothing* to me now."

Kurien had always used magic to puppet objects, most typically the weapons she employed in her murders, but never to the extent of controlling something this big and complex. If she wasn't lying about sailing the ship—and Church didn't think she was—then her power and control really had grown. By a lot.

"And, of course, there are the *other* instruments I've acquired."

Shadowy black tendrils swirled around them, engulfing the ship on all sides and swallowing the sky above them. All at once, everything went dark, and the sounds of the ship and sea that they'd been hearing went silent. The air became stale and stiff, and the tropical temperature dropped away to a completely neutral, temperate nothing. Neither hot nor cold. There was no smell of salt from the sea. There was no smell of anything.

"Brass?" Church's voice sounded too flat, devoid of any reverb as if the air itself was swallowing the sound and stopping it from bouncing off of anything.

"You're gonna have to speak up. I can't see," came Brass's reply. He was still directly behind him but just as oddly flat sounding.

Church prayed for vision to pierce the darkness for Brass and himself and was rewarded with a black and white view of the deck of the ship—and nothing but black void beyond it. The ship still moved and rolled as if it were on the water, but there was no sound and no sign of the waves beyond the rails.

"A wonderful toy, isn't it?" Kurien's voice called out to them, the only sound so far to have any kind of echo. "I'm only just beginning to experiment with what this Heart can do. But already, it's borne such wonders.

"When you first stopped me from completing my task and saved the young Prince Roland from his untimely demise, I *despaired*," Kurien admitted. "If ever there was a family that needed to be humbled, it was the 'Great Unifier' Roland and his illustrious 'Warrior Queen' Katherine. And yet, I was foiled. I thought that perhaps my tale would be a tragedy. The genius stopped at the height of her potential. If my defeat hadn't at least come with the honor of christening the kingdom's greatest heroes, I might not have stayed sane."

Church opted not to voice his opinions on Kurien's sanity.

"To be the force which forged a set of legends—that was a respectable legacy. How ironic then that it would be *you* great heroes who humbled the crown as even I never could! What is the crippling of a son compared to the annihilation of a city! I'll say it, I was jealous of you. I have broken the powerful and the proud. Reduced queens and emperors to sobbing wreckages. But now, everything has fallen into place just so. My target, clinging desperately to dignity in the Parthican capital. My weapon, forged by one of my greatest foes. And now, you, the perfect opposition. This will be my true denouement! The masterpiece that sears my name into the mind of every seat of power in the world."

As quickly as it emerged, the black void vanished, and a world of light and color and sound and smell came rushing back at them in full force. It was so disorienting, it took them a moment to notice Kurien, now standing before them, a dozen different weapons floating in the air behind her, arranged in a neat, slowly rotating circle of blades and spikes. She had one hand poised behind her back, and the other was wielding a kitbashed cross between a crossbow and an Old World force blaster that Church and Brass both recognized in an instant.

"Is that—?" Church never got a chance to finish the question as Kurien aimed Phoenix's old weapon and pulled the trigger.

A bolt of pure force launched out of the weapon, striking Church dead center and sending him flying back with a hole in his breastplate. Brass advanced, only to be forced to halt and parry as a chakram came flying out from behind Kurien's back, nearly taking his head off. The bladed disc circled Brass like an angry hornet, forcing him back while Kurien casually backed away and aimed her next shot.

On the ground, Church coughed out a healing prayer to seal the hole in his sternum and staggered to his feet. Phoenix's current wand had a regulator built into its force blasts, letting him dial the power up or down as needed. His old weapon only ever fired with lethal force, and it was a small miracle Kurien hadn't killed him with that first blast. Before he could even thank Beneger that he'd lived, a flying scimitar came whirling through the air for his neck, and he only barely managed to block it.

Church and Brass fought against a small swarm of animated flying weaponry hounding them on all sides and forcing them back whenever they tried to get close to Kurien. Meanwhile, the Prince Killer danced at the edge of the fight, taking pot shots with Phoenix's weapon whenever she fancied. They dodged what they could with Zealot even managing to parry one blast out of the air, but for the most part, they used what obstacles there were on deck as cover. At least until Kurien inevitably sent a flying weapon to drive them out of it.

Brass found an opening first. In between parrying away a chakram and ducking under a greatsword, he hurled a knife from his belt straight for Kurien, only for Kurien to blink out of sight right in front of them and reappear behind Church.

Church swung and had his blow intercepted by another of Kurien's puppeteered blades. Zealot created a spectral copy of itself in midair, forged from its own divine energy, but it, too, was intercepted by one of Kurien's weapons. The Prince Killer answered with a lunging step forward, shoving Church hard in the chest with an outstretched palm.

For a moment, the void returned, and the world went black and white around Church as he fell backward. Then color and clarity returned as he crashed into Brass, who only a second ago had been on the other side of the ship.

No, Brass hadn't moved. Kurien had moved *Church*.

Brass and Church both tumbled to the ground in a tangle of arms and legs, and Kurien vanished into thin air with a cackle. So did every weapon that had been flying around the ship. Experience told them it was too much to hope that Kurien was simply gone.

Sure enough, Brass yelped as something slashed through his shirt and left a fresh gash across his ribs. One of Kurien's swords reappeared, its edge now wet with his blood.

"Shit!" Brass swore.

He sidestepped on instinct and swung through the space he'd been standing in a second ago. Either by luck or perfect prediction, Brass's sword found another invisible weapon in midflight, knocking it off course and rendering it visible once again. Between Brass's instincts and Zealot's supernatural sense of the battlefield, the two of them revealed most of the weapons before they could land a hit.

The operative word being *most*. Church tried to heal the wounds they did incur, but he'd only recovered so much after the Red Lady, and he'd burned most of that reserve fighting the Cord. He was already starting to feel the early onset of fatigue from overuse of divine power. The dizziness, the feverish heat behind his face, Beneger's worried expression hovering at the back of his mind.

They had to end this quickly. Or Kurien was going to end it for them.

"On me!" Church yelled to Brass before praying to turn his skin as hard as stone.

As soon as he felt the prayer's effects take hold, Church charged straight at Kurien. Weapons flew through the air to intercept him, but he paid them almost no mind, only raising an arm to shield his face and letting Zealot and its hovering spectral copy do what it could to parry without slowing him down. Brass, picking up on Church's plan, moved to cover him, since the priest clearly wasn't going to cover himself.

Brass and Zealot managed to parry a few attacks, but the rest of the weapons all found their targets. The prayer kept any of the hits from going deep, but every weapon still left a wound in his flesh. Brass ignored it, powered straight through, and finally managed to grab a hold of Kurien while using Zealot to knock the weapon out of her hand.

For a moment, he had her.

And then Phoenix's blaster froze in midair, righted itself, and fired a blast, straight through Brass and into Church.

The two men staggered, and Kurien, like a maestro conducting the end of a symphony, drew her arms up and then out, commanding every weapon at her disposal to follow the same, sweeping arc. Each weapon gave a spin in midair to flick blood off their edges and then flew back into a resting, upright position behind Kurien, framing her like a set of jagged metal wings.

The two Starbreakers were both lying on the deck, surrounded by their own blood.

"Okay," Brass grunted. "I'll admit. That was a nice move."

Kurien chuckled and held out her hand. Phoenix's weapon spun around and flew grip-first back into the Prince Killer's waiting palm.

"Well, this has been fun, but destiny awaits us in Parthica." She raised the weapon high, almost as if in salute. "You can keep this ship if you like. There's a faster-looking one a little ways out I can use instead, and I've got another trick with my new toy I want to try."

A wave of black shadow rolled across the ship. The dark, silent void returned once again, and when it passed, Kurien, all of her weapons, and every chest from the warehouse were gone. For a few seconds, the only sounds were the waves of the ocean and the pained, exhausted pants of the two men lying bleeding on the deck.

Brass broke the silence first. "Church?"

"Hm?"

"I think we just got our asses kicked."

THE DREAD KNIGHT

Out of the five members the Seven Gates had sent to apprehend Lestrade, Angel had only found three. And only two were alive.

Angel didn't really know anyone in the knightly order so much as know of them. But she'd fought alongside them at the Battle of Loraine, and from that and the scattered accounts she'd heard over the years, they seemed like decent people. Good in a fight. She hoped the Church of Avelina could do something for them.

She told herself it was the element of surprise that had been the order's undoing. They'd expected a scribbler. They'd gotten something far worse.

She knew what she was walking into. More than that, she was Angel. She'd kicked the ass of every other escapee she'd tracked down without breaking a sweat. She was the reason the Starbreakers had won half their battles.

She could handle this.

"All right. Stay fucking put," she said, looking pointedly at the two stowaways who'd developed a habit of sneaking out of the Star to watch her fights. "And find a barrel or box we can put the helmet in when I bring it back."

Thalia nodded. "Be careful."

"Yeah," Angel responded.

She marched out into the mountains, wondering if she shouldn't have just left the three of them back at the Church of Avelina when she had the chance.

Too late now.

The helm of the dread knight housed a spirit—of what, the Academy wasn't sure. But it possessed whoever wore the helmet, and it was drawn to places where armies had fallen, where it usually raised an army of undead to wage war on anything in a hundred-mile radius. Now that the helm had Lestrade's body, that would be its next move. She had to stop it before that happened.

A quick talk with Ink over the message coil gave her the location of a mountain pass not too far away that fit the bill. Some two hundred years ago, a historically massive raiding band from Frelheim had pushed its way south into Corsar, only to be routed and near-slaughtered by the Order of Saint Ricard. If the Dread Knight wanted an army of fallen warriors, that would be the closest place to get it.

Angel had brought the Rusted Star as close to the pass as she dared and then walked the rest of the way. There was only one real path leading to the site. All she had to do was find a spot along it with decently favorable terrain and wait.

The Dread Knight didn't keep her waiting long.

Only an hour passed before a dark armored figure rounded the bend, marching straight toward her. Even at a distance, Angel felt the shift in the air as it approached. The same sickening wrongness that permeated the vault the helmet had been stored in followed it like a stormfront, growing stronger with every heavy metal footfall. Its armor was slimly profiled, black and jagged, evoking a skeletal bird of prey in its design. Tattered strips of cloth that might have once been a cloak fluttered off it, like the last molted bits of feather on long-decayed wings. Despite all that, it cut a surprisingly lanky figure, exaggerating the stretched, spindly silhouette of his shadow in the setting sun.

Her whole body was burning now, from her fingertips to her collarbone to her toes. Every fiber of her screamed for her to fight, but she held it back. She kept it contained, just a little longer.

It came to stop maybe twenty yards down from her. Eyes like blue-burning coals glowered at her from underneath its helmet. It spoke with two voices at once: Lestrade's and the helm's. One old and raspy, the other a rolling, metallic baritone.

"Sentinel. You cannot stop me. Not alone."

So, this thing knew what she was, and it wasn't worried. "We'll see."

Now her own voice echoed, doubled in much the same way as the Dread Knight's.

Finally, she let the pressure inside her release. Divine fury flowed through her veins like a drug, explosive and searing. A corona of golden light danced across her skin as her eyes became a pair of blazing suns, and a burning halo roared to life over her head. Everything else went up in a flash in her mind, leaving only the Dread Knight and a single set of truths: there was good, and there was evil. Where there was good, it must be protected. Where there was evil, it must be destroyed.

She leapt from her perch with a growl, aiming straight for the Dread Knight. It caught her glowing fist in its gauntlet, and they both flashed with light where they touched. Loose dirt around them danced from the impact, but the Dread Knight itself did not budge an inch.

It answered with a cross and a backhand, both across her face, each one landing with a resounding crack. Angel grunted, caught the next blow before it hit her, and landed a punch dead center in the knight's chest. This time, she staggered it, but not by much. It brought both of its fists down on top of her head and then kneed her under the chin.

She stumbled backward, unsteady on her feet and tasting blood. She was barely able to keep track of the Dread Knight as it lurched after her and unleashed a flurry of blows. She blocked some, answered a few. But most found their mark, cracking her across the ribs, the arms, and the face. All the while, the burning, searing divine wrath flowed through her veins. Normally, she would at least try to temper it, reign it in and keep it from burning right through her. But now, she just let it keep flowing, letting the fire inside her grow brighter and hotter, until she was blazing like a sun as she traded blows with the cursed helm and its puppet body. Because the more her power hurt her, the harder she hit.

It was a good way to burn herself out, but she was far past the point of caring about that. There was only the monster in front of her and the need to see it wiped from the face of the world. It didn't matter how much she hurt, so long as the Dread Knight went down sooner than she did.

It hit her again and again, but the longer the fight dragged on, the less she felt it. And when she hit back, she felt its dark armor buckle beneath her fists. With every punch, she willed the bastard to fall. To die. To burn.

The Dread Knight slammed her face-first into the rocky mountainside, cracking the stone and causing a brief shock of pain as her messenger coil crunched into scrap metal under the blow. She shoved him off and returned the favor, but she went the extra mile and dragged it across the rock, carving away stone with its metal face. When she ran out of mountain, she jerked its head back and let loose twin beams of light from her eyes straight into its face, screaming as she did.

Its hands groped meekly at her wrists as its knees began to buckle. The faceplate of the helmet began to glow red hot. Then yellow. Then white.

And then a tusk twice the size of her body slammed into her, and she went cartwheeling through the air.

Her halo fizzled out, and the light faded from her body as she tumbled across the dirt and rock, losing track of which way was up, until she finally came to stop face down in the ground, smoke curling off her body. Her breath came out in ragged fits and starts. All at once, she felt lighter than she was supposed to.

One thought cut through the fog of pain and exhaustion fast forming in her mind:

The fuck was that?

She staggered to her feet and wondered whether it was the heatstroke or blows to the head fucking with her.

Because bearing down on her was a reanimated, undead mammoth. Its bones were wrapped in long dried out, decayed strips of flesh, and the patchwork remnants of armor clattered like chimes against its body. Its eyes had long since rotted away, but in their sockets were two bright orbs of light identical in color to the Dread Knight's. With a sinking feeling in her stomach, Angel realized that they must have been closer to the fallen Frelheim army than she'd thought.

A lifetime ago, Angel had gotten to see a Frelheim war mammoth up close and thought it was actually kind of cool. Now, she changed her mind.

She widened her stance, dug in her heels, and bent low just in time to catch hold of one of the monstrosity's tusks with both hands. Her arms and legs buckled under the impact, and she went skidding backward, but she stayed on her feet. With a groan, she shifted her weight and pushed with everything she had, using the mammoth's own momentum to throw it aside. As she struggled to right herself, her chest heaved and her lungs burned. She prayed the thing would stay down, at least long enough for her to catch her breath.

"Weak."

The Dread Knight extended a hand, and blue-black wisps of smoke curled out of its gauntlet until they formed and solidified into a two-handed sword, its black blade shining like a mirror as wisps of smoke trailed off its edge. It crossed the gap between them with a burst of speed, and Angel only just managed to sidestep its swing. Refusing to be forced into a retreat, Angel tracked the next swing and caught the blade in her hands, feeling it bite into her as she did.

The weapon shook as each of them tried to yank it away from the other, leaving them both held in place. Blood ran down Angel's palms, but she only tightened her grip and pulled harder.

"You cannot contain your own power," the Dread Knight taunted. "Your mortal coil cannot withstand it. My helm has no such limitation."

"Shut. Up," Angel growled through clenched teeth.

She kicked the Dread Knight in the knee, buckling it and throwing him off balance enough to pry the sword from his hands. It dissipated to nothing between her fingers and rematerialized in his hand once more. She charged, hoping to get a hit in before he could force her back. She was too slow.

The tip of the knight's sword sank into her shoulder and then twisted as he yanked it out. As she stumbled from the hit, the Dread Knight neatly stepped around her and raked its blade across her back, tearing a scream from her throat.

"Do you know why your power is so ill-suited to your form? Why you are so hampered? Because I *chose* this path. I conspired to have this vessel forged to be my means of remaining in this world without violating the Laws. But you had no choice."

Angel screamed and let out another burst of light from her eyes, which the Dread Knight deflected with the flat of its blade.

"Humans think Sentinels are blessings from the gods. It is a lie told to hide the great shame of all your kind. There is no room in the armies of the gods for any who cannot fulfill their duty. True soldiers of the gods remain at their posts, but your kind obsesses with this world. With the scavengers that call it home. You were banished to the place of your obsession, condemned to rot in a human form. You did not descend from the heavens as a savior. You were flung from them in disgrace."

Angel surged forward, propelled more by pain than determination. She managed to dodge and weave through the Dread Knight's guard, knock the sword from its hands, and wrench it into a headlock. The helmet was the vessel for the Dread Knight's spirit and power. Deprive it of a host and it was just a brooding, self-righteous metal bucket. It could say whatever it wanted about her. It wasn't anything she hadn't heard before. It couldn't hurt her. Not more than her family had. Or her order. Or her company. Or herself.

At least, that was what she thought. Until it formed its sword in its hands once again and drove it into its own chest and straight on through into hers.

Her breath hitched, sending shooting pain up and down her nerves. All traces of fire and fury she'd felt still inside her were snuffed out at once. She couldn't breathe right. She was tired. And cold.

The Dread Knight yanked its blade back out, removing the skewer that held them together. Angel staggered back, unsteady on her feet. Blood dribbled down her chin. If the Dread Knight noticed the wound it had made in its own chest, it gave no indication. It made no advance on her. It simply stood, sword in hand, waiting. Its eyes burned their cold, unfeeling blue.

Angel clenched her fists, trying to will some power back into them. Light sputtered across her skin, only to give out. Her head spun, and she nearly collapsed then and there. And then, the dirt around her began to stir.

It was just one spot at first. Then several. All around her, things began to poke out from the earth. Bony, weathered hands. The top of a skull. The jagged, rusted remnants of a sword.

They were *much* closer to the fallen Frelheim army than she'd thought.

All around them, skeletal warriors were clawing their way out of the ground, every one of their eyes matching the burning orbs of their master. One hand coming out of the ground grabbed her ankle, and in trying to kick free, she tripped and fell face-first into the ground. Not nearly far enough away, the mammoth began to rise to its feet.

Every heartbeat felt like a hammer driving another nail into her coffin. Angel grit her teeth, unable to taste or smell anything but her own blood as she willed her rapidly numbing arms and legs to move, to act, to stand up and fight. They refused to obey. The Dread Knight and its rapidly rising army stood over her, not even bothering to finish her off themselves.

With a last, desperate cry, Angel tried to leap to her feet and was rewarded for her efforts with a boot to the face that sent her sprawling backward. Her forehead cracked against a rock, and the wind was knocked out of her good lung. As she tried and failed to push herself up, Angel thought back to the Rusted Star, which wouldn't be far from here. She thought about Thalia and Ruby and Bart still waiting for her to return, blissfully unaware of the undead army that would be headed right for them now. They would be dead before they could even understand what was happening.

It was enough to get her onto her hands and knees, not that she had a damn clue what she would do even if she could stand. She was outnumbered, outmatched, and out of strength. She was—charitably—missing half a lung and too much blood. But she refused to die lying down.

Her eyes flickered and flared. The Dread Knight cocked its head.

"It is over, Sentinel." It leveled its sword at her, readying for a final stroke. "You are going home now. Perhaps this time, they will let you stay."

"Fuck you."

Her whole body erupted in a corona of golden light as her halo returned, and beams from her eyes carved into the mountainside surrounding them. She only managed about a second of a burst, but it was enough. The rock groaned and rumbled under its own weight, suddenly too weak to support itself. With a thunderous crack, a portion of the mountain sheared off, tumbling down onto all of them in a massive rockslide. The Dread Knight growled in sudden fury, and Angel smiled as she collapsed.

She never hit the ground. Instead, pricks and stings of pain danced across her skin as something wound tight around her whole body and yanked her off her feet and away from the Dread Knight. It took her a second to find the source—a long, sickly black vine with red thorns biting into her. And holding tight to the other end was Ruby, pulling like her life depended on it.

Bart was at her side, pulling on the vine right along with her even as the thorns sliced his palms open. And behind both of them was the Rusted Star and Thalia standing in its doorway, shouting for them to hurry.

Son of a bitch. They had one job.

She tried to yell at them, but the only thing that escaped her lips was more blood. Ruby and Bart finally dragged her close enough for them to grab her. Angel was vaguely aware of skeletal figures chasing after them as they all retreated into the Star and shut the doors behind them.

"Is she alive?"

"She—I think she's breathing."

"Oh my gods. Oh my gods."

Banging on the walls. Undead maybe. Bad maybe. She was so tired.

"We need to move! Thalia!"

"I'm trying! Just worry about her! Don't let her die!"

"Bart, what do we do?"

Her pain was gone now. Gone away, numb and cold and tingly. She breathed out. Forgot to breathe back in.

"Bart? Do something!"

"I am! I just—I'm trying to remember the words!"

"What words! What are you—?"

A dull warmth trickled through her chest, removing the numbness and leaving her with a deep, throbbing ache. The faintest hint of energy came to her, like a little fit of movement in between trying to fall asleep. It was enough to keep her awake just long enough to feel her stomach lurch and to hear a sound like rumbling earth all around her.

Then everything went quiet.

SENTINEL

"**O**^{w.}"

Monica winced as Sir Richard wiped the scrape on her arm with an alcohol-soaked rag. The cleaning stung, but it wasn't nearly as bad as her own pride, which was in shambles. She'd hurt herself training.

Again.

It was almost impressive how many times she'd done it, given how ostensibly durable she was. But as it turned out, one of the few things strong enough to hurt her was herself, and it was starting to look like that was the only talent training with Sir Richard was honing. It was such a simple, basic technique for a paladin: funneling the divine power of Renalt into her body and weapon to enhance her strikes. The worst an apprentice should have been able to mess it up was not summoning enough power and being left with a weak attack.

Monica's practice axe had exploded in her hand.

"Stop your whining," the knight said. "Getting the wound hurt twice as much, and you made half as much noise."

"That was different," the girl muttered. She winced again but managed to stay quiet this time. "Can't we just let the priest heal me?"

"There are better uses of Renalt's power than cleaning up your messes," Richard scolded. "And besides, there isn't always going to be a priest around to pray you all better. Best to learn how to get by without one now."

"This is so stupid," Monica said. Another wipe, another wince. "Why can't I just stop?"

"And let all your progress be for nothing? I won't allow it. You were born for this, Monica."

"If I was born for it, why am I so bad at it?"

"You've only just started your training. Mastering most of these techniques takes years of—"

"That's not what I meant, and you know it!" Monica yanked her arm free of Richard's grasp as her threadbare patience broke, and she shot him a demanding glare. "Why am I like this? Why . . . why does it hurt?"

Her voice cracked for just half a syllable. In seconds, all traces of the fire in her glare melted away, leaving only a young girl, tall for her age and yet so small. Sturdier than some armors, stronger than half a dozen men, and scared out of her wits.

Richard leaned back in his seat as his brow furrowed. They weren't talking about her arm anymore.

When Richard or even Hilda called on the Vigilant Saint for power, the strength of Renalt flowed through them and their weapons. Using it tired them, sure. Hilda especially could barely maintain it for a few swings. But it was still pure empowerment while they were using it. Whenever Monica summoned power, she got stronger, but it felt like she was burning up from the inside out.

She knew it wasn't supposed to be like that. From the moment she was old enough to understand the world around her, she'd known she was different. Her parents, her village, and Richard all said she was special. But the more she trained under Sir Richard, the more aspects of being a paladin she managed to fuck up or just hate, and the more she just felt wrong.

"It's likely my fault," the old knight said.

"How?"

"At its core, you use the same power the same way as any paladin. Divine presence fills your body, makes you stronger and faster and harder than you could ever be on your own. And because of that, I've tried to teach you to use it the same way I've been teaching Hilda," Richard explained. "But the more this keeps happening, the more I've thought about it, and by now, I have to conclude that even in this, you aren't like Hilda. Or me or anyone."

"Because I'm a . . ." Monica paused, trying and failing to remember the word Richard had given it.

"A Sentinel, yes," Richard finished for her. "You have the body of a human, Monica, but you have the soul of an angel. And that soul comes with power. I've been acting under the impression that angels draw on Renalt's power at least similarly to how we do. But there is another theory regarding them and the Sentinels who bear their souls. That they don't need to call for power because it's already inside them."

"I'm leaking my soul every time I try to power up?" Monica's face paled.

"No! Renalt spare us, no. Your soul isn't getting leaked or spent, it's . . . manifesting." It occurred to him that explanation wasn't particularly easy to comprehend, so he tried again. "Think of it like a lantern. The light is always there inside of it, but to really see its full brilliance, you have to open the hatch and let it out. That doesn't mean you're using the light up any quicker."

"That still doesn't explain why it hurts me and not you."

"If you're not simply calling on Renalt for strength, if you are manifesting your own divine power, then you have the opposite of Hilda's problem. She struggles to draw enough power in. You may be bringing too much out. You might simply have more power than a mortal body was meant to wield."

"Well, that seems like a pretty big design flaw," Monica muttered. "Whose idea was it for me to be like this anyway?"

"If the texts are to be believed, yours."

"Shut up." Monica buried her head in her hands. Supposedly, Sentinels only came about by the choice of the angel who decided to be born as one. Not that Monica could ever recall such a decision. Certainly, she couldn't imagine making it if she'd known this is what it would be like. "This sucks. I hate this. I hate being like this. I want to stop!"

Richard said nothing for a moment, letting Monica calm down.

"Do you remember the first day we met?" he asked. "Hilda and I arrived at this place, the two of you waited outside while I spoke to your parents. And when I came out—"

"I was beating the shit out of some punks."

She hadn't started that fight—or any of the fights from her childhood, she'd argue. But that day, a group of kids her age saw a knight's apprentice from out of town hanging out with the freak and thought they had a chance to act tough without actually engaging Monica directly. Poor Hilda had been so new to her training, she'd yet to so much as throw a punch, and her attempts to talk the gang down had only managed to make them more aggravated. So, Monica gave them what they wanted.

That was the first real introduction Sir Richard had gotten to Monica. Bloody knuckles, glowing eyes, and half a dozen kids laid out all around her. Her parents, along with the rest of the village, were livid. Hilda herself took three days just to get over her terror enough to say thank you. But Sir Richard had been calm. He'd talked Monica down until the glow faded from her eyes, and once he'd gotten the full story from the girls, he'd smiled.

He was wearing the same smile now.

"You can't help yourself when you see someone who needs defending. That's the real reason I'm here, Monica. Not because of what you are but who you are. You might have the body of a normal girl, but you have the soul of a protector. Someday, you're going to have to figure out what that means for you. I want to make sure you're ready when that day comes."

HOMECOMING

A ngel's eyes shot open.

"Oh gods, you're awake!"

Angel barely had time to orient herself before Thalia's arms enveloped her and she got a face full of the bartender's curly hair. It was a terrified, desperate embrace, one Angel answered as gently as she could manage.

Ruby was at Angel's bedside by the time Thalia pulled away, offering an apologetic look.

"Sorry for hovering. You scared the shit out of us."

"*I* scared the shit out of *you*?" Angel muttered. "I told you to stay away from the fight."

"Well, we ignored you," Ruby said. "You're welcome."

"We could hear the fight all the way from the Star. It sounded bad. Really bad," Thalia said.

"So, you went *toward* it?"

Angel shook her head in disbelief, feeling it swim as she did. Much as she wanted to chastise her tagalongs for running straight into danger, she held off. Suicidally stupid as it was, it was hard to argue with the results.

"You're all insane," she muttered, her voice devoid of any real malice or criticism.

"No arguments there," Ruby said. "I still can't believe we got you out."

"Yeah . . ." Angel's memory of the end of the fight was foggy, addled by darkness and pain. "How exactly did you manage that? Actually, scratch that, how am I still alive?"

Ruby jerked her head toward Bart, who'd yet to get up out of his chair. "You can thank him for most of it."

Bart's face looked red from exertion, a dizzy expression smeared across it as he propped his head up with his arm. He gave a weak smile and a weaker wave.

He was still clutching a pendant of Saint Beneger tight in his hand.

Angel connected the dots. "You used a prayer?"

"I . . . yeah." His voice came out weak and raspy, one more telltale sign that he had *severely* overdone it.

"He used like half a dozen," Ruby spoke up. "He wanted to do more, but then he passed out."

"And I managed to move the Star to get us out of there before they could break down the doors," Thalia said. "We're clear. We're safe."

Angel cocked her head slightly. Thalia had never actually moved the Rusted Star before with it usually being Angel's job. She was amazed the bartender even knew how. "Where did you move us?"

A nervous, deflecting smile appeared on Thalia's face. "I'm . . . not sure? Best I've got is mountains and trees outside and no zombies. I couldn't find any instructions for steering this place, so I just went with 'away.' Seemed to work out."

"And I repeat myself: You're all insane."

"And I repeat *myself*," Ruby retorted. "You're welcome."

Angel let out a sharp laugh that her abdomen immediately protested. She barely registered the pain over the inexplicable feeling of pride. The girl had guts. All of them did, really.

"Thanks," Angel said, making sure to look each of them in the eye. "All of you."

They offered her worn, weary smiles in return. There was relief in the air now, but things had been harrowing, and it showed on their faces.

"Now get that one in a fucking bed before he kills himself from over-exertion," Angel said, jerking her head toward Bart.

"I'm fine." He waved off their concerns even as he teetered precariously in his chair. "I'm more worried about . . ."

He trailed off as he slumped over in his seat, only saved from face planting into the floor by Ruby's timely arrival.

"I got him," Ruby said, lifting the half-conscious young man into her arms. "You get some rest too."

"Sure."

Thalia waited until Ruby and Bart were out of the room before speaking again. "We both know you're not going to rest."

Angel groaned as she shuffled out of bed. "I'm gonna see where you parked us, figure out if it's actually safe to stay here for a while. Beyond that . . . I can't stop that thing. Not on my own."

"So, what's the plan?"

Angel touched her ear where her messenger coil should have been, and its absence left a cold feeling in the pit of her stomach. The memory of it being smashed to bits in her fight came back, and she grimaced.

"I don't know," she said.

Even as she said it, a thought came unbidden into her mind, and she realized it was a lie. There was one solution she could think of. One card she could try to play. Because there was one group of people who were strong enough to face the Dread Knight who she knew exactly where to find. And per Lupolt's own words, she also knew they weren't busy with their own fight since they had refused Roland's summons.

If she wanted help, she could try asking the Order of Saint Ricard.

". . . fuck me."

REPAIRS

O f all the odd things Snow had come to appreciate over the years since leaving home, waking up in immense pain had to be one of the more distressing entries. But the numbing nature of the Heart of Ice had made pain an infrequent presence in her life, and its sporadic reappearances felt oddly nostalgic. And, more to the point, pain was the surest sign possible that she was still alive.

She sat up in a dingy, straw-filled bed and immediately found herself face-to-faceplate with Gamma's expressionless metallic visage.

"You are awake," he observed.

"Where am I, what happened, and why are you here?" Snow asked, getting all of her questions out up front.

Metallic shutters closed and opened again over the autostruct's eyes. "You are in room four of the Drunken Prospector, a tavern in the provincial city of Loraine. You were attacked by multiple assailants, and I intervened. The assailants were dispatched, but you lost consciousness due to acute deimofloros poisoning and internal trauma. I carried your body into the largest local church and entreated the priests to aid you. They successfully neutralized the poison and repaired the worst of your internal damage. However, their power was limited, and you retain multiple, non-life-threatening injuries. I have been instructed to accompany and observe you on your mission."

"How in the hells did you find me?"

"I maintained an accurate reading on your location at all times using the beacon provided to you by the High Inquisitive."

Of course he had. She almost felt stupid for asking. Even if carrying it had effectively saved her life, she couldn't wait to be rid of the thing. Then the realization struck her.

Ink's autostruct had saved her life. The damn wizard was never going to let her hear the end of this one, she just knew it.

"Your expression indicates displeasure distinct from physical pain," Gamma said. "I reiterate my previous request that you do not decapitate me."

Snow sighed. "You get a pass for saving my life. Besides, it's not you I'm upset with."

"But you are upset."

"Ink's going to try to spin this into me owing her one again, which I don't," Snow said. "Once I get her Silas, she can rope someone else into working for her for free."

"You intend to continue your pursuit of Silas Lamark?"

"If the Cult of Stars wants me to back off, it's all the more reason to stay on him."

"You will be facing the Cult as well as Silas Lamark and his allies," Gamma said. "The tactical imbalance created by their numbers will make this dangerous."

"My life is dangerous."

There was a space where the only sound came from the soft whirr of Gamma's internal workings before the machine spoke again. "I have insufficient information to draw conclusions. Please inform: Why are you alone?"

"What?"

"You are undertaking a dangerous objective but actively resist working with others to achieve your goals. High Inquisitive Arakawa was originally sent to make contact with you because you are difficult to find or contact, even for those you are allied with. Observable data indicates your isolation is by intentional choice. This runs counterintuitive to your odds of success and survival, and I am unable to determine a reason to do this. Is there an advantage I am unaware of?"

Snow mentally responded to the autostruct a hundred different ways. She told it to fuck off and mind its own business. She explained smaller numbers actually helped in operations that required stealth or secrecy. She admitted that after so many years on her own, always moving, she didn't know how to be around people anymore without constantly watching for their betrayal or plotting her own. That, even now, she struggled to wrap her head around the fact that there were people who could and would help her if she asked. That the idea of having friends again terrified her, and she didn't trust herself not to ruin everything all over again.

What she actually said was, "I have trust issues."

"Acknowledged." Another pause. "What will you do now?"

"Everything I've got says Silas is headed for Nikos for some kind of deal," Snow said, pushing away the burlap blankets and scooting out of bed. "I need to get there and find him before he disappears again."

"Nikos is a large city. Finding a single individual will be difficult," Gamma noted.

"Silas is a wanted man. Any deal he makes at this point has some kind of underworld or black market connection, especially if he had to leave the country to make it," Snow said. "And I know black market business. Give me a few hours in that city, and I'll know where to find him."

"I request that you permit me to accompany you in closer proximity for the remaining duration of your mission," Gamma said. "Maintaining the distance necessary to avoid detection limits my ability to perform my duties, and in your condition, you will require assistance to both reach Nikos and conduct an investigation."

Snow was about to tell the metal man that she could handle herself just fine on her own, but given that she'd be dead without him, the statement felt hollow. And he wasn't done talking.

"Additionally, I am an autostruct. In my estimation, I lack the human variables to contribute to your trust issues."

And at that, Snow felt something give way in her mind. She had to admit, the autostruct might have a point there. The machine did not lie. Its adherence to its own assignment and directives was simple, clean, predictable. And given their history, and the fact that it had saved her life anyway, it didn't seem capable of offense or holding a grudge. He was almost perfect for her.

She decided not to think about what that said about her.

THE ORDER

When Angel explained her plan to try and recruit the Order of Saint Ricard, Thalia, Ruby, and Bart had all insisted on coming along. Ostensibly to help try to persuade the knights who had already rebuked a king's summons, though Angel suspected the real reason was for moral support. It wasn't hard to tell this wasn't something she was looking forward to.

Deep down, she appreciated the support, and the fact that these three had saved her life only a few hours ago. Their presence did slow the hike up Turnstone Pass to the order's keep, but in truth, Angel was grateful for that too. It let her put off facing the order for a little while longer.

"Remind me why," Ruby panted, "we couldn't just . . . tunnelport?"

Whenever Angel saw Brass again, she was going to clock him for coining that stupid word.

"The Order of Saint Ricard has one job," Angel said, holding up a finger. "Watching for invaders. They keep an eye out for any kind of big or unnatural movement out here, including magical traversal. If a whole fucking inn just popped onto their front doorstep, it's even odds whether or not we'd even get a chance to say 'don't shoot' before they blew us off the mountain."

"They sound . . . pleasant."

"They take their job extremely seriously, even when other people don't. Actually, especially when other people don't." Angel recalled the stories

Sir Richard had taught her, the groundwork that would have become her introduction into the order's philosophy, had things gone differently. "Ricard was a slave from Antem who escaped to Corsar to warn them an invasion was coming, that the Horde of Digax would sweep over the kingdom in twenty years. Almost nobody listened to him, and years went by without a peep from the east. But he got a spot in the army anyway and worked his way up until he was in charge of the kingdom's border defenses."

"What happened to him?" Ruby asked.

"Same thing that happened to every other saint from back then," Angel said. "He died. Twenty years to the day, the horde came. But all his prep kept Corsar from being completely wiped off the map. His surviving subordinates founded the order, and ever since, they've been ready to fight at the first crack of trouble. They used to do more. Kept the nobility in check. Helped out when things got rough here at home."

"Not anymore?" Bart asked.

"They still *act* like they're a check on the nobility, but there isn't a single member of the order left that isn't stationed here anymore," Angel said. "Telling Roland to shove it might have been the first time they'd interacted with a noble since the Battle of Loraine."

"What happened?"

"For starters," a new voice echoed through the mountains, "she did."

The voice's owner was a white woman, as tall as Angel, wearing a crimson-trimmed white cloak over worn, silver armor. She had an axe in hand but still at her side as she glowered down at them from farther up the mountain, one leg propped up on a rock and her elbow resting on her knee.

And with her stood a dozen others, all clad in similar colors and all bearing somewhere on them the crowned shield crest of the Order of Saint Ricard, the Vigilant. Some of them, like their leader, carried axes. Others held polearms and crossbows. The one closest to their leader carried no weapons but kept one hand on a saint's pendant dangling from their neck.

The hiking party froze. Thalia's hand darted to the knife on her belt while Bart gripped his walking stick tight, preparing to use it as a club. Ruby, for her part, retreated into the group, the normally confident redhead suddenly looking very afraid. Only Angel was unperturbed by their sudden appearance, as if she'd been expecting it.

With a rueful expression, she met the glare of the woman in charge, who also happened to be her ex-girlfriend.

"Hi, Hilda."

"Monica." Hilda's voice was as hard as stone. "You need to leave. Now."

"Sorry," Angel apologized. "Can't."

"Why not?"

Angel wished she'd brought a bottle of whiskey from the bar. She settled for a deep breath. When her stomach was as settled as it was going to get, she put on the most level, important sounding voice she could muster.

"I bring a warning. Under the Edict of the Vigil, you have to hear it, and I can't leave until you have."

"You broke every oath binding you to the Edict a long time ago," Hilda said.

"But you haven't."

Hilda's jaw tightened before she remembered herself. She stood up straighter, wiping away almost all traces of resentment from her face.

"What warning?"

For the first time since she'd started hunting down Oblivion escapees, Angel wished the rest of the Starbreakers were here. At the very least, Church and Phoenix. Hells, even Brass knew how to work a crowd better than she did. She knew enough about the order's customs and laws to have gotten them this far, but past this point, she was out of her depth.

If there was any law or tradition that could compel them to act, she didn't know it.

Which only left her with the old-fashioned way—asking.

"I need your help."

The words tasted bitter in her mouth, but they at least got a reaction out of Hilda as she leaned forward and cocked her head ever so slightly. Angel kept going before anyone could tell her to stop.

"The Helm of the Dread Knight has been unleashed, and it's already got an army. I give it a few days before it hits a town and wipes it off the map," Angel said.

"You've seen it?"

"I fought it. I lost."

That got a few of the other knights to take notice. Some of them had probably never heard of the Dread Knight, but there wasn't a soul in this order who wouldn't know that Angel of the Starbreakers was a force to be reckoned with.

"And yet, here you are," Hilda said, not bothering to hide the accusation in her voice.

"It had me dead to rights," Angel said. "My friends here got me out. They're the only reason I'm still alive."

She was saying in so many words what she could have said in three: *I didn't run.*

"And it doesn't matter. This thing is out there, and someone has to stop it. You have to."

"We do not."

It was like the mountain fell out from underneath her. It wasn't just that Hilda said no. It was the callousness, the speed. There wasn't an ounce of concern or guilt or even malice in her voice. Just cruel, empty indifference.

"What?"

"I'll tell you what I told Roland when he asked for the order to help him wrangle his escaped convicts," Hilda said. "The Order of Saint Ricard has a clearly defined mission: We stand vigilant against the threats of invasion and tyranny. We are not a blunt instrument to be hurled at whatever problem you happen to be facing."

"What do you call a fucking undead army marching through the kingdom?"

"When it's being helmed by a monster the kingdom's mages chose to keep in a cage, rather than properly destroy?" Hilda asked. "Inevitable. Homegrown. Not our duty. Take your pick."

"People are going to die, Hilda!"

"If Roland can't protect his subjects from the dangers his own mages create, then maybe he's the one we need to deal with," Hilda said. "An incompetent ruler clinging to power is just as much a tyrant as any other."

"Oh, fuck off," Angel snapped, aware in the back of her mind that probably wasn't going to score her any points. "Roland's doing more for Corsar than you are, which you'd know if any of you ever came down from your fucking mountain."

"Every saint has their domain. Every order, their duty. Roland runs the kingdom. We guard its borders."

"From what?" Angel said. "The queen of the Frelheim's a friend; there's no hordes left in Antem, and the dwarves have better shit to deal with than a kingdom they're just gonna outlive!"

"For now. As far as we know," Hilda argued. "We stand ready to face threats whether we see them coming or not."

"There are threats—here, now. There are people who need help—here, now. You want to protect them? You don't need to sit up here waiting for something scary to cross the border, you need to get off your asses and do something!"

"I will not have this order abandon its post, its mission, to cover up other people's failures," Hilda said.

Something about the way Hilda looked at Angel when she said that told her she wasn't talking about Roland anymore.

"What's that supposed to mean?"

"If Roland doesn't have the resources to stop the Dread Knight, I can only assume it's because the military capital of the kingdom was wiped off the map," Hilda said. "And if I remember the outcome of the trial correctly, that was *your* fault."

Light danced across Angel's fingertips, threatening to spill out. Her face, her whole body, felt hot.

She only barely forced it back down. If Hilda wanted to go low, so could she.

"Richard would have helped."

Hilda was down from her perch before anyone could react, and in Angel's face in another instant.

"My father is dead," Hilda spat. "Which is also your fault."

When she was sixteen, those words had ripped Angel's heart out of her chest. Now they made her blood boil.

"He knew what being a knight was really about," Angel said, ignoring Hilda's accusation and twisting her own verbal knife even harder. "It's about doing good. Helping people. Not some four-hundred-year-old mission statement from a dead man."

"He also never led this order, for good reason," Hilda said. "Every time we've stepped out of our charge, *every time*, we have suffered for it. I won't take us down that path. I refuse."

Angel's eyes were glowing, but Hilda matched her glare without so much as blinking. The knight's axe was in her hand while Angel's fists had already ignited with golden light. Each of them dared the other to make a move.

"Monica."

Thalia's voice pulled her back. Just one word, her name, but so laced with fear and concern it consumed her senses. Suddenly, the only thing that mattered to Angel was making that fear go away.

She recognized the fury in Hilda's eyes. The stubborn, righteous indignation that would not budge an inch no matter the opposition. In that moment, she knew there was nothing she could say to make Hilda change her mind.

Her glow faded, even as her glare remained. "Then we're done here."

"Good."

Hilda returned her axe to her belt and began backing away. The other knights collected themselves, starting back up the mountain path while Angel glared at their backs. Thalia put a hand on her shoulder, and Ruby and Bart stared, jaws slack.

"What?" Ruby balked. "They can't . . . they can't just let this thing kill people."

"Can and will, apparently," Angel muttered. "Gonna need a new plan."

"This was the new plan!"

The image of Angel, lying bloody and broken on the ground as a mob of shambling husks came to finish her off flashed in Ruby's mind. She remembered the horror of their soulless, burning eyes. Their withered, tattered bodies jerking in profane mockery of normal movement. Those things were coming for everyone, and these people, these knights were just going to let it happen. They were going to leave them all to die.

The same sense of fear and helplessness came for her again, and she remembered something else. The fire, burning all around her after Pitch left her to die. The smoke, choking her lungs. She could still remember begging not to die, knowing there was nothing she could do to save herself. Her stomach twisted in rebellion at the recollection.

Never again.

"Stop!"

Ruby's shout echoed as all of the knights closest to her froze in place. The others kept marching until they realized they were leaving their companions behind. Heads turned in confusion.

"We're leaving. Now," Hilda said.

The knights who'd listened to Ruby stayed completely still, and Hilda's gaze hardened.

"That was an order. Move," she barked.

They didn't move. They didn't do anything.

The knight with the saint's pendant held up a hand, asking for a moment. She spoke a prayer in the language of the gods, and a moment later, the knights began to stir again. Some of them were staring at their own bodies in confusion. Others immediately swiveled around to stare at Ruby.

The color had faded from her face, though it was rapidly returning, as the faint remnants of black veins faded from her skin. Bart and Thalia stared in surprise while Angel's expression grew grim.

Hilda stepped forward. "What was that?"

Angel placed herself in between Hilda and Ruby. Unconsciously, Thalia and Bart closed ranks around her. "Nothing. We're leaving."

Hilda ignored her, turning to her priest. Slowly, the priest reached into their sleeves and withdrew from them a foot-long, narrow, golden rod etched with a pattern of thorny vines and open eyes. Too late, Ruby recalled where she'd seen a rod like that before as the priest twisted it to activate it and held it out toward Ruby.

The demon detection rod gave off a blood red glow, and all of the knights drew their weapons.

Thalia's eyes widened. "What the fuck?"

"Hilda, don't!" Angel shouted.

The fury in Hilda's eyes wavered just a little, and she held up a fist. The knights halted their advance, but they kept their weapons trained on the group. At a nod from Hilda, the priest spoke another prayer, and change swept through the air, leaving a smell of fresh rain and the feeling of a hand on everyone's shoulder.

A truth prayer.

"You have six seconds to explain why you have a demon with you," Hilda said.

"She's not a fucking demon!" Angel protested.

"She just used the Hell Tongue on my knights, and the rod is glowing red," Hilda stated. "Either she is or she's consorting with them. And either way, we will not stand for it."

"What do they mean by that?" Ruby asked.

Angel ignored her, lest the truth prayer make something unpleasant slip. "She's not consorting with anything. Something happened to her. It was an accident. We're handling it."

"If you're handling it, why hasn't she been exorcized already?"

Angel paused as she saw the rest of the conversation laid out in front of her. She could see exactly where this was going, and exactly how it would end, unless she steered the conversation in a very different direction, very quickly. Unfortunately, she'd never been great at dealing with this prayer, and before she could think of a better way to phrase it, the truth spilled out of her mouth.

"We can't."

"What?"

"Nothing Church has tried has worked," Angel said. "And he's running out of ideas."

Renalt shit in her dinner, she hated this prayer.

"Then whatever hold is on her will only grow stronger," Hilda pointed out.

"I know."

"She'll only grow more and more corrupted by it."

"I know!"

"That only ends one way."

"I KNOW!"

Angel's eyes flared again, bright enough to force even Hilda to look away for a moment. She could feel herself shaking, struggling to keep it in now. She couldn't let it out. Because if it came out right now, Angel would only be able to see a bunch of people targeting a scared, confused, innocent girl. And she would not react diplomatically to that.

"We. Are. Handling. It," she said, forcing herself to stay slow and in control.

"And if you're not fast enough, whatever demon has its hooks in her will use her to cross over, and where there's one, there will always be more," Hilda said. "*That* is an invasion. That is something this order will stop by any means necessary. And if you can't exorcize her, there is only one option left."

"I am not letting you kill her!"

"I don't need your permission!"

And this was exactly where she knew things were heading. The knights of the Order of Saint Ricard were nothing if not zealously devoted to their mission. Ruby was, for all intents and purposes, a ticking clock on a demon incursion. It might be years from happening. It might be a few weeks. They weren't going to wait to find out.

"Test of strength!" Angel spat.

Hilda cocked her head. "What?"

Angel could hear it in Hilda's voice that she had her off balance now. She pressed that, hoping to take the wind out of Hilda's fury and her own.

"You want to kill her. I want to try to save her," Angel said. "Let's see who Renalt agrees with."

Renalt was the god of strength and justice, the ruler of the gods and patron of Corsar. Strength, in all its forms, was held as a sign of Renalt's favor and even a mandate from the god, depending on which church you asked. So much so that in the oldest traditions, it was not uncommon for disputes between two people in Old Corsar to be settled by tests, each party's strength against the other.

The practice had eventually morphed into Corsar's modern court system where disputes were settled by the strength of arguments and conviction, but in particularly rural or traditionalist places, more basic, physical tests of strength were still sometimes employed. And it didn't get much more traditionalist than the Order of Saint Ricard.

The leader of the order considered Angel for a moment before offering a slow, solemn nod.

"I accept."

Angel returned the nod, slowly relaxing her posture.

"Will someone explain what the fuck is going on, like now," Ruby demanded.

Angel didn't answer, still trying to keep herself calm to avoid ruining the temporary peace she'd just bought.

Technically, any kind of strength that could be tested was permitted to settle tests of strength. Mental fortitude, tolerance for pain, or even talent in a particular art were all options. But Angel and Hilda both knew exactly what kind of test they would pick.

They were going to fight for Ruby's life.

DEMONS

Ruby hadn't stopped pacing since the knights had left the four of them alone in the armory. The girl had been a nervous wreck the entire hike up to the order's keep, where they insisted on holding Angel and Hilda's duel. If it hadn't been for Bart holding her hand and the stern looks from Angel, she might have run before they'd ever gotten here.

Actually, she still looked like she might bolt.

"This is insane," she said, still pacing. "This can't actually be happening to me. Why are we here? Why did we agree to this?"

"Because if we didn't, they probably would have tried to kill you right then and there on the mountain, and there wouldn't have been a whole lot we could do to stop them," Angel said as she strapped on a gauntlet. "I'm good, but I'm not fight-an-entire-order good. At least this way, I only have to fight one person."

"But did we have to do it *in their keep?*" Ruby said. "Now we're stuck. I can't even run if I wanted to."

"That's probably why they wanted to do it here," Thalia pointed out.

"Not helping!" Ruby snapped. She ran her hands through her hair, twisting it around her fingers. "You've got this, right?" she asked Angel for the hundredth time. "Tell me you've got this."

Angel sighed.

She understood the girl's fear, but she only had so much patience with this sort of thing, especially when she'd really rather focus on not getting her ass kicked for the second time in as many days. She missed the others again. Church was always better at comforting people in distress. Snow might have even been able to find a way to sneak Ruby out of the keep while the order was focused on the duel.

But it was still just her. She was going to have to manage on her own. She put her hands on Ruby's shoulders and looked her dead in the eye.

"Ruby. I am not going to let them hurt you," she said. "I promise."

She prayed it was enough. She did not want to be the asshole who told a woman terrified for her life to shut the fuck up, but Renalt help her, she was about to.

Mercifully, her words seemed to get through to Ruby as she visibly relaxed. Not much but enough. "Okay."

Angel offered one last pat on her shoulder and went back to armoring up. It wasn't much, just some protection for her arms and chest—a full suit had never been her thing—but it might make the difference, and she was going to take every edge she could get. Thank the gods the order was too devoted to their ideals to make sure her and Hilda's fight was anything less than as fair as possible.

Thalia helped her with the last few buckles while Ruby and Bart broke away to talk among themselves.

"I know you have to act tough for her, but are you good?" Thalia asked.

Angel glanced over Thalia's shoulder to make sure Ruby was distracted. "Good as I can be."

The truth was she didn't know. She'd fought Hilda plenty of times before and had won more than she'd lost. But that was a long time ago. And Hilda had spent the last seven years as a knight, fighting and training every day. Angel had spent the last seven years running a bar. Even after the mess from last spring, she was a lot shorter on practice than Hilda. Plus, she'd already taken a beating from the Dread Knight, and she'd be lying if she said she couldn't still feel it.

The look in Thalia's eyes said she already knew all of that.

"What do you need me to do?" Thalia asked.

"Keep an eye on those two," Angel said, jerking her head toward Ruby and Bart. "Don't let anyone try to pull a fast one if I win."

"You think they'll go back on the deal?"

"No. Not the whole order anyway," Angel said. "But one idiot in it might. You can't proof against idiots, but you can keep an eye out for them."

"All right. I've got them." Thalia finished securing the last of Angel's armor and handed her the axe she'd picked out earlier. It had a cherry wood haft, wrapped in bands of steel to reinforce it, and a head that looked like it could split a person in two.

Thalia gave her a nervous nod. "Good luck."

Angel returned the nod, and the four of them all exited the armory.

Unsurprisingly, the Order of Saint Ricard had a room in their keep specifically for holding duels separate from their normal sparring grounds. The open, otherwise sparse space featured a central ring flanked on all sides by tiered benches, where several knights of the order were already sitting, talking in hushed tones that grew even quieter as Angel and the others arrived.

Two knights moved to intercept Thalia, Ruby, and Bart, ushering them to sit while Angel was left to walk into the ring. Hilda was already waiting for her there.

She'd abandoned her hooded cloak, revealing short, sand-blonde hair that created an asymmetrical frame around her face. Her silver armor, and really the armor of most of the knights in attendance, was surprisingly dull under the lightstone lamps, worn and scuffed from years of abuse and repair. It only made Angel's loaned armor look all the more out of place for how cleanly it glinted on her.

The two fighters took their positions.

The duel was first to yield or until someone was unable to fight, and neither had any illusions about getting the other to yield. The order had a cleric on standby to deal with injuries once the fight was over. That was it as far as rules went.

Make the other stop fighting. However you had to.

"You can still back down," Hilda said.

"I never back down." Angel rolled out her shoulders and assumed a fighting stance.

Hilda raised an eyebrow before settling into her own stance. "Liar."

Even though the barb stung, somewhere in the back of her mind, Angel knew that if anyone in the world had the right to call her that, it was Hilda.

The two of them had both been training under her father, Sir Richard, to become paladins and members of the Order of Saint Ricard. They fell for each other, hard and fast like teenagers always did, complete with naive promises to be together forever. And then, one day, what should have been a routine training patrol went horribly, horribly wrong. Angel had been overzealous in following a trail and led the three of them into a hobgoblin ambush.

Under Sir Richard's orders, a terrified Angel had carried a wounded Hilda kicking and screaming from the battle that followed, leaving the knight behind to die. Those screams, so fresh in her mind from her visit with the Oracle, sent a shiver down her spine. On that day, she'd broken both of their hearts. Not long after, Angel left the Order altogether. The only times they'd seen each other since then had been when the Order's business and the Starbreakers' briefly intersected. And none of those occasions had borne anything between them but dark looks and curt words.

And now, here they were. They stood still, eyes locked on one another, axes at the ready. Total silence fell over the room. For a single moment, no one breathed.

Angel and Hilda moved at the same time, rushing forward and swinging with their axes as both of their bodies were consumed in auras of light. Their weapons crashed together with a shattering clang loud enough for the spectators to feel it in their bones, and the whole room was consumed in a blinding flash.

Their axes deflected each other, and both fighters took a half step back before circling each other and swinging again with similar results. On the third swing, there was screech of metal on metal as their two axe heads interlocked.

Hilda reacted first, delivering a jab that caught Angel on the shoulder and sounded off like a cymbal as her gauntlet sang against Angel's pauldron.

Angel staggered back with a dent in her armor. She'd been thinking of doing the exact same thing, but Hilda had been faster. Treating it like a wakeup call rather than a bad sign, Angel rolled her shoulder and charged again.

Every blow traded was a crack of thunder. Each one echoed in the room, several giving off flashes of light that forced spectators to look away. Their exchange rattled the walls, made the lightstones flicker, and on one occasion, the stone cracked under their feet. Angel hit harder. Hilda hit more often.

Just as Angel was beginning to think it was an even fight after all, it all went to shit. She braced her axe in both hands and used the haft to block a downward chop from Hilda, and the weapon bent in her hands. Cracks ran the length of the wood, and it was only the steel reinforcements that kept it in one piece.

Her surprise slowed her, letting Hilda take another swing. The axe buckled further. Panic gripped Angel as she fell back and kicked with everything she had—too late.

Hilda's third swing of her axe cleaved Angel's weapon in two, burying itself in her chest. At the same time, her kick landed smack into Hilda's stomach, and the knight was catapulted back, only coming to a stop after a long tumble across the ring.

Slowly, both women clambered to their feet. Blood ran from the fresh gouge in Angel's armor, and her collar bone throbbed with pain. It hurt to move her left arm. And now her weapon was broken in two.

Somehow, Hilda had managed to hold on to her axe when she got hit, and though her armor had been caved in around her abdomen, she looked steady on her feet. Then she coughed, and flecks of blood spattered across the floor.

It was Angel's turn to react faster than Hilda as she reared back and hurled her axe head as hard as she could. Hilda, still winded, barely brought her own weapon up in time to deflect, and even then, it clipped her forehead before sailing past and embedding itself into a wall—just above the heads of some of the knights watching the fight.

It was a good hit, but a lucky one, and it didn't change the fact that Hilda had a weapon and Angel didn't. Pressing her advantage, she rushed forward and grabbed hold of Hilda's axe with both hands. But Hilda had the same read on the situation and wasn't about to give up her edge without a fight.

With a savage yell, she reversed her grip on her axe and used it as leverage to throw Angel over her shoulder and down to the floor. Before Angel could even orient herself, Hilda was on top of her, bashing her in the face with the shaft of her axe before using it to pin Angel to the floor by the throat.

"Yield before I break your neck!" Hilda shouted.

In answer, Angel drove her knee into Hilda, knocking her loose enough to relieve some of the pressure on her throat. Hilda answered immediately with another bash to Angel's face before trying to pin her again, but this time, Angel was able to get a hand between the axe handle and her windpipe.

"Why?" Hilda asked. "Why are you fighting so hard to put us all at risk?"

Angel struggled to grunt out a retort as she pushed back against the weapon threatening to crush her. "Why are you fighting so hard to kill someone who doesn't deserve it?"

With a grunt and a punch to Hilda's already broken ribs, she managed to shove the woman off and scramble back to her feet, her own injury screaming in protest the entire time. She felt like shit. But as long as Hilda looked as bad as she felt, there was a chance.

And Hilda looked like shit. A stream of blood ran down her face from the head wound Angel had given her, her armor was bent and buckled in half a dozen places, and her lips and teeth were stained red. And yet, none of it seemed to slow her down.

"It's not about deserving it," Hilda protested. She charged forward, swinging her axe like a madwoman. The form and precision were gone from her attacks. Now it was nothing but pure, fanatic strength. "It's about my duty! To Renalt! To this order! To everyone in Corsar!"

She punctuated every sentence with another wild swing. With nothing else to block with, Angel gave her best attempt at deflecting the blows with her gauntlets. The first time she tried it, she felt her collarbone explode in pain.

The second, Hilda cut a gash into her arm. The third, she didn't even try, only just managing to duck out of the way. The fourth caught her in the ribs, biting into her armor and sending her tumbling to the floor.

Pain and exhaustion welded Angel to the floor, her only saving grace that Hilda was too winded to press the assault. If she just stayed down long enough, it would be as good as yielding, and the fight would be over.

And Ruby would be dead.

Angel barely knew Ruby. Before this mess, they'd sat at the same table with a bunch of other people for lunch, once, months ago. She was supposed to be Church and Brass's problem. Maybe she felt some sympathy for her current predicament, bombarded with problems because of a power she never asked for, but there was a line for what sympathy could explain. Letting her stay in the Star instead of taking her back to Aenerwin? Sure. This? This was insane. At the rate this fight was going, she was going to get herself killed for a woman she barely knew, who was probably going to end up summoning a demon by the year's end anyway.

As she lay there on the floor, battered and bleeding, she caught sight of Ruby among the rest of the spectators. Out of her seat, a look of horror on her face. It was the face of someone who thought they were going to die. And next to her, Bart and Thalia, both seeing the same thing Angel was and knowing there wasn't a damn thing they could do about it.

Hilda's words echoed in her head. *It's about my duty! To Renalt! To this order! To everyone in Corsar!*

Angel grit her teeth and crawled up onto her knees as divine fire spread through her veins. The pain from her wounds was eclipsed in an instant by a searing, all-consuming burn spreading through every fiber of her being. Her eyes blazed, twin golden suns, and a burning halo ignited over her head. Her whole body glowed, too bright to look at for long.

When Angel spoke, it was in an echoing, doubled voice.

"Fuck your duty. Fuck Renalt. And fuck your order!"

Hilda realized what was coming in time to shield her face with her gauntlets and axe as beams of light surged from Angel's eyes. Hilda was a paladin of Saint Ricard, trained to funnel divine power into her body and weapons. Her equipment was made to handle that power. But it could only take so much.

Hilda's axe exploded in her hands, shredding her gauntlets.

The paladin stared at her arms for a moment, the ruined metal around them leaking blood in a dozen places.

Angel struggled the rest of the way to her feet, taking slow, pained steps toward Hilda. Her whole body shaking, Hilda raised her bloody fists. Angel matched her.

Angel's first punch dented Hilda's breastplate. Hilda's split Angel's cheek. Angel broke Hilda's jaw. Hilda cracked another of Angel's ribs. Angel grabbed both of Hilda's arms, spread them wide, and delivered a headbutt that put Hilda on the ground.

Angel all but fell on top of her, less out of aggression and more because she ran out of strength to stand. With more desperation than anything else, she threw her weight into one last elbow, and Hilda's eyes rolled back as her body went limp.

The light dissipated all at once from Angel's body as she gasped. Her halo vanished, and her eyes returned to normal as smoke curled off her body. She rolled off of Hilda, on to her back, and blacked out.

Total silence took the room, broken by a muted whisper from a lone redhead, equal parts relieved and terrified by everything she'd just witnessed. Her words cut through the still air, echoing the thoughts of everyone present.

"Holy shit."

ADRIFT

Too tapped to call on the power it would take to heal them, Church had fallen back on mundane treatments for his and Brass's injuries, cleaning and bandaging them as best he could. It wasn't perfect, but it kept them alive and stable long enough to crash the ship back into Puerto Oro's harbor, by which time Ink and Quint had managed to subdue the rest of the Cord of Aenwyn.

Kurien was headed to Parthica, but the fastest way to catch up to her was waiting and recuperating until Ink was feeling strong enough for another teleport. The wizard was with Quint, helping him and the Cord settle affairs with the city they had just terrorized. Fresh from a trip to a local hospital, the two Starbreakers were out of danger but sore, tired, and feeling sorry for themselves. Which, of course, meant they had sought out the closest cantina.

An exhausted silence hung between the two men as Brass smoked his way through a nail and Church nursed a cup of wine, his head propped up on one hand. Brass blew out a ring of smoke into the air above him and stared into it, as if it were a window to another time and place. Given what he was smoking, it might actually have been to him.

"Are you really just going back to Aenerwin after all this?" Brass asked.

Church sighed. He'd been wondering when they would have this conversation. Versions of it had come up early into Brass's stay in the town as the glintchaser grew restless. But things were different now. Going back to freelancing wasn't just an idea in Brass's head, sprung of boredom and nostalgia. They'd gone and done it. The others might be thinking of it as something different in their minds, but to Church and Brass, this job working for Roland was freelancer work, plain and simple. From the moment he'd agreed to work with Brass, Church knew that sooner or later, he was going to ask for more.

And the priest was going to have to break his friend's heart.

"Yes, I am," Church said. "It's my home. Maybe not where I was born or raised, but it's where I've built a life, a purpose. I have people who depend on me, I have work that needs doing. And I'm happy there."

"I just figured, after these last few days . . ."

"Brass, there are things I miss from freelancing. Really. But it's not for me. Not anymore."

"I know *that.*"

"I'm sorry?"

"Church, I'm a big boy. I know my moms and dads got divorced and went their separate ways and people change and move on and all that other stuff you and Phoenix never stop spouting. I get it. I can't say I'm not disappointed, but I get it. I've known since we were kids none of you wanted to do this forever. And if it's really over and you're all really done, then that's that."

"Then . . . I'm confused now. What's wrong with me going back to Aenerwin?"

Brass looked directly at Church now.

"Oh, come on. Have you seen yourself the last few weeks? You convinced an immortal wizard to help us *by asking nicely.* You prayed hard enough to drop a casino full of people without killing a single one while they were all beating the shit out of you. You've got a heart so golden dwarves want to eat it for breakfast and more power in your back pocket than most bishops, and you're just . . . sitting on it.

"Not that Aenerwin's not nice, but it's one town. One tiny, boring town. And maybe you needed that for a while—after Relgen—but forever? You used to have dreams. Plans. Big ones! You could be archbishop of wherever you wanted. You could have a hundred churches. You could change the world. Or at least put a hell of a lot more good in it than one town's worth."

Silence fell between them as Church stared at Brass, mouth agape. The priest sat there, struggling to process Brass's words. And more to the point, struggling to process how deeply they'd cut him.

How many times had he stood in front of the people of Aenerwin and told them that when Renalt gave a person a strength or talent, he did it so they could use it? That when a person found their calling, it was their duty to pursue it with everything they had? And for all of that talk, all those sermons, Brass was right.

Seven years he'd been in Aenerwin. Not once in those seven years had he ever tried to reach out beyond it. To do more. Aenerwin was small and manageable and, quite frankly, easy. Apart from his usual drain from public speaking, being the vicar of Aenerwin was barely work at all. There was no shame in reaching a limit, in doing all he could. But in his heart, Church knew he had more in him.

And Brass knew it too.

Only a few months spent with the priest in Aenerwin and a few weeks back on the job and Brass, of all people, had seen what he couldn't about himself.

Had believed in him on a level that he hadn't even believed in himself.

And Church had absolutely no idea what to do with that.

"That was . . . a lot."

"Well, I am smoking something to pass the time. I can get very profound when I'm high."

Church smiled. "Thanks anyway. It means a lot. Knowing you think about me that way."

Brass shook his head as if to say no thanks were necessary.

"I think about all of you that way. I mean, I know what I am. I'm a fun night in a purple vest and perfect eyeliner. But you? Phoenix? Snow? Angel? I was so thrilled to be in a company with the rest of you. Because I knew I was working with people who were going to change the world one day. And when the history books talked about all of you, I'd get to be in the footnotes as one of the lucky people who got to watch you do it."

"Brass . . ."

"I also thought you were all really hot. Like, aggressively hot. Phoenix kinda lost it a little bit, but he's also kind of making the gruff-dad thing work now. But the rest of you? Gorgeous as ever."

"If you two are quite done flirting," Ink interrupted as she sauntered into the bar. "We've got work to do."

HURT

When Angel woke up, she was greeted by an unfamiliar face and the all-too-familiar grinding sensation of her bones unbreaking. No matter how many times she'd been given healing prayers, she never got used to the feel of them.

After taking a second to collect herself, she recognized the woman hovering over her as the priest who'd been with Hilda up on the mountain and standing by during the duel.

Given how much better Angel felt, it seemed the woman was good at her job.

"Thanks," she muttered, her voice hoarse.

Before the priest could say anything, she was cut off by Thalia.

"You're insane. You know that, right?"

She was wearing a relieved smile, same as Ruby and Bart, as for the second time, Angel found the three of them surrounding her bedside. All of them looked unscathed, free of any chains or other signs of impending execution.

Ruby was the first one to hug her, with a surprising amount of strength for her small frame.

"Thank you."

"You were . . . that was . . ." Bart's tongue stumbled, at a loss for words. "I've never seen anything like that."

Angel gingerly peeled Ruby off of her and waved off Bart's praise, uncomfortable at the gratitude and awe being thrown at her. At least Thalia wasn't losing her shit.

"So, I won?"

"That was the judgment," the priest said. "Though there were some disagreements."

"One guy tried to call it a draw and made a move for Ruby," Thalia explained. "I punched him."

"She's underselling it," Ruby said. "She almost knocked him out."

"Okay, me dueling Hilda was not an invitation for all of you to start fist fights," Angel said, immediately worried.

"It's all right," the priest assured. "Marcel is . . . new. He needed a reminder to behave himself."

Angel raised an eyebrow as she sat up. "You know, you're pretty congenial considering I almost caved your leader's skull in."

"Not everyone in this order thinks the commander is right about everything," the priest said. "For what it's worth, I had hoped you'd win."

"But if I hadn't, you wouldn't have stopped Hilda, would you?" Angel asked.

A small frown overtook the priest's lips. "No."

"Figures," Angel said. She pushed her way out of bed, waving off the others before they could try to help her stand. "So, are we done here?"

"It seems so," came Hilda's voice from the doorway.

The whole room bristled, and Ruby's hands immediately balled into fists at her side. Thalia put herself between the knight commander and everyone else while the priest looked suddenly concerned.

"Hilda—Commander," the priest said, catching herself and earning questioning glances from everyone in the room but Thalia, who immediately recognized the concern and carefully placed boundaries in the priest's voice. "You should be resting."

"I'm fine, Naomi," Hilda dismissed, her eyes never leaving Angel.

The two of them stared at one another, neither moving.

Their eyes searched each other, each looking for something different and neither finding it. In the end, it was Angel who broke the silence.

"You still won't help."

"The girl is your charge," Hilda said. "But the order is mine. And I won't let you drag it down again."

Angel shook her head. "I get that you hate me. But are you seriously going to turn your back on the world just because it hurt you?"

Hilda narrowed her eyes. "You did."

Angel felt the self-righteousness leave her sails. Hilda had her there. She might have come here talking a big game, riding high off her little streak of playing a knight, but for however much she slagged off Hilda and the order for sitting on their asses, what had she done the last seven years?

And just like that, the argument was over. In the end, Angel and Hilda really were too alike for their own good.

After a few seconds of tense silence, Naomi cleared her throat. "I can walk all of you out."

"I remember the way," Angel said pointedly.

Naomi took the message and hung back with Hilda as the four of them left. Thalia lagged behind and lingered in the doorway for a moment. Her soft brown eyes found Hilda's piercing blues.

"You're wrong about her," Thalia stated.

Hilda looked mildly offended that some bartender thought she knew Angel better than she did, but Thalia didn't waver, meeting Hilda's questioning look with resolute conviction. Without another word of elaboration, she hurried to catch up to the others.

DIVIDED

Roland swung himself through the halls of the Corsan embassy, grateful for some time away from the chancellor's mansion where he had been staying since his arrival in Nikos. This summit might have been vital to the recovery and prosperity of Corsar, but his fellow heads of state were, put bluntly, a bit much.

Big and boisterous, Chancellor Kleitos of Parthica dressed himself extravagantly in multi-hued purples and an excess of gold jewelry, ate a full pie with every meal, talked loudly, and laughed even louder. And he kept trying to set Roland up with his son, which the king was running out of ways to politely dodge.

Though she wasn't technically the leader of Iandra, Princess Diane Recpina had taken charge of the delegation from Her Lady's City. Maybe it was just her recent stay in Olwin, but she was particularly fond of talking Roland's ear off.

But they were both preferable to the sultan of Gypten. Far and away the oldest member of the summit, Tariq the Immortal's cheerful condescension toward the rest of them and tendency to bring up meeting the other delegates as children was a constant drag on discussions.

In a way, finding out about Kurien had been a minor blessing. Nothing bought a reprieve from diplomacy like news of a deadly assassin on the prowl.

"If you would permit me to say so, I think you handled that quite well," Lupolt said. "You warned everyone of the danger without revealing the full scope of the breakout, and your suggestion to postpone discussion rather than end the summit leaves the door open to continue our work here once the situation is resolved."

Roland halted, took a moment to stabilize himself on his crutches, and stared Lupolt down. "What did you do?"

Lupolt considered trying to soften the truth but decided against it. Roland was too straightforward a man for it anyway.

"The Starbreakers are here."

Roland's jaw tensed for a moment, and he closed his eyes.

"They might be the only ones capable of stopping Kurien," Lupolt stressed.

"I know."

"Coordinating with them for this might mean the difference—"

"I know. I just . . . need a moment." Roland drew in a deep breath, did his best to bury the reflexive flare of pain and guilt, and focused his eyes on the task ahead of him. "All right."

The two men entered the embassy's office where Ink, Brass, Elizabeth, and Phoenix were all assembled. A hush fell over the room as whatever conversation had been going on before Roland and Lupolt arrived abruptly ceased. At an encouraging nod from Elizabeth, Phoenix cleared his throat.

"Your Majesty."

"Phoenix."

"I know that—"

"It's probably for the best if we focus on the task at hand," Roland said, sensing the direction Phoenix had been about to take things. "You're here. You can help. And we need it. The past, and how we feel about it, can wait."

"Right."

"Where are the others?"

"Angel hasn't been answering her messenger coil," Ink reported. "Church is trying to make contact with a prayer now."

"What about Kurien?"

"Kurien stole an arsenal's load of arcane weaponry from collectors and other organizations on her way out of Puerto Oro along with the Heart of Shadows from the Cord of Aenwyn," Ink said.

"It's more weapons than even she could use, so we're still not sure why she wanted that many. But the Heart explains why the Oracle couldn't see her," Phoenix said. "When the Servitor had that thing, we could only track the trail of stuff it destroyed. We also know she's coming here to kill you."

"I still don't know how I feel trusting the word of a serial killer," Wings said. "She could be lying to get us looking for her in the wrong spot."

"Kurien's a drama queen," Brass said. "She's not going to send us in the wrong direction when she *wants* a fight with us."

"And if she's *not* coming here, we have nothing to go on. No information, no plan," Phoenix said. "For now, we assume she's telling the truth, that she's coming here, and we plan and act on that."

"Do we have any idea where she is beyond 'coming here'?" Roland asked.

"Local authorities are searching any location that fits her profile," Ink said. "Theaters, music halls, coliseums—"

"Like I said, drama queen."

Ink shot Brass a look that said she didn't appreciate being interrupted before continuing. "But it's a big city. We've put feelers out into less scrupulous circles, but that's going to be even slower going than the authorities."

Roland frowned. "Do we have any faster methods?"

"Well, actually—" Phoenix began, only to be cut off as Church burst into the room, pale faced and panting for breath. The room tensed, reading the fear on the priest's face.

"The Dread Knight," Church said. "Angel couldn't stop it. It has an army, and it's headed straight for Loraine."

Stunned silence gripped the room by the throat. Lupolt was the one to recover his wits first. "How long?"

"Less than a day."

Roland suddenly felt very unsteady. He adjusted his grip on his crutches and started talking. "Lupolt, get word to the baron of Loraine now. Tell him what's coming, tell him to hold his town, and then get the garrison outside Olwin marching *yesterday*."

"Hold the town?" Elizabeth said. "Shouldn't they evacuate?"

"They'd never outrun the undead," Roland said. "Their only chance is to hold the enemy until the army can arrive to wipe it out."

"Or," Brass offered, "skip that noise and send us."

"What could you do against an army?" Lupolt asked.

"It's undead. Just kill the thing that raised them, and the rest of them pop," Brass said dismissively. "Easy stuff."

"Somehow, I doubt that," Lupolt said. "And even if you could, you're needed *here*."

"Lupolt, if they think they can stop the undead, they should go," Roland said.

"Absolutely not," Lupolt said. "You are more important than one settlement."

"What?" Church gawked.

"It's the calculus of rule," Lupolt said. "Every day, people die. I don't like it, but that's the way it is. All we can do is try to make the decision that keeps the number as small as possible. If Loraine falls, it falls. But if Roland dies, what's left of Corsar dies with him. If that happens, it's anarchy, if not war."

Phoenix opened his mouth to offer a solution, but Brass got a word in first.

"Uh, have you *been* outside a city lately?" Brass asked. "Anarchy's already the default."

The glintchaser didn't mean it as an accusation, but Lupolt took it as one anyway, and the royal attendant immediately snapped a response before Phoenix could say anything.

"I know what's outside the walls. But it will only get worse without someone leading the kingdom," Lupolt said. "Roland's safety is our priority."

Now it was Roland's turn to interrupt Phoenix before he could get a word in.

"I decide whose safety is priority," the king snapped. "And I won't sacrifice my people for my own safety. That is not the kind of king I am."

"With all due respect, it's the kind you need to be. You are too important."

"So are the people I'm sworn to protect."

"Then we don't choose!" Phoenix's shout cut through the noise, driven by his frustration and the anxiety caused by everyone's arguing. It hit everyone like a slap, stunning them to momentary silence.

Roland was the first to recover his wits. "What do you mean?"

"I mean we don't choose. We find Kurien, take her down, and then teleport to Loraine to stop the Dread Knight. We don't leave anyone to fend for themselves, everybody lives."

"Well, that's a nice idea," Ink said. "First hurdle: we don't even know where Kurien is, and magic's useless for tracking her with the Heart of Shadows involved."

"I think I have a way around that." Phoenix eyed both the High Inquisitive and the King of Corsar. "But I'm going to need your help to do it."

Roland met Phoenix's gaze, and they locked on to one another. Their previous agreement to let the past be vanished, and each felt a tide of emotion roll over them. Grief, not only for the lives lost but for the bond between them that severed. The sting of betrayals, real and imagined. Frustration at finding something so hard that should have been easy. They were friends once. Phoenix could still remember the brilliant smile on Roland's face when the prince first tried out his new leg braces. The mixture of terror and pride he felt when the prince had recommended the Starbreakers as the heroes the kingdom needed to face the Servitor. Phoenix's only saving grace was that he'd been here before. Facing a friend he'd lost because of Relgen. When interacting with another person got complicated, similar experiences to draw on were a godsend.

"We can't change what happened," Phoenix said. "But we can help with this. We can do something here and now."

For a heartbeat, the king of Corsar was impassive. Then Roland straightened as much as he could on his crutches and choked back the knot of regret and resentment in his throat. "What do you need?"

"As many illusionists as the Academy can spare and for you to have a talk with the chancellor."

LORAINE

In a few hours, everyone in this town was going to die.

The Rusted Star had cropped up on an empty space at the end of a thoroughfare, giving a good view of the unrest spreading through the ruintown. Town guards marched through the streets with a crier, calling for anyone who could to report to the guard's headquarters to aid in the defense. Some people heeded the call. Plenty more were too busy boarding up their homes or packing their bags.

Even in crisis, Loraine was still a ruintown.

One particularly enterprising individual was already selling "emergency travel packs," advertised to contain everything someone would need to survive on the road. Another right across from him was selling "genuine Old World personal defense weapons."

Both men's stalls had crowds in front of them.

"Do they stand *any* chance?" Bart asked as the group spectated the chaos. The kid had a big heart, full of compassion for seemingly everyone he met. Right now, it was audibly breaking.

Angel shook her head. "If it was just the army of undead coming for them? Maybe. It'd be a fight, but provincials can be pretty resilient when they have to be. But there's the Dread Knight. Even if they could stand up to that thing, as soon as he got close enough, he'd turn this whole place against them.

The ruins are bound to be full of bodies, especially after the fight against the Servitor a few years back. Fuck, even their cemeteries. It'd be a slaughter."

"Did the king not tell them what was coming?" Ruby didn't like this any more than Bart, but she expressed it differently. His bleeding heart left him despairing at the fate of so many. She was angry.

She was angry at the thing that hated humanity so much it would see them wiped off the map. She was angry at everyone who had failed this town through their inaction or absence. She was angry at how utterly powerless she felt.

"He probably did," Angel said. How was it that despite having such a grudge against Roland, she kept finding herself defending him? "My guess is he or the baron likes the town's chances of fighting better than running."

"Are they idiots?"

"Maybe not. It's a long way to Olwin, and an undead horde doesn't eat or sleep or get sick. They run, it's good odds it just catches them on the road instead of in town. And that's without even mentioning everything else that would come for them out here."

"So, they're screwed if they stay and screwed if they run?"

"Basically."

"How does this even stop?" Bart asked. "How does this thing not just kill . . . everything?"

"If Roland throws everything he's got at it—between the army, Seven Gates, the independent knights like Wings, and the Academy—they can probably take it down," Angel said. "As long as they can get to it before its army gets too big."

"But in the meantime, it just . . . keeps going? Keeps killing?"

"Other towns will have more warning than Loraine. More time to evacuate to Olwin or across the border or just out of the fucking way."

"Right."

For most of his life, Bart had found comfort in the teaching that Renalt did not allow evil and injustice to go unanswered, even if sometimes the answer was not immediate. Knowing that, eventually, things would be all right had been a comfort to him, especially in hard times. But never before had he been confronted so directly by the gap between the evils of the world and the answer of Renalt.

Someone *would* stop the Dread Knight. But until they did, people were going to die.

For the first time, Bart had an understanding for the people who didn't much care for Renalt and his churches. "Everything will be all right in the end" was cold comfort to all the people hurt until that end came along.

Thalia spoke up for the first time since they'd arrived in Loraine.

"What if they didn't have to make a whole trip to evacuate? We've got a tunnelporting bar right behind us. We could get people out, drop them somewhere safe, and come back for more before the Dread Knight even gets here."

"Do you have any idea how hard it would be to convince even one trip's worth of people to listen to us, pile into the mysterious inn, and let us just take them away?" Angel asked. "And that's just the first group. As soon as people see their friends get swallowed up by the ground and not come back, they're gone."

At the mention of convincing people, Ruby's eyes glinted like newly minted coins.

"What if I made them listen?" she asked. "Like I did to the knights on the mountain?"

"You did that once, by accident, to three people. You can't just jump from that to an entire town."

"I don't have to," Ruby said. She found herself channeling her mental image of Brass who so often seemed to fabricate plans as he was speaking out loud. "If . . . if it's the right person, I only need to do it once." She had to wait for her brain to catch up to her mouth. But when it did, the light came on in her head. "The baron lives in Loraine. All the guards take their orders from him, and people will listen to the guards. If they were on our side, working with us—"

"You do remember this is demon magic you're talking about using, right?" Angel asked. "We still don't know what using those powers does to you."

"I don't care!" Ruby snapped. "Whether or not it's bad for me, however it makes people see me, until somebody figures out how to get rid of them, I'm stuck with these stupid powers. And if I am, I'd rather do something with them than sit around being scared. We can do this! We can help these people!"

"Some of them," Angel said. "You can help some of them. Even with the Star, even if we get the guard to help, we can't get everyone out of here before the Dread Knight shows up."

"It'd still be more than we'd save if we did nothing," Bart said. "And that's enough."

"Then start figuring out who gets to live and who gets left to die," Angel said. "Because once he gets here—"

She paused, mentally crashing into a conclusion she should have seen coming. Once the Dread Knight itself arrived at the gates of Loraine, that would be the end of the town. But every second until then was an opportunity to get more people out. The slower it came, the more people lived.

And she could think of only one way to slow that monster down.

"Son of a bitch."

This was it. The reason she had been trying to get this whole business over with as quickly as possible. It happened every time. She would do one thing. One tiny good deed that barely even counted, because it took basically no effort on her part and her only other choice had been to let someone die. So, she'd do it, and inevitably, the next thing would come. And then the next thing and the next, and each one would be a little bigger and she wouldn't be able to stop until suddenly she'd blink and everyone was expecting her to be some grand hero.

Thalia saw the look on Angel's face and immediately understood the decision she'd reached. "Hang on. You don't—"

"Of course I fucking do," Angel said.

"No. Hey!" Thalia protested. "I'm not letting you do this. All right? Not with me."

"Do what?"

"I've listened to you talk over and over about all the things you felt forced into. By your family, the order, Renalt. You hated it. You hated everyone forcing you to be something you didn't want to be. I am not going to be that to you, okay? You don't have to fight that thing. And I won't think any less of you if you don't."

"Bullshit."

"I won't. Fuck, *I don't want you to*," Thalia said. "It almost killed you last time. And you have done enough. Ruby is alive because of you. All over the kingdom, people are safe because of the monsters you put back behind bars. You didn't have to do any of that, you sure as hells don't have to do this."

"But if I fight that thing, more people live than if I don't."

"And you probably die," Thalia said. "Or come close and hate all of us for making you feel like you had to do it. Well, you don't. All right? You don't have to die for this town, you don't even have to fight for it. If you want to, you're not an angel, you're a fucking saint. And if you don't, you're a normal person who wants to live and be happy and there is nothing wrong with that. There's nothing wrong with whatever you want to do, and whatever you pick, I will still be here. So, forget about what you think you're supposed to do. Forget about what anyone else thinks. What do *you* want?"

It wasn't that no one had ever asked Angel those words before. But in the few times she'd heard them, no one had ever so vehemently demanded she consider the answer. Or given her permission to answer as honestly or free of consequence or judgment. Thalia understood something about Angel that no one, maybe not even Angel herself, ever had before.

She had spent too much of her life caught up in what other people wanted from her. What other people expected her to be. She'd lost sight of what she actually wanted until all she knew for sure was that she *didn't* want anyone else on her case.

One question. Four words. And it was like a set of shackles was finally removed from her soul after decades of having been there.

Angel cast her mind back to her fight with Hilda and the look of fear on Ruby's face that had stirred a fury in her stomach. The moment the mimic had lunged for Thalia, and her heart had lurched out of her chest. The day, so many years ago, a crowd of idiots had picked on a blonde girl for the sin of trying to be Angel's friend.

And she knew what she wanted to do.

OPENING NIGHT

With a thunderous boom, a massive shower of arcane sparks sizzled across the sky over the city of Nikos, briefly banishing the stars behind a curtain of shimmering, crackling lights. From elsewhere in the city, another ball of light streaked into the sky before erupting into a similar display. Then followed another and another after that as the arcane fireworks show truly got underway. All across the city, Corsan mages of the Academy were positioned, slinging spells into the air to create a dazzling display of lights and sounds.

And with each detonation, another swath of the city was covered in a thin sheen of magical residue from the spells.

Phoenix, Church, Brass, Ink, and Wings stood gathered in the belfry of a church that overlooked the city, watching it all unfold. Waiting.

Brass whistled. "Gotta hand it to the Academy. They know how to put on a show."

"I still can't believe Roland managed to get approval for this so quickly," Ink said.

"But are we sure Kurien's going to take the bait?"

"This whole show was publicly stated to be a sign of enduring friendship and that the members of this summit are not afraid of their enemies," Phoenix said. "We may as well have just spelt out 'Kurien, we dare you to try something' in lights."

"How's the coverage?" Wings asked. In response, Phoenix pulled his goggles down onto his face.

With the Heart of Shadows, Kurien was going to be completely concealed from any magical detection, along with anything near her. It made scrying on her impossible and any other direct detection or location method completely useless.

But it also meant that if, for some reason, the entire city showed up as magical under an arcane detection filter, then it would be very easy to spot the Heart and by extension, Kurien, as the one part of the city that didn't.

Technically, the fireworks weren't strictly necessary for that plan to work. The Academy mages Ink called in could have simply blanketed the city in the same amount of residual energy with significantly less flashy magic, and they still probably could have found where Kurien was hiding.

But a cloudless night, illuminated by pyrotechnics celebrating the fearlessness and friendships of Roland was a setting Kurien wouldn't be able to resist. Whatever hole she was hiding in, whatever plan she was forming, it would all be abandoned or hastily adapted so she could make her move. Tonight.

It was the perfect time to catch her off guard.

When Phoenix activated the arcane detection filter on his goggles, the entire city suddenly became a sea of glowing white light—save for one spot on the far side of the city, near the river, where what looked like a small amphitheater showed up as completely dark.

"Got her."

Silas wasn't sure what the occasion was beyond hearing something about the summit of world leaders in the city, but the fireworks were more than appreciated. While everyone's eyes were glued to the sky, he and his escorts were free to move through the crowded streets of Nikos completely unnoticed.

The Millionaire's Forum was packed with people and ringed on all sides by businesses and stalls eager to take advantage of the foot traffic. Unlike other forums of Nikos, it sat just at the base of the steep cliff that hosted several of the city's finest mansions. The forum was a respectable place, where the wealthy could descend down to experience more quaint and common pleasures in relative comfort and safety, and businesses could reap the benefits of customers with deep pockets.

René and Rosa remained on high alert, constantly sweeping their surroundings, each one covering the other's blind spot. They'd studied their meeting place extensively the night before, planning multiple escape routes in the event things went wrong. They were, by any metric, prepared, alert, and ready to make the transaction.

And yet, no matter how many times he glanced over his shoulder, Silas couldn't shake the feeling that something was wrong. For the time being, he kept it to himself. René and Rosa were already being as vigilant as they could be. And there was still every chance he was just being paranoid, like he always was when making underworld deals. He'd long since hardened his moral fiber against the grimmest aspects of the path he walked. He could do terrible things, like what he did to Pitch or others before him. But doing business, trusting and negotiating with criminals and cutthroats as if they were equals, still left him unsettled.

Their contact was waiting for them near a travel outfitter's shop, leaning against a collection of flimsy, disposable-looking carts laden with covered goods. Assuming that was what they'd come for, it was going to be cumbersome to maneuver through the streets, at least until they met up with the rest of their group.

True to his word, their contact had brought two hangers on with him. Like their contact, they were big men, dressed in clean linens and adorned in brightly colored sashes that seemed in vogue here in the city.

"They're armed under their sashes," René said. "But then again, so are we."

"I don't see any kind of ambush on our flanks," Rosa reported.

"Then for now, we take it as innocent precaution," Silas said.

He was still on edge, but he didn't get a sense of imminent betrayal from these men. He would have expected a more conspiratorial look to them or else maybe a blank expression to hide their deception. Instead, they simply looked relaxed. Not in the way that suggested they were careless but rather that they were completely unafraid in their current situation. That boded well.

And yet.

"Keep your eyes out for anything," Silas warned.

The three of them made their approach, quick and direct, and their contact shoved off of the cart to stand up straight to greet them with a slight frown.

"Did you have to be so obvious?" the man asked in Parthican.

Silas cleared his throat before speaking, still uncomfortable with the language. *"Did we do something wrong?"*

The contact sighed, shaking his head. *"Foreigners. It's too late now. Let's just be quick."*

He nodded to one of his associates who pulled back the canvas cover on the cart's goods to reveal stacks of cases that looked made to store instruments and selected one from the top of the pile. He flicked open the case to show Silas and the twins the contents, which gleamed under the dazzling, multicolored lights above them—two swords, each with Arcania lettering etched along the face of the blade with grooves near the edges that gave a faint, white-gold glow. An unmistakable, almost intangible hum came from the surface of the blades along with the faintest whiff of ozone.

When the plan had first been proposed, Silas had doubts about using a madwoman murderer as an intermediary in acquiring their arsenal. But now the results were right there in front of him: Old World weaponry, the most coveted kind of artifacts across the world. The greatest of them could let one man fight like one hundred, and even the simplest put any implement made by modern hands to shame.

And the carts were full of them.

Silas presented the bottomless bag he had been carrying—which contained no less than ten thousand crowns in hard bullion. Their contact took the time to make sure everything was there. It was a tedious process, during which Silas had nothing to do but sit, wait, and shiver at the evening chill that was rapidly descending on the forum.

Silas's whole body suddenly went rigid as he truly processed the sudden cold in the middle of a previously temperate summer evening, and he whirled around, making everyone else in the meeting jump in surprise as he searched wildly around the forum.

He spotted her not ten feet away, standing with her daggers drawn, the blades dancing with different colors as the frost clinging to them caught the light of the fireworks. Already, the crowd was parting around her, warned of her presence by the sudden cold snap in the air. Her eyes were like two glassy white orbs as they bore into Silas.

"You," Silas growled.

"Me," Snow replied.

From a perch atop the remains of a crumbling wall in the ruins outside of Loraine, Angel waited for the Dread Knight and his undead to arrive. Like any approaching army, they started as little more than a dark line at the edge of the horizon. Then, slowly, over the course of a few hours, she watched them take shape.

A shambling horde of long-desiccated corpses, clad in the tattered remains of armor and clinging to chipped and corroded weaponry, marched toward her, forming a sea of burning cobalt eyes. Reanimated war mammoths towered over the rank and file, lumbering along as their rusted armor jingled against their hulking forms.

Near the front of the army were two undead that still looked human, except for their deathly pale skin and burning eyes, their armor and weapons whole and bearing the crest of the Seven Gates of Sasel. With disgust, Angel realized what had become of the missing members.

And of course, leading the macabre procession was the Dread Knight itself.

Angel slipped off the wall and down to the ground, beginning the slow walk out to meet them, just far enough to get their attention. The Dread Knight slowed his march, eventually coming to a stop a few hundred feet away.

"You survived," the Dread Knight's voice boomed across the field. "But you have not learned."

Angel's heart hammered in her chest, and heat rose up in her body. She should have been terrified. Should have been begging and praying for Renalt to spare her soul. By any sane metric, this wasn't heroic, this was suicide.

But when she looked out at the army before her, all she saw was a sea of victims, killed without last rites, their souls twisted into the horror and torment of undeath. She saw a tide that would wipe an entire town of people off the map and probably sweep them up into the same fate as the things that destroyed them. She saw a single, malignant entity behind it all.

And her blood boiled.

Her hands, her whole body, were trembling. But not from fear. Every fiber of her being was shaking, burning, screaming with pure, unbridled rage.

In that moment, she didn't care what Renalt wanted her to be. She didn't care what anybody else thought she was or what mistakes and failures were behind her. All that mattered was making sure the Dread Knight didn't hurt anyone else ever again. For most of her life, she'd blamed other people for dragging her back into this life, into these fights. But Thalia putting the choice back in her hands had made her realize something.

She wanted to be here. To fight. To rend the Dread Knight from the world with her bare hands for daring to inflict its evil on the innocent souls of this world. Her world. A golden halo ignited over Angel's head as her whole body began to glow and her eyes became twin suns.

"So be it," the Dread Knight said. "You die today. My promise, one fallen of heaven to another."

In answer, Angel screamed.

The feral sound ripped through the air, echoing through the ruins behind her and carrying all the way back to Loraine itself. Angel's whole form was swallowed in a blinding beacon of light before twin beams lanced out from her eyes. They cleaved through the ranks of the Dread Knight's army, reducing swathes of it to ash as she swept her head from left to right.

In a blink, the entire front rank was gone, along with much of the lines immediately behind them. Only the Dread Knight and the reanimated members of the Seven Gates remained of the vanguard.

As quickly as it came, the light extinguished, leaving Angel with only a dim glow in her skin and eyes. The initial burst of power was good for a statement, but this was going to be an endurance match. Already, Angel felt like the inside of her body was on fire, and that was just the easy part of this fight.

She'd just kicked the undead hornet's nest. Now, she had to keep its attention for as long as she could.

PERSPECTIVE

Hilda's footsteps echoed in the otherwise silent halls of the keep. Except for those assigned watch duty or chores, after dinner was free time for the members of the Order of Saint Ricard. Some used the opportunity to unwind, indulging in simple hobbies like reading or playing music. Others, particularly the newer members, used the time to study and train. Hilda had been hoping to spend the evening with her girlfriend. But apparently, she'd taken someone's monitor shift.

Naomi hated monitor shifts.

The monitor room was a small chamber near the heart of the keep with walls decorated in red and white banners bearing the insignia of the order, and the center of the room was occupied by a pool filled with shimmering silver waters.

At a touch, the pool could be made to show anything within the power of Saint Ricard to see, and often, it would show things entirely of its own volition, bringing news and warnings to the order as Ricard saw fit.

But it was a temperamental thing, and it could also sometimes show nothing, leaving whoever was on duty with nothing to look at but their own reflection while simultaneously requiring that they not let their attention wander, lest they miss something critical. It was the kind of boring work Naomi usually avoided unless she was already avoiding something else.

The priest was sitting on the rim of the pool itself, her finger drawing lazy ripples across the water's surface. She didn't acknowledge Hilda when she came in, her eyes glued to the silver pool. In training today, Naomi trounced her sparring partner with an almost impatient efficiency, and at dinner, she'd eaten in silence at the edge of the table, cleared her plate as soon as she was finished, and left the room. And now, this.

Hilda dared to hope this was just about Naomi missing home or doing a favor for an overworked squire or that maybe Hilda had forgotten one of the seven anniversaries Naomi liked to keep track of. Anything but the one topic that had been hanging over them since yesterday.

Anything but Monica.

The knight rapped her knuckles on the doorway, finally getting Naomi to glance in her direction for a moment.

"Commander."

Hilda frowned at Naomi's formality, but she soldiered on. "Missed you after dinner. Searched half the keep before somebody told me you took monitor duty tonight."

"I wanted to give Cole the night off."

"So, you're not avoiding me?"

Instead of answering, Naomi turned her attention back to the pool. Hilda sighed, bracing herself.

"What did I do?"

"What did—" Naomi's face flashed with indignation. "Hilda, you wanted to murder an innocent girl."

"To protect the world."

"And now you're letting a town die!"

"I am following our oath!" Hilda said. "We stand—"

"I know what we stand for. I also know we could help the people of Loraine, and we are choosing not to," Naomi said.

"You think I don't know that?" Hilda asked. "You think this isn't a hard choice for me to make?"

"I think you chose wrong," Naomi said.

"We have our mission."

"Then *the mission* is wrong!"

Technically speaking, Naomi had just spoken heresy. Again.

Even though she served as a member of the Order of Saint Ricard, it was the pendant of Saint Robyn that hung from Naomi's neck. Robyn, the Saint of Revolution, was a symbol of change and rebellion against unjust rule. So, of course Naomi chafed against traditions and constantly questioned Hilda's decisions. It was practically sacrilegious for her not to.

And of course Hilda had fallen in love with her. Why did she always fall for the troublemakers?

"Every time this order has gone off mission, things have gone wrong," Hilda said. "When the order stepped in to help Roland I and Katherine claim the crown of Corsar, war broke out. When we answered the crown's call to stop the Servitor, we were nearly wiped out, and the Horde of Stone invaded from Antem while we were weakened. When my father abandoned his post to train Monica, he died."

"So, we sit here and do nothing while your ex dies trying to save the town we abandoned?"

"Monica's not dying doing anything," Hilda said.

"She came *here*, just for a chance to find help for that town," Naomi said. "You really think she'd turn her back on it just because she couldn't get it?"

"You don't know her like I do," Hilda said. "She acts tough because she's stronger than almost anything she runs into, but when things actually get hard, she always runs. She tried to fight the Dread Knight, and it almost killed her. She's not going anywhere near it."

"Then explain this!"

Naomi splashed her hand against the silver surface of the pool, and as the ripples faded, an image of the streets of Loraine came into focus. The town's guard had assembled on the street, manning makeshift barricades that enclosed a massive crowd of people. Desperate, terrified screams filled the air as the guards picked off the reanimated dead that were beginning to stalk the nearby streets.

The Rusted Star took in dozens of people at a time, closing its doors only when it began to get too crowded to move safely, after which it would disappear into the ground, returning a few minutes later. Manning its doors, alternately ushering people inside or consoling those left just short of the cutoff, were Bart and Ruby.

"Every time this thing has decided to show me something, it's been Loraine," Naomi said. "That's her inn. She's there."

Hilda failed to hide her surprise. "She found a way to help without fighting."

"Except they can't save them all," Naomi said. "The fringes of the Dread Knight's army are already starting to enter the city."

"Nobody ever manages to save everyone," Hilda said. "Monica's saving who she can, which is more than even I thought she would. The people who protect Corsar's interior will do their job, and we will do ours."

Naomi's shoulders sagged, and Hilda's frown deepened.

"You still think I'm wrong."

"You're the commander. You've made your decision."

Naomi's voice had a bitter tinge to it, but however much she disagreed with Hilda, she didn't take it as far as desertion or insubordination. Hilda wondered whether it was because Naomi ultimately trusted her decisions as commander or she just couldn't bring herself to stand against Hilda.

She prayed it was the former.

"I have. I'm sorry if you disagree with it."

Naomi turned her back, refocusing on the pool. Hilda decided that it might be best if she gave Naomi some space and turned for the door.

"Hilda."

The knight commander froze in place and instantly felt embarrassed. All Naomi had to do was say her name, and she could stop Hilda's heart. For a moment, her chest tightened in anticipation, waiting for Naomi's next words.

"You need to see this."

The commander obliged her partner, coming back to the pool. She didn't know what to expect. A new threat that they could ride out to meet felt like too much to hope for. Maybe things were taking a turn for the better in Loraine. Or a turn for the worse.

What Hilda saw instead was her one-time lover, surrounded by ruins and the scattered remains of undead soldiers, her eyes ablaze like white hot flames, in the middle of a fierce melee with what could only be the Dread Knight itself. The longer Hilda stared at the scene, the more insane it was to her. Monica, who'd taken the name "Angel" as a sarcastic joke, who'd run from the Order of Saint Ricard not once but twice, who'd spent the last seven years hiding and hoping the world forgot about her, was fighting a monster she knew she couldn't beat.

And where she was doing it—their surroundings were too dilapidated to be Loraine itself. Which meant she was fighting it outside the town's defenses. She recalled the earlier scene from inside Loraine, where the guards were holding back only the small beginnings of an undead incursion, and suddenly the pieces began to fit together.

She was going to get herself killed. She had to know that. But every second she didn't was one that the Dread Knight would be fighting her and not the town. Hilda had been half right. Monica was saving everyone she could. But she was doing it at the cost of herself.

Hilda watched as Monica swung a haymaker that went wide, resulting in her taking an elbow to the head that sent her sprawling. She was up on her feet a second later, screaming bloody murder. This time, she landed a good hit, sending the Dread Knight through a wall that crumpled on top of it. It burst out from the rubble, unphased.

Only a brief exchange and Hilda knew. Monica stood no chance. She was going to die in those ruins. But every second she fought, the number of people who would die with her shrank.

In the face of that kind of sacrifice, all Hilda could feel was shame. While Monica fought and died, the order stood still. Would stay still.

Unless Hilda moved it.

"Hilda?"

"Get everyone ready to depart," Hilda ordered. "Now!"

FIREWORKS

The Lysander Theater was a dilapidated mess of a place. The doors and windows had all been boarded up, and the paint on the marble walls was chipped and cracked in places where it wasn't missing outright. The giant mask over the main entrance hung at an off-kilter angle, threatening to fall off completely even as it continued to cast its lopsided gaze over all who entered.

"Say one thing for Kurien, she really knows how to stay on brand."

"I thought the authorities were searching theaters?" Church asked.

"We're in Nikos," Phoenix said. "Every building here is either a theater, a bath, or a courthouse."

They searched the theater slowly and methodically, starting with a full sweep of its exterior before moving inward. The four of them split up, each making their way through a separate part of the theater. Though they wanted to be thorough and sweep the entire building, they all knew that there was really only one place Kurien would be waiting for them in a place like this.

And so, they all converged on the main stage itself.

Phoenix came in through the main entrance, staring down a wide aisle flanked on either side by a semicircle of stone bench seating. Brass came in from the west wing, Church the east, while Wings crept out onto a balcony seating box overhead. Tattered, midnight blue curtains framed the edges of a slightly dilapidated wooden stage, while a small hole in the ceiling let a shaft of shifting light and colors shine down on it. And standing center stage, still as a mannequin and patiently waiting with her back turned, was none other than Kurien.

As the door closed shut behind Phoenix, Kurien brought her hands together in a slow, hollow clap.

"As soon as I heard about the fireworks, I knew you had some sort of trick to find me," Kurien said. She turned around with a flourish, spreading her arms wide. "Well? Here I am."

At the same time, Phoenix drew his wand and Wings knocked back an arrow. They shot as one, just in time for Kurien to vanish in a burst of ink-black darkness, leaving nothing but an echo of her laughter. Four heads moved at once, looking in every direction for any sign of where she'd gone.

"And yet, still I find myself disappointed."

Kurien's voice echoed, sourceless and omnipresent. "Am I not worth a proper reunion, gentlemen? Did I not warrant the full troupe? You'd have me settle for the three of you and one of the king's lapdogs?"

"Rude," Wings muttered.

"Honestly, how am I supposed to stage a grand return without proper antagonists? The Prince Killer versus the Starbreakers is a story worth telling. An iconic clash for the ages. The Prince Killer versus *some* of the Starbreakers and someone else doesn't even roll off the tongue!"

Wings nocked and fired an arrow, a gust of wind banking it hard to the right in midflight, sending it straight into a seemingly empty dark corner in the theater.

With a flash of steel, the arrow was sliced out of the air, and the shadows in the corner coalesced into the form of Kurien.

The Prince Killer cocked her head. "Well now. The lapdog knows a few tricks."

"That was a warning shot," Wings said. "Call me lapdog again and see where I aim the next one."

The Prince Killer straightened her posture as, one by one, a row of weapons unfurled behind her like a set of razor-sharp, metal wings. There were even more now than there had been when Church and Brass had fought her. When she spoke, there was a new twinge of excitement laced into her voice.

"I suppose I can make do with the players I've been given." With a flourish, she reached behind her, producing the final piece of her arsenal—Phoenix's old blaster, crackling and ready to fire as she extended it toward her assembled adversaries in mock salute.

"Come now, everyone! Give me a show!"

Kurien punctuated her challenge by vanishing into a cloud of darkness as her weapons scattered off in four directions, each one moving to harry a different opponent.

As a trio of polearms came racing toward her, Wings dove from her balcony, her ethereal wings bursting to life behind her and carrying her into a quick, rolling turn to avoid them. The weapons altered their course to follow her, forcing her into further evasive maneuvers in the tight space of the theater.

Down below, the boys were having their own problems.

Brass was retreating backward, hopping over seating rows as he parried one errant flying sword after another. At the opposite side of the room, Church was struggling to keep his footing under an onslaught of attacks from a maul and a mace. And down in the center, Phoenix was being completely overwhelmed. A small swarm of daggers, along with a single chakram, were coming at him from every direction, darting in and out to make quick slices at him. For every one he blocked with his force shield or shot out of the sky with his wand, it felt like two more slipped through his guard and cut another slit in his armor. The arcane weapons were more than a match for the protective enchantments in his armor, and taking them out one by one was going too slowly. Sooner or later, one of them was going to hit something important, which meant he had to end this quickly.

Holstering his wand so he could keep his shield up, Phoenix dug as many dispelling discs as he could out of his belt and tossed them out in a wide circle around him. With a flash of light and a crash, the discs dissolved into embers, and every single weapon attacking Phoenix dropped to the ground, completely inert—along with every enchanted piece of equipment on his person.

Dispelling discs couldn't destroy the kind of permanent magic woven into Phoenix's equipment, but they could absolutely disrupt it. In that moment, Phoenix's armor, his wand, even the bottomless pockets in his belt and coat, all briefly became ordinary steel and leather.

And then Kurien reappeared center stage.

On an intellectual level, Phoenix understood that Kurien was using his old weapon. When Brass and Church had first told him, it hadn't taken him too long to work out a chain of events that might have led to the old thing ending up in some wealthy individual's private artifact collection. He'd even prepared to deal with it, tuning his armor to resist the energy the blaster fired.

But it was different *seeing* his own creation pointed at him, charging to fire, and knowing that not only had he built the thing that was about to put a hole in his chest but that he'd also just disabled the one thing that might have protected him from it. As Kurien pulled the trigger, Phoenix recalled the old fable of the Architect of Oblivion and the old adage about creators always being undone by their creation.

It really was a stupid way to go.

Luckily, if there was one person with plenty of experience saving Phoenix from himself, it was his wife.

Wings dove down from the air, bringing both feet onto Kurien's back in a flying mule kick, and Kurien's shot went wide. She disappeared into a cloud of darkness again, reappearing a few feet away. With a twitch of her finger, the weapon fired itself once again.

Wings almost got clear of the shot, taking a blast aimed for her heart in the shoulder. She ducked out of the way of the next one and was back in the air by the time the third went off, dodging blast after blast.

Brass and Church both tried to close the gap on Kurien, only to be cut off by more flying weaponry as Kurien conducted her arsenal against them. Her hands twirled in a flourish of movement, all while she still found time to mentally aim and fire Phoenix's blaster at Wings.

Back in the stands, Phoenix was deeply annoyed at Kurien and himself. None of his equipment was functioning yet, but after years of working with it, he'd become a particularly accurate throw. And Kurien had given him plenty of weapons to choose from.

Phoenix scooped the bronze chakram off the ground, waited for a moment where Kurien's head was transitioning to look up at Wings, and threw the weapon straight into the Prince Killer's face. It struck dead on, snapping Kurien's head back as it took a chunk out of her previously pristine mask.

Kurien staggered backward, cackling.

"Oh, very good!" Her head snapped forward once again, displaying the deep, jagged crack running down the side of her mask and the massive nick at the top of it. "That's talent! Delivering even when diminished! Don't disappoint me now! It's time for the grand finale!"

Kurien's remaining weapons retreated from their bouts, returning to their position at her back as the shadows of the theater began to warp and pool around her, seemingly unaffected by the fireworks from outside. Brass, Church, and Wings all rushed the stage as the darkness seemed to swallow Kurien, closing in just as she vanished from sight.

"Oh, come on!" Wings cried. "Is she just going to keep doing this the whole time?"

Phoenix looked around, thinking. This was different from Kurien's other disappearances in the fight. She wasn't taunting them from the shadows, and her weapons weren't attacking them to create any kind of opening. That, and her mention of a grand finale, pointed to one conclusion.

Kurien wasn't in the theater anymore.

"Ink, she's on the move," Phoenix barked into his messenger coil. "If she's covering her tracks with the Heart, you should be able to see the gap she's creating with a detection spell."

"*Well then, we've got a problem,*" Ink's voice came back. "*Because I'm seeing four gaps leaving the theater in different directions.*"

"Is she trying to distract us?" Church guessed.

"She'd have to know how we were tracking her to game it like that, and I don't think she does," Phoenix said. "This isn't her trying to throw us off her trail, this has to be part of her finale somehow."

"How?" Wings asked.

"Enough of this. I'm following the one headed for Roland," Ink said.

As soon as Ink spoke, a realization struck Phoenix. Kurien was here to make a statement, to reinstall herself as the terror of nobility and leaders everywhere. Everything they knew said Roland was her target.

But that didn't mean Roland was her only target.

"No!" Phoenix shouted. "We need you here, now!"

"Why?"

"Because Roland isn't the only world leader in the city!"

For a split second, neither Snow nor Silas moved as they stared each other down. Snow took in her surroundings.

Three people were here to sell weapons to Silas, all armed but visibly skittish, and they already had their money. When violence broke out, they'd run. Silas had two identical women with him to make the exchange. Silas and the twins all wore wristpockets, and the twins were also each wearing another piece of Old World jewelry around their wrists that Snow couldn't place. The associates of criminals in hiding didn't usually wear Old World jewelry purely for the sake of fashion, so it was safe to assume they did something magical. She'd have to keep an eye on them.

"Both of you get the cargo out of here," Silas ordered. "I'll handle this."

"We're not leaving you."

"René, go. That's an order."

The argument was over as quickly as it started, but it was all the opening Snow needed.

In a blink, Snow was gone, reappearing behind Silas with daggers already drawn. He was slow to react, but someone else pushed him out of the path of Snow's blade.

There was movement to Snow's right and footsteps behind her. She blinked away before either could become a problem.

René and Rosa drew up on either side of Silas as their wristpockets flashed, summoning their weapons into their hands. Rosa wielded an Iandran rapier while René brandished a pair of stiletto parrying daggers. Silas himself drew two shortswords whose pommels were connected by a thin metallic cord.

Sure enough, the weapon sellers ran, taking their money and leaving their carts full of goods. Most of the other people in the forum had the same idea, fleeing while shouting for help. Those who stayed kept their distance, not interested in getting involved but unable to look away. Sooner or later, someone, probably a local guard, was going to do something stupid like get in the way.

Snow needed to finish this before that happened.

The next time Snow blinked in, René and Rosa were ready, positioned on either side of her as she reappeared behind Silas again. With a dagger in each hand, she blocked both of their attacks and still reacted in time to parry Silas. She kicked him in the chest and blinked away again, and Silas and the twins made the mistake of turning around.

Instead of reappearing behind Silas for the third time, Snow turned up at René's side, blades flashing. Snow's knife sank into René's shoulder, and ice immediately began to spread out across her arm. In another second, Snow would have had her, but that was when René's mysterious Old World bracelet lit up.

René's whole body became a blue-white silhouette before condensing into a single spark and zipping over to Rosa's side where René rematerialized in a flash, out of Snow's reach.

So that's what they do.

René and Rosa fought in almost perfect sync, each one creating space for the other. René came fast and reckless, putting a lot of aggression behind weapons traditionally built for defense. Rosa, in contrast, was patient and precise, every thrust, parry, and feint expertly done. Regularly, one twin would teleport to the other's side, often as a way to dodge Snow's advance or try to gain an angle for attack.

In their brief exchange, three things kept Snow alive.

The first was that she knew their game. One attacker employing steady, decisive swordplay, the other coming at the flanks with daggers as fast and mean as they could—it was the exact pattern she and Brass used when they fought together.

The second thing was, of course, the Heart of Ice. Just a touch of Snow's weapons could send ice spreading across their weapons and bodies, impairing their movements. As an added bonus, the open and rampant displays of magic had scared off what straggler observers had remained of the crowd.

The third thing was more straightforward: She was better than them.

Even two on one, the twins struggled to keep up with Snow, and even with both of them teleporting back and forth between their positions, they never seemed to actually put Snow off balance long enough for it to matter.

The wrench in things was Silas.

Wide open as he might have been at first, he learned fast. She hadn't caught him off guard with a blink since engaging René and Rosa, and he was careful to never let his blades stay in contact with hers for too long. The cord between his swords wasn't just for show either. More than once, he used it to block her attacks, and if not for her own reflexes, he'd have entrapped one of her arms with it early on in the fight.

Any two of them, Snow was confident she could have taken. But all three at once was proving to be a problem. Parrying both the twins meant she had to retreat to dodge Silas.

Going for an attack on him necessitated relieving whatever pressure she had on the twins. For a moment, she considered abandoning her original plan and playing her trump card early. But apparently, she wasn't the only one getting desperate.

As Snow blocked another stab from Silas, ice raced out from her feet across the ground, snaring René by the ankle. Rosa immediately retreated, giving René room to teleport to her and to safety, at the cost of giving up a lot of ground. But instead of letting the twins rejoin the fight, Silas deliberately moved to position himself between them and Snow.

"Go! Now!" he shouted.

René still looked ready to charge in, but Rosa grabbed her by the arm, pulling her toward the ramshackle carts loaded with weapons. Technically, Snow's only job was bringing in Silas. But if he wanted the carts out of here, she wanted them to stay put. So as soon as the twins threw their backs into getting the carts rolling, Snow blinked around Silas and onto the top of the closest cart, looming over the twins.

She leapt just as Rosa sliced with her rapier, sailing over the attack and both the twins's heads with an aerial front flip. She readied her daggers to come down swinging.

But then, something wrapped taut around her waist, and she was yanked out of the air.

Just before she hit the ground, she caught sight of one of Silas's shortswords, only now the cord attached to it was much, much longer, wrapping around her waist multiple times and reaching all the way back to Silas who held fast to the other sword on his end.

With another yank from Silas, the cord uncoiled from around Snow and shrank back. Only instead of returning the flung shortsword to Silas's hand, the cord went thick and rigid, becoming a polearm capped by a sword at each end. He twirled the weapon once overhead with practiced ease before leveling it at her.

His eyes sent a clear message: *If you want them, you have to go through me.*

"I'll just take them when I'm done with you," Snow said as she got back to her feet.

"I don't think so," Silas said.

Behind him, Rosa reached into the folds of her linens and produced a small, circular device that struck Snow as familiar. As glyphs on the device began to glow, the air around the twins and the carts took on the distorted, fractal appearance that accompanied imminent teleportation.

Snow threw a dagger, trying to knock the device from Rosa's hands, but René was ready, deflecting the attack with her own dagger. In the instant before the teleportation finished, Snow realized why Rosa's device looked familiar; it was a beacon.

The very same kind Ink had given Snow to carry. The twins weren't teleporting the cargo. They were signaling someone else to.

And then, they were gone.

Lupolt was in the impromptu war room he and Roland had set up when Phoenix's warning came through the message coil. The king's right-hand man stiffened. When he spoke, his voice was tense.

"Roland."

For the first time all night, the king looked up from the table of maps and reports he'd been poring over. "She's coming?"

"Yes."

Lupolt tested the draw of his weapon from its scabbard. It was as smooth as ever. Good. He couldn't afford to go into a fight with its mechanisms even the slightest bit faulty.

Phoenix had tried to be optimistic about being able to find and capture Kurien before she could make a move on Roland, but they had all acknowledged that it was still a strong possibility that the assassin would make her play tonight. The fireworks were too perfect a backdrop not to at least consider it.

And as much as Lupolt detested the idea of putting the king in danger by daring his would-be killer to come for him, Roland insisted the risk was worth it. How much of that belief was pragmatic bravery and how much was his wounded pride, Lupolt didn't feel like debating. Roland was the king; the decision was his.

But that didn't mean Lupolt had to like it.

"Get away from the windows."

"I'm nowhere near them, and the curtains are drawn."

"You're still in their line of sight. If she has a way to see through the curtains, you're a clear target. Find a corner, or—"

"I don't know whether to marvel at your paranoia or be offended that you think I'd do something so gauche as a shot through a window."

Kurien sat in a plush chair in the corner of the room with one leg crossed over her lap, as if she'd always been there. She shook her head in mock disappointment.

"I mean, honestly, who do you think I am? The Bowman?"

Lupolt positioned himself immediately in front of Roland, one hand resting on the hilt of his weapon, the other holding its short, rectangular scabbard in place. If Kurien was really in the room in front of him, she had gotten in through locked and sealed points of entry, countless alarm wards, and an army of security. However she'd managed it, she might very well use the same means to slip past Lupolt to get to Roland the second the king's retainer charged forward.

For now, Lupolt's best course was to hold his ground and stay close to the king.

Kurien drew in a deep breath, letting it out long and slow. "No. I prefer my art to be more . . . personal. I want to see the look in my victim's eyes when their end comes. I want to know how they meet it."

"You're not going to touch him."

"Obviously." Kurien gestured to the weapon in her hand. "That's what this is for."

She leapt to her feet, drawing her spindly frame up into an upright posture with one hand tucked behind her back and Phoenix's weapon at the ready.

"I like the look in your eyes, dear servant," Kurien murmured. "The devotion. The fear. You're going to make this so much more enjoyable."

Lupolt tightened his grip on one of his weapon's hilts as he gauged the distance between him and the Prince Killer. Not yet.

"Now. Are you ready to die for your king?"

Roland tensed in his chair. "Lupolt—"

Kurien took a single step forward, and Lupolt drew. The blade exploded from its short, box-like sheath with a metallic chittering as piecemeal segments of steel joined together to form a narrow rectangular blade the length of an Iandran dueling rapier—more than double the length of the scabbard on Lupolt's hip.

In a perfect imitation of Brass's own technique, Lupolt leveled his sword and thrusted straight for Kurien's face. The Prince Killer dodged with an effortless tilt of her head, nimbly ducked under Lupolt's follow-up slash, and parried the third strike with Phoenix's blaster.

Lupolt narrowly dodged the point blank blast Kurien offered in response and was quickly forced back as Kurien fired off several more. Before a shot could land on him or Roland, Lupolt kicked over the table Roland had been working at, turning it into cover for the both of them.

"Roland?"

"I'm okay!"

Lupolt couldn't afford to take time to confirm that. He shoved his weapon back into its scabbard, the blade clicking and clattering as its segments disassembled to fit back inside. He immediately drew once again, but now, the weapon came out in a different configuration.

Instead of a single, long, thin blade, Lupolt's weapon now boasted a short, wide profile akin to a square butcher's knife. When he stood up from the cover of the table, he aimed it like Phoenix aimed his wand.

With a hiss, Lupolt's weapon fired off a blade like a missile, returning fire against Kurien. The first blade went wide as Kurien's whole body became a cloud of darkness and shifted out of the way, and the next several that Lupolt loosed were all similarly avoided as Kurien's shadowy form crawled across the walls of the room, always managing to move just clear of Lupolt's shots.

By the time Kurien reformed, Lupolt's weapon was out of blades to shoot. A dark, throaty chuckle echoed behind Kurien's mask as she took aim at Lupolt's chest. Lupolt returned his hilt to his scabbard and charged forward.

Kurien fired once, and Lupolt ducked. A second shot, he narrowly avoided with a sharp lean to the side. By the time Kurien fired a third shot, Lupolt was nearly on top of her. And as the blast came, Lupolt leapt into the air, flipping over the blast and Kurien's head as he drew not one but both hilts from his scabbard, each one now boasting only a single blade segment the length of a dagger. Lupolt came down swinging with both blades, a relentless blur of steel Snow would have been proud of. When one swipe missed, he flipped the knife in his hand and came back in with a reverse grip stab. He cut with one hand, thrust with the other. More than once as Kurien tried to line up a blast, Lupolt shoved the blaster high or to the side, sending the shots wide.

After a brief struggle, Lupolt managed to lock the wrist of the hand holding Phoenix's blaster in between his two blades and with a clean cut, severed Kurien's hand. The Prince Killer snarled as she staggered backward, bleeding from her new wrist stump, only to be pinned to the wall by Lupolt holding a blade to her throat.

Kurien let out another chuckle, though it was underpinned less by a sardonic edge and more by a hiss of pain.

"Well played. You're almost as good as the originals," Kurien congratulated. "Roland?"

There was a scuffle and clack as Roland struggled out from behind the table and back to his feet with some difficulty.

"Still alive."

Lupolt risked the briefest of glances over his shoulder to confirm Roland was unscathed, nodded, and turned his attention back toward Kurien.

"It's over," Lupolt said.

"Let's not get ahead of ourselves," Kurien said. "I did say you were *almost* as good as the originals. Shouldn't you have heard something hit the floor by now?"

Lupolt's brow furrowed as he searched Kurien's masked face for her meaning. The realization came too late.

A warped sound like a stone on a frozen lake cut through the air, and his abdomen exploded in pain. Hovering a few inches off the ground, Kurien's severed hand still clutching it, was Phoenix's blaster.

A warm wetness quickly began to soak Lupolt's shirt. His legs wobbled beneath him. As Kurien's laughter filled his ears, the whole world went black, and the madwoman slipped from Lupolt's rapidly weakening grasp.

Lupolt stumbled forward in the dark, flailing to try and find Kurien with his blades, but he met nothing but empty air. When the darkness receded, Lupolt was standing in the middle of the room, and Kurien was right behind him. Roland shouted a warning that came too late. Kurien kicked Lupolt in the same place that he'd been shot, knocking him down and sending his blades clattering across the floor. Lupolt groaned and tried to stand back up, only for Kurien to force him back down with a boot to the back of the head.

The Prince Killer knelt down to Lupolt's level, shaking her head.

"Really, it was a noble effort. But this was never your fight to win," Kurien said. "Do try to stay alive for the finale though. You won't want to miss it."

Roland came forward while Kurien was still crouched, putting all his weight on to one crutch as he swung the other straight into the assassin's face. The crack that rang out carried the rage of a man pushed to his limit and harboring a decades-long grudge.

Roland moved with his own swaying balance, transitioning into a move to drive the end of his crutch down and into Kurien's foot hard enough to break bone.

But then the blaster, still hovering off the floor, swiveled in place before firing again, this time shattering one of Roland's crutches and sending him toppling over.

Roland growled, more in frustration than pain. He couldn't get up, not quickly, but he refused to stop fighting. He spotted one of Lupolt's fallen blades and scrambled to pull himself toward it, but just as his fingertips brushed the hilt, Kurien's boot crunched down on his hand. Roland screamed.

"Well played, Your Majesty! Not as helpless as your servant thinks!"

Kurien kicked the blade away from Roland's hand and then kicked Roland in the face.

"I've thought about you so much. My one that got away. You've come a long way from the sniveling little boy bleeding to death in the snow. But not far enough."

Kurien used her one remaining hand to grab Roland by the hair and drag him across the room to prop him up against a wall. Roland fought the entire way, punching and thrashing to no avail. When Kurien finally had him in a sitting position, she let go, switching to planting a boot on Roland's chest to keep him upright.

"Roland!" Lupolt dragged himself across the floor, leaving a trail of blood as he did. He didn't notice.

He didn't care.

"Lupolt," Roland coughed. "Stay back."

Kurien cackled, flinging blood from her wrist stump around the room as she threw her arms out in delight.

"You see? *This* is art! So much better than shooting through a window!"

As if in protest, every window in the room chose that exact moment to shatter into a million pieces, and a rush of warm night air threw open the curtains to reveal the dazzling green light of another firework—and of Wings, flying in with both swords drawn.

As it turned out, having Ruby convince the baron to support their evacuation plan had been the easy part. Distressingly easy, actually. When it was done and everything was in motion, Ruby was disturbed by how simple it had been. How intoxicating the control had felt. There was a lot to unpack there, but it would have to wait. The undead had come.

When they had committed to rescuing as many people in Loraine as they could, Angel had warned Bart and the others that she might be able to hold the Dread Knight's attention, but she'd never be able to keep an entire army from getting past her. Inevitably, the undead would enter the city, all bent toward the same, single-minded purpose of killing every living person in the town. She told them they needed to be ready for that.

She never actually said how.

The undead lurched around in unnatural fits and spasms, bellowing and croaking with warped, hollow voices. A pair of angry blue flames burned in every one of their hollow eye sockets with fathomless, all-consuming hatred.

The first time Bart had seen undead, rescuing Angel from them on the mountain, he'd barely had time to register them before turning tail and running as fast as he could. This was different. This time, not only were they everywhere, but he couldn't run. He had to stand, staring into those burning blue orbs and watching their twisting, writhing bodies come closer and closer.

He could barely breathe.

Most of Loraine's still-present population was gathered in the makeshift evacuation center they'd erected on the town's thoroughfare, forming a vaguely queue-shaped crowd down the length of the street as people waited for the Rusted Star to return and accept another load of evacuees.

Barricades had been erected at every intersecting street, hastily constructed out of wagons, luggage, and whatever bits and pieces could be torn off of nearby buildings. Here, the members of the town guard stood, keeping back the undead as they trickled in and helping late-arriving citizens up and over into relative safety. The few not on the barricades were all at the Rusted Star's lot, trying to keep at least a vague semblance of order.

Bart found himself with them, doing his best to console those who just missed an evacuation load's cutoff and reassure them that they were going to get everyone out safely, just as long as they were patient.

The longer things went on, the more Bart felt like he was lying.

The trickle of undead had slowly turned into a steady stream, and already that stream was threatening to become a tide. The guards were doing their best, and their leader actually knew how to fight undead, instructing his men to target the enemy's heads and spines. But knowing how to fight undead and putting it into practice while they were bearing down on you were two different things. And there were a lot more undead than guards.

Every time the Rusted Star returned, Bart could hear a voice in his head telling him, begging him to get inside it. To take the ride out of this nightmare before he lost his chance. But then he would see the face of someone on the verge of panic, and he would stay to put his hands on their shoulders and tell them they weren't going to die. Not today. Every time he did, he risked a glance to Ruby. And every time, she made the same choice as him.

A scream came from the barricade closest to Bart as undead crested the blockade, and the guard manning it tumbled onto his back, dropping his war hammer. The first undead scrambled toward the guard with a broken sword, stabbing him in the stomach while clawing at his face with a rotten hand. All around, people screamed.

For Bart, everything moved in slow motion. The hands of more undead pulling themselves up and over the barricade. People fleeing in every direction. The face of the guard, contorted in pain as the undead drove its weapon deeper into the man's stomach.

And then Bart spotted the guard's fallen war hammer.

Before the idea was finished forming in his mind, Bart's hands were wrapping around the haft of the weapon. Before he could think about what a terrible idea it was, he was rushing toward the undead attacking the fallen guard. And before he could get too scared to move, he swung the hammer with everything he had and shattered the undead's skull like a cheap vase.

The world went back to normal speed. People all around him were still screaming and running. The closest guards were rushing from their posts to meet the assault. But none of them would get there before the withered husks of pure malice collapsed onto the closest threat to them—Bart.

As half a dozen skeletal frames bore down on him, the hammer suddenly felt a million times heavier in Bart's hands. It finally dawned on Bart just what he'd done.

"Duck!"

When Bart heard Ruby's voice, he didn't question it, he didn't even turn around, he just obeyed. A whip of thorns lashed out, crashing straight through the skull of one undead and wrapping around the second before lifting it off its feet and using it like a bludgeon to smash into the rest of them.

With all six destroyed, the vine retracted back into Ruby's shaking arm. A look of shock and exhilaration consumed her face. Just as Bart recovered enough of his wits to shoot her a smile in gratitude, her own face turned to a look of horror.

More undead were coming over the barricade. Over multiple barricades.

Bart found himself surrounded on all sides by terrified people, penned in with no escape as monsters closed in all around them. They hugged one another, cowered behind the guards' lines of defense, and cried for help.

Bart stared down at the hammer in his hands, unsure where to even start.

"Renalt, please," Bart whispered. "Help us."

Typically, priests used very specific prayers to be granted very specific results. There was a prayer for healing wounds that was different from the prayer that completely restored a person's body, and they were both different from the prayer to cure a person of disease. Such was Cosmic Law. But all of that required study, training, virtue in accordance with a god's tenets, and of course practice channeling divine power so it didn't cook you from the inside out.

Bart's words were closer to how laypeople prayed. No formalities, just a person with a problem they very desperately needed solved, and faith—hope—that if he asked hard enough, he'd get an answer.

Those kinds of prayers were, quite honestly, a complete roll of the dice, which was why the clergy hadn't been put out of a job centuries ago.

But sometimes, a roll of the dice came up exactly the way you needed it to.

A beam of light descended straight from the heavens, crashing down directly between a group of civilians and an oncoming mob of undead. It was gone as quickly as it came, but where it had struck, a priest dressed for battle stood. Bart recognized Naomi as the priest gripped her saint's pendant tight with one hand and extended her other hand, speaking a prayer in the language of the gods. Divine authority carried with her voice, and a shimmering wave of golden light radiated out from her. As it washed over the advancing undead, they turned to dust.

Another beam of light lanced down from the sky elsewhere on the street. And then came another. And another. With each one, Bart's shoulders grew a little lighter, and the smile on his face grew.

After their last experience with them, Bart never would have expected to be so happy to see the Order of Saint Ricard.

Angel crashed against the base of what was once a statue's pedestal, leaving a spiderweb of cracks and getting the wind knocked out of her. As she coughed, gasping for air and getting a faint taste of copper on her breath, she took a brief moment to reflect on the fact that, if nothing else, this was going better than last time.

Angel had a lot of faults, but she wasn't stupid. She knew she couldn't hold back an entire army by herself. Not even in the tight, labyrinthine quarters of the ruins. No sooner had she retreated into them than the shambling undead began to ignore her, breaking past her nonexistent line in the sand and moving on the town itself. But as long as she held the Dread Knight's attention, the army was the only thing threatening the town. And that was as close to a fair fight as Loraine was going to get.

She knew from firsthand experience that coming at the Dread Knight with everything she had wasn't enough to put it down, so she instead focused on hit-and-run tactics. She came quick and fast, exchanging a few blows or throwing the nearest hunk of rubble at its stupid helmet and then retreating to a different part of the ruins.

She stayed just close and aggressive enough to be a nuisance that couldn't be ignored but did her best to avoid a prolonged battle that would be the end of her.

It was the perfect strategy for buying the people of Loraine more time without just getting herself killed—in theory. In practice, things were a lot messier. Even though most of the undead masses were marching on the city, plenty were still flooding the ruins, hounding Angel from all sides. Every time she thought she had a moment to breathe, she'd round a corner into another group or another undead hand would burst out of the ground and grab at her ankles.

Holding back bought her time, but it also meant the Dread Knight was stronger and faster than her. Even in short exchanges, it was dangerous, and keeping them short was its own problem. To disengage, she had to put distance between them. Sometimes, that meant throwing the Dread Knight. Sometimes it meant taking advantage of *getting* thrown. And most recently, it had meant luring it into an empty building, smashing its few remaining supports, and diving out as the whole place came down on top of it.

She knew that wouldn't be enough to stop the Dread Knight, because it wouldn't have stopped her. But it had given her time to deal with the other wrinkle in her plans—the Seven Gates. Or, the reanimated corpses of their fallen.

For whatever reason—and Angel didn't know enough about necromancy to have more than a wild guess as to why—the former knights had come back not as simple skeletal husks but as wights. Their eyes burned with the same cold blue flames, and their incoherent voices were every bit as feral and hollow, but their movements were faster and more fluid, their tactics more coordinated. And most annoying of all, they could still use magic.

Angel pried herself off the side of the pedestal, glowering at the two knights in question. One with a burning sword whose flames matched his dead, hateful eyes, and another with hands that sparked and popped with erratic pyromancy.

When the knight with the sword swung, his weapon broke apart, stretching out into a long, blazing whip of segmented blades that sliced clean through the stone behind Angel as she dove out of the way. She grabbed a loose stone out of the streets and hurled it in response, only for the mage to blast it out of the air so strongly that the shockwave lifted Angel off her feet. She tumbled across the ground, losing track of which way was up until she finally came to a stop face down in the dirt.

A low, pained groan escaped her lips, and the golden light in her eyes flickered out. Bruises, burns, cuts, and scrapes screamed to be heard in the din of pain that had become Angel's awareness. Her fight in the ruins had lasted a lot longer than the one she'd had in the mountains. But it was starting to feel like it was going to end the same way. That feeling only grew as the Dread Knight burst out of the remains of the building that had been dropped on it.

Somewhere in her mind, a voice begged her to simply stay down. To give up and let it end. She'd fought the good fight. Done her part and then some. The number of people who were going to live to see tomorrow because of her had to be in the hundreds by now, at least. If she rested, no one would think any less of her. She'd die a hero, past sins be damned.

And as those thoughts swam through her head, one thought snuck past all of them straight to the forefront of her mind.

Fuck that.

When she pushed herself up off the ground, her arms shook the whole way up. As she brought her fists up, she got a good look at her knuckles, bruised and split.

Blood dripped down her chest from a shallow gash left by the Dread Knight's sword. It hurt to breathe.

The Dread Knight remained still, watching her stand for what was sure to be the last time. The wights of the Seven Gates stayed back, watching and waiting.

"Any last words, Sentinel?"

Angel cracked her neck and straightened her posture. "When you get to hells, tell the devils I'm sorry."

In a way, it was liberating, knowing she'd run out of time. There was nothing more to gain by conserving her strength for later. For however long she could manage it still, Angel was ready to fight with every ounce of power she could manifest.

What she wasn't ready for was a beam of light cascading down from the sky, striking the ground between her and the Dread Knight, or for the gleaming silver and crimson of Hilda's armor to be standing there once it had faded, a shield emblazoned with the symbol of Saint Ricard in one hand and a gleaming white and gold axe in the other.

The mage immediately fired another blast, and Hilda raised her shield. A wall of golden light erupted from its surface, mimicking the shield's shape as it grew into a fifteen-foot barrier. The mage's fireball splashed harmlessly against the divine shield, producing little more than a ripple in it. With a growl, Hilda slammed her axe into the back of her own shield like it was a gong, and the barrier shot forward like a battering ram, plowing straight into the Dread Knight and his minions and launching them backward.

With the enemy temporarily dealt with, Hilda turned her attention to Angel, grabbing her arm and speaking a healing prayer. Instantly, Angel's wounds began to mend, and her breathing came easier again. She wasn't as good as new, but it put a bit of life back in her movements.

"So not only did you decide to face down a legion of undead alone, you opted to do it unarmed," Hilda chastised.

"In my defense, it's hard to find an axe that won't explode when I swing it."

"I know," Hilda said. "So, give this one back when we're done."

Angel stared down at Hilda's axe as the leader of the Order of Saint Ricard held her weapon out to her. The milky white and smooth gold materials, along with the subtle incorporation of feathered wings into its design, gave it away as a blessmetal weapon. Now *that* was an axe that wouldn't explode in her hands.

And Hilda had another one ready to go on her hip.

"Thanks," Angel said. "What made you change your mind?"

"It was pointed out that, since the Dread Knight is technically not of this world, even if its host body is, its presence constitutes an incursion from another world, and we are within our charge to stop him."

"No, but actually, what changed?"

"Do you really want to know, or do you want to kill it?"

"Fair enough," Angel said. "Just one problem."

Angel pointed her axe in the direction of not just the Dread Knight, not just the wights of the Seven Gates but a growing crowd of shambling undead all converging on their position, their voices a jumbled chorus of anguish and rage.

"Right," Hilda said. "Legion of undead."

"You again," Kurien snarled as Wings arrived.

"Try not to sound so disappointed," Wings said. "You want a finale? You just got a one-on-one with the Winged Lady of Sasel."

"If you think this is the finale, you're in for quite the surprise," Kurien said. "Still, you'll do until the real heroes arrive."

"They're busy with more important things," Wings said. "It's just you and me, Barn Owl."

Kurien's birdlike, masked visage cocked to one side. "I don't know which part of that to be more offended by."

Wings shot forward as she transformed her bow into scimitars, a blur of ethereal feathers and gleaming steel. Kurien laughed, dancing between her strikes before melting into the shadows of the wall. A moment later, the entire room was swallowed into complete darkness.

As soon as the darkness blinded her, Wings stopped moving, raising her swords in defense. The Heart of Shadows might block most magical detection, but it didn't get rid of the air or the Heart of the Sky's connection to it. Every breath someone let out, she could hear and trace back to the exact spot it came from. Every movement created subtle disturbances in the air she could feel, as clearly as if they'd brushed against her own skin.

She reached out with her own awareness, searching, distinguishing one source of disturbance from another. Just in time, she singled out the quick, zipping movements of Phoenix's blaster as it darted behind her. She moved her sword in response, bringing its flat to bear just in time to block a blast from it. The blast sparked off the enchanted blades, creating a flash of light that briefly illuminated the room.

It tried, again and again, to land a hit on her, moving and shooting faster and faster, and each time, Wings matched its pace and movements, her swords sparking and flashing in the dark over and over with each deflected shot. After a few seconds on the defensive, she heard the one thing she'd been waiting for—a grunt of frustration from Kurien, giving an exact read on her position in the pitch-black room.

Sidestepping another blast, she recombined her swords, drew an arrow, and loosed it straight into the corner where she'd heard Kurien, receiving a shout of surprise as her reward. The darkness in the room evaporated like black mist, revealing Kurien once again as the blaster retreated to hover at her shoulder. She'd dodged her arrow, but she'd lost the dismissive posture she'd gone into their fight with.

"The Winged Lady of Sasel, was it?" Kurien said. "How is it I've never heard of someone like you?"

"You *were* in prison for a while," Wings said as she transformed the bow back into swords. "Don't feel too bad. The dragon I killed hadn't heard of me either."

Kurien cocked her head again. "Oh my. You're not lying."

The blaster fired, and their dance resumed for another volley of shots. Kurien was getting more creative now, blasting chunks out of the walls and ceiling to create distractions or forcing Wings to redirect her attention by taking aim at Roland and Lupolt instead of her. Whereas before she'd let her get close, tauntingly evading her strikes, now Kurien kept her distance as much as she could.

Wings did her best to overcome her caution with speed, pressing even harder, constantly forcing Kurien to retreat and cover herself. And for one perfect moment, it seemed like her assault had won out. She parried a blast with one scimitar and lunged forward with the other. But rather than dodge, Kurien thrust her own hand forward, meeting the tip of her sword with the tip of her finger.

And just like that, Wings's sword froze in midair, twisted out of her grip, and swiveled around to point directly at her. She leaned back, just managing to avoid running herself through on her own sword, and quickly retreated as the blade began slicing, now puppeted by Kurien.

"I admit, I'm impressed," Kurien said. "But I think I've reached my patience dealing with extras. What exactly is so important that the Starbreakers couldn't be here by now?"

Even as she locked blades with one of her own swords, Wings couldn't help but smirk. "What do you think? The grand finale."

CURTAINS

On the other side of the city of Nikos, in a mansion being rented by the delegation from Her Lady's City, Diane Recpina was about to die. Most of her bodyguards were lying dead, their throats slit by flying swords being puppeteered by a shadowy silhouette of a woman, and the few who were still standing weren't faring particularly well. Running had done little good as the shadow woman moved like liquid, and her swords were barely slowed by the opposition mounted against her.

Now, cornered in her bedroom, she watched the last person charged with keeping her alive fall to a flying sword to the stomach. By now, the princess was out of screams, falling back on terrified whimpers as she backed away, desperate for an avenue of escape.

As a trio of floating blades slowly glided into the room, Diane ran for the bedroom's balcony. It wasn't much of a plan, but she wasn't planning. She was just trying to get away as she desperately prayed to Lady Luck to once again show her favor. Instead, as she threw open the balcony doors, she was shown the shadowy silhouette of her murderer.

She yelped, backing away, only to stop when she realized she was backing straight into the waiting points of the animated swords. Her head turned back and forth, finding herself cut off on either side.

She was trapped.

"Princess." The shadowy figure bowed, speaking fluent Iandran. *"Hearsay spoke often of your ambitions and beauty. I do hope this great and tragic end will see both suitably immortalized in the imaginations of your fellows. I promise you, it will most definitely be in mine."*

"Who are you?"

"Me? I am the great equalizer. The reminder to those at the very top of society that they are as mortal as those at the bottom. I am the untimely tragedy that rings through nations' histories for generations. And from this day forward, I am no longer merely the Prince Killer. I am the—"

The shadow's words were silenced as Brass leapt into the room through the open balcony window, and he scattered the shadow with a slice of his sword. Immediately, all three blades at Diane's back surged forward, and she let out another scream just before Brass tackled her out of the way.

They rolled to a stop on the floor with Brass hovering over Diane, offering her a reassuring smile.

"Princess," Brass greeted. "We've really got to stop seeing each other like this."

Elsewhere in the city, the Chancellor of Parthica was running for his life, hounded by a set of flying polearms. He fled through his home's grand halls, desperate to reach more of the guards somewhere on the premises before the weapons or their shadowy puppet master could catch up to him.

Unfortunately, he was not the athlete of his youth anymore, and his leg seized in a cramp so severe it dropped him to the ground. As he lay on the ground, cursing and writhing in pain, he rolled over to find himself staring down the length of a possessed spear. And then, just before it could stab down, a golden, spectral image of a sword manifested above him, batting the spear aside before cleaving it in two.

Church entered the hall from the opposite end as Kurien's shadowy doppelgänger, holding Zealot at the ready.

The Sultan of Gypten had been annoyed by the needlessly ostentatious pyrotechnics display so late in the evening, but that annoyance quickly vanished from his mind when a cloud of daggers burst into his penthouse suite. No guards came when he shouted, but the weapons quickly fanned out in a ring that encircled him.

Before he could even make sense of that much, a metallic disc flew into his suite, letting out a low thrum. Suddenly, the sultan found himself falling—toward the ceiling. The daggers closed in on the space he'd been in a moment ago, and a crash rang out as a barely visible blast of force sundered one of the daggers, followed by several more in rapid succession.

The metallic disc's thrum died, and the sultan fell back to the ground, now surrounded by the shattered remains of a dozen broken blades.

Outside the sultan's window on an adjacent rooftop, Phoenix cycled his wand and shot a line of spider silk out that he could use to swing over to the sultan's inn. As long as Kurien's shadow was still in the area, his job wasn't done. But he was off to a good start.

Back in Roland's own room, Wings couldn't see Kurien's face, but she could see the way the Prince Killer froze up like she'd just been startled, and Wings could hear the shift in her voice. All dismissal was gone.

"So, you figured it out after all," Kurien said.

"It's over, Kurien," Wings said. "You lost."

In four locations scattered across the city, Kurien and her shadows recentered their stances. Wings, Brass, Church, and Phoenix each squared off against an array of flying weapons, the only thing standing between the summit's participants and death. For Kurien's part, she found herself nearly bouncing in anticipation, even through the growing pain in her wrist. She was about to have a duel for the fate of four nations beneath a blanket of fireworks.

She couldn't have asked for a better stage.

"Please," Kurien said. "All you've done is make this interesting."

Annoyed as she was over losing his helpers and as many questions as she had about who could have teleported them and their cargo out like that, Snow took solace in the fact that she had been right. One on one, even with his fancy quicksilver weapon, Silas was no match for her.

But he did put up a fight.

With René and Rosa gone, Silas was free to swing around his weapon like a whip, cutting wide, sweeping arcs through the air to try and keep Snow back. After only a few swings, though, Snow had his pattern down, and after one last dodge, she vanished in another shadow blink, reappearing inside the arc of his swing. He reacted, trying to alter the attack's course to hit her, only for her to sidestep the attack and grab the sword out of the air.

Ice spread across the quicksilver cord linking Silas's swords, locking the weapon up and racing along it to capture him as well. He countered by retracting it, shattering the ice and converting his weapon back into a sword staff.

He stayed on the offensive, alternating between short lunges and spinning slashes with the sword staff. Snow dodged every one of them, sidestepping, ducking, and weaving around each one. With every miss, he grew more frustrated, attacking faster and sloppier. He was so tunnel visioned on her, he forgot to pay attention to his footing and didn't see the ice until it crawled up his boot.

Silas moved quickly, jabbing one end of his staff into the ice, gripping the shaft tight, and extending its length so that it propelled him into the air, breaking the ice on his foot in the process. By the time he landed, he was back to paying attention to everything Snow was making contact with. He even avoided parrying her weapons with his, knowing the contact would only let her cover his weapon in more ice.

The problem, Snow eventually realized, was that Silas only ever fell for a trick once. But she still had a few more tricks up her sleeve.

She blinked to get behind him and to get enough distance to throw both of her daggers. He, of course, spun around in time to see the attack coming and dodged—anyone who'd been in a fight with her longer than a few seconds knew to expect an attack from behind when she blinked. But hitting him wasn't the point of the throw.

The next time she blinked out of sight, Silas reacted exactly like he did before, whirling around in anticipation of an attack from behind. Only this time, he found nothing, as Snow reappeared in the exact same spot she'd disappeared from.

With his back exposed, she grabbed him by the shoulder, immediately spreading ice across his body.

Still, he fought back, elbowing her off of him with his unfrozen arm and turning to face her. The ice made his movements awkward and easy to dodge and left him wide open for her last trick. She willed Companion Piece back into her hand, calling it to come back to her—and straight into Silas's back. With a thunk, the dagger sank into him, and he seized up. His staff fell to the ground.

Just for good measure, Snow sprinted forward, leaping into the air at the last second to deliver a flying mule kick straight into Silas's chest and sending him crashing through the window of the closest building. She sprang back to her feet in one fluid motion and shook her hair out of her face.

Silas didn't get back up.

Glass crunched under Snow's boots as she stepped through the broken window to collect Silas, who she found prone in the remains of a broken shelf, shattered pottery, and loose soil. Going off that, and the flowers that were absolutely everywhere, she must have kicked him through the window of a florist. Or a homesick druid.

Most of the ice on Silas's body had broken up, letting him slowly roll onto his stomach and try to drag himself to his feet. Before he could even get on all fours, Snow's boot was on the back of his neck, pinning him down. Already, some of the frost began to fade from her face, and her eyes slowly began to shift back to a pale blue.

"One chance," Snow warned. "Stay down."

"Why?" Silas grunted. "Why are you doing this?"

"You put a hit out on me," Snow stated, as if that alone was justification for hunting a man across two kingdoms. A bit more blue came back into her eyes as she recalled last spring. "And you hurt my friend."

"You killed mine," Silas spat.

Silas squirmed and struggled beneath Snow's foot, but he got nowhere. After a moment of holding him down, Snow spread ice out from her boot and froze him to the ground.

"Kill me if you're going to," Silas said. "It won't change anything."

"Don't tempt me," Snow said. "I already promised to deliver you alive."

"You'll do no such thing."

Snow hadn't heard any clink of any weapons or armor. No tremble of fear or hesitance, which any normal person would have had in this situation. The fact that they were unarmed and unafraid to confront her should have tipped Snow off even before she turned around, but the Cult of Stars was something she still hadn't gotten back into the habit of expecting.

Two hooded figures stood behind her, hands folded neatly in front of them. With a flick of Snow's wrist, Companion Piece sank into one of their forehead carvings like it was a bullseye.

The other didn't so much as bat an eye. Crackling silver smoke began to leak out from beneath the folds of his robes, quickly filling the florist shop. Snow summoned Companion Piece back to her hand, searching for any sign of the cultists in the crackling smoke surrounding her.

"How many of you do I have to kill before you figure out this always ends the same?" Snow asked.

"Kill as much as you like. Nothing will change." Snow ignored everything but the cultist's voice, trying to locate him amid the constant echo and shift in the sound's origin. "I told you, I will not allow your hunt for Silas Lamark to succeed."

"You think you can stop me?"

"I defeated you when you were five strong. Alone, you are nothing."

"About that," Snow said. "I'm not alone."

Gamma couldn't have timed his shot better if they'd rehearsed it. A blue-white beam of light cut through the fog surrounding Snow, and a surprised grunt echoed from the smoke as the cultist took a direct hit. Snow dove out of the way as more blasts followed, each one finding another target in the smoke. On the rare occasion Gamma didn't land a kill shot, she finished his work for him with Companion Piece.

Silas may have had a bunch of starborn-worshiping lunatics watching his back, but she had an autostruct with arcane eyesight. The crackling smoke that normally provided them cover and made them so difficult to fight did nothing to impede Gamma's vision, and in seconds, the autostruct's shots fell off in pace as he started running out of targets. The fight was over. Even the Cult knew it.

"Another time, Starbreaker," a voice snarled at her, rapidly withdrawing deeper into the smoke.

The blasts from Gamma ceased, and the smoke thinned out as quickly as it had arrived. When it vanished, she found herself in the florist shop with Gamma as the only standing figure in sight. Too late, Snow realized she couldn't hear Silas struggling anymore. The ice that had encased him was still unbroken on the floor, but he was nowhere, as if he'd slipped out without disturbing it. There was no sign of where he or any of the cultists had gone.

"Where did they go?" she demanded.

"Teleportation," Gamma reported. "The effect was consistent with their movements within the atmospheric disturbance they created. I could not determine their destination."

Frustration simmered inside her, slowly growing into full blown anger. Weeks tracking Silas. Nearly getting killed by the Cult. Spending all day and all last night finding where Silas would be tonight, and she had nothing to show for it. Not Silas, not his accomplices or the weapons they'd bought, not even a lead on where to find them.

For once, she didn't let the cold take over. She only did that when she wanted to focus or to block out feelings she didn't want to deal with. She *wanted* to be pissed. She wanted to stab something, ideally several somethings. But before she could properly start swearing or throw Companion Piece into a wall, the ceiling of the florist shop broke apart.

Across all her bouts, Kurien was a flurry of energetic, almost erratic movement. In one part of the city, she crossed blades with Brass as the glintchaser desperately juggled defending himself and keeping Princess Recpina out of harm's way. At the same time, she overwhelmed Church with a halberd assault and forced Phoenix on the defensive with a storm of daggers. And she did it all while dancing around the attacks of Wings right in front of her, alternating attacks with Phoenix's blaster and the sword stolen from Wings.

"I want to thank all of you," Kurien said, her voice projected across her shadows. "I had my doubts, but you've played your parts to perfection. This was a better show than even I could have envisioned."

"Not sure I like the use of past tense there," Brass said.

In four places at once, Kurien made her move. All three of her swords fanned out around Brass and Diane, preparing to stab from all sides at once. Exploiting a poorly judged block, she knocked Zealot out of Church's hands, sending it cartwheeling across the hall out of reach. With the cleric disarmed, the halberd turned its attention to the chancellor himself. A comparative slouch in close combat, it was trivial to send blades around Phoenix's guard and rake him across the back before immediately boomeranging toward the sultan. And after finally maneuvering Wings out of the way, Kurien used a shadow blink to change angles, and took aim at a now exposed Roland.

Wings's eyes widened. Phoenix dropped to his knees in pain. Church clutched at his amulet, speaking as fast as he could. Brass grabbed Diane's hand.

Each of Kurien's scattered weapons lunged as she fired a blast at Roland.

And, in that moment, the battles were over.

Brass yanked Diane straight down, letting the arranged swords pass over them. As he dropped to the ground, he stabbed with his own sword, threading it through the handguards of all three weapons, catching them in one move, and pinning Kurien's blades into the floor.

Church's skin became hard as stone. It wasn't enough to stop an enchanted weapon. But it was enough to survive jumping directly into the halberd's path, taking a stab meant for the chancellor right in the chest. The halberd lodged in Church's own chest, not deep enough to kill him, but deep enough to get slightly stuck trying to pull back. Church seized the opportunity, grabbing the halberd with both hands and holding it in place. Every twist and jerk of the weapon sent lightning bolts of pain through his body, but as long as he held it, it couldn't hurt anyone else.

Even as he fell, Phoenix cycled his wand, took aim, and shot out a line of spider silk, catching a blade inches from opening the sultan's throat. With his free hand, Phoenix dug into his belt and tossed another dispel disc at the briefly trapped sword. When he set it off, the spider-silk line he'd created disintegrated, and the possessed weapon dropped to the ground.

Meanwhile, the blast Kurien fired tore through the air as Wings dove forward to try and block it with her remaining sword. By inches, she was too slow, and the blast struck Roland in the chest. The king was knocked back, crashing into a wall.

"No!" Lupolt screamed.

Wings rolled, recovering from her dive and coming up with her sword at the ready, only to freeze as she saw Roland lying slumped against a wall. Phoenix's blaster clattered to the ground as Kurien released her control over it and took a bow.

"Goodnight, Your Majesty," Kurien said.

"Renalt preserve me."

Kurien's head shot back up at the sound of Roland's voice. He sounded as if he were in pain, out of breath. And yet, the King of Corsar lifted his head with a smile on his face.

"That's two apologies I owe Phoenix," Roland said.

"Roland." Lupolt breathed a sigh of relief. Nearby, Wings beamed with pride.

Kurien shook her head in disbelief. "How?"

Roland reached into his shirt, producing a large, silver and onyx medallion engraved with arcane sigils. White energy arced back and forth across its face, absorbed from the blast that had struck Roland.

"A last-minute gift from an old friend. He made it so fast, I didn't think it would actually work," Roland said. His smile briefly took on a sad quality. "You'd think I'd know better than to doubt him by now."

Wings took the opportunity to slam the hilt of her sword into the floating one Kurien had taken control of. In a flash, her weapons transformed back into a bow in her hands. Wings reacted immediately, drawing an arrow.

"Roland!" she shouted.

The king threw the absorbing medallion at Kurien.

The Prince Killer saw the medallion tumble through the air toward her. She should have reacted. She could have. But she was mesmerized by the thing.

It was rather unwieldy in size, impractically so for an actual medallion. A scant three screws seemed to hold the whole thing together, and its pieces rattled slightly as it flew. All in all, it had an extremely cobbled-together look that absolutely would have thrown its viability into question. But there was also a care to it. The glyph inscriptions and arcane circuitry were immaculate. It was unmistakably the work of the very same hands which had constructed the weapon Kurien had tried to use to kill Roland.

A protective enchanted item, designed specifically to counter Kurien's intended murder weapon. Had she simply used Wings's blade, Roland would be dead. But of course, she couldn't have done that. Killing Roland with the weapon of the man who foiled Kurien's last attempt was too great an irony for the Prince Killer to pass up. And the Starbreakers knew that and exploited it.

Kurien couldn't help herself. She laughed.

She laughed as Wings loosed an arrow into the medallion, shattering it just as it reached her. She laughed as the ensuing explosion of force flung her from the room, out a window, and into the night air. All the way down as she fell, and as the last of the fireworks above exploded into the crests of every nation present at the summit, Kurien laughed.

She'd been outplayed. Or rather, she had played her role perfectly.

Then she crashed through the roof of a florist's shop.

Wings descended down through the hole in the roof as Ink teleported into the forum with Brass, Phoenix, and Church. For a moment, when they saw the broken window, they thought that Kurien had gotten away. But then they found Snow and Gamma standing over a prone Kurien who had been frozen to the floor.

Snow looked at each of them in turn, ignoring their shocked looks and searching for anyone with enough sense about them to offer an explanation. When nothing immediately came out, she pointed to Kurien with a dagger.

"You guys drop this?"

Phoenix looked around at the forum, which was covered in swathes of ice and full of concerned faces. At the far end of the street, he could see guards racing toward them, weapons already drawn.

"We . . . should compare notes," he said.

"Quickly," Church said. "We're not done yet."

Snow cocked her head, curiosity piqued if Kurien, the gods damned Prince Killer, wasn't even the end of their day.

This should be good.

THE STARBREAKERS

Angel cleaved three undead in half with one swing. With a sweep of her shield, Hilda knocked half a dozen more aside. They were almost completely surrounded, impossibly outnumbered, and in full retreat. By now, the Dread Knight had dedicated its full attention to drawing forth more undead from the ruins beneath their feet, largely to replenish the forces the two women had hacked to bits.

"You were going to fight against this by yourself?" Hilda asked.

"Didn't exactly have much choice," Angel shouted back.

"You could have not fought."

"Like I said. Not much choice."

"You're unbelievable." Hilda shook her head. "Monica, if we die—look out!"

Hilda shoved Angel back and raised her shield just as a fireball crashed into them. With its magic long since drained from the fight, there was no golden wall to block the blast this time, leaving the raw wood and metal to take the brunt of the blast.

It didn't fare nearly as well.

Hilda was blasted off her feet, landing on the ground, smoking and covered in soot. Angel was at her side in an instant, cleaving away anything that came near her.

She bought them a moment of breathing room, during which she stood guard over Hilda's body. The source of the fireball, the mage wight, descended down from the roof of a nearby tower, slowing its fall with jets of flame from its hands. More undead were marching toward them up the streets, howling in a loathsome chorus.

"You all right?" Angel asked.

"I can stand," Hilda said, trying to prove that wasn't a lie.

The wight gathered magic in her hand, preparing another fireball. Angel tightened her grip on her axe, preparing to charge. And then a pair of daggers whizzed past her ears, followed by a spectral image of a sword and a blast of force, all unleashed on the wight.

One of the daggers simply struck an undead down with a clean strike to the forehead, but when the other hit the wight, ice exploded out from the point of impact, leaving it teetering off balance and a sitting duck for the ethereal sword and force blast that tore it to pieces. Arrows rained down, twisting and turning midflight as each one found an undead's skull, dropping it.

Angel watched, dumbstruck, as the searing pain inside her faded away, replaced by a fluttering in her chest. Her halo vanished, and her glow subsided. At least for right now, she didn't need them. Hilda and the Order had been a nice relief, but now, the real cavalry was here.

Standing behind her, weapons drawn and magic at the ready, was Church, Phoenix, Brass, Snow, Wings, and even Ink. Angel couldn't help it. In spite of her pain, in spite of the situation, in spite of all the years she'd spent hating every person there except Wings, she smiled.

"What took you assholes so long?" she asked.

"Had to stop a few regicides," Wings said, before eyeing Snow meaningfully. "And pick up a stray."

"I *will* leave," Snow threatened.

"No you won't."

"We came as soon as we could," Phoenix said before looking at their surroundings. He loved a happy reunion as much as the next person, but it seemed like there was a job that needed doing. "So. What's the situation?"

"We've got the Rusted Star in the town, tunnelporting people to safety," Angel reported. "But it's not that big of a bar. The town militia and the Order are doing their best to protect the evacuation, and everything that's not trying to kill them is here, trying to kill us."

"The Dread Knight?"

"Somewhere in the middle of all this."

Phoenix looked around as he mentally conjured a map of Loraine and the surrounding ruins. Without even meaning to, he began sorting information. The undead. The townspeople. The Dread Knight. Them. It all slotted in like parts of an equation to be balanced. It wasn't until he caught a glimpse of Wings's smirk that he realized he'd subconsciously walked to the front of the group, and now, all eyes were on him.

When no one else said it out loud, Snow asked what was on everyone's mind.

"What's the play?" she asked their leader.

For a split second, Phoenix felt the weight of every one of their eyes and the thousands of souls in Loraine. Then he took a breath.

He had this. *They* had this.

"Wings, get in the air and get us the Dread Knight's location."

"On it." Her wings flapped once and she was gone.

"Ink, get the commander to the rest of her order, and then get to the edge of the ruins. Box the army in and turn it back toward us. Hopefully, we can give Loraine room to breathe."

"Do you have any idea how much energy it takes to teleport you people all over the place?" Ink asked.

"Can you do it or not?"

"Obviously," Ink said, already preparing another teleportation spell to take her to the edge of the ruins. "I just like to be appreciated."

"I can still fight," Hilda protested.

"Which is why I need you to rally your order for a counterattack," Phoenix said. "We should be able to draw enough attention to create an opening, and our two groups can pincer the enemy between us."

Hilda narrowed her eyes for a moment, but eventually, with a glance at Angel, she nodded. With a flash from Ink's spell, they were gone.

"The rest of us are the spear," Phoenix said. "As soon as Wings gives us a heading on the Dread Knight, we punch through the army straight to him. Angel and Church, you're the vanguard. Snow and Brass, keep our flanks clear. I'll support from the rear. Problems?"

"Just so we're clear, the plan is for the five of us to fight half an army?" Angel said.

Phoenix thought about arguing the nuances of the kind of army it was and just how much of the enemy they'd have to fight at any given time but decided it wasn't worth the pedantry.

"Yeah."

"Seems a little unfair for the army," Brass said.

"Got eyes on the Dread Knight, due southwest of your position," Wings's voice came through the message coil. *"Just on the other side of a river of uglies."*

"That's our cue," Snow said.

"Please, no theater references," Church said. "Ever again."

Angel scoffed, shaking her head as she shouldered her axe. "Let's do this."

Ink teleported to the top of a tower that overlooked the main road leading out of the ruins and into Loraine proper. Overhead, dark clouds were already gathering as Wings soared across the sky, emerald wings spread wide. Below, a tide of reanimated bodies marched down the road, a sea of rattling bones and hollow wails.

The truth was, she had been doing a lot of teleporting today. She'd stayed out of the fight with Kurien just to make sure she conserved enough energy to get the Starbreakers to Loraine. She was tired, and it was going to take a considerable amount of magic to stop an army of undead in its tracks. But she couldn't go and let the Starbreakers and the Order of Saint Ricard get all the credit for saving the day.

So, Ink dug deep, summoning every ounce of strength she could muster, and began to weave threads of magic together over her head. With every sweep of her hands and gesture of her fingers, the threads grew longer and longer, drifting higher and higher into the air as they increased in numbers until she had a titanic net.

With a yell, Ink threw her hands down, bringing the threads whipping down with them. They wrapped around the tower she was standing on before spreading to the buildings closest to it. From there, the threads spread out to the next closest buildings, and so on and so on, wrapping and winding over and over again.

The threads sliced through undead until the entire border region of the ruins became choked in a glowing tangle, like a massive cloud of luminescent cobwebs. Undead that attempted to push through them succeeded only in slicing off pieces of themselves.

Sweat poured from Ink's brow at the effort of maintaining such a massive spell, and her head swam. Even fully rested, she wouldn't have been able to hold something this enormous for long. But she wasn't planning to.

"And now, for my next trick . . ."

With all the strength Ink had, and probably some that she didn't, she pulled on the threads until her fingers bled. Some of the threads snapped as her concentration was pushed to its limit, but most held. All across the ruins, the threads tightened. Biting into masonry. Bending metal. Cracks began to form in several buildings.

Then, with an ear-splitting screech of rock being sheared in two and a roar like a rockslide, the first of the entangled ruins gave out entirely, collapsing in a shower of rubble onto the closest undead. Other structures swiftly followed suit, one at a time, then two, then all at once.

As the tower Ink was standing on began to list, she finally released the spell and more or less stumbled to the edge of the tower before leaping off, using one last thread to rappel down the side of the tower as it collapsed. She hit the ground, rolled, and used the last dregs of her strength to form a shield over her head, deflecting the stray debris that rained down from the tower as it toppled, crushing a swath of undead on its way down and blocking the road to Loraine.

Even as her ribs ached and she tasted copper on her breath, Ink beamed with pride. But her opportunity to bask in her own success was cut short by a cacophony of feral shrieking and scuffling footsteps as the nearest undead who hadn't been trapped behind the wall of rubble began scrambling toward her. Ink suppressed a groan.

"Right. The rest of you."

Just as arcane threads began to materialize on Ink's fingertips, Wings came tearing onto the scene in a sharp dive, and with a flap of her wings, the entire oncoming crowd was cleared away with a single gale.

"Nice work," Wings said. "Guessing you need a second to catch your breath?"

"Just a second?"

"Well, yeah. Can't let those five have all the fun, can we?"

Ink smiled through her exhaustion. "You read my mind."

———

The undead choked the corridors of the ruins in every direction; a tide of rotten, reconstituted flesh and pitted weaponry. And yet for all the numbers and relentless nature, they barely slowed the Starbreakers down.

Angel charged with reckless abandon, hacking into the undead like a scythe through wheat. Church followed close behind, Zealot and its spectral copy in constant motion. When enemy numbers threatened to envelop them, the two of them fell in together, fighting back-to-back until Church finished a prayer. A wave of divine power radiated out from him, rending the bindings that trapped the victimized souls within the undead bodies, freeing them and leaving nothing but empty husks which quickly withered away to dust.

On the flank, Snow darted in between enemy ranks, only staying in place long enough to jam a knife into the closest undead and leaving it there before blinking to another spot as far away as she could to find a new target. After a dozen stabs, she blinked to the roof of a nearby building and immediately created a short wall of ice to use for cover.

Down below, every knife she'd left behind began to glow red from the miniature fire spheres Phoenix had stuck to them, and an instant later, they detonated in a chain reaction that cleared the entire flank in a single, rolling blast.

Brass was a blur as his steel flashed in every direction, taking down another corpse with every stroke. He reached into his vest pocket, produced three knives, and threw them all at once, each one finding a target's head. A low thrum tipped him off to a crowd of enemies suspended in midair by one of Phoenix's gravity discs, and he dashed underneath it, taking the heads off of every one of them as they helplessly dangled. When the last one had been decapitated, the gravity disc powered down, and the bodies rained back to the ground behind him.

Phoenix himself had his hands full—literally. With one hand, he fired blast after blast into the horde, while with his other, he furiously collected the components for a new idea he'd come up with. He took a gravity disc from his belt and tucked it under his arm while he dug out another miniature fire sphere and a pinch of adhesive putty. It took another second of fiddling to get the bomb attached to the disc, and then he holstered his wand for a moment as he adjusted the settings on the disc and activated the fire sphere's fuse.

He threw the ad hoc device, and the gravity disc pulsed, pulling all the surrounding undead toward it just before the fire sphere exploded, taking the cluster of enemies out in one blast.

"Yes!" Phoenix pumped his fist and made a mental note to iterate on that design the next time he got back to his workshop.

"Undead with a flaming sword up ahead!" Snow shouted from her perch on a rooftop.

"I got him!" Brass shouted. "Angel, give me a boost!"

Angel buried her axe in the nearest undead, locked her fingers together, and turned just as Brass came sprinting toward her. He jumped, planting a foot on her hands, and she immediately tossed him into the air.

Brass sailed overhead, coming down in an arc on top of the undead knight. Their swords clashed before Brass had even hit the ground, and Brass twisted in the air to land on his feet, not missing a beat as he seamlessly transitioned into crossing his own blade against the wight's flaming sword. The maneuver had gotten Brass straight into a duel with the wight, but it had also left him in the middle of the enemy, cut off from the rest of the Starbreakers. But if that worried him, it was completely absent from the massive grin on his face.

"You know, it might be too soon to ask since you're not even totally dead yet," Brass said. "But did anyone in your order have dibs on that sword?"

As the wight attacked and the surrounding undead began to close in, Snow blinked in behind Brass, immediately spreading out ice to freeze the encroaching horde in place and give Brass space. At the same time, she dragged her hand across Brass's left forearm, coating it in a protective layer of ice.

Brass immediately used his now-frozen arm like a shield, blocking the wight's sword and creating an opening to counter. Snow blinked again, reappearing behind the wight. That was all it took: a touch to let him know she was there, a quick blink for her to get into position, and they fell into their old rhythm.

René and Rosa wished they were as coordinated as Snow and Brass. He blocked an attack, she moved in to slash. She dodged a swing, he stabbed where an opening had presented itself.

In no time at all, Snow slashed the wight behind its knees, and its legs buckled. It gave a wild swing in retaliation, forcing Snow to dodge but leaving Brass free to twist the sword from its grip with a quick swirl of his own. Snow caught the sword out of the air and hacked the wight's head off with a final stroke.

As the wight's body slumped over, Snow and Brass took a moment to look around at the undead and realized just how surrounded they were. Making things worse, the undead were starting to break their own feet off to escape the ice that was keeping them from collapsing on the pair.

"You went too deep," Snow chided Brass as she tossed him the confiscated sword.

Brass caught the sword, gave it a test swing, and shrugged. "I knew you had me."

She rolled her eyes. Without explanation, she slapped one of Phoenix's gravity discs onto Brass's chest and then blinked to safety.

Brass had just enough time to appreciate that he was now alone and completely surrounded before the gravity disc pulsed, lifting him clear of the assorted swords and spears bearing down on him.

The first thing he noticed while airborne was a fallen tower at the far end of the road completely obstructing the path into Loraine itself. There were some undead piling up against it, but already, it was clear that the masses were turning around, shifting priorities from the blocked road to the five individuals absolutely shredding their rear lines. The plan of turning the army back toward them had worked.

The second thing he noticed was even more encouraging. Looming in the center of the countless undead soldiers, not much farther ahead, was the Dread Knight itself. The other undead gave it a wide berth, making it easy to spot among the crowd. It stared up at Brass as he drifted through the air. At his current distance, it was hard for Brass to tell if the Dread Knight was preparing to somehow take to the skies and cut Brass down itself or if it was just staring up at the floating glintchaser with complete and utter befuddlement. He really hoped it was the latter.

The third and most pressing thing he noticed was the massive bulk currently charging full tilt toward the rest of the Starbreakers with other undead scrambling to get out of the way of its armored tusks.

"Is that a zombie war mammoth?"

Angel, having taken over Brass's job of keeping the flanks clear, whipped her head back toward the front, just managing to spot the beast over the heads of the surrounding horde. She knew firsthand how hard those things could hit, and she was not keen for a reminder.

"Church, overkill!" she shouted.

For the first time since the Starbreakers had arrived, Angel's halo reignited, and her whole body was consumed into golden light as she sprinted forward. She drew out every bit of power she could handle, letting her veins and muscles burn with divine strength. At the same time, Church clasped his amulet and said a prayer to grant Angel even more strength.

It was a combination they'd discovered a long time ago, made possible by the slight difference in how Angel's power and Church's prayer worked. There were principles of divine power behind it, but at the end of the day, what mattered was that, for as long as Church focused on maintaining the prayer, Angel could exceed even her own impossible strength.

The result was Angel plowing through the surrounding undead like they weren't there, bearing down on the undead mammoth at a full sprint as it charged to meet her. With a guttural yell, Angel planted her foot, twisted her hips, and delivered a punch straight to the mammoth's face that completely shattered its skull, crumpled its spine, and sent what was left careening backward, knocking over everything in its wake.

In doing so, she cleared a path straight to the Dread Knight. Its eyes bore into hers.

"You."

The Dread Knight surged forward, bringing its sword down on Angel. She caught the blade with the haft of her axe, though the impact rang out through the ruins around them.

"I have had enough of you."

The Dread Knight's sword moved like a blur, too fast for Angel to parry. Church switched prayers from enhancing Angel's strength to hardening her skin. It was the only thing that saved her from losing her head as the Dread Knight's blade sent her reeling. Another swing, skipping off her shoulder and leaving a red gash. The next one she managed to block and even took a swing of her own, only for it to go wide and be answered by another three from the Dread Knight, all of which struck home.

"You will change nothing. Inevitably they will all die."

"Probably not today, though!" a voice shouted from above.

The Dread Knight looked up in time to see Brass dropping down from above, a line of spider silk still attached to his chest from Phoenix yanking him into position. The Dread Knight slashed, and Brass twisted in midair to avoid the blow before driving the wight's flaming sword straight through its armored chest.

Brass rolled as he hit the ground and came up with his own sword drawn. "You can keep that, by the way. Too heavy for my tastes."

The Dread Knight let out an annoyed snarl which grew into a bellowing growl as force blast after force blast from Phoenix's wand began to pelt its armor. When it dashed after the spellforger, flaming sword still buried in its chest, it was stopped after only a few steps as Angel hooked its pauldron with the crook of her axe and yanked it back toward her to deliver a haymaker to its armored face.

With a roar, the Dread Knight gripped its sword in both hands and swung in a wide arc, managing to catch Brass in the leg and Angel on the shoulder. Brass dropped to the ground, bleeding from a gash in his thigh, while Angel was sent spiraling through the air. Having bought a moment's respite, the Dread Knight finally pulled the flaming sword out of its chest and tossed it aside.

Instead of moving to finish off either fallen glintchaser, it whirled around, wrapping its gauntleted hand around Snow's throat just as she appeared behind it.

"Shadows cannot hide you from me, thief," the Dread Knight said.

Flames washed over both of them as Phoenix unloaded the fire cell of his wand, knowing Snow wouldn't be hurt. Unfortunately, the Dread Knight quickly picked up on that and swiveled around to use Snow as a shield from the flames before hurling her straight at Phoenix.

At the same time, Zealot's spectral copy materialized to take a swing at the Dread Knight, which he blocked without even having to look. When it turned, it was the sword in Church's hand, and not its wielder, that the Dread Knight addressed.

"Zekiel. Ever the servant," it seethed. To Church, it said, "Do you even know what that blade *is*, sycophant?"

"I know it doesn't like you," Church said. "And neither do I."

All around, the Dread Knight's forces closed in, threatening to reach the Starbreakers who were still recovering. Church held his amulet in the air as he shouted the same prayer as before, releasing the undead around them and dusting their remains. It bought time, but it left him exposed, and the Dread Knight surged forward. Zealot moved Church's arm for him, bringing itself to bear just in time to block what would have been a death blow.

Immediately, the Dread Knight shoved against Church as hard as he could, sending him to the ground before raining down blow after blow. He blocked them all with Zealot, but each one came closer to striking true. Their blades locked once again, Church lying on his back, desperately pushing against the Dread Knight as it loomed over him, threatening to drive the crossguard of its spectral sword through Church's chest if his arms gave out for a second.

"This was over before it began," the Dread Knight said. "I have defied heaven itself. You are all nothing to me."

Maybe it was the fact that he was three inches and a muscle cramp from death. Maybe it was the will and fire of Zealot's own personality bleeding into his. Or maybe it was something else, something Brass had said to him, that reminded him of something he'd forgotten. But when Church heard the word "nothing," he rebelled.

"If that's what you think of us," Church said, "you have no idea who you're dealing with."

"The Starbreakers," the Dread Knight said. "My host knew your names. Ambitious. Powerful, for vermin. But still vermin."

"Not us. The people. Of this city. This kingdom. This world," Church said. "You're up against all of them. And they've survived worse than you. The Servitor. The dragon. Relgen. None of it broke them. It barely slowed them down. The mages of the Academy. The knights of the crown. All the men and women of this kingdom, ready to fight and die for their home. Even if you beat us, you can't beat them."

Church's speech was punctuated by a scream from Angel and her axe crashing into the Dread Knight's torso. The priest clambered to his feet as the Knight was thrown off of him, while around him, the other Starbreakers also rose. Brass had his vest tied around his thigh in a tourniquet. Phoenix stood with help from Snow, his arm now in a cast made of ice and supported by a sling of spider silk.

As the five of them stood assembled against the Dread Knight, Church ended his speech with one last line.

"But you're not going to beat us."

At the far end of the road, just over the wall of rubble that separated the ruins from the city of Loraine, a voice cried out that echoed across the stones, demanding to be heard.

"For Renalt! For Loraine!"

Hilda's battle cry was followed by a droning shout that nearly matched the violent shrieks of the Dread Knight's undead. The Order of Saint Ricard crested the wall Ink's destruction had erected and charged down to meet the enemy. A wall of golden light and flashing steel, the order tore into the undead's ranks. Along with them, Ink's threads danced and weaved through the horde, stringing up dozens at a time before pulling them apart and slicing them to ribbons.

The gathering clouds overhead bellowed as Wings soared through the air, her eyes turning to pure green orbs of swirling power. With a battle cry that drew thunder from the sky around her, she dove into the heart of the enemy ranks. As if guided by her movements, the sky let loose a torrent of white-hot lightning, vaporizing scores of undead and clearing the path for the charge.

The Dread Knight looked at the Starbreakers, wounded but defiant, and at the Order, buoyed forward by righteous zeal, and it was forced to confront two competing facts: It was more powerful than any human force. And it was losing anyway. Impossibly outnumbered, many of them already ragged from battle, the humans were pushing in and winning.

With a bellow of fury so loud the Starbreakers felt it in their stomachs, the Dread Knight drove its sword into the ground, sending out a shockwave that shattered the ground and flung all of them off their feet. While they were down, it leapt into the sky, carried on skeletal wings that rattled with every undulating flap as he flew away from them and toward their reinforcements.

"No you fucking don't!" Angel shouted. She shoved herself to her feet, charging after him and hacking down any undead that got in her way. The whole time, the glow cascading off her grew brighter and brighter.

By now, she didn't even feel it when skeletal hands and rusted blades scraped against her skin, trying in vain to drag her down. There was nothing but the burning, screaming pain.

Phoenix fired a line of spider silk, snagging one of the Dread Knight's legs. Rather than hold the Dread Knight down, though, he was lifted off his feet, and it took Church and Brass grabbing his legs just to keep him from being carried away. On the opposite side of the battle, Ink sent out as many threads as she could, wrapping them around nearby structures before converging on the Dread Knight as well.

Ink dug her heels in, fingers bleeding from where the threads originated. Phoenix had to frantically coach Brass through using a gravity disc to make them all heavier while Church used a prayer to enhance their strength. Even then, the Dread Knight stayed in the air. But together, the four of them managed to hold it.

Snow blinked out ahead of Angel and slammed both her hands into the ground. Ice spread out in front of her, forming a series of misshapen pillars that resembled a haphazard staircase.

Angel picked up on the plan, leaping from one pillar to the next as Snow dissolved the ones behind her and made new ones out in front, carrying her up toward the Dread Knight. Down below, Hilda caught sight of what was happening and threw her axe as hard as she could.

"Monica!"

Angel caught Hilda's axe out of the air. She made one final leap off of the last of Snow's ice pillars to close the gap between her and the Dread Knight. By now, Angel's vision had gone almost completely white. Most of the world left her awareness. Sounds like the screams of undead, the clash of weapons, and the shouts of her companions all faded away to a distant drone. Even the pain of her power dulled, like it was happening to someone else. Her whole body felt impossibly light.

But even as everything went fuzzy, she kept her eyes on the two burning blue orbs of the Dread Knight's eyes.

With one last visceral, violent scream, Angel slashed with both axes and cleaved the Dread Knight's head from its body. In one shared moment, every undead still on the field seized up and then collapsed as the Dread Knight's helmet and body tumbled limp and lifeless to the ground.

Then Angel's followed.

UNFINISHED BUSINESS

Kurien was bound tightly to her chair by thin but resilient Old World chains, recovered from a derelict prison sky ship that had once specialized in holding mages. The chains resisted all magical power and influence, impossible for Kurien to either control or destroy. Her arms were trussed tight against her body, her ankles locked together, a shock collar around her neck. She could barely move, and at a word, her entire body could be locked into electrically induced convulsions.

Ink still felt uneasy around her.

It was the way she sat, so unbothered, as if everything had somehow gone exactly according to her plan even though she hadn't killed a single one of her targets and she was now back in Oblivion. That shouldn't have mattered to Ink. But her confidence in Oblivion and its ability to hold Kurien, to hold anyone, had been shattered. And with it gone, she couldn't shake the feeling that she was missing something.

Then there was her mask. They'd taken it from her when she'd been captured, but without it, Kurien became a gibbering mess, babbling incoherently, scratching at her own face, and laughing at nothing. Even Church's attempts to heal her mind hadn't helped; the mask was the only thing that restored her coherence. The fact that they *still* didn't know what was wrong with Kurien, and what the mask had to do with it, troubled the High Inquisitive.

Her now wearing it just gave her that much more of the impression that she knew something they didn't, that she was hiding something from them. And somehow, the new cracks in it only made it more unsettling.

"With faces like those, you'd think you'd all failed," Kurien taunted. "Don't tell me Roland went and died of a weak heart after the whole affair."

"The king is alive," Ink said. "As is every other world leader you targeted."

"Disappointed?" Wings asked.

"Somewhat," Kurien said. "I admit, to be denied a life not once but twice is rather galling. But then, killing Roland with something so paltry as fright would be anticlimactic. And oh, what a show we put on! You must pass along my thanks to the others. I'll be riding the high of that performance for years. Perhaps it's even better I retire now. I don't know how I would ever top it."

"Where's the Heart?" Ink asked.

When they'd captured Kurien—or, technically, when Snow had—Kurien had been missing the Heart of Darkness. And so far, none of the searches for it had turned up any results.

"I don't know."

Ink's nostrils flared, and she snapped her fingers at the priest sent by the Church of Avelina, asking for a truth prayer. The priest complied, and Kurien laughed.

"Please. Don't insult me by insinuating I have a soul your precious prayers could afflict, little god botherer." She cocked her head teasingly. "You'll just have to take me at my word."

"She's . . . the prayer isn't affecting her," the priest reported, sounding afraid.

"But she *is* telling the truth," Wings added.

"Of course I am. I may use misdirection for dramatic effect, but I never lie," Kurien said. "After all, where would the fun in that be?"

"So, you just lost it? One of the rarest and most powerful artifacts on Asher?" Ink said.

"On my back one moment, gone the next," Kurien said. "It was rather surreal."

"Who took it from you?"

"I didn't see. By the time I had my wits about me, I was already on ice, and it was long gone."

"Let's talk about the breakout, then," Ink said. "How did you escape?"

"I didn't."

"Listen to me and listen well, you—"

"That is to say, I didn't orchestrate my escape," Kurien quickly elaborated. "I took no action to make it happen. I was merely a beneficiary of some other generous soul's actions."

Both Ink's and Wings's eyebrows shot up.

"Keep talking."

"They came into my cell, and they offered a proposal. In exchange for my freedom, the opportunity to continue my work, and a lead on an artifact which could elevate my talents—the Heart of Shadows, of course—I would secure a shipment of arcane arms and transport them to a waiting buyer on the mainland. With such generous terms, how could I say no?"

"Who was it?"

"Now, now." Kurien shook her head. "*That* would be telling. And I would never spoil someone else's grand reveal. But I suspect you'll be hearing from them very soon."

"Not good enough," Ink said.

"It's the best you're getting," Kurien said.

The High Inquisitive narrowed her eyes. "We'll see about that."

She turned to leave, but Wings stayed behind, evoking a raised eyebrow from the mage. The knight of the crown stepped forward.

"Just so you know, it wasn't that special," she said.

"I beg your pardon?"

"Your performance. It wasn't anything special. Not to Roland, not to us, and definitely not to them," Wings said. "It wasn't even the biggest thing we all dealt with that day."

"You . . ." Kurien leaned forward as much as her chains allowed, a sneer in her voice. It rapidly faded, though, as her mask's painted-on eyes stared into Wings's swirling emerald ones. When she spoke again, it was like she'd deflated. ". . . aren't lying."

Now Wings walked away, leaving Kurien squirming in her chair as she shouted after her. Sudden desperation overtook the Prince Killer as she shook and strained against her chains to no avail. "Wait! What else did they do? What was it! Tell me!"

Ink and Wings left the room, the cell door slamming shut behind them.

"I'm impressed," Ink said. "You've got a bit of a sadistic streak in you."

"I just wanted to knock the smug out of her voice at least once," Wings said with a sigh. "Thanks for letting me sit in, even if we didn't get much out of her."

"You know, I could have just sent along everything she told me," Ink said. "You've all earned that much after everything."

"They'll trust it more coming from me than you," Wings said.

"Of course." Ink rolled her eyes, then grew quiet. "I . . . hope she wakes up. Really."

"We all do," Wings said. She cleared her throat, hoping to change the subject. "Any idea who she might be talking about? Her mastermind?"

Ink *did* have an idea, especially now that Kurien had told them that whoever had broken her out of Oblivion had also been the one to order her to collect so many arcane weapons. Such an arsenal seemed like a perfect fit for the mystery cargo Snow had seen Silas's accomplices escape with.

"I have a few theories."

THE KNIGHT IN EXILE

A cold, wet sensation ran along his spine, sending tingles down his body. All around him, there was only silver. Endless churning silver, crackling and flashing like thunderless lightning deep within a cloudbank. Tiny pinpricks of light coalesced and swam around him.

No. Not lights.

Stars.

Silas lurched awake in bed, gasping like a drowning man. He thrashed, throwing off covers that felt like a smothering net, and frantically sat up, trying to reorient himself.

He'd been fighting Snow. Losing to Snow, trying to cover René and Rosa's escape with the weapons. Nothing he tried bought him more than a second's reprieve, never made her so much as furrow her brow.

She was so aloof. So incredibly above him, as if she barely registered him as a threat. And her eyes. He didn't know if he would ever get those placid, murderous white orbs out of his mind ever again.

Confusion rose up within him the more he thought about the fight. He'd lost to Snow. She had him dead to rights. And then . . . and then . . .

He recognized this bedroom as one located in their new headquarters, so graciously provided by one of their benefactors. But that headquarters was back in Corsar, nowhere near Nikos.

"You are awake."

Silas jumped at the voice of a thin, hooded man with parched lips and pallid skin. The man's eyes had a foggy texture, as if covered in scratches, and yet they stared straight at Silas. As soon as Silas saw the man, it was like the air suddenly went still, and a tingle with a familiarity he couldn't place rolled down his spine.

"Who are you?" Silas demanded. "How did you get here?"

"A prisoner of the cosmos's making," the man answered. "And would you rather not know how *you* got here?"

Silas said nothing, trying to get any kind of read on the man. He seemed old and frail and appeared unarmed but carried himself as one who had nothing to fear. Uncertainty plagued Silas. If the man was a threat, he needed to be dealt with. But what if he wasn't? Or worse, what if he was a threat Silas couldn't deal with?

The self-labeled prisoner gave a pitying shake of his head. "The answer to both is the same. I brought us here."

"How? Why?"

"Space and distance mean little to someone like me. As for why, it's just as I told the Starbreaker," the prisoner said as he pulled back his hood to reveal a twelve-pointed star carved into his forehead. "It pleases me for your work to continue."

Silas felt the blood drain from his face. "You . . . you're from the Cult of Stars."

As soon as Silas saw the symbol of the cult that had killed his home, any caution and uncertainty fled his mind, and he tackled the man to the floor, immediately wrapping his hands around the weathered man's throat.

"Give me one good reason I shouldn't kill you now," Silas said.

"Because . . . I bring . . . gifts," the prisoner croaked.

He held out a trembling hand as crackling silver smoke billowed in his palm. When it dispersed, there was a long, narrow, bronze cylinder, with constant wisps of ink black smoke drifting off of it. There was no mistaking the device. It was the core of an extractor, used to contain a Servitor Heart.

Silas stared at the Servitor Heart, at the cultist, and at the horrid insignia on the cultist's forehead before finally relenting, releasing his grip on the prisoner's throat. He snatched the Heart away, feeling his hand go numb just holding it. In a blink, the whole world became black and white. Every sound became flat and wrong. Surprised, he dropped the Heart, and the world returned to normal.

"The Heart of Shadows," the prisoner explained. "Taken from Kurien, the Prince Killer, who stole it from the Cord of Aenwyn, who took it as a trophy when the Servitor fell. Just one of many such artifacts you and your order have long coveted. Were it not for me, it would now be in the hands of your enemies."

Silas shook his head. The Cult of Stars *were* his enemy. They'd murdered everyone he had ever known. None of this made any sense.

"Why are you giving this to me?" Silas asked. "Why did you help me?"

"It pleases—"

"No!" Silas barked. "I want to know. *Why?*"

"Because when I first met your master, I was shown a possibility. Something I'd never seen in all my gazes into the stars. I saw a mortal, human man, who recognized the fragility of humanity's place in the world. But rather than bow to it as I had, he vowed to become powerful enough to change it. So, I gave him power. I taught him to walk between spaces and conceal himself from scrying eyes. And I watched to see what he would do."

"You're lying," Silas said. "Haegan devoted himself to eradicating people like you. He would never—"

"Oh, he objected to receiving my gifts. Quite strongly. But I did not need his permission to bestow that power upon him. And once he had it, he was too pragmatic not to use it. And he used it well."

Silas thought back to all of the things he had seen Haegan do even before they'd acquired the Heart of Force. The way he seemed to intuitively know things about people and events, without ever having seen them. The way no investigation ever seemed to find him. His powers of teleportation that eclipsed even what Silas had heard the strongest Academy mages to be capable of.

"Did you really never wonder where he learned such things?"

"It never mattered."

"It *always* matters where power comes from, young man," the prisoner said. "Now, you are not the man your master was. But you carry on his work. I have watched your order as it grew and stumbled. And you have achieved much. But if you truly want to protect your home, to save humanity, you will need to do so much more. You will need to upset the balance of power written in the stars themselves. I can help you become the kind of man who can do that."

Silas was quiet for a long time. "You said you brought gifts. Plural."

The prisoner smiled.

RETURN

The door was open for her, but she was gently held back from it as an alternative offer was made.

"You can rest now, if you'd like."

There was a seductive air to the word "rest." And yet, with almost no hesitation, she shook her head. "They still need me."

"Yes. But they will always need you."

The truth in the words was nearly overwhelming in its purity, its certainty. But they hadn't stopped her the last time she made this choice either.

"I know."

The Rusted Star sat off the northern road leading out of the town of Aenerwin, close enough to walk to the Church of the Guiding Saint if need be but far enough away to have some privacy. Four former Starbreakers, a church acolyte, and an unemployed escort gathered in the bar room, passing time by swapping stories, catching each other up on what each of them had seen and done. Snow was quiet, listening to Brass and Phoenix give overviews of their respective missions, nodding as everything in their stories played out more or less how she expected.

Church was equal parts proud and horrified at Bart's recounting of traveling with Angel and the role the young man himself had played in defending Loraine.

"I'm sorry, but are we really not going to talk about what happened?" Brass asked.

"Literally, all we've done is talk about what's happened," Snow said.

"No, not about all that other stuff. I meant what happened—oh shit."

A set of slow, heavy footsteps plodded down the stairs of the Rusted Star. Gripping the railing tighter than she ever had, hair hastily tied back with a borrowed scarf, and both confused and irritated was Angel, upright and awake for the first time in three days. Thalia followed close behind her, though, the bartender paused a few steps up, letting Angel greet her old company by herself.

"The fuck are all of you doing here?"

A weight lifted off the room, and relief spread like a ripple. Brass immediately sprang to his feet, beaming in victory.

"And there's the woman of the hour! I told you all she'd wake up!" Brass said. He slapped a table, loudly declared, "I'm making drinks!" and darted behind the bar.

While he began pulling bottles off the shelves, the others quickly swarmed Angel, Church even going as far as hugging her. Angel allowed the hug and even half-heartedly returned it along with a mutter of, "Saints, you're worse than Thalia."

A half-dozen variations of "You're awake!" and "I'm so glad you're okay," flew at her, turning into a frenzied swarm of well-wishes that she physically winced under the barrage of.

"No, but seriously. The fuck?" she asked when she was finally able to get a word.

"You died," Phoenix said. "Church brought you back after, but you weren't waking up."

"I got that part from Thalia already," Angel said. "I meant why are all of you here?"

Phoenix opened his mouth, but nothing came out beyond a flustered, "Well, we, uh . . ."

"We were worried about you," Church said. "We wanted to wait with you, to make sure you were okay."

Angel let the words sink in, driven home as they were not just by Church's face but by everyone's. They were all here. All worried about her and happy to see her alive. Angel's insides fluttered, but not from any kind of divine radiance. Just a brief, fleeting moment of uncomplicated happiness. She didn't trust it. Not for longer than a second. But after the week she'd had, it wasn't unwelcome.

There was one part she absolutely could not believe though. She shot Snow a pointed, questioning glance. The assassin shrugged.

"I wanted to leave," she said. "They didn't let me."

"Fuck you too," Angel said.

"Bitch."

"Dirk."

The two women held each other's stare, not quite glaring, as a mutual understanding passed between them. They did not get along. But that was its own kind of dependable constant that helped the world keep making sense. It could be nice to have something like that around when things got crazy. And, though neither would ever say it, they'd both rather keep butting heads than attend the other's funeral.

"And that's enough fighting for now," Brass said, shoving a cup into Angel's hand and another into Phoenix's. "We're all alive. We won. Bottoms up."

"What is this?" Angel said, staring at her glass.

"I call it 'I Came Back From the Dead, and All I Got Was a Lousy Drink,'" Brass said. He clinked his cup against hers. "Welcome to the club."

Phoenix sighed, took a sip, and nearly coughed it back into his cup. "Brass, what's in this?"

"Unclear. I just chucked in a bit of every bottle that looked expensive. I figured it was an appropriate recipe to go with the name."

A knock on the Rusted Star's door saved Brass from Angel's reaction to the news. It creaked open, stunning everyone in the bar to silence as two new arrivals appeared.

"Am I interrupting something?"

King Roland II of Corsar walked into the bar, carried in upright by a pair of softly whirring and freshly polished spellforged leg braces. The monarch wore no indicator of his identity, clad in plain clothes with no jewelry or insignia in sight. And yet, he held his head high. Similarly dressed, a healed and recovered Lupolt hung at the king's right, the slightest hint of a smile breaking through his stoic facade as he watched his friend and ruler.

Angel sighed. "An idiot is trying to waste my booze. Come in, I guess. Everyone else let themselves in."

"Thank you," Roland said, letting Lupolt close the door behind him. "I heard about what happened. I'm glad you're awake."

"Been hearing that a lot," Angel muttered. "Shouldn't you be doing king stuff somewhere?"

"An Academy illusionist is filling in my presence in a return tour of the kingdom," Roland said. "We'll be rejoining soon but, while we were nearby, I wanted to come here. I wanted to pay my respects, say thank you and . . . to apologize.

"When you needed me after Relgen, I turned my back on all of you. I let the world brand you as traitors and menaces, and I supported it. I was hurting. I was confused. And I was wrong. And despite all of that, when Corsar needed you again, you came, you gave everything, and you saved countless lives. Maybe even the sanctity of this kingdom. I can never repay that."

"The money was a nice start," Brass said.

"For legal reasons, you were not given that money by the crown," Roland said. "But those laws and my own reactions aside . . . Lupolt made the right decision, calling all of you. You all more than earned what he promised you."

"We appreciate that. Truly," Church said. "And we're happy to have helped."

"There is another reason we are here," Lupolt said.

"What happened now?" Phoenix asked.

"The five of you did," Lupolt said. "Please understand, I am as grateful as Roland for what you've done for us. But your battle at Loraine was very . . . visible. There are hundreds if not thousands of witnesses putting the Starbreakers, together and reassembled, on the field of battle doing exactly what a very public royal ordinance forbade them from ever doing again.

"For now, these are just rumors. Stories to be told and disbelieved and to slowly die out as more interesting things take their place. But if word were to get out about what actually happened and people began to suspect the Starbreakers had returned, the consequences could be . . . messy."

"So, 'Thanks for your help, but please go back to the rocks you were all hiding under before people start to talk.' Is that about right?" Snow asked.

Lupolt noted the hostility in her voice. "Essentially, yes."

"I know you're not the menaces we made you out to be at the trial," Roland said. "I know how much you've done for Corsar . . . and for me, and I swear to you I will never forget it again. But most of the kingdom doesn't know that. So, I'm asking you, now that this crisis is over and the escapees are back where they belong, to lie low. Go back to the lives you've built for yourselves . . ." He paused, wondering if he should amend that when his eyes drifted over to Snow. "Or maybe find quieter ones. Whatever suits you. Just . . . let the rest of us take things from here. At least for now."

"Ink has asked me to look at some notes she had regarding the breakout. She wanted a spellforger's eyes on the prison's security measures," Phoenix disclosed.

"That should be fine," Roland said. "Appreciated, even."

"I was planning to meet with some of the other vicars," Church said. "To see if they had any insight on a problem I'm looking into."

The king frowned. The last thing he wanted was to have to stand here and give a stamp of approval to every move the Starbreakers were planning on making.

"Just . . . use your best judgment. As long as the world doesn't think the Starbreakers are back, everything should be fine."

"Won't what happened at Loraine get in the way of that?" Church asked.

"Despite what rumors might say," Lupolt said, "the official word that will be carried by all dispatches to the provinces is that the Winged Lady of Sasel, along with the Academy and the Order of Saint Ricard, were able to repel the attack and stop the Dread Knight. We cannot convince everyone, but for most people, you were never there."

"Wings, Ink, and a bunch of knights get all our glory?" Brass said. "I don't know how I feel about that . . ."

"We'll double your pay."

"I think I can swallow my pride this once. How about the rest of you?"

"No complaints from me," Phoenix said. Nobody else had any either. With the possible exception of Brass, none of them had actually done this for money or glory or really any reward at all. Their home had been in danger. They had people counting on them. That was reason enough to fight.

Though the money *was* nice.

Roland nodded. "Thank you all. Truly. For everything."

"Yeah," Phoenix said, before deciding that probably wasn't the right thing to say, given he was talking to a king. "I mean, you're welcome. Your Majesty."

"Please. To all of you, it's Roland," the monarch said.

The glintchaser nodded, processing the meaning behind the request. Names had always been important to Phoenix. What he called himself, around who, and what others in turn wanted to be called by him had always carried an extra layer of meaning in a line of work where nobody used their real name if they could help it.

But this was different.

Roland wasn't another freelancer, revealing his name as a sign of trust or respect. He was a king, the divinely anointed ruler of a nation giving some of his subjects permission to address him as a peer.

Not even his father had ever held the Starbreakers in high enough regard to do that.

"Roland."

"Arman."

The king gave a farewell smile to the company. "I wish we could stay. But as Angel said, 'king stuff' awaits. I'll have Lupolt set up a discreet line of communication in case something like this should ever happen again. Or in case any of you ever need my help for a change."

"Which should only be called on in an emergency," Lupolt immediately stressed as he held the door open for Roland. "It is *not* an invitation to ask the crown for favors."

"What if I've got a few outstanding bounties I need cleared?" Brass asked.

"Or business taxes we want to dodge?" Angel added.

"Goodbye."

The door shut behind the two, leaving a comfortable silence to descend on the bar until Ruby broke it.

"That was the king," she said.

"Yep," Angel said.

"The King of Corsar was here. And he ditched his own personal welcome home parade to come here, just to say thank you and offer you all a favor whenever you need it. Like you're drinking buddies," Ruby reiterated.

"More or less," Phoenix confirmed.

"And that's not even the craziest thing I watched happen this week," she said, utterly bewildered. "My life officially makes no sense anymore."

Angel shook her head. If not for the sake of the girl's soul, then at least for her sanity, they really needed to get her normal life back. Otherwise, she was going to develop a taste for this sort of thing.

"They are going to be so pissed when they realize we're back," Brass said.

"We're not back," Phoenix said. "We're just . . . coordinating our efforts on some unfinished business."

"What business?" Angel asked.

"The Cult of Stars," Snow said.

"What?"

"They're back," Snow repeated. "And they're mixed up with Silas, who's mixed up with whatever was really going on with the breakout."

"You're shitting me."

"I've got the scars and mindfire hangover to prove it."

That got Angel's attention, and so Snow, Church, and Phoenix laid out the working chain of events they'd compiled from their compared notes and the information Wings had sent Phoenix. The breakout. The weapons Kurien stole and delivered. Silas's deal in Nikos. The Cult of Stars. All tangled together. One problem after another, all spiraling in on each other. Brass jokingly pointed out that at least Ruby's demon magic was probably its own thing, but that just reminded them that they had another problem to deal with.

Everyone who hadn't already was eager to see Ruby's new abilities in action. Phoenix and Snow were intrigued, and Brass crossed all the way over into excitement, but Church was only concerned. For the last few months in Aenerwin, Ruby's powers had remained essentially the same. Now, they'd expanded by leaps and bounds.

"I still know a few people in the Infinite Library," Phoenix said. "They usually keep anything connected to demons under a pretty tight lock, but I might be able to get access."

"We could always just break in again," Snow said.

"I'd rather not make them hate me *again*," Phoenix said. "I think it would actually stick this time."

"You guys don't have to do all of this for me, really," Ruby said. "I don't wanna cause any more trouble for you."

"We're the reason this happened to you in the first place," Church said. "And I promised I'd help you. So, I will."

"We all will," Phoenix said.

Brass sat back, listening to his companions. This was what he'd been trying to talk about earlier. All five of them, together in the same place at the same time, had faced off against a rampaging menace, saved an entire town, and been handsomely rewarded for their efforts. Not because the rampaging menace had been out to get them. But just because it was a job that needed doing, and somebody important enough to afford them had asked them to do it.

They'd just completed a freelancer job together. They'd fought side by side against impossible odds and had come out the other side just like they always used to back in the day. And now they were all sitting together in a tavern, shooting the shit, discussing options, and plotting next moves. Moves they were going to make together.

They could pretend it wasn't true all they wanted—and for the sake of keeping peace with the crown, they probably should—but as far as the glintchaser was concerned, there was no denying it.

"We are so back."

THE END

GLOSSARY

CHARACTERS

Angel/Monica Falone: A former Starbreaker with the divine powers of a Sentinel, and the owner of the Rusted Star tavern.

Bart: A young acolyte at the Church of the Guiding Saint.

Brass: A former Starbreaker of unparalleled hedonism, irresponsibility, and skill with a blade.

Church/Arno Farnese: A former Starbreaker, priest of Saint Beneger the Guide, and the vicar of the Church of the Guiding Saint in Aenerwin.

Princess Diane Recpina: Princess from Her Lady's City and the representative of Iandra in the summit at Nikos.

Dietrich: The town warden of Cutters Place, a village on the edge of the Iron Forest. Was rescued by the Starbreakers as a child.

Edelfric: Oblivion escapee. Former servant of King Roland I, transformed in death into a plant monster and the Scourge of the Iron Forest. Was originally stopped by the Starbreakers.

The Handler: An underworld middleman and facilitator boss who managed the contract on the Starbreakers. Famous for employing Faceless as servants and bodyguards.

Hilda: Commander of the Order of Saint Ricard, daughter of Sir Richard, and Angel's former training partner and lover.

Gamma: An autostruct belonging to the Academy, formerly attached to the Golden Shield, and now a direct servant of Ink.

Sir Haegan of Whiteborough: Silas Lamark's mentor. A former knight of the city of Relgen who witnessed its fall and swore to make Corsar strong enough to prevent anything like it from happening again. Stole the Heart of Force from the Academy and put out a contract on several individuals connected to the Servitor Hearts, including the Starbreakers. Killed by the Starbreakers.

Ink/Kira Arakawa: High Inquisitive of the Academy, formerly a member of the Cord of Aenwyn, and a powerful wizard. Brought the stolen secrets of Hidoran wizards to Corsar.

Julian: One of the brokers who circulated the contract on the former Starbreakers.

Lord Kaiden Roso: Oblivion escapee. Iandran hellborn who uses Hell Tongue to control others through verbal commands.

Katherine: The former queen of Corsar and the mother of Roland II.

Chancellor Kleitos: The elected leader of Parthica and its representative at the summit in Nikos.

Kratz: Vera's half-orc bodyguard and enforcer.

Kurien: Oblivion escapee. A notorious masked murderer who earned her reputation as the Prince Killer by targeting the heirs of nobility. Was stopped from killing Roland II by the Starbreakers.

Lexos: Oblivion escapee. The human mimic—part man, part shape-shifting monstrosity.

Lupolt: The advisor, attendant, and bodyguard to King Roland II. His sister died in the fall of Relgen.

The Oracle/Apollius: An ancient elf who sought to use the Oracle's Sanctum to take over the world. Defeated and imprisoned within the Sanctum by the Starbreakers.

Phoenix/Arman Meshar: A former Starbreaker and scholar of the Infinite Library. Sole keeper of the secrets of spellforging in Corsar. Husband of Elizabeth/Wings, father of Robyn, and ex-lover to Snow.

Pitch/Highwater: Oblivion escapee. Former member of the Cord of Aenwyn turned assassin. Possesses the Heart of Flames and burned down the Crimson Lilac in pursuit of the contract on the Starbreakers.

Quint: Former prince of the kingdom of Kaberon, now the leader of the Cord of Aenwyn. Ex-lover to Ink.

Renalt: The Corsan god of truth, justice, and benevolent strength, and the patron deity of the kingdom.

René and Rosa: Twin sisters who work for Silas Lamark.

Sir Richard: Hilda's father and the person who trained Hilda and Angel to become paladins. Killed in battle defending the girls.

Robyn Meshar: The daughter of Arman/Phoenix and Elizabeth/Wings.

Roland: Former king of Corsar, born in the city of Relgen. Abdicated the throne after the city's fall and passed soon after.

Roland II: The current king of Corsar, son of Roland. Unable to walk unassisted after an attack by Kurien in his youth.

Ruby: Former escort at Crimson Lilac. Left to die in a fire by Pitch and had her prayers for salvation answered by a demon. Granted power in exchange for an unknown price.

Silas Lamark: A former knight who worked for Sir Haegan and has since taken up his mentor's mission of remaking the nation of Corsar.

Simon: Server at the Broken Cask, de-aged by a witch's curse, and only just now reaching adolescence for the second time.

Sinnodella: An elf who lives in the forests of Corsar and trained a young Elizabeth/Sable in druidic magics.

Snow/Chloe Guerron: Former heiress and Starbreaker, now a notorious assassin. Possesses the Heart of Ice. Ex-lover to Phoenix.

Tariq the Immortal: The sultan of Gypten and its representative at the summit in Nikos.

Thalia: The bartender of the Rusted Star.

Vera: Former owner of the Crimson Lilac, a brothel that was burned down by Pitch.

Wendel Lestrade: Oblivion escapee. Used his knowledge of the Disassembly Council's work to find the location of the Helm of the Dread Knight and became its host.

Wings/Elizabeth Meshar/Sable: Former member of the Broken Spear. Now a skilled archer, practitioner of druidic magics, knight of the crown, wife of Arman/Phoenix, and mother of Robyn. Possesses the Heart of the Sky.

LOCATIONS AND ORGANIZATIONS

The Academy: The Tarsim Academy of Arcane Studies, better known simply as "The Academy," located in the capital city of Sasel, is the foremost institute of magical knowledge and study in Corsar and one of the greatest in the world.

Aenerwin: The town where Arno/Church currently lives, site of the Church of the Guiding Saint, and the first town the Starbreakers ever saved from the Cult of Stars.

Akers: A small village on the outskirts of the city of Olwin where Arman and Elizabeth Meshar live.

Asher: The name of the world.

The Broken Cask: A tavern in the city of Sasel, formerly frequented by the Starbreakers.

The Broken Spear: An all-female freelancer company Elizabeth Meshar previously belonged to, during which time she used the name "Sable." Now disbanded.

The Church of the Guiding Saint: The church in Aenerwin, dedicated to Saint Beneger the Guide.

Clocktower: A criminal organization that facilitated the hits on the former Starbreakers and clashed with the company many times in the past.

The Cord of Aenwyn: An internationally traveling freelancer company that developed a bitter rivalry with the Starbreakers. Currently led by Quint with former members including Ink and Pitch.

Corsar: The kingdom now ruled by Roland II. Only recently unified by the previous reign of Roland I and Katherine of Sasel and still reeling from the fall of the city of Relgen.

The Crimson Lilac: Vera's former luxury hotel and brothel in Olwin; burned down by Pitch.

The Cult of Stars: A cult dedicated to the return of the Starborn. The Starbreakers earned their name by foiling their schemes and hunting their members years ago. Thought to have been wiped out by the fall of Relgen.

The Disassembly Council: A council within the Academy tasked with keeping dangerous artifacts secured from the rest of the world and destroying them when possible.

Faceless: Grey-skinned, shape-shifting, telepathic beings believed to come from another world.

Future's Road: The artery that links Corsar's capital city (Sasel) to the rest of the interior.

Gypten: One of the nations present at the summit in Nikos. A land of deserts, mountains, and elemental rifts fueled by trade and ruled by the sultan. The native homeland of Arman's family.

Her Lady's City: Shorthand for Her Lady Excellent's City of Corrinverno, the capital city of the Iandran Empire.

Hidora: The great empire of the Far West, and the former home of Kira Arakawa.

Iandra: One of the nations present at the summit in Nikos. The self-proclaimed center of the world, famous for its passionate people and their love of the arts. Arno Farnese's birthplace.

Infinite Library: One of the greatest repositories of knowledge in Asher, situated off the coast of Corsar. The place where Arman Meshar worked and studied before becoming a freelancer.

Loraine: One of the largest ruintowns in Corsar, which was previously nearly destroyed by the attack of the Servitor and now well on its way to becoming a true city.

Nikos: The capital of Parthica and the host city of the first international summit of Asher.

Oblivion: A prison of incredibly advanced physical and arcane security features where the most dangerous criminals and monsters are kept.

Olwin: The largest city in Corsar's interior now that Relgen has fallen. Home to countless refugees from the area surrounding the fallen city.

Parthica: Host nation of the first international summit of Asher. One of the only nations in Asher to elect its leaders.

Pearl Palace: Home palace of King Roland II.

Puerto Oro: An independent port city on the shores of Tecah, originally established by Iandran colonization efforts.

Relgen: Formerly the military capital of Corsar and Bastion of the North. Its entire population was wiped out by an Old World weapon during the Starbreakers's final mission together as a company.

Rusted Star: Tavern owned by Angel/Monica.

The Sanctum of the Oracle: A great Old World machine housed in a floating fortress of ice and rock built to provide perfect knowledge of the past, present, and future. Home of the Oracle.

Sasel: The capital of the kingdom of Corsar; City of Yesterday and Tomorrow; Jewel of the Coast.

Seven Gates: An order of knights who serve the crown.

Tecah: A large island landmass located to the southeast of Corsar with an interior of impenetrable jungle and independent port cities along its coast.

OTHER TERMS

Company: Most common name given to a group of freelancers who work and travel together.

Extractor: A device created by Phoenix to siphon the energy of a Servitor Heart. Only a few unused models remain, held by the Academy in the event of their need.

Freelancer: An itinerant mercenary-explorer who finds employment in everything from delving into Old World ruins, recovering artifacts, hunting monsters, and serving as hired muscle. Infamous in many places for bringing trouble wherever they go but nevertheless invaluable for their skills and expertise.

Glintchaser: Colloquial, semi-derogatory name for freelancers used most commonly in Corsar.

Hell Tongue: A fiendish power to control others with verbal commands.

The Old World: The days when the elves ruled an empire of several worlds that included Asher and humans were little more than servants.

Paladin: One who is trained to funnel divine power into their body and weapons.

Ruintown: A typically temporary settlement that rapidly springs up around the community of opportunists who come to exploit newly discovered Old World ruins. Often the host of all manner of strange people and occurrences.

Sentinel: An angel who incarnates in human form to battle evil on the mortal plane, forgetting its previous life as an angel in the process.

The Servitor: A war machine of the Old World which rampaged through Corsar until stopped by a joint effort of multiple freelancer companies and the forces of the crown.

Spellforging: Old World practice used to create arcane machines and weapons.

Starborn: Ancient cosmic beings from beyond the farthest human understandings of the universe, believed by some to have existed before the gods.

Servitor Heart: A power source of the Servitor, each one keyed to a specific type of power, such as Force, Flames, Ice, Sky, or Shadows.

ACKNOWLEDGMENTS

I have wanted to be a writer for most of my life, but because it was more a dream than an actual goal for so long, I've spent a long time wondering when I'd feel like a "real" writer. It used to be I thought it would happen once I got my first book published. But then I did that, and as momentous as that occasion felt, pretty soon I started to think, *Well, anybody can get one book out. You're not a real writer until you have books out.*

Well, I now have books, plural, out in the world. And even more writing than that besides. And I guess I do feel a little bit more like a real writer. But, probably honestly, this is never going to feel real. This is a journey. One I intend to walk for the rest of my life, and one I absolutely could not walk alone.

Thank you to my beautiful wife, for reading this thing almost as many times as I did. I genuinely do not think I could have properly revised this story without you. You are, as ever, the reason I write and the reason it comes out half as good as it does.

Thank you to God, for giving me a gift and a chance to share it. You are the reason my first and greatest goal is to add some goodness to the world. I hope I made you proud.

Thank you to my editor, Donna McKeever, for your fresh perspective and sharp eyes on the story of the Starbreakers. You had the unenviable task of filling the shoes Bridget left, and you more than stepped up to the task.

Thank you to Sue Arroyo, Helga Schier, and the rest of the team at CamCat Books. Before everything began, I had reservations about working with a publisher, but working with you all has never been anything less than wonderful.

Thank you to Naomi Novik, Will Wight, Drew Hayes, and Marina Lostetter, for writing stories that filled me with delight and renewed my drive to pass that feeling on.

Thank you to Brendon Urie, Katy Perry, Billie Eilish, Taylor Swift, Kesha, Macklemore, and every other musician whose songs helped to birth the scenes, themes, and characters. You are the spark that lit some of my favorite fires in these books.

Thank you to my beta readers, Christy Gasner and Megan Kalinsky. Your aid is invaluable, and your desire to beta read for me in the first place is an immense boost to my own drive.

To all of you, from the bottom of my heart, thank you. This journey gets a little more real every day because of you.

ABOUT THE AUTHOR

Elijah Menchaca is a Puerto Rican author, born and raised in Bakersfield, California, and has been writing and telling stories since he was five.

To chase a few dreams and learn to put his own pants on, he attended the University of Louisville where he minored in Creative Writing and discovered a love for Dungeons and Dragons. When the group of friends he'd made began to go their separate ways and their adventures around the table reached their conclusion, Elijah sought to explore his relationship with his past and the people around him, which eventually gave birth to the Glintchasers series.

Now based in Ohio, when he isn't exploring the world of Asher with more stories both in print and online, he's making new memories around the virtual table with his old friends, pondering the worlds of speculative fiction with everyone who will listen, and doing his best to be a good husband to a woman far too good for him.

He's still working on the whole pants thing.

If you enjoyed
They Split the Party by Elijah Menchaca,
we hope you will consider
leaving a review to help our authors.

Also check out
Ghost Tamer by Meredith R. Lyons.

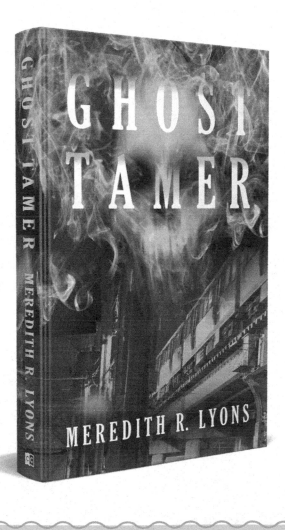

CHAPTER ONE

It's coming. Let's run."

Joe and I both sprinted through the thick snowflakes toward the train platform. Pounding up the salt-strewn stairs two at a time. Scanned our passes, lickety split, and leapt onto the very first car just as the doors glided shut.

"Winners." Joe held his gloved hand up without turning around, and I smacked my mittened palm against his for a muffled high five. He pointed to the front of the car. "Hey, Raely, your favorite seats. Must be your lucky day, girl."

"Excellent!" I clamped onto my friend's shoulder and wove after him through the standing passengers as the elevated train bobbed and swayed.

It was just after rush hour. The train was not uncomfortably packed. Joe and I lucked into those first two seats at the front behind the driver. I loved being able to see out to the tracks in front. Made it almost like a carnival ride. As soon as I was settled in my seat, leaning back against the side window, Joe launched into an impassioned critique of my stand-up set in between gasps. We were both still out of breath from our sprint. Still buzzing from the adrenaline of recent stage time.

"I mean, you have to feel good about that bit with the birthday cup," he said. "That one is solid . . ." We had just done our five-minute solo sets at an early evening open mic.

I liked the earlier ones. Fewer people, although Joe was trying to get me to commit to a "real" one sometime before spring.

Other passengers surrounding us in our little section of the train either stood reading or plugged into music or podcasts. Everyone created their own space. Joe's ardent critique of my set didn't register to the average commuter, although a few smiled to themselves, glancing over at Joe. Perhaps catching some of his clever turns of phrase. Since he was in impassioned flow, he was still standing, gesticulating, while I gazed up at him.

I flung my legs across the seat he had not yet taken and studied him. He was one of those guys who would always be okay. He could easily transition from his office job to any bohemian shenanigans that he may get the urge to dabble in with a simple change of clothes and an alteration of mousse pattern. His set had been perfect. He'd nailed every bit. And for some reason, he always wanted me to do just as well.

"Okay, now you do mine," he demanded, one gloved hand gripping the upright post as he swayed with the train, the fluorescent overhead lights gilding his dirty-blond hair. "What did you think? Where do I need to tighten it up? I thought the part about the reunion email was a little meh . . ."

"Joe, none of it was 'meh.'" I'd spent much of his set resisting the urge to tell people next to me, *That's my best friend up there.* "I think you should just go for the whole ten minutes next time. It was spot on. The whole audience was with you. I think they were disappointed when you were done, honestly."

"I still think if we got into Second City, it would take our skills to the next level." He scooted a little closer as the train made another stop, but only a few people pushed through the doors before they slid shut again. "Improv is an essential skill."

"Oh, for sure," I said, doing a quick check of our surroundings to make sure I didn't need to move my feet to make room. "I just don't know that I'm—"

"Stop saying you don't think you're ready; you never think you're ready for anything. You just need to *do.*" He leaned toward me, grinning and pointing. The train jostled, but he swayed with it. I couldn't help but smile back. The city flashed by in the windows behind him.

Bright lights against the winter dark sky. It had stopped snowing. I peeked out the front window, watching the line of track before us gobbled up ever more quickly as the train picked up speed.

"So," I nudged his leg with my boot. "We're done with our sets, no more secrets. What's the big exciting thing you're doing this weekend that trumps game night?"

Joe's smile broadened. He smacked my boots, shoving them to the floor, and took the seat. "I'm proposing to Mia."

I straighten away from the window. "Shut. UP!"

He grinned and pulled a glove off, reaching for his inside coat pocket. "Wanna see it?"

"Yes I wanna see it! Oh my God! Joe!" I scooted closer, a silly grin taking over my face, and extended my palm toward him. I loved Mia. And I loved who Joe was *with* Mia. Joe grinned back at me and unfastened the first two buttons of his coat to access the pocket.

The full moon gilded the metal of the tracks ahead of us as the train whipped past the river. There was a curve just ahead. The hairs on the back of my neck stood up.

"Joe," I said, catching his eye. "The train is going too fast."

We turned away from each other, gazes locked on the front window. The curve was looming. Shiny, bright metal, arcing gracefully to the left. And the train wasn't breaking. My heart expanded, uncomfortably filling my chest. Electricity shot through me. We sped forward relentlessly. The moonlight flashed over the wind-roughened river.

My eyes found Joe's. The metallic taste of fear coated the back of my tongue. I meant to say that we should grab on to something, even as my body compelled both hands to grasp the railing of the seat beside me. Joe opened his mouth to say something, and then . . .

There was a wrench. A screaming of metal fighting metal. The train tore off the rails. For one second, we were all suspended together. As if existing inside a gasp. Not a human sound. Conversation ceased. Silence was our collective scream.

Then chaos. Everyone yelled, cried, cursed. The lights strobed. Then cut out. Every body and bag on the train hurtled toward the front of the car. Tagging every metal guardrail along the way. Gravity found us again with a sickening crunch. Pain sliced into my side, but I couldn't move. Couldn't make space. Pressure increased. I couldn't breathe. Panic clawed at my ribcage. I wanted to fight but there was nowhere to go. Blackness. When consciousness found me again, I was disoriented and my head hurt. My lungs heaved as if I had been underwater. I wheezed like a drowning victim. Someone pulled at me. Under my arms. Hauling. My feet were caught. Yanked free. A yelp died escaping my throat. I struggled to open my eyes, my eyelids impossibly heavy.

"Joe?" Raspy. Rusty voice.

"I'm getting you outside. They'll find you easier outside. You need to stay very still."

I wrenched my eyes open. I watched my legs being pulled through the shattered window of the train as if they belonged to someone else. I had never given thought to how big the trains were when I rode them every day, but now, seeing one crashed in a snowbank, it was like a blue whale.

"Joe . . ." I croaked.

"You need to think about surviving. You're hurt. You need to stay relaxed and then you need to do what the medical people say. Look up. Look up and stay calm."

The stranger laid me down in the fresh snow. I looked up. I could see the moon. Full. I could even see a few stars. *Never see stars in the city. Not downtown.* I heard sirens. Helicopters. Someone was in trouble. I knew I should help. But I was so tired. Lying in the snow and looking up seemed the right thing to do. The edges of my vision blurred. Whoever had been pulling me out was no longer nearby. I heard voices.

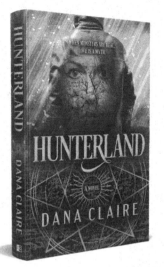
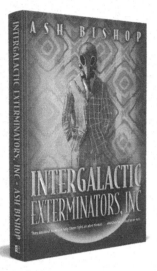

CamCat
Books

VISIT US ONLINE FOR MORE BOOKS TO LIVE IN:
CAMCATBOOKS.COM

SIGN UP FOR CAMCAT'S FICTION NEWSLETTER FOR
COVER REVEALS, EBOOK DEALS, AND MORE EXCLUSIVE CONTENT.

CamCatBooks   @CamCatBooks   @CamCat_Books   @CamCatBooks